We're coming to get you, Lulu . . .

I began to hear something . . . the sound of rapid footsteps, someone running.

Now I could hear other footsteps trailing the first. I was shaking.

The first runner came into view, really moving. I watched as she ran deliriously toward me, dress flapping. Her open mouth an obscene black hole. Then it clicked . . .

"M-mummy?" I cried, stumbling backward.

I ran into the kitchen just in time to see my mother yank the screen off its hinges and smash the little window high on the door. Her whole arm snaked through, heedless of broken glass . . . in search of the lock. Her terrible half face was visible in the opening . . .

"Lulu," she grunted. "Help Mummy, Lulu. Come out."

As I whimpered there in the dark, the door beat hard against my shoulder. *That door's not gonna hold, it's not, it's not . . .*

XOMBIES

WALTER GREATSHELL

BERKLEY BOOKS, NEW YORK

This is a work of fiction. Names, characters, places, and incidents either are the product of the author's imagination or are used fictitiously, and any resemblance to actual persons, living or dead, business establishments, events, or locales is entirely coincidental.

XOMBIES

A Berkley Book / published by arrangement with the author

PRINTING HISTORY
Berkley mass-market edition / August 2004

Copyright © 2004 by Walter Greatshell.
Cover design by Jill Boltin.

For information address: The Berkley Publishing Group,
a division of Penguin Group (USA) Inc.,
375 Hudson Street, New York, New York 10014.

ISBN: 0-425-19744-1

BERKLEY®
Berkley Books are published by The Berkley Publishing Group,
a division of Penguin Group (USA) Inc.,
375 Hudson Street, New York, New York 10014.
BERKLEY and the "B" design
are trademarks belonging to Penguin Group (USA) Inc.

PRINTED IN THE UNITED STATES OF AMERICA

10 9 8 7 6 5 4 3 2 1

To Cindy

prologue

MY NAME IS Louise Alaric Pangloss, I am seventeen years old, and I suffer from Chromosomal Primary Amenorrhea. I am not in the habit of announcing that to the world, but there is so little of the world left now that it scarcely matters what I say. I am very slight of build—that is to say, flat as a board—and frequently mistaken for a girl half my age. In part this is due to my neotenic, waif-like features, but in the past it was also a product of my wardrobe, which over the years had become an increasingly specific costume calculated to elicit sympathy from bill collectors, truant officers, social workers, and other bureaucratic functionaries. It consisted of a plush green velvet dress and bodice, with a lace collar and puffy-sleeves, white knee-length stockings, and shiny Buster Browns. With my milk-white skin, wide-set amber eyes, and pigtailed black hair, these elements combined to create an archetype of Edwardian innocence, which my mother was only too happy to wield like a voodoo doll. The effect was particularly brutal if I feigned tears or affected a British accent. I should say that out of costume I was not a particularly adorable child—my head is rather large for my body, giving me a slightly dwarfish aspect. At one elementary school I was nicknamed "the alien" because of my supposed resemblance to the little gray men of UFO lore; at another I was "Lucy," after the prickly Peanuts character.

How I came to be lying in state, under glass, with a procession of men and boys paying their respects to my magnificently preserved body—and all of this taking place aboard an Ohio-Class nuclear submarine—is the basis for the story I am about to tell.

It is the only known record of these events.

one

MY MOTHER AND I missed the news about Agent X because we spent most of that January cooped up in a beach bungalow outside Jerusalem, Rhode Island. Prior to that, we had been living in Providence, stalking an elderly man that Mummy had tracked all the way from Anaheim, California—a man she contended was my father. I found her crusade embarrassing and pointless: If she had been so foolish as to get knocked-up by an old goat who ran off at the first chance he got, it was more an expression of her character than his. Having lived with her for seventeen years, I knew all too well what a pain in the ass she was. The guy had my sympathy.

When we began leafletting his Pawtucket neighborhood, the codger spooked and fled to his summer cottage by the sea.

"You can't get away from me that easily," Mum muttered nefariously, late into the night. "Oh no, buster. If that's what you think, you got another think coming. Yes indeedy." We had to pack up and leave our little Gano Street apartment during the wee hours of the morning, a drill I was quite familiar with after a lifetime of covert maneuvers.

"Isn't this fun?" Mum said breathlessly as we loaded the sputtering Corolla. Her eyes were bright and wild. It was cold.

"Oh, sure," I said. "What am I supposed to do with my bike?" I had just gotten it for Christmas—a new Huffy.

"Just leave it chained under the stairs, honey. We'll get it later."

That was the thing about her. She knew we would never set foot within a mile of this place again, not with all the back rent and utility bills we owed. Caches of our abandoned pets and possessions now stretched from coast to coast, and she acted as if someday we would follow it all home like a trail of breadcrumbs. Did she even realize we were butting up against the far side of North America? The only place left to run was the Atlantic Ocean.

In reply to my grinding contempt, she said, "Come on, sourpuss! It's an adventure! Show a little spirit!"

It wasn't hard to find off-season rentals in summer resorts. Owners of such properties were usually so happy to have winter tenants that they made no bones about leases, first-and-last, background, or credit histories. Add to that the discount rates, few nosy neighbors, and attractive, out-of-the-way locations that tended to discourage process-servers, and you understand why such accomodations were a staple of ours. Poor old Mr. Fred Cowper had no idea that by retreating to the seaside, he'd all but put out the welcome mat.

Mum soon had us in a treeless village of white clapboard cottages strewn like apple crates across a grassy common. Bare clotheslines and backyard LPG tanks made up the view. It looked like a mining camp during the Gold Rush, or at least the abandoned remains of one. The sea wasn't exactly at our doorstep, but you could smell rotten eggs when the tide went out; to me that meant clams, oysters, and other littoral delights, of which I was an avid hunter ever since reading *Stalking the Blue-Eyed Scallop,* by Euell Gibbons. (Over the years I had practically memorized the book, and still felt a guilty twinge every time I read the words "Property of Oliver LaFarge Public Library.") Aside from a few seldom-seen retirees like Cowper, and a house down the road occupied by hard-partying stoner types, the place was a ghost town.

We didn't have a TV or a radio, not even in our car, because my mother couldn't bear commercials of any kind, and most popular music disturbed her *chi.* Instead we relied on an old Capehart record-player and her collection of movie soundtrack albums, so that my childhood memories are all scored by Henry Mancini. Mummy painted watercolor still-lifes and I wrote poetry in the style of Emily Dickinson, whom I identified with to a nearly pathological degree. Consequently, by the time we heard what was going on, it was already old news. Here is what happened:

It was the first week of the month, and Mummy had gone to our P.O. box in Providence to retrieve and cash the interest check from my trust-fund. This was money left for my care by her father, and it galled her no end that she had no control over the principal, which would be mine when I turned eighteen. For a period of several years she actually contested his will, an Ahab-like quest that almost drove her mad. Mum's ever-changing, grandiose plans for that money made me glad she couldn't get at it, though the shopping binge would have been fun. As it was, we had just enough to live on three weeks out of the month, and ran up debts on the fourth.

On that particular fourth week we had been subsisting on pancake mix, basmati rice, and whatever I could forage from the ocean, so I was looking forward to unpacking a carload of groceries and all the magazines we subscribed to. After weeks of picking over old ones, new magazines were like fresh meat. But I knew something was wrong when I didn't hear her get out of the car. The engine stopped and she just sat there, as if formulating another bogus tale—I knew at once she had blown the money, or been conned out of it. Something. My bird chest constricted and my eyes swam with tears of frustration: *Not again.*

But when she finally came in, I could tell it was something else. Something new. There were no groceries, and I was determined to be indignant, but the look on her face gave me a feeling I thought I had long outgrown: childish fright—the fright that only comes from seeing adults fall apart.

Clinging for dear life to my petulance, I demanded, "What happened?"

"Honey?" Her look was dreamy, detached. Unbalanced. "Something weird is going on."

"What? Shut the door, it's freezing in here."

"Lulu . . ."

I avoided looking at her. "What?" I said. "What's wrong?"

"I couldn't check the mail. Everything's blocked off."

"What do you mean? Why?" I thought she meant it was road construction or an accident. That was it: She must have seen a terrible accident. Such things had disturbed her before—once we passed a bad wreck while riding the bus, and she covered her eyes and moaned, "Oh, oh, oh," for long minutes, while the other passengers stared at us and I tried to reassure her that the body under the bloody sheet was only covered up "to keep the sun off him," and that "I swore I saw him move."

Creepily blank, she said, "There's nobody out there. I couldn't even get to the highway. Traffic was all jammed up."

"I don't get it. There's nobody where?"

"Anywhere."

Growing impatient, I said, "You just said there was a lot of traffic."

"Yes." She looked at me, slowly nodding her head. Now I could see that she was vibrating like a scared kitten. As if correcting a preschooler, she said, "The cars are all abandoned, sweetie. They were all just left in the road."

Now I felt a twinge. "Give me a break," I said, annoyed by my own reaction. "You're just having an anxiety attack."

She seemed to catch her breath and get centered. Focusing on me in the hyper-earnest way she knew I disliked, she said, "Lulu, honey, I don't mean to scare you. Dammit, sometimes I forget you're only seventeen. But I *promise* you I won't let anything happen to you. I know the last couple of years have been difficult, with me going through the 'change of life,' but this is different. This is not a hot flash."

I was completely lost, could only shrug helplessly.

"I stopped at the gas station on Route One," she said. "There was no one there, but I found this." She set down her big Guatemalan bag and pulled out a Hello Kitty portable radio. "I also found cartons of those army rations, those MREs—they're in the trunk. All kinds of things were just lying around loose, and I started wandering the street trying to find someone. All I could think was terrorists, you know, maybe a bomb scare or something, and I thought we should know what to do. I couldn't find a soul. Then I got the bright idea to try the radio." She shook her head, chewing on air for a second. "I thought it was a prank or something. April Fools' Day. Only it's not." Her teeth had started chattering.

My scalp bristled. "What? Mom, you're freaking me out!"

"They say if we just stay out of sight we're safe . . ."

"Safe from *what?*"

She stared at me, wildly conflicted, then let it all spill out. "From *women,* honey. Sick women! I'm not kidding! It's called Agent X, but it's some kind of disease like rabies. It's a real epidemic. It infects everyone, but it starts with women. They're out there like—like Typhoid Mary or something, crazy, and if they catch you, you get it. Or you can also catch it from men, once they've been infected, but either way we're not supposed to go outside. 'Beware any aggressive, unusual, or disheveled-looking people' they said. She giggled hysterically. "That's us, isn't it?"

With that it hit me that my mother had flipped. She was imagining all this, was lost in some kind of paranoid, psychotic episode. The fear I had been feeling now turned inside-out and became an entirely different kind of terror, one bound up in pity and loneliness and infantile need. What was I going to do? I was still a minor—what would happen to me? Ward of the state? I had no relatives to take me in, we had no money. I could feel the tears spilling down my cheeks.

"Mom," I begged. "Come on. It's okay. It's gonna be okay." I gingerly took her by the arm. "Come on. Come sit down and rest. You're okay. See? It's okay, you just need to take it easy. Everything's going to be fine . . ."

She was resisting my gentle attempts to pull her.

"What do you think you're doing?" she erupted at last. "*I'm* not crazy!" The way she said this—the wry edge to her voice—was so completely normal that it cut through the strangler-vines of fear like a machete. I continued to try to lead her by the arm, but my own arms had gone wobbly, and she wouldn't budge.

"Come on," I insisted weakly, suddenly flashing on the "Bring out your dead!" scene from *Monty Python and the Holy Grail*.

"No. Lulu, let go." Somehow she caught wind of the loony direction things had taken and cracked a smile.

"What's so funny?" I said, grinning back against my will. That opened the floodgates, and we were both wracked with weeping laughter, expelling the suffocating fear like bad air. After a few minutes it died down, and we sat on the nubby orange couch to catch our breath.

Mum got ahold of herself first. "Phew! Honey, I swear I'm not crazy. This is real. I wish it weren't, but it is."

Those words came as a cold soaking, though less utterly oppressive than before. "Okay," I said, wiping tears off my face. Then I frowned and shook my head. The cabin's cheap wood paneling totally belied anything extraordinary. "Mum, I'm still confused. When did this happen? How long has it been going on?"

"I don't know, but it's all over the country, so it wasn't just overnight."

"All over the country!" Disbelief cushioned the blow. Part of me was still absolutely confident that this would all turn out to be a load of crap.

"That's what they said: 'All population centers nationwide.' It's martial law, honey!"

"Well, what are we supposed to do? You said women carry it. Does that mean we're quarantined or something? Is there an inoculation we're supposed to get?"

"No, they just want us locked up."

"Are you kidding? What about men?"

"They said men can catch it from women, but I think it's all the same thing once you're infected. I'm sorry, baby; I couldn't make sense of it either. It didn't sound like they had a whole lot of information themselves."

"They must have said what to do. What if we come down with it? What are the symptoms?"

"They didn't say anything about that. Just that we're to stay indoors and keep listening to the radio."

"What if we get sick and have to go out for help?"

"They said not to go out for any reason."

"Well, that's nice. And what if some of those—what did you say it was?—Agent X women come knocking on our door? What do we do then?"

She could only shrug, saying, "We hide, I guess."

two

THOSE MEALS READY to Eat were actually not bad. The food was all right, but more than that they exhibited a sense of fun that I wouldn't have credited to the military. Their olive-drab wrappers concealed playful items like miniature bottles of Tabasco, instant cocoa mix, premium-quality cookies, and candy. Each MRE had a little surprise of some kind, and for two days my mother and I did nothing but sit at the kitchen table with the radio squawking horrors between us, peeling open MREs at mealtimes, and idly trading the contents. From time to time we would cry really hard.

This is what we heard on the one station we could find, repeated over and over in English and Spanish:

"This is the Emergency Broadcast Network. This is not a test. Repeat, this is not a test. You are listening to an official broadcast by your Federal Government. The epidemic of Maenad Cytosis, also known as Agent X, has infiltrated all

but the most isolated pockets of the country. Due to a catastrophic breakdown of civil authority, a state of martial law has been declared, and all citizens are ordered to remain indoors so that comprehensive decontamination efforts may be undertaken. At this time, all population centers nationwide are under quarantine until further notice, and the Interstate Highway System remains closed to civilians. All government services have been suspended, and emergency officials have been moved to secure locations. A network of 'safe zones' is being established for civilians, but until these are officially operational, no one may seek refuge outside of their home—all civil-defense shelters, military facilities, and government compounds are classified as shoot-to-kill zones. This is for your protection. Do not approach military cordons. Stay indoors and keep a low profile. Barricade all windows and doors, and make every effort to give your dwelling an abandoned appearance. For your safety, all women must be segregated and contained, even if they do not exhibit symptoms of Maenad contagion. Once exposed to the airborne disease agent, they may change without warning, *transmitting the contact form of Agent X to men and women alike. Beware any aggressive, unusual, or disheveled-looking people. Likewise,* anyone *with serious injuries or who is critically ill is a potential source of infection, as it is thought that their weakened immune systems make them vulnerable to the airborne pathogen. No matter how apparently weak, unconscious, or near death, they must be securely contained and treated with extreme caution. If you are low on food, water, or essential medical supplies, do not venture into the open, even if you hear military convoys or other official movement. All efforts are being made to come to your relief, but the scale of the crisis demands patience. You* will *be saved. Stay tuned to this station for news and official information. This is not a test."*

The numbing sameness of the reports was frustrating, as well as the lack of specifics. It was like a tape loop that had been left playing. "They must be blowing everything all out of proportion," I said. "Are people dying like flies, or is it some kind of mass hysteria? You said you didn't see any bodies or anything when you were out there."

"No."

"And obviously neither of us is sick, so the whole airborne thing can't be as bad as they're making it out to be. And what the hell do they mean, women may *change?* Change into what? It all sounds fishy."

"Don't swear," my mother said, stirring her coffee.

"Well, it makes me nuts."

"I know. I feel there's something we should be doing, but I can't imagine what."

"We can't sit here forever, that's for sure."

"Where can we go? I don't want somebody taking pot-shots at us."

"I know," I said. "But we're going to have to let somebody know we're here. We don't even have a phone. What about that old guy, Cowper, or even those guys over at Stoner Central? As long as we don't sneak up on them, I think they'd at least talk to us. We could bring them a couple of MREs."

"We might need those. And if they were home, don't you think we'd have seen them by now? We haven't seen a soul in weeks. And by the way, Lulu, he's not some 'old guy,' he's your father."

"Whatever, it's worth a try. I've seen his car there. Besides, even if nobody's home, they might at least have some food or something."

"You mean break in? Good heavens no!" My mother—paragon of virtue.

"Oh please."

"And be caught looting? Uh-uh, thanks but no thanks."

"Well, can we at least see if they're home?"

"I don't like it. What if some of that Agent X is floating around? I think we should stay put, like the radio says."

"Mum, if Agent X is as bad as they say, we'd have it by now. That is, if there was anyone to catch it from. I bet this whole area's deserted—all you have to do is look out the window." I flipped up the curtain. The view was like an overexposed photo of bleak suburbia. "We're like people in the Middle Ages who went to the countryside to escape the Black Death. Maybe we lucked out, but we can't just sit here forever. There may be help out there." I wasn't sure if I believed this myself.

But my mother thought about it, bit her lip, and nodded.

Bringing her die cast toy Luger made Mummy feel less vulnerable, so I didn't say anything. We drove to the cabin of my "father" first, a private little place tucked in its own cul-de-sac. He had a reinforced steel mailbox to ward off bat–wielding joyriders, and it was made quaint with an old lobster-trap, buoys, and a jigsawed wooden sign that read, COWPER'S REST.

The cottage looked all shut up, but his big utility vehicle was parked in the driveway. I wondered if it might be possible to siphon gas out of it.

"Let's just sit in the car for a few minutes," I said. "Give him a chance to look us over."

"Okay," Mum said, turning off the motor.

We sat watching the house for any sign of activity, but no one peeked back at us through the blinds.

After a few minutes, my mother said, "I don't think there's anybody there."

"I know."

"I feel funny lurking out here."

"Well, let's go knock."

"You think so?"

"Sure, why not?" As we got out, I added, "But I think you should leave the gun in the car."

"I'll put it in my purse."

We cautiously climbed the porch and rang the bell, listening to the faint chimes within.

"Hello?" my mother called hopefully.

There was nothing. It was kind of a relief. I'd been tricked into meeting Mr. Cowper during one of my mother's confrontations, and to his credit he was cordial, but chilly. What was odd was how desperately coquettish she had been, flattering him and making her painstaking pursuit seem like a casual visit. It was pathetic. He went along with the small-talk, humoring her like a doctor in an asylum, and I could feel his sympathy for me like a chintzy gift from a rich relative. When he started asking me how I was doing in school, and Mummy began to boast about what a genius I was, I felt physically ill—it was the sensation that he and I were watching her with the same pity.

In the distance, I could see the bulbous water tower by the highway. It made me wonder how long we'd have water pressure . . . and electricity, for that matter. A lump rose in my throat. My anxiety was interrupted by Mum plopping down on the steps.

"I can't take this," she said. "I just can't *take* it."

Trying to sound reassuring, I said, "It'll be okay. I'm sure there are other people like us around." I could tell she was on the verge of one of her meltdowns. It was something I didn't think I could handle just then, barely keeping it together myself. *Give her a few minutes to cool down,* I thought. "Listen, you take it easy for a little while," I said. "I'm just going to run over to the stoner house and take a look. I'll come right back."

"No! By yourself? No way, buster, we'll drive."

"Mum, it's twice as long to drive. From here I can just cut across the field, and I'll be back in five minutes. You know how careful I am."

She was wavering, not sure what to do. With her graying hair and her housecoat, she suddenly looked very old and sad. Seeing her like that made me want to kill myself.

Trying to clinch it, I said, "You know nobody's even going to be there. I mean, look around!" I waved at the ranks of empty cottages. "I'll be right back, I promise."

With a worn-out nod, she said, "Okay, but don't scare me."

"I won't." I bolted from the porch.

Cutting across backyards and sparse woods, I felt exhilarated, freed. At times my mother was a planet unto herself, with a dense, claustrophobic atmosphere and heavy gravity. She needed company, and it was my lot to provide it. Being alone never bothered me; I often thought I would do well in solitary confinement, as long as I had access to books. Of course, being cooped up in that cabin with her for more than a month didn't help. As my head cleared I even began to wonder if the whole Agent X business wasn't pure delirium. Not that I believed that, but it was so unreal.

I stopped to take a pee beside a vine-covered stone wall, listening to the trickle in the silence. It was so damn peaceful—yes, maybe there was nothing to be afraid of.

Crossing the meadow under the power lines, I found Hull Street. It was a narrow dirt lane with more summer houses on either side. My feet crunched on the gravel, and I found myself treading lightly without quite knowing why. If there was no one around, why did I care? And if there was someone, shouldn't I make myself heard?

Stoner Central lay at the end of the street, a double-wide trailer strung with Christmas lights. I had seen it at night, all lit up and booming vapid techno music to a throng of future tinnitus cases. Now the place was quiet, nearly invisible, set far back under the trees, and surrounded by a low chainlink fence. Drifts of unraked pine needles covered the property. Whitewashed tires served as planters, and might have been taken off the stripped car in the driveway. Around back, a decrepit patio set was visible under the pines, where there was a lingering icy crust from the last time it snowed.

Worried about dogs, I made a racket opening the gate and waited. Just as before, zero. I looked back down the road to see if anyone was watching, but nothing stirred except the trees. Standing still was the worst thing to do—it made me imagine all kinds of things. Never being one to let my imagination get the best of me, I mentally slapped myself and went up the walk.

A cold gust of wind swept through, slamming a screen

door somewhere and making me turn my face away. It had been a very mild winter, but in the afternoons the wind always picked up. I entered the zone of shade around the house and climbed to the front door, kicking pinecones off the step. There were cigarette butts everywhere. *We're all friends here*—that's what I tried to communicate with my spritely knock.

Once more there was nothing. The sunlit street looked a long way off, and I was ready to call it quits. I turned to go, but while turning absently gave the doorknob a twist. It opened.

Darn, I thought.

three

FEELING MY SKIN crawl, I pushed the door in and said, "Hello?"

Rank, housebound air puffed out. It smelled like damp ashtrays and rancid milk. I felt for the light switch but it was dead, so I leaned in to let my eyes adjust. For a second my heart seized up at what I thought was the shape of a person in the gloom—*Oh God, oh God*—until the shape resolved itself into a life-size cardboard cutout of Pamela Anderson. Getting a grip, I stepped inside.

Not much to see: mustard-colored shag carpeting, a bunch of baggy old furniture, TV, stereo—typical guy stuff. Pamela was the only decoration. These were the kind of men who could argue heatedly about which pro athlete should be president. I tried the TV and got nothing, but there were several remotes and it's possible I didn't do it right.

So this was Stoner Central. I was a little disappointed—except for a few cigarette burns the place was pretty clean.

I'd always pictured something a little more exotically nasty. To tell the truth, I'd had a secret yearning to come in here since Mummy and I first arrived, and had gone so far as to spy on their New Year's Eve party, skulking around under the trees as the place roared like a bonfire: sleazy-voluptuous tattooed women slithering against crude rough-necks, none of them much older than me, yet as confident in their skins as royalty, while music and laughter and the clink o˙ bottles pushed back the solitude. I had fantasized about walking into that circle of light, all of them falling silent and the most scarily beautiful couple, the branded boy with the pierced lip and his languid, stunning gangsta princess, coming up and taking me by the waist. Welcoming me in.

That party was the last peep we'd heard out of the house, and I now realized it was likely that no one had been here since. I crept across the living room and peered into the kitchen. Not too bad. The contact paper was peeling here and there, likewise the Formica, but on the whole it was at least as clean as our place. No dirty dishes or pizza crusts—these guys wanted their security deposit back. Spotting a wall phone, I snatched it up, but it was dead. This was getting to be annoying. I checked the refrigerator with a sense of trepidation, but it contained only basic condiments and a few cans of beer. I hate beer.

There was a collection of tools laid out on the dining table as if on display: axes, hatchets, pruning saws, cleavers. The sight of all those sharp blades was vaguely unsettling, so I returned to the living room, thinking I ought to get back before Mummy panicked.

Crossing to the front door, I was struck again by the pu-trid milk smell. I had forgotten about it in the kitchen—obviously it wasn't coming from there at all. I looked down the wood-paneled hall . . . the smell was definitely stronger. The only room I could see into was the bathroom, on my right. Some idiot had broken the toilet seat, but other than that it looked empty and clean. No, the smell was further down, in the vicinity of those closed doors. It had to be pretty ripe behind one of them. You had to wonder what was causing it.

With terrific economy of motion I was back outside, tugging the front door shut behind me. That I neither left it open nor slammed it in haste should put to rest any idea that I panicked. I was fairly secure about the source of that smell being nothing but, say, a rotting damp mop. But what would be the point of finding out?

Kicking through a drift of pine needles halfway down the walk, I began to hear something. A pattering sound from the road. I slowed to listen. It was the sound of rapid footsteps—someone running.

A jogger? There was something alarming in that ordinary sound, but I didn't want to jump to any paranoid conclusions. Chances were it was someone else who was feeling a bit marooned. Perhaps someone helpful. I couldn't see the person yet through the screen of trees, but in a moment our paths would intersect at the front gate. As the footsteps neared, I felt a strong, instinctive impulse to hide, but limited it to stopping well short of the fence.

Now I could hear other footsteps trailing the first. I pictured a whole gaggle of runners, a cross-country team sprinting by in their shorts as if nothing was wrong. God, that would be good. I was shaking.

The first runner came into view, really moving, and it took me a moment to recognize her. I just watched stupidly as a blue woman—her face the bruised color of a sparrow chick—ran deliriously towards me, dress flapping. Her open mouth was an obscene black hole. Then it clicked: *That housecoat . . .*

"M-mummy?" I cried, stumbling backward.

As she attempted to lunge over the fence, her dress became entangled in the hooked wires and she fell. Senseless with shock and grief, I cried out and jumped to help her, but froze again at the sight of her rolling and heaving in the dirt like a wild animal. She was so *blue,* blue as someone in

the throes of strangulation . . . but she was not suffering.
All the while she struggled to get loose, the huge black
pupils of her glaring eyes were fixed on me. It was such a
manic, predatory look that I shrank back with fear. Then
the dress gave way like a shed skin.

I don't remember screaming or running or anything else
that happened for the next few seconds, but somehow I
wound up crouched in the trailer, gasping for breath, with
my back against the front door. The door rattled in its
frame. I must have been in shock, because the strongest
feeling I had was that I was overdue, that my mother would
be worried.

The door stopped shuddering, and the thing outside
leaped off the stoop to circle around back. The back door. I
ran into the kitchen just in time to see my mother yank the
screen off its hinges and smash the little window high in
the door. Her whole arm snaked through, heedless of broken glass, a crab-like blue hand skittering in search of the
lock. Half her terrible face was visible in the opening, the
mad dilated eye bulging with furious greed.

Weeping, I jammed a chair under the doorknob and
shakily said, "Mom, stop." I couldn't look at her.

"Lulu," she grunted. "Lulu help. Help Mummy, Lulu.
Come out." Her voice was gutteral, masculine. The sound
of it made my hair prickle like static electricity.

"Mom, please," I wailed. "It's me! Try to remember.
Try."

Her efforts became more frenzied, but it was no use—
she couldn't reach the knob. Her arm withdrew like an eel
and I lost sight of her. Heart racing, I looked out the window over the sink just in time to catch a blur vanishing
around the front of the house. There was a loud crash of
breaking glass—the living room window. Forcing myself
to move, I arrived there just in time to see not only my
mother, but two more frenetic human monsters floundering
in over the high windowsill. One of them had no eyes. It
was a freakish feat of agility, this squirming invasion, and

in a way it cleared my head, because it was nothing my real mother could ever have done in her wildest dreams.

Flying on pure instinct, I barely spared them a glance as I rushed past and into the first door off the hall. I half shut myself in the bathroom before I realized the knob was missing, then I lunged for the next nearest door, one that opened on a shelved linen closet packed with canned goods and emergency supplies. *Damn it!* Footsteps pounded my way—the little daylight filtering through from the living room was suddenly blocked by the press of approaching bodies. I didn't dare look back, just barrelled through the next door and locked it behind me. As I whimpered there in the dark, the door beat hard against my shoulder, shaking the whole house: BAM! BAM! BAM!

My crying was a high-pitched whistle from deep in my throat, broken up by violent hiccups. *That door's not gonna hold, it's not, it's not . . .*

What was that *smell?* I was in the last throes of animal desperation, but even that had to yield before the stench. The *stench.* It filled the dark room like a dense, gamy vapor, like cut bait left in a tacklebox all summer. I couldn't see anything, just a thread of light under the heavy blackout curtain, but I knew there was something rotten in there.

I could hear the maniacs laying waste to the room next to mine, searching for a way through. It freed me to leave the door for a second and open the curtain a crack, just enough to admit a little light. I did this with trembling caution, not wanting anyone outside to notice and come crashing in. But there was no sign of them—the yard was empty. I turned and screamed.

The room looked like a slaughterhouse. It had been a bedroom, with a futon on the floor, CD racks, and a high chest of drawers, but everything was spattered with black congealed blood, all the way up the walls. The center of the futon pad was a lava-like mass of gore, mixed with teeth and hair. Several blood-smeared yellow raincoats were draped on a chair alongside gloves, overshoes, and other protective gear. Wads of duct tape and cut plastic police restraints lit-tered the floor. Remembering the tools on the dining table, I suddenly had a bizarre revelation: Where were these guys when I needed them? Instead of dropping dead from the hor-ror, my brain seemed to rise to the unspeakable and take unexpected strength from this scene—not everybody was squeamish. I could choose here and now whether to fall apart or whether to live . . . and be this kind of person. Be-cause the carnage before me was not the work of Agent X mental cases. It was the work of hard-hearted men.

This was not a conscious thought process so much as an emotional rush that got me moving.

I dragged the sodden, reeking futon over against the door and prepared to move the dresser in front of the win-dow. Then I thought, *Why*? Barricading myself in this aw-ful place wouldn't save me for long. Screw that. Instead, I tipped the dresser onto the mattress and went to unlatch the window. It slid open easily, presenting a clear field of flight. Then I frowned: I'd never outrun those things. Not even my own mother. Anxiously, I started searching for a weapon, a club, anything to hold them off until I could get back to our car . . . and maybe away.

The maniacs were going crazy in the hall, having heard my yelp and the dresser falling over. Still looking for any kind of weapon, I opened the closet and leaned in, then I reeled backwards as if slapped. Amid a heap of women's shoes stood a green plastic garbage can, filled nearly to the brim with purplish-blue human remains. Amid the offal I could make out part of a jaw, ribs, hair, intestines. But that wasn't what had made me jump.

The remains were *alive*.

Though every joint seemed to have been severed, the whole mass seethed like an octopus. It made wet smacking sounds, and I had the insane impression that it was *aware* of me—that those veiny, glistening lumps were surging in my direction.

The bedroom door was coming apart. Moving like

a sleepwalker, I closed the closet, casually crawled out the window, and dropped gently to the ground. Fresh air! Nothing was weird at all out there; it looked exactly the same as when I'd first walked up. I was pretty sure I hadn't been dreaming, but I still felt self-conscious running for the road under that prosaic winter sky.

Going through the gate, I made the mistake of looking back and caught a glimpse of herky-jerky figures emerging from the window like bats from a crevice. They were so *fast*. Chrome-bright panic knifed through the cobwebs, spurring me to run harder than I ever had, harder than I really could for more than a short sprint. I'd never been much of an athlete, except for diving, and that didn't require much stamina.

I came to the first crossroads and broke right, not daring my earlier shortcut. White noise began to fill my senses— the rush of blood to my head as my breathing shredded. I could taste iron. *Please, God,* I pleaded. I'd been avoiding backward glances, but as I ran I began to feel that perhaps the creatures were no longer after me, that they had lost interest. Lungs burning, I risked a glance and lost equilibrium, skidding, going down, skinning my hands and knees. Grit powdered my sweaty face and funneled down my dress. I hated myself.

But there was no sign of any pursuit. Heart galloping, I got to my feet and scanned the road. Nothing. Nothing but—

Movement flickered to my left, among houses and yards. I flinched, drawing a sharp breath. It was them, all three of them, coming across the lawn nearest the road and splitting up to cut me off. My mother was the closest, shamelessly charging up the center in her underwear, as rapid and jerky as a wind-up toy. Next was a man, a swarthy, unkempt soldier in tattered fatigues, whose face was the frozen scowl of a tiki idol. The last was a tall, limber boy who looked about my age, but whose eyes were just hideous black sockets. He moved as surely as the rest.

With their blue-gray complexions, they resembled a trio of rubber-limbed Hindu deities. Where I had turned right, they had come across diagonally to intercept me, demonstrating at least an animal cunning. They weren't tired. Their loony, distorted faces showed nothing but wild obsession. Not even cruel glee—I got no impression that I was sport; just a commodity.

I doubled back, legs shaking, trying to duck the enclosing snare. The one angling to block my way was the blind boy, whose unhindered, gangly agility made me think, *No fair*! Tongue lolling out as he ran, he was wearing a tattered sweatsuit and a gold medallion around his neck. He had an erection.

They had me: I was blocked and had to stop in my tracks. My only hope now was the field I had cut through to get here, though I didn't feel good about running over uneven ground. Eyes stinging with sweat, I launched myself over the roadside ditch and landed, scrambling on all fours, halfway up the far embankment. I grabbed at dead stalks of last year's milkweed, but they pulled out of the loose soil like bathtub plugs and I sprawled to the bottom.

It was all over. My legs were spaghetti, my heaving chest a box of coals. I sat upright and dug fruitlessly in the cold sand for any decent-sized stone, watching them come.

They didn't slow down the way a person would when he knows he's won, but converged on me with the same hyper-animated haste they'd shown all along. From low in the ditch, I watched first their gargoyle faces, then their torsos, then the rest come speeding at me. Covering my eyes, I whimpered, "I love you, Mum . . ."

Then a car hit them.

At first I only heard its engine and the snarl of its wheels churning gravel. The driver must have crept up slowly and floored it at the last minute, because I uncovered my eyes barely in time to see all three of my pouncing attackers swatted aside like chess pieces off a board. The sound was a triple impact, a mighty drum flourish—BADABOOM!—and a tinkle of headlight bits as the vehicle hammered through. Pebbles showered down on me. Immediately, the driver stood on his brakes and fishtailed to a stop. I was dimly aware of a crashing in the roadside brush, and I realized that the bodies of my mother and the others were only now hitting the ground.

Spinning its tires in reverse, the car backed through the dustcloud until it came up even with me. It was Cowper's blue Expedition. From my low angle I couldn't see the driver.

The passenger-side window powered down. "Hey, girlie! Lulu!" It was the nasal voice of Mr. Fred Cowper.

"Yeah?" I said, loathe to move.

"Where are ya? You okay?"

"I think so."

"Then what you waitin' fah? Get in the damn cah before them bastids come back!"

I almost said, *You're talking about my mother,* but I didn't. I climbed painfully to my feet, peered grimly through the window at Mr. Cowper—who looked owlishly back at me through ashtray-thick prescription glasses—and yanked at the door handle. It wouldn't open.

"Unlock it," I said.

"It's unlocked," he replied impatiently. "Pull hahd!"

I yanked and yanked and shrugged at him.

"Sonofabitch!" He leaned across the seat, fumbling with the door handle, but it wouldn't budge. I could hear him muttering, "Son of a bitch bastids wrecked my cah." The right front end was slightly crumpled from the collision; the door and fender were buckled together, but it didn't look that bad.

Glancing behind the car, I spied a number of people, eight of them, running toward us. Even from a distance it was very easy to tell what they were. Mr. Cowper dithered angrily, stretching his bony legs across the passenger seat to try and kick the door loose. The back was crammed with boxes or I would have just jumped in there.

"How about the window?" I asked, fidgeting.

He ignored me, rocking the car with his futile kicks.

"How about I climb in the window?"

"Keep ya shirt on," he said. Then he glanced in the mirror. "Crap. All right, get on in."

The window was not as easy as I hoped. It was gym class all over again. I made the mistake of climbing up one foot at a time, but it was too high and I found myself in the awkward position of hanging from the sill by one leg and one arm, with my dress bunched up around my waist. "I can't do it!" I cried.

"Aw, fa Christ's sake," he snapped, bolting from the car and hurrying around to my side. I thought he was going to try shoving me through, and had a flash of Winnie the Pooh stuck in Rabbit's hole, but he pulled me off and sent me around to scoot across from the driver's side. Doing this, I was unnerved to see that he hadn't followed, but was trying to jimmy the passenger door loose with a pocket knife.

Behind him something moved in the underbrush. Like a jack-in-the-box, the blue soldier popped out of a thistle patch and stood there, slowly swaying. His body was a squeezed-out toothpaste tube, his head an oozing Picasso. Then the eyeless boy jerked to life nearby, even more of a wreck . . . then my mother. I lost my breath at the sight of her.

"Sir, they're coming, they're coming," I choked, tears flying from my eyes. "You have to hurry right now, get in—"

"Don't worry, I see 'em back there." He wasn't even looking.

"No, the others, the ones you hit, they're up there, look . . ."

The three mangled carcasses started for us, thrashing through the weeds and across the ditch.

Mr. Cowper made a final effort and the door clunked open.

"Outta the way fuh Crissake!" he hollered, throwing himself over me and scrambling behind the wheel. He was nimble for his age, but it still took him a minute to get settled in place. In that time, the three creatures reached my side of the car, dragging broken limbs and dirt-caked loops of intestine behind them.

I watched them come, my window open, my door unlocked, simply because I didn't know which button was which and I didn't want to make a fatal mistake. In the sideview mirror I could also see the other eight, a tribe of capering goblins rushing up from behind to join the party.

Cowper hit the window button. As it began sliding shut, a face suddenly rose up in front of the mirror and wedged itself in the window. It was the dust-floured harpy that had been my mother. She was unrecognizable now. The whites of her eyes were inky black, crying dark blue tears that streaked a clownish face so swollen it was featureless, all eyes and lips.

Those balloon-lips parted, croaking, *"Lululululululu-ulu,"* until her breath ran out. Then she wheezed and continued, *"Lululululululululu,"* all the while fighting me for the door. She still had strength but no dexterity, and her grip on the handle kept slipping loose. The other two arrived beside her, crowding each other in their eagerness to worm through. Strings of black spittle fell on me, and I leaned as far away from the door as I could without losing my grip.

"Lock the door!" I screamed. "Lock the door!"

Even as I said it, the locking bolts shot home with a deliriously gratifying *ka-chunk.*

"Ya don't have to wait fa me, ya know," Mr. Cowper grumbled. Twisting around to face backward, one hand on the wheel, he said, "Fasten y'seat belt," and gunned the big Ford in reverse. Like magic, the three ragged creatures were left rolling in the dust. The sight of them dropping away was so sweet it was agonizing. But I wasn't ready for hope, and might never be. I was leaving my mother behind.

We kept going backward at a fast clip, swerving a little as if taking aim, until there was a jarring multiple thump and the car bounced over something. We passed through the line of maniacs, half of them clutching hopelessly after us, the rest stretched out in the road. Once we were safely clear, Cowper stopped and turned the car around, proceeding away at a more leisurely pace.

"Do I have to tell ya to close that window?" he griped. "I got the heat on."

"Sorry," I said, finding the button. All of a sudden I started trembling so hard I was afraid Mr. Cowper might think there was something seriously wrong with me and put me out. But he wasn't paying attention. He was looking out the rearview mirror with grim intensity, nodding to himself.

"And *that's* why I drive an SUV," he said.

four

MY MOTHER DIDN'T believe in cars. She owned a car as a "matter of survival," but thought the world would be a better place without them. Cars figured prominently in her "Penis Patrol" theory: Most men are not mature enough to handle any extra reach, and to give the average jerk a platform by which he can increase the radius of his stupidity is asking for trouble. I found this hilarious coming from her, but couldn't argue with the logic. "Civilization is so *boring*," she liked to say, spying some example of male profligacy— from thudding car stereos and roadside litter to mad gunmen and rogue jetliners, "Let's break stuff." Any time a new atrocity occurred that illustrated her case, all Mummy and I had to do was look at each other and say, "Penis Patrol," and that explained it. Over the years, I even found myself doing it when I was alone.

Now, as Mr. Cowper's giant vehicle enfolded me in cream-colored leather, I realized I was muttering, "Penis

Patrol," every couple of minutes, like a weird tic. I wasn't aware of it until he said something.

He said, "You sound just like ya motha."

Shocked out of my passivity, I grunted. I didn't want to talk about her; didn't think I could without screaming. My placid demeanor was just the slag on a roiling cauldron; perhaps when cooled it would crumble away, exposing tempered steel, but in the meantime it threatened to spatter everything in sight.

"She and I didn't really see eye-ta-eye on a lotta things," he continued, "but I gotta give her this: she was one tough lady. She didn't give up, no how, not when she wanted somethin'. You got that in you too, little girl, and it's gonna get ya through."

He went on with the pep talk, but I couldn't listen. Much easier to skate the powerlines and guardrails, bodiless and afloat, muffled, in a corridor of gray winter maples. But as we ventured up the coast, my detachment began to shred. There were blue people out there. *There! By that farmhouse! That donut shop! The strip mall!*

Every time I saw them I was so repulsed my stomach muscles spasmed, causing me to double over in pain. Cringing as we swerved to avoid one, I yelled, "Don't stop!"

"I ain't about to stop," he said dryly. "Don't worry."

His gas gauge showed less than a quarter-tank. "Where are we going?" I asked.

"Hopefully where there ain't gonna be no Xombies."

It was as if I'd been pricked by something sharp. Under my breath, I said, *"Zombies."*

"Xombies, yeah. With an X, like Agent X. Every damn thing's gotta have an X nowadays."

"Is that because of the women? The X chromosome?"

"Hey, maybe so," he said. "I just thought it was one a them Generation X things. Good thinkin'."

Even in the midst of unbearable grief, his approval tickled a reaction out of my girlish pride. I stamped it down like a cockroach. "Why don't I have it?" I asked. "Agent X?"

He became very uncomfortable. "Well, I, uh . . . from what I've heard, they think it's got somethin' to do with that time a the month . . . I don't really know. They say little girls and, uh, olda ladies don't catch it that way, spontaneously, the way menstratin' women do. And I know you have a . . . problem in that area."

"You mean I'm immune because I don't get a period?"

He winced. "Immune, no. You're immune the way I am, the way anybody is who didn't automatically go bad on Sadie Hawkins Day. That doesn't make us safe from catching it off 'em. Half the things runnin' around now are men."

"Sadie Hawkins Day?"

"That's what they wa callin' it when all the women turned, the first week a January."

"Is that when this happened? God, we had no clue."

"Oh yeah. They went off like they wa synchronized. Afta that, everything went all ta hell pretty quick—I'm not surprised you missed it. They say the original women carriers are different than the ones they infected, not so re-tahded, but I don't know. To me it's all the same if they're afta your ass."

"But . . . my mother just went through menopause . . ." My voice quavered; somehow I'd blundered into facing the Gorgon. Thickly, I said, "How do those things infect you?"

"Now there's no use goin' inta that. I gotta pay attention to the road. You just sit tight."

"Mr. Cowper, how did you know to find me?"

He didn't acknowledge the question for some time, giving jittery attention to his driving.

Grimly, I said, "You were home, weren't you? You heard us."

He scowled, nodded. He didn't look at me. "You shouldn't a been out there," he said gruffly.

"We didn't know."

"Well God damn it, you *shoulda* known!" Suddenly he was spitting with exasperation. "Don't you think I'da let you in if I hadn't known them bastids were out there? They were there the whole time, and you two standin' on my porch like there's nothin' funny!"

"I'm sorry."

"Sorry!" His temper abruptly dwindled and he shook his head, saying, "I was gonna let her in. Afta you left, I was gonna take a chance and let her in." The old man's face contracted as if squinting into a high wind. "But *they* came first. They came runnin' like a pack a hyenas, and she saw 'em before I did. Before I could do anything, she was gone—"

"Okay," I said sharply, not ready to hear everything.

"That was when I got it in me to go. Take Sandoval up on his offer. Why not?" His cactus-bristled cheek quivered. "I figured maybe I could get to you before . . . uh . . ."

He was very upset. It scared me and took me out of my panic. Trying to sound strong, I said, "And you did. You did it, Mr. Cowper. You saved me." I started to cry.

"Don't thank me just yet," he said.

SUBURBAN SPRAWL GAVE way to industrial blight. Fenced-off tracts of land were posted, PROPERTY OF U.S. NAVY—KEEP OUT and WARNING—RESTRICTED AREA—USE OF DEADLY FORCE AUTHORIZED. It was reassuring in a way, though there was no sign of life. Any authority, however brutal, sounded pretty good. I craved the sight of men with guns the way a person lost in the desert craves a drink. For that matter I was thirsty, too.

Coming to a dusty crossroads jammed with abandoned vehicles, Mr. Cowper was forced to slow down to a reluctant stop.

"Don't *stop*," I said shrilly.

"I hafta," he said.

"What about that median strip?"

"It's too narrow. Hush up!"

There were no zombies—*Zombies,* that is—but adrenaline lanced through my veins like quicksilver as I scanned all the myriad hiding places. I tried to remind myself of how much time my mother and I had spent out in the open without knowing the risk, but that only alarmed me more. Cowper, too, showed nervousness as he bounced us through a rough three-point turn, squealing the tires. Finally, we were on our way. It was a short respite: after backtracking a couple of miles, he stopped the car between two empty pastures and got out.

I thought he was angry, but he leaned in and said, "Ya want a bite ta eat?"

Surprising myself, I opened the door without hesitation. My legs supported me. It was late in the day, but enough light penetrated the hills on either side to give ample warning of any threat . . . I hoped. Skittish as a rabbit, I joined Mr. Cowper at the rear. He was making a great deal of noise manhandling some devices of wood and chainlink—they looked like screens for sifting clams. Leaning them against the bumper, he took out two small coolers and a rolled-up blanket.

"Spread this out on the grass, will ya?" he said, handing me the picnic items. Seeing my disbelief, he added, "Go on, I'll be right with ya." Then he began placing the screens on the car, and I realized they conformed to the shapes of the windows. He had devised them to belt across the top and fasten by hooks beneath the fenders. When the job was complete, the SUV resembled some kind of demolition derby hotrod. "Shoulda really had these on the whole time," he said. "Looks like a damn lobsta trap, but at least they fit like I hoped."

The daredevil look of it scared me, as if we were going to attempt a stunt. I wanted no contact with Xombies, however protected. As he came up the embankment to join me, I said, "Won't they just hang onto those?"

"Nah . . . well, as long as they don't get in. Hey, it's better than nothin'. It was all I had to work with."

"No, it's good. It's great."

Less reassured than I would've wished, I kept my peace as we shared a meal of Rhode Island delicacies: cheeseless slabs of cold pizza, stuffed quahogs, pickled snail salad with yellow peppers and mozzarella balls, and gritty little cornmeal patties called johnnycakes. Once I got the first few bites down, I found I could eat, though I kept crying all over everything. To drink there was bottled lemonade— "For scurvy," he said—and a Thermos of coffeemilk. It was chilly to be outside, the dead of winter, but as we sat and ate I could feel my dread loosen its grip. In shock or not, I could breathe again.

"I thought this was crazy, but it's okay," I said. "Thank you."

He replied offhandedly, "Might be our last meal. Oughtta make the most of it."

I stopped chewing, feeling the food like a brick in my stomach. "Where are we going?" I asked.

"I don't wanna get your hopes up. You'll see—we're almost there."

Just as the sun began to set, moving figures appeared in the distance, and we packed up and got underway.

Returning to the traffic jam, Mr. Cowper slowed to bump the car up onto the highway divider as per my earlier suggestion. But as soon as we were on that narrow island I realized why he had taken the extra measure with the screens: the median was scarcely wider than the car itself, hemmed in on both sides by bumper-to-bumper traffic. Driving along that cramped passage was unnerving—there could be no U-turns, no reversing at any speed. And the soft, grassy track seemed to go on forever.

Cowper didn't seem unduly concerned. "Once we turn right at the innasection, should be clear sailing," he said. "Long as we don't get stuck in the mud."

I put my faith in the elderly gent, though as we neared the end I didn't like the look of things. This was no mere traffic jam, but an abandoned military roadblock. Through the misting windshield I could see relics of recent violence: shoes, broken glass, bullet-holes, and spent shells everywhere. No bodies.

Shadows flitted between the cars. I drew up my legs under me.

"Here they come," I said.

They came in droves, like paparazzi. One minute our path appeared to be clear, the next it was choked with rushing bodies that hurled themselves at us willy-nilly. Mr. Cowper accelerated, trying to mow them down, but even the most brutal impact did not seem to prevent many of them from clinging parasitically to the window cages. In minutes it became pitch-black inside the car, the windows draped with writhing, naked monsters. All credit to the driver for keeping us moving—I don't know how he did it.

"How can you see?" I yelled over the pounding.

He ignored me, scrunching up his gnome face to peer between the cracks. Absorbed in his futile task, Cowper was bottoming out, hitting the horn again and again like a cranky old codger. I wouldn't have minded, except his horn played the festive strains of *La Cucaracha* and seemed to energize them.

Several times we crashed into other cars, and I wasn't sure if it was accidental or Cowper's attempts to shake off our foe. If intentional, it failed, because for every Xombie we lost, we gained three by losing speed. It reminded me of a grisly nature film I'd seen showing cattle set upon by vampire bats. Also the car was falling apart: I could hear the *wup wup wup* of flat tires, and smoke began pooling around our legs. We didn't have long to live.

I remembered those radio reports referring to Agent X as some kind of disease, but it was incredible to me that these things could be in any way considered sick. They were superhuman; nothing stopped them. I could even tell that some were smart. One female Xombie—a blue woman who straddled the hood like a fierce, Celtic witch—had no trouble figuring out the arrangement that kept the screens in place, and began unhooking the straps. In seconds, the whole thing was loose, held in place only by other bodies, and she battered its frame against the windshield, starring the glass.

This is it, I thought.

The web of cracks burst inward, the witch's hands peeling apart the safety glass like a membrane and her grinning, black-eyed face thrusting through at me. Trapped in my seat, I could hear myself making a high-pitched whine from deep in my throat. Just then Cowper stamped hard on the brakes, causing the whole unmoored wire contraption and every Xombie on it to go flying off the car in a jangling heap.

Now I could see again. We were clear of the traffic, clear of Xombies, and dragging our flopping treads down a tree-lined drive toward some kind of factory complex. The trees gave way to parkland, then a high fence and a series of concrete barricades. It was the end of the road, in every sense. Mr. Cowper turned off the dying motor and we sat there in silence. My ears were ringing.

I was about to say the place looked deserted when a brilliant light filled the car. It beamed down from above the fence, from a hidden platform. Bathed in phosphorescent white smoke, we couldn't see a thing.

"Hold up your hands," Mr. Cowper said. He held up his own, fanning identification cards like a poker hand. "Fred Cowper here!" he shouted. "Referred by James Sandoval!"

For a long moment there was nothing, then a voice shouted, "Step out of the vehicle!"

We climbed free of the car, keeping our hands up. Mr. Cowper had an old leather satchel slung from his shoulder. Again, he called out, "Fred Cowper here! Fred Cowper—don't shoot!"

A different voice called down, "Fred Cowper? We thought it was the Mexican Army. What'd you do, take the scenic route?"

"Who's that? Chief Reynolds? Beau, you know I'm cleared with Sandoval!"

"That was three weeks ago. We gave up waiting for you."

"Goddammit, I'm here now! Open up!"

After an unbearable pause, the spotlight went off and we could see men with guns lined up on a high catwalk and makeshift guard tower. They were not soldiers, but some kind of private security force—what my mother called "rent-a-cops." Others below waved us toward a cagelike revolving door in the fence. "Hurry!" they shouted. "Run!"

As we made for it, something charged from the shadows between barriers, something naked, blue, and low to the ground. I barely saw it before gunfire erupted from a dozen places at once and the thing was knocked over, spouting flesh. It was a headless torso riddled with holes, trying to get back up on its hands. Then we were inside the door, pushing as hard as we could. But it only revolved a quarter-turn before crashing against the bolt, trapping us inside.

"Who's the girl?" demanded a stunned-looking sentry.

"Sandoval said I could bring someone," Cowper said. "Open the damn gate!"

"Girls are supposed to be quarantined."

"That's only if they might turn. She has a medical condition that stops her from maturing. Look at her—does she look seventeen?"

"She's *seventeen?*" All the guards nearly jumped out of their skins, as if I was liable to snatch their guts out.

Impatiently, Cowper replied, "Ya morons, if she was gonna, she already woulda. Don't you get it? Where's Reynolds?" As he spoke, I saw a ghastly figure appear out of the hazy twilight, racing along the outside of the fence toward us. We were pinned in place; it could grab us right through the bars.

"Let us in!" I screamed.

"I guess it's 'Bring Your Daughter To Work Day'," said Reynolds from above. "All right, go ahead," he ordered. "Let 'em in." The gate swung open and we were jerked through, half deaf from the fusillade around our ears. I had never heard shooting before. It wasn't like the movies. Something squishy slammed against the bars just as we jumped clear—I didn't want to look. I could've cried to be among people again, and tried to thank them, but any man I approached reared like a spooked horse.

"They're a little traumatized," Cowper observed, taking me aside. "Send 'em a thank-you note."

Reynolds announced, "Hold your fire—that thing's got more holes than the goddamn Albert Hall." At his command, a man swaggered past us wearing a tank on his back like an exterminator. Using a sparking device, he ignited a pale blue pilot light at the end of his weapon and pointed it at the writhing pulp outside. Liquid fire sprayed through the gate. Its oily yellow glow cast all the men's unshaven faces in gold, making them look like combatants in some Hollywood spectacle.

"Cowper!" called Reynolds from above. In the waning torchlight, he too looked heroic up on his crowded platform, like Napoleon reviewing the troops, but he was obviously extremely annoyed about us traipsing through the scene. "Get that girl out of here before somebody shoots her by accident. They'll fill you in at Building Nineteen."

"I have to go to the Front Office," Cowper said.

"The Front Office is restricted to company executives and NavSea."

"Since when?"

"Since you'll find out. Now go."

"I want to talk to Sandoval."

The other man's laugh was mirthless and distracted. "Sandoval's a little scarce these days, along with the rest of the suits in upper management. Talk to Ed Albemarle."

"Ed Albemarle? From Finishing?"

"He's in charge of you people. Better hurry—it's after curfew."

I had no idea what they were talking about, but Mr. Cowper was plainly troubled by it, and that was enough to disturb me. "What's wrong?" I asked.

"I retired here afta twenty years," he groused, nodding to himself. "That was afta serving twenty in the Navy, and you gonna tell me that son of a bitch won't talk to me? He'll talk to that asshole Coombs, but he won't talk to me? Bullshit. I served with Rickover, fa Christ sake! I got more experience than both a them assholes put togetha. We'll see about this . . ."

He started leading me away, but just then the man with the flamethrower was sent outside the fence, and we were caught up in the sudden, expectant lull. "Why is he doing that?" I asked, appalled.

A hyper young guard standing nearby said, "That's Griggs; he's hard-core. 'Have Flamethrower, Will Travel'— that's his motto. First time I saw it I was like, 'Whoa!' It's his job to make sure nothing's left wiggling on the doorstep that might creep into your bunk later on. Hey, somebody's gotta do it!"

In spite of his heavy fuel tank, Griggs moved lightly, a black silhouette against the settling dusk, pilot flame darting back and forth. Every few seconds he would let loose a dripping gust of fire down the concrete hedgerows, as if trying to flush game. Just before he reached the last one, there was a motion over the top of it: Something large, pale, more crablike than human, had been hiding in the smoldering wreck of the car. Now it rose at him from the murk.

He was ready for it, unleashing a billowing yellow plume that met the thing and swallowed it whole. But in that gorgeous light, Griggs must have seen what we all saw, captured in mid-air like a camera flash:

Four garish monstrosities, jittery-fast in the sepia light as creatures in a bizarro silent movie, coming at him from either side. In that split second, Griggs knew he was dead. I knew the feeling, too, and perhaps because I had been wrong I expected something to intervene, to save him, but when the nearest one—a feral harpy wearing a coat of greasy flame— caught Griggs up in her blazing rapture and bellowed into his face with a mouthful of fire, lips peeling back like bacon, black teeth gnashing, hair a crackling torch, then covered his mouth with her own as the others piled on, I could only whimper, *"No, no, no . . ."*

Shocked cries and gunfire rose from the men around us, then were drowned out by the double explosion of the car and Griggs's tank. A fireball like an immense Japanese lantern rose into the sky, radiating debris and baking heat. It enveloped the watchtower, ballooning men upward and dropping them like charred scarecrows. Reynolds was caught completely off guard. I saw him up there just before that firecloud hit, and he seemed to be looking off into the distance. Perhaps he didn't much care that the air was suddenly sucked from his lungs, or that the chill evening had become a blast furnace. Perhaps, like Griggs, he already knew he was dead, having seen in that baleful light the hordes of Xombies emerging from the trees and scrambling across the grassy divide toward the fence.

"Time to skedaddle," said Cowper, dragging me away.

five

SOMEWHAT RELUCTANTLY, I let Mr. Cowper lead me from the zone of frantic activity at the fence to the relative peace just beyond. The road continued, deserted, through tracts of no-man's land and widely spaced industrial buildings. Cries of unseen gulls echoed in the dark.

Much as I trusted Mr. Cowper, I wasn't sure I liked leaving the realm of the living so quickly. With crisp volleys of gunfire ringing behind us, I said, "Is it safe to be out in the open like this?"

"Long as that fence holds," he said, short of breath. "Ya can't see it from here, but this whole compound sticks out in the bay. That gate is the only way on the premises— that's why they've held out so long. Plus it's set way back behind a bunch a posted govament property—not many people know it's here. It ain't even on the map."

"It's a Navy base?"

"Durin' the war it used ta be a trainin' field fa the Naval

Air Station, but now it belongs ta a big defense contracta. They been keepin' it runnin' on an emergency basis as a matter a national security, offerin' safe shelta to families of employees if they stay on the job. I guess they wa pretty hahd up, because they came and tried ta talk me outta retirement. Fat chance. I couldn't see sleepin' on no concrete floor at my age. I said ta them, I says, 'I hope you fellas ain't tryin' ta turn that place inta some kinda refugee centa, because there's no potable wata and nowhere ta run if things get hot. Oughtta be a toxic waste dump from all the lead and cadmium that's leached inna the soil ova the years.'

"They say ta me, 'Fred, that's just it—we got all the water and power we could ever use, plus we got the whole Atlannic Ocean to escape to. We're authorized to use *any and all* facilities at our disposal ta safeguard sensitive technology. That includes movin' it offshore. Doesn't say nothin' about passengers. You can even bring a friend.'

" 'What are you sayin'?' I ast 'em. 'You gotta be kiddin' me.'

"They get all spooky and say, 'Just consider it, Fred. You think things are bad out there now? This ain't even a wet fart compared to the shit that's comin' down the pipe. Sandoval knows—that's why he thought a you. The company needs you, Fred. You're paht of the family.'

"I thought they wa crazier than bedbugs and sent 'em packin', but I remember Beau lookin' me in the eye as he left and sayin', 'This is privileged information, Fred, but Sandoval gives you his personal guarantee that if you come now you're a shoo-in for a seat on the Board. How can ya turn that down?' I says ta him, 'Just watch me.' "

We left the main road, turning right alongside a second fence and a row of low, shuttered buildings. Behind them was a storage yard strewn with heavy machinery and steel scrap, enormous items, but all dwarfed beneath the vast white hangar that towered like an iceberg over all. Many cars and trucks were parked before a second checkpoint, this one manned by only a few guards. Apparently they had been notified about us, because they let us through without any interrogation, keeping well clear of me.

"How ya doin', Sal?" Cowper called to one.

"What did you do?" Sal demanded. "I can't raise Reynolds."

"Reynolds is gone—ya must a seen the explosion. If I were you, I'd get ova there."

"You led 'em to us," Sal said coldly, clicking his gun's safety on and off. "We were doing okay until you led 'em up to us, Fred. You and that . . ." He couldn't bring himself to say it. Keeping his eyes averted from mine, the man said, "You shoulda stayed away. You're not gonna get what you came for."

"All I'm afta right now is Ed Albemarle. He in there?"

"He's in there, but he's not gonna be able to help you. Nobody is."

"Thanks, Sal. It's good ta see you, too."

To our backs, the man said, "I could shoot you for being out after lockdown! I'd be within my rights!"

As we crossed the tarmac toward the hangar, Mr. Cowper noticed my upset and whispered to me, "He doesn't know what he's sayin'. Don't worry, he won't shoot. And it's not true, ya know, what he said about us leadin' 'em in. Those things wa awready on their way—we just happened ta come along at the same time they did. It's that 'critical mass' the TV predicted; they saturate the urban areas, then fan out across the countryside when they run outta prey. Providence is spillin' ova—we just hit the wave-front is all." He was sweating.

"What does he mean, we're not going to get what we came for; nobody's going to help us?"

"Aw, nothin'—it's nothin' fa you ta worry about."

We approached a door and were buzzed through from the guard shack. At first all I saw was a cavernous room full of machinery—rows of giant rusty drums covered with scaffolding, multi-story steel frameworks like half-finished buildings, antlike workers toiling under bleak factory lights—but then the sound began to register: thrash-metal music and the familiar rasp and clatter of practicing skate-punks, punctuated by echoing cheers and catcalls. This was no longer a factory. I could see lots of hardhats, but no one was working. The door locked shut behind us.

It was a playground. An industrial-chic skate park. Curved steel plates weighing tons and cylinders wide as subway tunnels had been commandeered for aerial stunts by bike and skateboard fiends. People swung like Tarzan from dizzying catwalks in the rafters or, more alarmingly, bungee-jumped the hundred or so feet to the concrete floor, springing back just in time. A deejay standing on a huge, multi-wheeled platform—the mother of all flatbed trucks—plied his stylings before a scattering of headbangers and homeboys and someone wearing a big-headed chipmunk costume. The aisles between machines were Turkish bazaars full of tents and sleeping bags, with clotheslines slung like cobwebs overhead.

Everyone seemed completely unaware of the nightmare outside. What's more, they were kids, teenagers—boys. Hundreds of boys. A tough-looking bunch, many of them very "street" in hooded sweatshirts, baggy pants, and stocking caps. They were filthy as chimney-sweeps from life in the factory. Staring in wonder, all I could do was silently mouth, "Oh my goodness."

Our appearance on the floor began to have a ripple effect. As people saw us, saw me, they reacted in surprise, pointing us out to others nearby and gradually bringing a halt to all the activities. Some fell back, others began to come forward to meet us. Among the latter were many older men I hadn't noticed at first. They didn't look particularly friendly.

One exception was a burly, chinless guy in dirty denim coveralls who came running up, eyes wide, and clasped hands with Mr. Cowper. "Fred, you bastard," he said. "Where in hell did you come from?"

"Hell is right," said Cowper. He leaned toward the other man and said, "What's the bad news, Ed?"

The bigger man pursed his lips, bobbing his head. "It's like you said, Fred. They screwed us."

"When?"

"Last week. Had a big recommissioning ceremony, gave us a steak dinner, then dropped the bomb while we were all loosenin' our belts."

"Who did? Sandoval?"

The heavyset man nodded bitterly, saying, "Those bastards never had any intention of taking us along."

"Has she put to sea?"

"Not yet, but they're not telling us anything. Should be any time now."

"Coulda told ya."

"You did."

"Did they give any reason?"

"Yeah, we got a boatload of sensitive materials the day before from Norfolk—you know about SPAM?"

"Whattaya mean, Spam?"

The other man waved it away. "Sensitive Personnel and Materials—crap! All the stuff the government can't leave behind when it shuts down. Basically it got our seat. I don't care about me, but those kids busted ass for a month, and now they get bumped by a shipment of Top Secret nonsense? The future is riding with these kids, and they're fit for duty."

"Oh yeah?" Cowper said, eyeing the gritty playland. "Where at? Ringlin' Brothas?"

The other man perked up defensively. "Hey," he said, "don't knock 'em for blowin' off steam. After last week we're all on strike around here."

"Now Albemarle, that sounds like union talk."

Ed Albemarle laughed grimly. "Yeah, it's a union shop now. We're gonna start picketing. Give the Xombies signs to carry." Throughout the conversation he had pointedly avoided looking my way, though everyone else in the place was. Now he turned toward me, and I could see the nervous whites of his eyes. "And who's the little lady?" he asked.

Before Mr. Cowper could speak, I said, "Lulu. Lulu Pangloss," offering my hand. It almost killed him to shake it. Hoping to put him at ease, I added, "How do you do, Mr. Albemarle?"

He regarded me with the awe of a man seeing a talking dog. "God damn," he said, taking back his hand. "You know . . . girls are bad medicine these days. I'm surprised you got in."

And none too pleased, I thought.

"She's okay," said Cowper. "She has a condition that stops her havin' a period. Female trouble. She ain't gonna turn."

Though I understood the necessity, it was mortifying to hear him announce this to everyone. To those boys.

"Why?" Albemarle said suspiciously. "How old is she?"

"Seventeen," I replied, at which they all caught their breaths and seemed to backpedal, or at least lean backward. My age bounced around the group like heresy, triggering furious whispering and a few cries of "Uh-uh!" and "*Hell* no!"

Albemarle looked apologetically at Cowper. "Fred, how can we have her in here?" he asked. "I'm in charge of these people's safety."

"Then you betta forget about her and get these kids movin'. All hell's breakin' loose outside."

"What are you talking about?"

"You'd know if you'd turn off that racket." He meant the music. Albemarle complied, barking an order that was relayed back to the deejay. The boy, having come down for the commotion, mounted the crawler and killed the sound. At once it was possible to hear the faint sputtering of gunfire outside. Everyone in the room became transfixed.

"I'm tellin' you," said Cowper, "we gotta get 'em outta here, Ed. Beau Reynolds is dead, and Security ain't gonna hold that fence fa long. It's up ta us now. We gotta move, and fast."

A few people reacted strongly to the news of Reynolds' death, but Albemarle spoke over them. "Move where?" he said. "There's a lockdown in effect—no unsupervised activity. Set foot out of here and we'll be shot on sight."

"We're the last a their worries, Ed. This is our chance, while they're puttin' every available man on that fence."

"Our chance to do what?"

"Get down ta the pen."

"Down to the—oh no. Are you serious? You gotta be shittin' me."

"Why not? Take 'em by surprise, you neva know."

"Jesus, you are serious!"

"What choice do we have?" Mr. Cowper's voice swelled with surprising authority. "Dammit, Ed, listen! Alla you listen a me! Fuhget about them *things* out there, what's gonna happen to ya now that the company don't need ya no more? They got what they wanted—from here on out you're just dead weight. Tell me you haven't been worryin' about that! Is Sandoval gonna keep this place supplied and manned after he's gone? How long ya think that security detail is gonna stay on duty once supplies start gettin' short? I'll tell ya right now they got an escape plan a their own, an' it don't involve sharin' with you. Our only praya is to take what we can, right now."

Albemarle's face had gone darker and darker as Mr. Cowper's speech went on. Now he said wearily, "You know, Fred, they shot Bob Martino for that kind of talk. Shot him in front of everybody after the big dinner, then trussed him up and burned him, right there—you can see the spot. I'll never eat another steak. So if you think we have any illusions about our chances with the company, think again. But we've lost so much already . . . we're tired. *I'm* tired. All I want to do at this point is let these kids be kids for however much time they—" He was interrupted by a dull boom that rattled the walls. Dust sifted down.

Over the stunned murmuring, Mr. Cowper said, "Time's up, Ed."

"What do we got to lose?" This was shouted by a tall elderly fellow with white hair and a bushy mustache.

"He's right," said a stocky character who looked like an old-time circus Strong Man. "We're fish in a barrel sittin' here."

Albemarle became angry. "And what? We just march our kids out into the line of fire?"

A number of boys cheered the idea, one calling out, "Better than bein' stuck here!" a second saying, "Shit yeah!" and several more shouting, "Let's go!"

Mr. Cowper interceded, holding up his bony arms to yell, "Nobody's gonna get shot!" The crowd hesitated, listening. "They're not stupid enough to shoot us, awright? They're busy enough without makin' a whole mess a Xombies *inside* the fence. That's all they'd accomplish by killin' us, an' they know it." To Albemarle he explained, "Ya said yaself they burned Bob Martino. That means they know he woulda come back. We're more of a threat ta them than they ah ta us, an' that's the God's honest truth. Best they can do is keep us locked up in here, alive. Now who wants ta go and who wants ta stay?"

It was a landslide. Even Ed Albemarle grudgingly nodded, causing a cheer.

In the midst of the excitement, I bit my lip and tapped Mr. Cowper on the shoulder. Trying to speak privately, I said, "Um, Mr. Cowper? How can we get out if we're locked in here?"

He smiled thinly and patted my head. "Don't you worry about a thing, little girl."

GETTING OUT OF the building was a piece of cake. Albemarle dispatched a handful of the bigger boys to a supply room—the "tool crib"—and they returned with armloads of welding and cutting implements that they obviously knew how to use.

"Hey, Mr. Albemarle," one of the boys said, looking like a blacksmith as he donned protective leathers. "Is there an SSP for this?" The joking question raised a laugh.

"Yeah," Albemarle shot back, "Shipyard Standard

Procedure says kiss my ass. In case you hadn't noticed, we're not doing things by the book anymore, boys and girls. So stop screwing around and get that door open."

The door he meant was not the door we'd come in through, but the sixty-foot-high hangar doors. They'd been secured by a mammoth chain strung through holes in the metal like something out of *King Kong*. Trundled up to it on a rolling scaffold, the boys applied their blinding blue flare to one of the bagel-thick links, making a tremendous zapping sound and showers of sparks. "Don't look at it," Cowper said, a little late. Steel dripped like burning tallow, and then, just like that, the chain clanked apart.

"All right, roll 'er open!" Albemarle bellowed. "Everybody behind the Sallie, heads down! We're going on parade!"

The "Sallie" was the deejay's platform. It was a freight-carrying goliath, all wheels and deck (the word SALLIE cast in steel above its low front cockpit), which now started up with a groundshaking rumble and rolled forward on nine rows of tires. It reminded me of the vehicle NASA used to transport spacecraft to the launch pad, though somewhat smaller. Fathers and sons fell in behind its twin rear cab as it approached the parting doors. When it passed us, Mr. Cowper and I joined the crowd.

"Stay close," he said, pinching my bicep.

People gave me plenty of room, so for once I didn't feel claustrophobic, as I often did in groups, and in fact took comfort from the sheer size of the crowd. We were an army.

"*You're* not coming," someone said to me from behind, but I ignored him and kept moving.

We streamed out of the hangar at a fast walk, the crawler bearing right to make for the inner guardpost. It was now deserted. The main gate was behind us, mostly hidden by buildings, but we could hear the commotion there—sounds like rioting hooligans with firecrackers—and see the dim orange glow of flames illuminating the draped fence like a paper screen, on which life-size shadow puppets scrambled.

Men could be glimpsed running along a catwalk at the top, dodging mangled hands that lunged spastically at them through the razor wire.

After seeing a guard yanked into the lacerating coils by those obscene blue things I didn't dare look back anymore, covering my ears to muffle the screams. A wave of gibbering fear swept the crowd, causing some boys to fall and almost be trampled, but Cowper and Albemarle kept yelling, "Eyes forward! Keep moving! Eyes forward—look where you're going!" and it seemed to help, even though we could barely see where we were going.

Heading down a grassy slope, we descended into gloom, with pale, unlit buildings rising like sunken ships out of the fog and our only illumination the haloed caution lights of the Sallie. Smells of seaweed, tar, and diesel exhaust mingled in the air. It was a strange, ghostly parade all right, with the Sallie its unadorned float.

"What's it like out there?" asked a boy to my left. He was the one in the chipmunk costume, now carrying its head under his arm. It was a blue-collar chipmunk, I noticed, with work boots, protective goggles, and a plush hardhat. From the boy's intensity I realized he meant the outside world.

The question set me off again; I found it very hard to reply. Eyes dribbling tears, it was all I could do to shrug, turning away to wipe my face on my puffy sleeve.

"That's pretty much what I figured," he said bitterly. "How did you get through?"

I wasn't going to get into it. "Ask *him*. Where are we going?"

Before he could answer, another boy said, "You'd know, if you belonged here."

"Don't talk to her—she's a freak," said someone else.

"Shoulda stayed where you was, Little Miss Muffet."

"Nobody wants you here."

"Ya see any other women with us? That's 'cause they were quarantined. We hadda leave 'em behind—"

"Sisters, mothers . . . all of 'em."

"—all gone, an' you think *you* comin'? No way."

"My auntie can't come, you can't come, bitch."

Trying to stem the hostility, I said, "Wait a minute, I didn't ask to come here. I'm just along for the ride."

This was the wrong thing to say. The reaction was so vehement—*"She just along for the ride!"*—that some of the adults cast puzzled and annoyed looks our way. Frankly, I would have appreciated any adult intervention, but the grownups were deeply engrossed in heated business of their own. I resented Mr. Cowper for letting himself be monopolized this way.

We passed through an open gate and entered a field of massive rusty cylinders, large as redwood trunks. Above them, disappearing into the fog, loomed a huge inert crane; a skeletal Godzilla guarding her eggs. The Sallie stopped, and with it the abuse directed at me. Everyone's attention was suddenly focused on something down the road—some kind of winged, black monolith with giraffe-speckled antennae sprouting from its crest.

"Is that what I think it is?" I asked. No one replied.

It was a very, very big submarine.

six

AS IF DISMISSED from school, the boys broke formation and surged toward the sub. I was swept along in the rush, taking comfort in being momentarily ignored, lost in the crowd. Albemarle was yelling, "Hey! Hey! Wait!" but it wasn't until the shooting started that we all stopped short.

It was a bright spike of automatic-weapons fire from the vicinity of the submarine. I couldn't see much, caught in the sudden pile-up, but I could hear an amplified voice bellow, "HALT. YOU ARE IN A RESTRICTED AREA. WE ARE AUTHORIZED TO USE DEADLY FORCE, AND WILL NOT HESITATE TO DO SO UNLESS YOU TURN BACK NOW. LEAVE AT ONCE." As the voice spoke, a harsh spotlight cleaved the mist, probing us like a boy stirring ants with a stick.

People fell back behind the Sallie or jammed into the shadows between rusty cylinders, and as I took refuge in just such a trench amid dozens of grease-smelling boys,

I lost touch with Mr. Cowper. A squall of curses and complaints arose from the gang—"That's it, man, shit! We ain't gettin' in there! We're fucked!"—leading me to believe all hope was lost. Then they turned on me: "You and that fuckin' old man! What you gonna do now? Let them Marines fry our asses? Damn! Shoulda *known* you were fulla shit!" At once I was being manhandled, treated like a hot potato, shoved hand-to-hand out of the hiding place into the searchlight's bullying glare.

Now I was alone in the road, feeling very small beside the multiple tractor tires of the Sallie vehicle. One of my shoes had come off, and I could feel the cold, coarse macadam through my thin stocking. The spotlight was warm. In a reverie of hurt feelings, I shielded my eyes and began walking toward it. *Fine,* I thought madly. It felt good to let go. Tears streaming, I walked faster and faster, aware of nothing but my own feet and the baking noonday light. Swelling orchestral music seemed to accompany me, as if I was expected to break into some showstopping Broadway tune.

Suddenly someone snatched me off my feet and dove with me out of the light. As we hit the dirt I had a strange, strong sensation of being tackled by Santa. Then my senses returned, and I realized it was only the padded costume that made me think of Santa—it was the boy in the chipmunk suit, as if that was somehow less bizarre. Over his furry shoulder I could see row after row of great wheels lumbering by, close enough to touch.

"Sorry," he said, trying to catch his breath. "Jesus, you okay?"

My cheek stung from being scuffed on the ground. I wasn't sure what had just happened, but as the Sallie passed entirely, I saw the flattened chipmunk head in the middle of the road. Sitting up, I said, "Did you just apologize for saving my life?"

"Oh, sorry—I mean—" Before he could say more, rattling bursts of automatic gunfire broke out at the waterfront and he threw himself on top of me, crying, "Get down!"

But they weren't shooting at us; they were shooting at the advancing Sallie. Gleaming under the spotlight like a monstrous sowbug, the flat juggernaut maneuvered drunkenly toward the sub, where orange-vested figures could be seen running for cover. The gunfire was all coming from a white humvee parked at dockside, which was being used as a gunrest by two men in Darth Vader helmets. Flashing jets of ammo speared out from them in a twin stream, gouging nickle-bright pocks all over the crawler and leaving red afterimages hanging in the air.

The boy's body shuddered at each volley, his face screwed shut against the racket. *"It's okay, it's okay,"* he said, more to himself than to me. He was heavy, a big guy who needed a shave, but even without his mask he had a chipmunk quality that made me want to pet him and say, "There, there." For all the noise, I was strangely calm, and couldn't bring myself to turn away from the action, though I was afraid any moment a stray bullet might catch me in the eye.

There was no stopping the thing. At the last possible second, the soldiers gave up shooting and retreated to the submarine's gangway. Their humvee disappeared from view as the hulking tractor closed with it and bowled it over the edge of the landing with a junkyard crash. Continuing on, the Sallie then struck the pivoting base of the gangway, buckling the narrow span like a tinkertoy and causing the guards to fall out of sight. And still the machine kept on, jutting out further and further into space, making its own bridge to the submarine. I held my breath for the impending, catastrophic fall—*Penis Patrol*—but the Sallie stopped there, half its wheels frozen in mid-air. The sub's searchlight stayed trained on this precarious object as if staring in disbelief.

Now a voice issued from the deejay equipment left on the Sallie:

"THIS IS COMMANDA FRED COWPER, REQUESTING PERMISSION TO COME ABOARD."

A man emerged from the Sallie's unscathed rear cockpit

and stood holding a wireless microphone. He wore a stunning white military uniform, with black and gold epaulets and a cluster of medals over his breast pocket. In spite of the fog, the distance, and the masterful new costume, I could see at once that it was indeed Mr. Cowper. No wonder he almost ran me down—he had been driving backward. Amazed, I pushed the boy off and stood up. Hundreds of others were coming out of hiding around us, equally bemused, murmuring in the dark.

The submarine's loudspeaker replied, "FRED, THIS IS COMMANDER COOMBS. I DON'T KNOW WHAT YOU THINK YOU'RE DOING, BUT IN MY BOOK IT'S TREASON. YOU ARE INTERFERING WITH CRITICAL NAVAL OPERATIONS."

Cowper said, "HARVEY, THIS WAS NOT MY ORIGINAL PLAN, BUT I'M TRYIN' A MAKE THE BEST OF A BAD SITUATION. HERE'S THE DEAL: LET ME AND ALL A THESE PEOPLE ON BOARD, THEN PUT US ASHORE SOMEPLACE HALFWAY SECURE. IN RETURN, WE'LL EARN OUR KEEP—I KNOW YOU'RE SHORT A HANDS. THESE KIDS'LL DO ANYTHING YOU TELL 'EM, PLUS WE'VE GOT A CREW OF OLD FARTS WITH DOLPHINS WHO ARE JUST ITCHIN' TO GET BACK BEHIND THE WHEEL. HEY, I'LL RE-UP. WHERE ARE YOU GONNA FIND ANOTHER GUY WITH MY EXPERIENCE?"

"I'M NOT BIG ON EXTORTION, YOU SENILE SON OF A BITCH," said Coombs.

"WHAT EXTORTION? IT'S A HUMANITARIAN GESTURE. NOT TO MENTION KEEPIN' FAITH WITH THESE PEOPLE . . . AND ME FOR THAT MATTA. SANDOVAL PROMISED US—TAKE IT UP WITH HIM IF YOU DON'T LIKE IT. THE BASTID IS THERE, ISN'T HE?"

"AS A MATTER OF FACT HE'S OVERDUE. IT WOULDN'T SURPRISE ME TO HEAR THAT YOU AND YOUR MOB HAVE KILLED HIM."

"HEY, I'M TRYIN' A SAVE LIVES, YOU ARRO-
GANT PRICK, BUT IF YOU DON'T START LETTING
US BOARD RIGHT NOW I'M GONNA BACK THE
SALLIE OVA YA AND SCUTTLE THE WHOLE SHE-
BANG. WE GOT NOTHIN' TO LOSE." Cowper ducked
back into the low glass cab and started the engine. To us he
announced, "ALL ABOARD! NO RUNNING! BOARD
THE BOAT IN AN ORDERLY WAY—THE CREW
WILL DIRECT YOU BELOW . . . *OR ELSE*."

We were already moving. After the first tentative steps,
boys stampeded past, too rushed to give me a hard time. I
could see that the collapsed gangway didn't slow anyone
down—apparently it was just as easy to hop down from the
concrete ledge to the guano-caked timbers alongside the sub
and from there to the stern, where a plank had been laid
across. I just let myself be dragged along. Everyone else
was on fire with the instinct to survive, but I felt listless and
drained and totally clueless.

Fighting the malaise, I tried to blend in with the rest as I
waited for Mr. Cowper, staying close to Albemarle and the
other men who were shepherding the stragglers. Below I
could see the two fallen Marine guards being fished from the
water by the submarine's crew—they both looked shaken
but alive. Other sailors were now helping boys across that
finger of dark water. They didn't look particularly resentful of us, which I found reassuring.

It was a surprise when some of them suddenly pointed
weapons up at the landing and began to shoot. We were sitting ducks.

THE GUNFIRE CAUSED shrieks of terror, and everyone
dropped to the ground. No, I noticed that some of us didn't
duck, didn't stop, but simply charged ahead with manic
fury. They didn't look right. These were the ones the sailors
were shooting at.

Xombies.

There were Xombies among us, and many more coming down the hill.

Not everyone was as slow on the uptake as I—Albemarle and the other men had already created a defensive line at the rear of the crowd and were brandishing large hammers like those used for chiseling. I would learn that these were standard equipment at the plant. "Don't panic," they shouted. "Just keep moving!" When a skinless creature in burnt security clothes rushed up through the fog, they all raised hammers like Thor and clouted it down. The problem was, it wouldn't stay down, but rebounded off the pavement like a dented gingerbread man.

"It's Reynolds!" someone screamed.

"Just like you're marking studs, boys," shouted Albemarle, pelting the thing again.

More Xombies came tearing in, nimble as stage-painted acrobats. Keeping them off required a kind of assembly-line operation, a constant gauntlet of flying hammers, but our hundred-to-one advantage was quickly eroding. In places, the line started breaking up into fractal eddies of hand-to-hand fighting. To the boys up front, who were taking their sweet time boarding the sub, these must have seemed more like fringe disturbances at a rock concert than a desperate losing battle, but for us at the rear it was doom breathing down our necks: medieval combat and middle-school fire drill rolled into one.

Then Mr. Cowper was at my side. "Doin' fine," he said, splendid in his dress whites. Over my head, he shouted, "Don't nobody get trampled! We'll make it!"

"When did you manage to change your clothes?" I asked.

"I always come prepared."

"We can't all fit in that submarine."

"Sure we can," he said. "Ya see those big cylinders by the road? Those used ta hold ballistic missiles, but they wa taken out ta make room fa cruise missiles and SEAL teams. That refit's been postponed indefinitely, which leaves a big empty space inside the missile compahtment—you'll see. Don't worry."

I wished he looked more confident himself.

As the last of us were helped down from the platform by furiously yelling submariners—*"Get out of the way! Down, down! Move your asses!"*—the amount of shooting redoubled, and I was shocked to see how many Xombies were now massed on the landing above. We were becoming outnumbered. Spent shells tinkled down the sides of the sub like slot-machine tokens, and icy water splashed me as bullet-riddled demons stage-dived off the edge to fall into the depths beneath the pier. The water was soon packed with thrashing ghouls.

Passed bucket-brigade fashion along a line of jumpy crewmen, I finally made it up onto the sub's runway-like deck, its entire length crowded with milling refugees. Above us soared the mammoth black cross that was the vessel's conning tower, steel Golgotha beckoning the pilgrims with salvation.

Waiting my turn to go below, I prayed.

seven

THEY WEREN'T LETTING us below.

"The hatches must be kept clear," shouted someone at the head of the crowd. "Ship's personnel must have free access or we cannot cast off! Make room!"

A squall of protest and pleading met this development, but we were packed too tightly to riot, and in any case it was only those boys near enough to actually see the hatches who really objected—the rest of us knew we weren't getting below anytime soon. The sub was hundreds of feet long, and the Xombies all but upon us.

We watched helplessly as they spilled over the landing, scrambling for the best crossing and leaping like grotesque pirates for the stern. Albemarle's thinning rear-guard did its best to hold them off, but the footing down there was terrible: a slippery ramp to the sea. Men fell by the dozens, locked in death-grips with twistedly grinning monstrosities as they slid out of sight. Every loss set off a new a chorus of grief. Mr. Cowper was there, a luminous figure in his white suit, and I dreaded the moment I would see him grappling for his life or being dragged into the water.

At some point the shooting stopped, and I heard people say, "They're out of ammo." No sooner had this idea been relayed through the crowd than there was a commotion up front.

"What's going on?" I asked, as boys around me frantically craned their necks to see.

An obese, Buddha-faced kid nearby replied, "The crew have all gone below."

"Maybe they're getting more bullets," I said.

"They've closed the hatches."

A sickening weight seemed to press the air out of us.

"Well, that's it," someone said calmly. "We're dead."

"We been played," another boy agreed.

"They let us on the boat, wait until we good and trapped, then lock us out. All they gotta do now is wait—Xombies gonna do the rest."

"That is so not right."

"Shit, man."

I didn't know what to believe, and wasn't sure they did either. "Let's not jump to conclusions," I said shrilly. "We don't know what they're doing down there."

"Shut up. They got food, they got water, they got air, they got power. They sittin' pretty."

Not everyone was taking it as stoically as these few boys. Elsewhere on the deck the babble of panic could be heard: a hundred variations on the theme of, *"They can't just leave us out here!"*

Turning on me, a wild-eyed boy with a hairnet said, "This is all your fault."

"God, shut *up*," I groaned.

"If you hadn't come along, none a this woulda happened."

"You are so stupid."

They all closed in around me like hostile savages, grimy hands reaching for my arms, my hair, my throat.

Completely exhausted, I could think of nothing to say or do. Time stopped, and everything froze into a weird tableau, jittering like film snarled in an old projector. Wait. Vibration—the deck was vibrating. Whitewater boiled up around the rudder. From one end of the submarine to the other, a desperate, bedraggled cheer broke out.

We were moving.

IT WAS A sickening, slow race for time. The huge submarine took forever to get going, while Xombies were fast overwhelming the lowest part of the stern. It was a giant blender down there. After the propeller started, there had been a general retreat up to the safety cable, but the Xombies (mainly male ones, I should say) had no such qualms. They continued leaping to the slippery slope in droves, heedless of being sucked under, and because of it were picking off our rear-guard.

Yet the sense that we were moving, the renewed hope of escape, did seem to give strength to our defenders. They fought back with incredible zeal, sacrificing themselves rather than permit the enemy to breach their lines.

Once a Xombie had someone around the neck, it clamped on like a python and was all but impossible to get off. Many times I saw men throw themselves and their clinging attackers over the side rather than risk joining the Xombie ranks. For that was what was at stake, I belatedly realized, not death, but Xombie membership. They did not want to kill, but to multiply. They *lusted* for us. For them, strangling was a procreative act—there was even a horrific sort of deep kiss involved that suggested a perverse, rough tenderness toward the struggling victim. It was horrible to see.

The sub started to budge, glacially scraping along the landing. We were making the slowest getaway of all time.

As we passed the overhanging hulk of the Sallie, I had a good long look at its mangled rows of tires, the blown-out glass cockpit, and the heavily pitted SALLIE emblem. The thought of Mr. Cowper backing into that firestorm made me shake my head in disbelief—had my mother ever seen that side of him? She never told me anything that explained her fierce attraction . . . or excused it. I could see him down there now, a little old man taking his turn with a hammer, and felt something unlike any emotion I'd ever experienced: a raw amalgam of yearning and awe. Love. Was he really my father? For the first time, I wanted him to be. I desperately needed him to be.

My reverie was interrupted by shouts of "Look!" and fingers pointing ashore. At first I couldn't see anything in the gloom, but then a peculiar white shape came trundling across the grass, making a faint electric whine: a golf cart! It sped down toward us at top speed, faster than I thought golf carts could go, and skidded to a stop beside the Sallie.

"Jesus Christ," said Albemarle from below, "it's Jim Sandoval!"

Female Xombies on the landing raced for the well-dressed driver, who climbed, scrabbling for footholds, to the Sallie's freight-bed. They vaulted up after him, and he ran to its projecting front end, bald head gleaming in the spotlight. Cornered, he didn't hesitate, but used his momentum to leap across the water into the mass of us—it had to be a good twenty feet. People were knocked over like tenpins. Before we could learn if anyone had been hurt by this desperate act, we were distracted by a thunderous sound from the shore: thousands of trampling footsteps. We fell silent, listening.

They came. The foggy void boiled over with them like a Biblical plague—or perhaps extras in a Biblical epic—rushing forward in mute frenzy. "Xombierama," said a much-pierced boy in awe.

Fear sounded all over the deck as this inhuman host, this nightmarathon, swept across the field and down the landing in an avalanche of flailing blue arms and legs. People steeled themselves for the bitter end, but appalling as the enemy seemed, its numbers served only to clog the already precarious stern crossing, and a great many were simply crowded off into the propeller wash. Also initially alarming were the spastic multitudes swarming the Sallie, their rushing bodies spilling off as if from a sluice . . . but they were too late: Sandoval's leap had been lucky—the submarine was now just out of jumping range, and the naked throngs pummeled harmlessly down the ship's side like a lumpy waterfall, piling up at the waterline to claw against the passing hull.

It really began to seem that the handful of Xombies already on board were all we had to fear (which was certainly bad enough). But then the Sallie began to tip over on us.

"Whoa," people moaned, seeing the rig teeter from the weight of massing bodies. If they didn't keep jumping off like lemmings it would have gone already. My heart constricted, and I tried to will the ship to move faster: Come on come on come on . . .

So close. As the ship's big rudder fin finally came even with the Sallie, the great crawler tilted past the point of no return. Cracking sounds like gunshots could be heard as its plank bed flexed and the rear wheels levitated upward. Keens of mass dread erupted from all of us as the front end of the thing dipped into our surge, but still didn't topple—the banks of tires at its axis gripped the ledge until the last possible instant, until the vehicle was so improbably steep that the audio equipment on its back plummeted through the Xombies hanging below.

"It's gonna hit the screw, it's gonna hit the screw," someone jibbered.

The Sallie dropped.

It went loudly, each of its nine rows of wheels slamming first against the concrete ledge, then against the lower wooden pier—BABAMBABAMBABAMBABAM! As it jounced downward it must have just cleared the giant propeller, because the ringing, fatal blow we were all holding our breaths for never came. What did happen was scary enough: a mound of water engulfed the stern, carrying away Xombies but also rows of men. Some of them escaped the propeller and were left bobbing in our wake. We could hear them calling in the dark.

Not many of us had the energy to be mortified. I couldn't see if Mr. Cowper was still aboard or not, and for the moment I didn't want to know. A few hysterical kids were restrained rather impatiently. I understood: At that instant my biggest fear was that someone might include me in their compassion, might slow our flight. I would've gladly killed someone like that, even though we were safely out of reach of the Xombies.

But there was nothing to worry about. The boat didn't stop.

eight

IT WAS VERY cold and windy out on the open water; the only shelter we had was each other. Grief sounds threaded the night. A lot of people had to go to the bathroom, but unlike the others I couldn't just pee over the side. Albemarle, Mr. Cowper, and the rest of the adults came forward to see what could be done, which wasn't much. There was no one from the sub's crew to appeal to, except maybe hidden atop the conning tower, and they wouldn't answer our shouts. The searchlight had been turned off. When Mr. Cowper's uniform went by in the dark I grabbed a sleeve.

"Hey," he said, pulling away. "Not now, honey, okay? Sit tight."

Bereft, watching the dark shore recede, my initial flush of gratitude quickly passed and I began to get anxious. How long did the crew expect us to stay out here? A rough head-count was organized: there were about four hundred people on deck, less than fifty of them adults. At least half the older men we'd started out with were gone. Boys were the great majority, mostly teenagers like myself (well, not exactly like myself—these were more the Ricki Lake crowd), who seemed to have the same casual expertise about the sub that other kids had about Nintendo. Sea urchins. Listening to them, I quickly learned that the sub was the *boat,* the conning tower was called the *fairwater* or *sail,* and the leathery black deck was a *steel beach.* They had prepared for this nuclear orphanage. But obviously something had gone wrong . . . and I, the only female, was to blame.

"This is bullshit, man," said the hairnet guy. Turning on me once more, he groused, "This is all your fault. If you hadn't of come, things would be different. You're bad luck. You gonna throw a hex on this whole thing."

Vision swimming with pathetic tears, I said, "What is your *problem,* kid? I'm serious; are you off your medication or something? Because even the dumbest knuckle-dragging moron would see that this is not an appropriate time or place to be pulling this Slim Shady bullshit."

"Oh, you really auditioning to be my bitch now."

A voice over my shoulder said, "Shut up, Mitch." It was the boy in the chipmunk costume. He was a head taller than the other, but somewhat less menacing: Sesame Street versus Crenshaw. Squeezing between me and the homeboy, he added, "Give it a rest, man. She's been through enough."

"What you say?" Mitch exploded, shoving his furry shoulder. "Huh? You got somethin' to say, you clown? Pussy? Oh, she been through enough, is that it? Fuck you! You wanna do somethin' about it? What you gonna do?" The costumed boy didn't react, but just watched the other with tired patience. "That's what I *thought,*" Mitch said at last, spitting at his feet and pushing past us into the crowd.

After a moment the bigger boy said softly, "He lost his whole family, I mean we all have, so you know . . ."

I nodded in perfect understanding. After a short interlude I asked, "What's with the chipmunk costume?"

"I'm not a chipmunk. I'm Safety Squirrel."

"Aren't squirrels supposed to have a big fluffy tail?"

"It got caught in the machinery. That's the tragedy of Safety Squirrel."

Gruff sounds of an argument broke out under the tower. Men were shouting, "Throw the sonofabitch overboard!" and a raw voice beseeched, "SPAM, I'm SPAM—ask Coombs!" Making my way foreward, I practically tripped over a man sitting on the deck. He was the bald guy—Sandoval—who had jumped across from the Sallie. He looked stunned and was hugging his right knee as if in pain. The other men loomed all around.

"Quiet, Lulu," Mr. Cowper said brusquely when I found him. To the injured man he said, "We've had ta fight fa what we wa promised. A lotta men I've known fa years wa lost. Since you're the one who made the promises, Jim, ya kinda in a spot."

Gravel-voiced, the other replied, "I didn't have any choice, Fred. Jesus, I'm glad to see you."

"I bet you ah. We're all happy as clams to see you, too."

"Now just hold on. It wasn't up to me. When I made that offer to all of you I didn't think there was anybody left in Washington who would bother about a decommissioned, neutered boat. STRATCOM had her birds in Kings Bay— they weren't interested anymore. I figured she was a big fat windfall for us. Can you blame me? With communications all down, and the crazy talk out of Cutler: we were bombing Canada, or it was the Rapture—crap like that? I never heard back from Group Ten, much less the Nuclear Posture Review, so we decided to reactivate her as SSGN on Coombs' authority. Don't laugh—he was the most senior person we had. We never got any acknowledgement from COMSUB-LANT. Then all of a sudden a tender shows up carrying promotions and sealed orders for all the NavSea people—"

"Not to mention SPAM," Albemarle snapped.

"Right, SPAM—Sensitive Personnel and Materials. Tons of SPAM. Hey, I was as disappointed as anybody. Suddenly SPAM took precedence over everything else. In the absence of any other orders Coombs might have been willing to entertain the thought of an employee sealift, but after that it was his sworn duty to execute this SPAM operation. I lost my vote."

"But you run the company," said Cowper. "You're a civilian contractor, not his subordinate. You're the Chairman, fa God's sake, the CEO. You coulda stood up to him, and Reynolds woulda backed you."

"You think so? And be a traitor to his country? Maybe. I didn't see it that way, Fred. It's been my experience that some ex-Navy guys are pretty patriotic."

This was the wrong thing to say. Albemarle jumped in, "We're plenty patriotic, you asshole. This is about saving Americans. I notice you were pretty quick to save your own ass back there."

"That's because I'm Sensitive."

"You weren't too God-damned sensitive to let Bob Martino get blown away."

"No, I'm Sensitive Personnel. I'm SPAM—that's what I've been trying to tell you. That's why I'm here. Otherwise I would've shipped out with the rest of the Board a week ago."

"Whattaya mean, *you're* SPAM?" Cowper squawked.

"I mean I have been designated essential to the mission— Coombs is required to deliver me at all costs."

"Deliver you where? Why?"

"That I don't know. But it gives you guys a pretty sweet bargaining chip, doesn't it?"

"He's lying," said one of the other men threateningly. "He's just tryin' to save his friggin' neck."

"Give me a little credit, will you? I wouldn't lie about something that you can verify so easily. Ask Admiral Coombs."

"*Admiral* Coombs," Mr. Cowper scoffed. "That would be fine, if he'd talk to us. The maneuvering watch won't answer our hails."

Albemarle said, "He's up there and we're down here. That's the problem."

"Just because he won't talk doesn't mean he won't listen, Ed." Sandoval pointed to the top of the sail. "How about I let them know I'm here?"

Mr. Cowper rubbed his chin, said, "Go ahead."

"Topside watch!" he shouted weakly. "This is for Commander Coombs! Harvey, it's James Sandoval, requesting to come aboard! I made it! Harvey! Admiral Coombs!"

There was no reply. He tried several more times, straining harder with each effort, but the tower appeared to be deserted. Concerned muttering broke out among the bystanders.

"I don't think there's anybody up there," Sandoval said finally, discouraged.

"How can there be nobody up there?" demanded Cowper. "We're in the goddamn channel! Somebody's gotta be piloting this thing!"

Sandoval shrugged helplessly. "I know. I don't understand it."

"Maybe they're piloting by scope," a boy offered.

"And maybe we don't need no cockeyed opinions from the peanut gallery," Albemarle barked. To Cowper, he said, "Look, this bastard's just stalling for time. He'll say anything to keep us off him until Coombs gets things under control. SPAM my ass. For all we know—"

He was cut off by a falling body that slammed him to the deck. Two more followed in quick succession, plunging into the sea.

"Heads up!" Mr. Cowper shouted, pinning me flat against the tower. Other men followed suit, keeping the crowd back, but there didn't seem to be any more jumpers, and after a moment everyone rushed in to help Albemarle and the fallen man.

Albemarle was groggy, but the new man was wide awake. He wore a dark blue jumpsuit with gold dolphins stitched over the left breast pocket. Over the right pocket was his name: COOMBS.

"Xombies," he gasped. *"Xombies on board."*

"THEY'RE SPREADING DOWN there like weasels, ferrets, snatching men right and left," the commander babbled. He was a trim, swarthy man with a hawk nose and short, dense hair like Velcro. "So fast, so fast, there's no time to *think*. They suck the life out of you, you know that? Put their filthy mouth on yours and—" He shuddered violently "Then you're one of them."

"Easy there, Skipper," said Mr. Cowper. "How much a the boat have they got? Where ah they?"

"Wardroom—musta started in the wardroom with the injured. Yeah, one of those Marines who cracked his head, had to be." His eyes were glazed, feverish. "I'm on the bridge and all hell breaks loose—Montoya's screaming in the phone for armed support, the general alarm starts going off—I don't know what the hell's happening. I drop down to control and there's nobody there! Kranuski's on the com yelling to secure the forward bulkhead, and all of a sudden Stanaman comes running in from operations like he can't breathe, blue in the face, and just before he reaches me Baker and Lee come flying across the console and take him down, wham! I thought they killed him, but he's fighting back like a damn wildcat, and Lee yells, 'Get out, Cap! Up top!' Just as I'm thinking, *Xombies!* here comes Tim Shaye and Rudy after me like a couple of damn ghouls, and there's nowhere to go but up. They're right on my ass the whole way—I never climbed so fast in my life." He glanced around in fear. "Where the hell'd they go?"

"Into the drink."

"Thank Christ for that." Coombs suddenly became alert, listening, and we all felt it too: a queasy change in velocity. We were slowing down. It seemed to bring him to his senses. "Oh my Lord," he said. "Cowper! I have to get down there!"

Cowper just stood up in disgust. The dreadful news that

Xombies were in the sub swamped everything—after what we'd been through it was the final cosmic straw, our great escape debunked. There was no weeping or wailing, just helpless incomprehension. Limbo. Then Albemarle started laughing. For a long moment, his lone cackle was a kite in the void.

Finally he said, "Join the club."

"How many men are down there?" Cowper asked.

Coombs hesitated, and Sandoval said, "Forty-two. Just the NavSea team."

This caused a rustle of amazement—I gathered it was a shockingly low number. Later I would learn that it was less than a third of the normal crew complement.

"That's privileged information," Coombs retorted. He squinted in the dark, noticing Sandoval for the first time. Sandoval shook his head as if to say, *Don't ask.*

"And ya couldn't fit these kids in?" Cowper asked. "Jesus H. Christ."

Coombs began to reply, "Since when do I have to justify my orders—" but was interrupted by yelling from the stern. I could hear, "Stand clear, stand clear!" over a lot of nervous chatter. There was a heavy *clunk.*

Coombs said, "Missile compartment hatch," and began shoving his way through the crowd, followed by Cowper and others.

Meanwhile, someone new was coming forward, demanding, "Who's in charge up here? Where's Fred Cowper?" The parties met in the middle, and the new man—an officious-looking crew-cut type—seemed relieved to find Coombs.

"Commander! You're safe! We thought everyone forward amidships was gone!" He raised a walkie-talkie and said, "Found the CO unharmed, over." The reply was a crackling garble.

"What's the status, Rich?" Coombs asked impatiently. He seemed embarrassed to be found.

"Yes sir—well, we secured the forward bulkhead, and it looks like everything aft of the CCSM is clear. I ordered all

stop and station-keeping, and the men are rigging for aux-
iliary control right now. It's a miracle we're not aground,
but that could change when the tide goes out. I don't think
anyone but Mr. Robles and myself made it aft, and no one's
reporting from anywhere in the forward section now. No
one made it out with you, did they?"

"No."

The other man lowered his voice, ill at ease sharing this
information with us. "Then that's twelve officers missing,"
he said.

"All right," said Coombs, nodding furiously. "Well, we
have to get back in there. Assemble a team and we'll do an
armed sweep."

"But that's the problem, we—" He caught himself, eyeing us suspiciously as he amended, "I'll talk to you below."

"Speak up, Lieutenant," Coombs said with resignation.
"You might as well forget OPSEC; we're all in the same
boat. So to speak."

"Okay then, we can't spare the men. They're spread too
thin to run the boat and fight at the same time, and we sure
as hell can't afford to lose any more."

"I wish we had a choice."

Mr. Cowper stepped forward. "Don't stand on ceremony,
Mr. Kranuski," he said, offering the man a handshake. It
was ignored.

"You dirty traitor," Kranuski said softly, eyes burning
with loathing. "I hope you're happy."

"I'll be happy when these kids are all below drinkin'
bug juice. Until then, I'm just tryin' a survive, Rich. But
there's no reason our survival should be incompatible with
your mission. In fact, I think it's safe ta say that at this
point you need us as much as we need you."

"You're a disgrace to that uniform."

Coombs stepped in. "That's enough. We don't have
time for this. Fred, if you're offering us extra hands, I accept. Assemble your best conners and have them meet us

below. They'll be reporting to Mr. Robles. The rest of you stay up top until you get the all-clear. No shenanigans!"

Down the hatch. I never gave a thought to that expression before. It was rather forbidding, that bright hole in the sea, like a volcanic vent. Suddenly the cold deck wasn't so bad. Others were feeling it too: the eagerness I had seen in these boys back at the hangar seemed to have been cured by recent events—there was certainly no Alamo-like rush to volunteer.

It was worked out that twenty of our guys would go: ten technical people and ten big boys running interference. This was thought to be the biggest number we could field without creating a logjam below. "Ya gotta have enough room ta fight and still keep in sight a everyone else," Mr. Cowper explained. The technical ones were all older men who had served aboard subs at one time or another—Cowper and Ed Albemarle among them—and these were quick to step forward. The boys were another matter, since the only ones who really wanted to go were relatives of the men who were going, and the men refused to bring these. The deadlock was broken when Mr. Cowper announced he would take me, "just to shut everyone up."

"If we don't pull this off," he said, "we're all goners anyhow."

People looked to see my reaction, but if the choice was to stick by Mr. Cowper or remain on deck as everybody's scapegoat, I wasn't about to complain. The arguments sputtered out and a tenth boy was picked (presumably to make up for my inadequacy) bringing our total number to twenty-one. Blackjack.

PEERING DOWN THAT rabbit hole, I think even the seasoned veterans must have had second thoughts. Not that it was dark or creepy—it was a glowing chimney, what they called the "escape trunk," a cream-colored vestibule with a shiny ladder leading to a second hatch just below. And if you pulled open that inner hatch? All of us had seen enough by now to picture an unspeakably vivid Pandora's Box.

"Alla times I did this shootin' studs, an' all I was afraid of was a little inert gas," said a bushy-bearded man, climbing down.

"Argon'll kill you just as fast as those things," Albemarle replied. "Think of it that way."

"But they don't kill ya, that's the problem."

I could no longer see past the ring of intent spectators banking the light like cavemen around a fire, but I could hear the lower hatch open. A second man went down. Then a third. The boat rocked gently, waves lapping at its sides. No one made a sound.

Some of the teenagers started to go down, and I was pleased to see the chipmunk boy among them. *I should have known he'd volunteer,* I thought. Then it was Mr. Cowper's turn, and I followed along on his heels, pushing through the press of bodies. Someone gave me a shove, so that I barely kept from falling, bowling into the legs of several adults. Albemarle turned with an expression of pained surprise—I had hit his injured back.

"Sorry," I said, mortified. "I tripped."

"This is no place for games," he said flatly.

"I know, I'm sorry, excuse me."

Mr. Cowper was concentrating on finding his footing down the ladder. At bottom I could see a mustached man in khakis waving us down. In my ear, Albemarle said, "*He* don't come back, *you* don't come back." He handed me a big sticky hammer.

I nodded, climbing as fast as I dared.

It was like entering a pool. As light and warmth surrounded me, I experienced a brief, primal surge of relief—my animal instincts going, *Ahhh, shelter*. I was helped down the last few rungs to an institutional-looking Formica floor in a room like a well-lit basement. It reminded me of the boiler room at the Y. Though hardly exotic, the insulated plumbing and perforated acoustic tile were a dramatic change from the blustery ocean above. We were underwater! The guys already there motioned me aside, and I joined Mr. Cowper by the wall. Albemarle came down last, wincing in pain.

Once everyone was present, the man who had given us a hand down said, "Welcome aboard. Hi Ed. I'm Lieutenant Commander Dan Robles, among other things, and I'll be your guide today." He was a dapper-looking, pudgy man with a faint Spanish accent and an air of weary contempt, though not necessarily for us. I could tell he accepted me as just another in a series of disasters that fate was delivering upon him, and as such, unworthy of special attention. I liked him immediately. Brandishing a pistol, he asked, "Any questions before we get started?"

"What's the plan?" Cowper asked a bit shortly.

"The captain and Mr. Kranuski are standing by forward to brief you."

"Any more guns?" Albemarle asked.

Robles shrugged apologetically. "For reasons of safety, the captain is reserving firearms for active-duty personnel only," he said. "Not that they're any better than your weapons. Personally I'd like a chainsaw. All right? Watch your heads."

Following Robles, we crossed the room and passed through a heavy watertight door, which opened onto a sight so unexpected that my stomach lurched:

We were at least four stories up in a yawning tunnel that resembled a multi-tiered prison cellblock . . . or King Tut's tomb. It ran forward from us a hundred feet or more, piled high with plastic-wrapped cargo of every shape and size—boxes, barrels, cases, crates—under a vaulted ceiling inset with two rows of numbered white domes. Cables looped everywhere like jungle vines, giving the place an apocalyptic, overgrown look. They swayed with the movement of the boat.

Hearing my gasp, some of the boys smirked in the way of jaded old-timers, but Mr. Cowper nodded, whistling appreciatively at the view. He said, "We used ta call this

Sherwood Forest, but without the missile silos it looks more like Shippin' and Receivin'. You guys've been busy little beavas." Pointing down at the heaped freight, he asked, "What's all this crap? SPAM?"

"SPAM," Albemarle said, shaking his head.

"Yuh, I see. That *would* make things a bit tight," he sighed.

Robles led us along a steel-grated walkway to the far end, where we could see Captain Coombs and Mr. Kranuski waiting for us, armed to the teeth, beside another watertight door. As we came up they stared at me as though they couldn't believe their eyes.

"What the hell's going on?" Coombs demanded. "What's this little girl doing here?"

"Get her outta here," Kranuski told Robles darkly.

"Hold on!" Cowper said, holding him off. "Before you do anything, you oughtta know this kid may be immune ta Agent X. She has a genetic problem—Lulu, what's it called?"

"Chromosomal amenorrhea," I said.

"Right, and she's been survivin' on her own since this thing stahted—almost a whole month with them bastids. Ya know how I found her? *She knocked on my door!* I'm barricaded down there fa three and a half weeks, an' she just knocks. I'm tellin' ya, Harvey, she might have an advantage none a us has, not ta mention the possibility of a cure."

I couldn't wait to see how this would fly. Years with Mummy had taught me to keep my composure in the face of rampant b.s., but even she would've never attempted such a flimsy tale. Then it occurred to me that Mr. Cowper might really believe it.

Kranuski scoffed, barely listening, but Coombs said, "Wait. Are you saying they won't touch her?"

"No. I'm sayin' she an' I came through what you saw up there, and I don't think it's because of our sterling characta. If you ask me, *she* oughtta be SPAM."

"Captain—" Kranuski began.

Coombs looked hard at me, asked, "What do *you* think?"

"I don't know, sir," I said honestly.

"Tough nut, are you?"

"Well . . . I don't know."

"What happened to your other shoe?" Before I could reply, he said to Cowper, "Bring her, what the hell; there's no time. Just keep her out of the way—we're not here to babysit. Christ almighty!" He shook his head in giddy disbelief. "Okay, here's what's happening: You boys are going to do a Roto Rooter straight for the control center, with the rest of us bringing up the rear. Follow Mr. Robles. If anything blue gets in your way, you beat it down and move on. Don't stop to finish the job! Each guy in line will have his turn, but speed is more important than anything—keep moving, no matter what. Once we're all in command and control, we need to seal it off good. Then we'll go from there. Ready?"

We could never be ready, but they weren't waiting for a reply. Kranuski unsealed the door and pulled it open. "Go," he hissed. "Go, go, go!"

Holding his pistol with both hands, Robles ducked through. Coombs and Kranuski covered him from the door with rifles, but the way was clear, and boys began to follow at a brisk walk, hammers upraised. Any moment I expected to hear trouble, something to interrupt this madness, but before I knew it Mr. Cowper was moving, and I with him. Kranuski and the captain went last, securing the door behind us.

We were in a pastel-green corridor, its ceiling a baroque mass of ducts and wiring. A metal stair descended somewhere, and vented aluminum doors branched off to either side. Some of the doors were open, and inside I could see empty chairs facing banks of electronics; the last two rooms, however, were cozy adjoining cabins with beds, TVs, and a tiny shared bathroom. Small plaques on their doors read, CO—H. COOMBS and XO—R. KRANUSKI.

We went up a flight of stairs and the passageway opened out into a large compartment that I recognized at once from its glamorous central feature: a periscope. No, *two* periscopes. I didn't remember seeing that in movies. When I entered the room, our people were already jumping into action at various consoles and donning headsets to contact other parts of the sub. Mr. Robles was standing by the raised platform in the middle, issuing orders, while Albemarle and the boys checked various side compartments and closed off the area. Feeling supremely useless, I stood by Mr. Cowper as he took readings off gauges and called them out to Coombs. In that room full of busy, shouting people, I think I actually forgot for a second that the Xombies existed. Until I saw one.

IT TOOK ME a second to comprehend what I was seeing, another to react. I don't know if I was the first one to spot it, but I certainly felt alone as I watched that purple-faced thing hang upside down from an opening in the ceiling. With its hair sticking down and its wild-eyed grin, it looked almost childlike, in a florid, demonic way. It was *so darn happy* to find us.

One of the boys had just crossed beneath the hole. He was a tall kid, very gangsta with his gold front tooth, and he had to stoop to avoid banging his head. He never saw the thing or made a peep before it had him around the neck. Then he was gone. The bang of his hammer hitting the deck alerted everyone, and a few people made involuntary sounds of surprise.

"Look out!" I screamed, too late.

"God *damn* it!" shouted Albemarle. "Get 'im!"

"No!" Kranuski ordered, kneeling for better aim. "Secure the hatch!"

I suddenly felt a weird trickle down my leg. Almost jumping out of my skin, I realized I was peeing myself! It went all at once, uncontrollably, like a cup tipping over, and I danced in horror out of the puddle as if it was something alien to me.

Mr. Cowper yelled, "McGill! Where's McGill?"

"It took him up the sail!" Kranuski barked impatiently.

"Not *him,* damn it! George McGill! Big, bearded guy! He was right there!"

It was true—suddenly we were short a man. Two people gone.

Kranuski screamed, "Find out where it came from! *Get that hatch!*"

Mr. Cowper had already found out—an access panel had been removed from the floor of a small cubby, the opening concealed by a stanchion and bundles of cable. Seating the metal cover with a loud clang, he shouted, "Got it!" Coombs, meanwhile, was closest to the overhead hatch, bounding up the ladder to reach for it. As he did so, everybody watched in frozen horror as a pair of blue-sleeved arms unfolded from the hole and snatched him off his feet. But Albemarle was right there, grabbing his legs before they could disappear. For an instant it appeared that the big man might be drawn up as well, then Robles had *him* and together they wrenched Coombs down, fighting the thing for him.

"Hey!" Albemarle grunted. "Hey! Hey!"

Now boys were piling on. Coombs made a gargling noise, and I could hear his joints popping from the strain. The only visible part of the Xombie was its arm, which had him in a headlock, but the captain's own raised arm was also entangled in its grip, taking some of the pressure off his neck. He still didn't look good. There was no way to beat at the creature without pulverizing Coombs in the process, and two boys together couldn't loosen that constricting arm. There was just no leverage—it was like ten guys fighting to change a lightbulb.

The miserable futility of it was just starting to sink in— *He's dead*—when Mr. Cowper came up with Coombs's rifle, forced his way through, and blasted the Xombie's arm off at point-blank range. Coombs dropped free, the quivering limb still on him. Now Kranuski dashed in and began shooting up the hole. The shocking explosion of noise and sparks and hot shells on their shoulders caused boys to duck away, cursing, while Albemarle and Robles picked up the captain and hustled him clear. But the Xombie wasn't finished. It ballooned from its hiding place like a jack-in-the-box, the stump of its arm spurting inky liquid as it lunged for Mr. Cowper.

I didn't think; there was no time to. I just jumped forward and hit the thing as hard as I could, surprised at how light the big hammer suddenly felt. My blow fell on the creature's temple and seemed to spin its whole head around, causing it to become disoriented for a second and lose its balance. Before it could recover, there were a dozen hammers clouting it down, a rain of iron that turned bone and sinew to limply wriggling pulp. "Have a club sandwich, asshole," someone snarled, pounding. The sound was the worst—at least the sulphur smell from all the shooting masked the stench of blood. To the boys it was obviously some kind of catharsis: they were avenging their parents, their world, on this creature. I had to turn away.

"Seal that hatch!" Kranuski bellowed for the third time, reloading his rifle, but people hesitated, understandably leery about going near. They were staring at me, and I realized they expected *me* to do it! Since I was immune, no doubt. I shot Mr. Cowper an exasperated look, and he raised his eyebrows as if to say, *Yeah, so?* and gave me a boost to the opening. "Don't take all day," he said.

I could see way up the narrow shaft, the inside of the sail, and smell seawater. Reaching for the gleaming valve wheel, I began to pull the heavy hatch cover down, only to have it yanked from my hand. What happened next is a blur, but suddenly I was on the floor with the wind knocked out of me, and some kind of brawl was going on.

The kid with the gold tooth was at the center of it, struggling wildly as men and boys hung off his back and grappled with every limb. They weren't having an easy time—he had freakish ways of squirming loose, impossible contortions like a Chinese acrobat. The expression on his gray face was one of pure intensity, not fear. He wanted them bad.

"I can't get a clear shot!" Kranuski was yelling, and the people with hammers were almost as stymied, trying to land blows without braining the guys hanging on for dear life. Also they were tentative, as anyone would be who had to kill someone they knew.

"Come on, Jerry," sobbed the old guy who looked like a carnival Strong Man, holding the boy from behind. "Ya gotta go with God—we talked about this. Don't fight, honey." Other cries of "Hold 'im still!" and "I got 'im!" were fired back and forth as the battle migrated into a corner, where I think they hoped to trap the boy and give him the old club sandwich. But just as they turned him loose, the teenage Xombie seemed to vanish into thin air. The men were left standing there, hammers aloft, staring in confusion at the place where he had been.

"*Shit,*" someone said.

"Ah, hell," Albemarle said. He was cautiously peering between the thick trunks of black cable that filled the corner. "There's an open penetration from when we pulled out the CIP."

Kranuski probed the narrow gap with his gun muzzle. "How could anything fit through there?"

"Who the hell knows? You saw it as well as I did. We better put a boot on that before others come popping in."

Kranuski jumped back. "And check every inch of this place!" he roared, red-faced.

Albemarle looked at Kranuski, then at the unconscious Coombs. "You better see to your skipper, Mr. Kranuski," he said. Then he pointedly turned and addressed Mr. Cowper: "What are *your* orders, Commander?"

Laying the rifle on a table, Mr. Cowper sighed, "You and the boys make sure there aren't going to be any more surprises, Ed. Everyone else resume your stations—let's get this boat under control fast."

Kranuski couldn't believe his ears. "What do you think you're doing? *You're* not giving the orders here," he said threateningly.

Mr. Cowper was totally matter-of-fact. "As the only man on board with command experience, I'm acting captain until Mr. Coombs is fit fa duty."

"Like hell you are. You're a goddamned traitor who has jeopardized this vessel and compromised its mission, and now you think you're going to make it your private little Navy. Well, that's not gonna happen. *I'm* in command here."

"Mr. Kranuski, you haven't been XO long enough fa that promotion, but I will need you to continue your duties, stahting with a fix on our position. Lulu will look afta Mr. Coombs. Mr. Robles, will you man periscope one and scan for traffic?"

"Stay where you are, Mr. Robles," Kranuski ordered.

Robles looked from Kranuski to Coombs and back again. Then he crossed to the periscope and began working. Kranuski cast about furiously and realized not a single person was paying attention to him. He was alone. I was afraid he would kick up a fuss and upset everyone, but something seemed to click in his mind and he became very calm. Without another word he went to the other periscope and flipped down the handles.

His grace in defeat was awesome to see—I could have kissed him for taking it so rationally. You can't usually count on people being dignified, and to me there is nothing in the world more important, because isn't dignity the soul of reason? It's what makes us human.

I felt Coombs grasp my ankle, and I looked down expecting to see that he had recovered consciousness. I might have been smiling in relief. But Coombs was still passed out, arms motionless at his sides. The arm that clutched my leg like a predatory squid had no body. It seemed to want mine.

Even after I managed to wrest the nasty thing loose, then hammered, stomped, and mashed it into something resembling day-old roadkill, it was a while before I stopped freaking out. People gave me plenty of space.

nine

AFTER EVERYTHING POSSIBLE had been done to stabilize the sub and barricade us in, the men discussed what to do next.

"I know there isn't a lotta useful information about this Maenad thing," Mr. Cowper said, looking dreadfully tired, "but if we pool what we know, maybe we can think of a way to slow them bastids down. I know we can't suffocate 'em, because that's how they spread the infection, by stoppin' you from breathing. They give ya that kiss a death and the disease moves in. That's why they all look cyanotic, because Agent X somehow takes the place of oxygen in the bloodstream and uses it like a highway ta attack ya brain and nervous system. That's the last I heard outta USAM-RIID. Anyone else hear that?"

A white-haired man with a walrus mustache said, "I saw on TV that the Center for Disease Control was *treating* it with pure oxygen. They said it slowed the disease. That was the only good news I heard before everything went off the air."

Others chipped in, saying they had heard the same thing.

"Well, that's gotta be our first move then," said Cowper, encouraged. "We pump the oh-two content way up and see what happens."

Kranuski was skeptical. "Are you serious? This boat has just been gutted and rebuilt. You wouldn't believe the half-assed repair jobs I've witnessed over the last four weeks—I'd hardly dignify it as a refit. More like something out of Dr. Frankenstein's lab. Enriching the oxygen mixture under these circumstances is asking for it."

"He has a point," said Albemarle. "One spark and we're toast. We know the smoke barrier's compromised too, not to mention the Xombies crawling around in the works. I don't think we can risk a fire. Especially since we don't really know if it'll make any difference. I'm no scientist—what do we really know about this? Enough to stake the boat on it?"

"I agree," said the Strong Man. "It's not worth it. We're better off fighting hand-to-hand, section-by-section."

Cowper shook his head. "We've lost two people, and we've secured one compahtment. Now we're gonna abandon that compahtment and open ourselves to attack? There's too much boat ta cover; they'll whittle us down ta nothin'. That's how they get ya."

"Have you ever *seen* a flash-fire?" asked Kranuski.

"I've seen enough ta know we got no choice."

"Well, you're acting CO," he said scornfully. "You give the order."

Mr. Cowper didn't take the bait. "Keep ya shirt on. Commanda Coombs must have had some plan. What'd he have in mind?"

"He intended for us to use this as a base to spread out from, gradually expanding our area of control until we could seal off and quarantine the rest without hampering critical operations."

"See, that just don't work fa me. The Xombies won't

cooperate unless we have some kinda clear advantage . . . which we might, if we just think about it. Look, this is a *submarine*—a highly adjustable environment. We can play with it. How can we make it uncomfortable for 'em?"

"CO," I said.

"The problem is, whatever hurts them, hurts us," Kranuski said.

"Which brings us back ta oxygen," Cowper replied.

"I'd rather go down fighting than blow myself to kingdom come."

"CO," I repeated, a bit louder. Boys in the room frowned at me. Chipmunk boy gave me a wide-eyed inquiring look and shook his head: *Don't.*

Mr. Cowper said, "Quiet, Lulu. What about controlled flooding? Or changin' the air pressure? The temperature? How can we make climate control work for us?"

"Or a big dose of radiation?" another man offered gloomily.

I said, "Excuse me, but what about CO? Carbon monoxide?" My skin crawled with embarrassment, but I had to speak up. "That won't burn, and it mimics oxygen in the bloodstream."

All the boys rolled their eyes at my impertinence. One of them said, "God, shut *up,*" and another said, "It's poisonous, stupid."

Forging ahead as I had so many times in school, I tried, "But there are emergency air masks, aren't there? Like on airplanes?" Almost apologetically, I added, "Isn't that what these nozzles are for?"

There was a sudden hitch in the men's discussion. Annoyance and confusion played across all their stubbly faces. Mr. Cowper said, "God-dammit, Lulu . . ." then trailed off in consternation.

Albemarle scratched his big head. "Kid's right," he said.

WITHOUT BOTHERING TO thank me, Mr. Cowper, Mr. Kranuski, and the others applied themselves to the problem of how to fill the boat with carbon monoxide gas. It turned out to be very simple, much simpler than I expected when I made the suggestion. All I had known was that submarines, even modern nuclear submarines, are equipped with back-up diesel engines. But my trivia-packed brain did not know that these were specifically Fairbanks-Morse engines, nor that they suck air from the living spaces inside the sub (drawing it in through vents at the top of the sail) and expel exhaust gases out a retractable tailpipe at the stern, creating a powerful suction that can replace the boat's entire volume of air in minutes.

Or, by blocking the exhaust, can just as quickly flood the boat with suffocating carbon monoxide.

After a rather heated phone conversation with the engineers in back, Mr. Cowper made an announcement over the PA system:

"Attention all hands. We are about to fumigate everything forward amidships with cahbon monoxide. The CO burner is to remain off. Unless you want to die, close off all vents from the foreward bulkhead and don EAB apparatus. Do not remove it until I give the all-clear."

After this message was repeated a few times, orders were given to disconnect the exhaust coupling. The fresh-air intake was left shut, and the open hatch that we had entered through was ordered closed. I felt bad about this because of how it must have looked to the people stuck above, but I consoled myself with the knowledge that we were doing all this for them . . . and if we didn't succeed, they would live longer than any of us.

We then put on the air masks that had been handed out. They looked like World War I gas masks, and could be connected to oxygen-giving metal nipples anywhere in the room. The men went around checking and re-checking them to make sure they were fastened correctly, giving the one on the unconscious Coombs extra attention.

While inspecting mine, Mr. Cowper winked at me

through our foggy faceplates and said, "Lookin' good, sweethaht." His gnome face was all scrunched up from the tight seal. I wanted to ask him, *Are you really my father? Would you be?* But I couldn't find my voice, and he moved on.

When all was in readiness, he sat down on his dais, saying, "A-gangers, give Clyde a kick."

"Engage diesel, aye," Kranuski barked.

"Engaging diesel," Robles said.

A deep rumble could be felt through the deck. The tension in the room was fierce—it was like sitting in a gas chamber. Hollow-voiced, Kranuski announced, "Diesel engaged, sir."

"Very good, Mr. Kranuski."

"You want gas levels, commander?" asked Robles.

"Nah, no smog alerts. All we need ta know is if it'll kill ya. Everybody keep breathing nice and steady. Don't anybody tense up and fool themselves that they can't breathe. There's good clean dedicated air comin' through those pipes. Relax."

A piercing alarm started to go off. Everyone jumped, thrashing around for the source.

"Nothin' to worry about!" Cowper said loudly. "Nothin' to worry about! Cahbon monoxide detector—that's what we want."

It was an annoying noise. Kranuski and Robles roamed the various control stations, making adjustments and conferring with quiet intensity. Long minutes passed, and the air became dense and warm, causing the light to waver.

"Mr. Cowper?" I said, indicating the remains of the Xombie. Its squashed fibers were relaxing, turning from purplish-blue to bright, meaty red. He nodded, trading looks with the other men. Some of the boys made muffled sounds of disgust.

Robles said, "Carbon monoxide above lethal concentrations, sir."

"Thanks, Dan. We'll let it go a little while longa."

The smooth thrumming of the engine began to stutter.

"She's starting to skip," said Kranuski. "Not enough air."

"I know," said Cowper intently.

"Gonna run her until she stalls?"

The old man held up a finger, as if counting down in his head. Then he said, "No. Hopefully that's enough. Kill it, but leave the cahbon dioxide scrubbas running."

"Diesel off."

"Diesel off, aye."

"And mute that damn alahm."

Once it was still, Cowper addressed the whole ship. His amplified voice sounded thin and distant under the mask, like an old-time radio program. "Gentlemen, you a now surrounded by toxic gas. The gas is oduhless, culluhless, and tasteless, so you may be tempted to adjust ya mask or scratch ya nose. I advise you to refrain from this, because doing so will cause you ta fall asleep and neva wake up. In case some a you a wondering, this is *not* an attempt to smotha the Xombies—as fah's we know, they a not vulnerable to suffocation. In fact it's ah guess that Agent X can't invade the bloodstream if there's too much oxygen present. Respiration is a buffer against the disease, which is why we don't all catch it like the flu. No tellin' why women did—we'll probably neva know.

"In light a that, you may be curious what we're doing. Well, I was plannin' on flushing the boat with pure oxygen, when one of the nubs made the brilliant suggestion that instead a blowin' our asses ta Timbuktu, we oughtta try cahbon monoxide instead. Or she mighta just said the new CO is a deadly gasbag, and I misundastood a. If what we think we know about Agent X is true, then this should suppress the disease in some way. We don't really know how, but hopefully it'll give us a chance to retake the boat." He hung up the mike. "Lulu, come up here a second. Watch ya air line."

I stepped up on the periscope platform with him, and he

beamed at me benevolently. I felt like a squire about to be knighted.

"Since this was your idea," he said, "I'd like ta give you the honor of locating a Xombie."

"Excuse me?"

"We need you ta flush out a Xombie for us. See if ya plan worked. Chahley, put a tank on her, will ya?" A man came forward bearing a stubby yellow oxygen tank.

"Alone?" I asked. I was thinking, *This is a joke.*

"We can't all go. What if it didn't work? Nah, we really just need somebody ta test the wattas."

I looked around at their tired faces, some mocking, some troubled. Mr. Cowper's was the most indifferent, and for that I carelessly shouldered the heavy tank, saying, "Okay. Where to?" At that moment I would have jumped off a cliff to spite him.

"Ya see that door there?" To the others he said, "The rest a you tend goal an' make damn sure nothin' gets in."

There was a brief interruption of my airflow as Albe-marle switched the line. Kranuski handed me a walkie-talkie and said, "Lulu, take this radio and leave it on talk, like this, so we know how you're doing. You've got twenty minutes of air, but start heading back after five. You won't even need that much time. Just go forward to the radio shack and come back. It's a straight shot; you can't get lost."

It was strange to have him call me Lulu, like he thought he had to be chummy with the condemned. "Louise," I muttered.

He either didn't hear or ignored me. "You ready?" he asked.

"Just hurry up."

Cowper signalled them to turn the wheel. It was like a bank vault, but even more like the door of a submarine. Robles kicked it outward, gun at the ready. I pictured a wall of water on the other side, water that became a white hori-zontal column, blasting these people down and drowning them so that they drifted about the flooded green room like wide-eyed statues with flowing hair. But nothing came through.

Robles patted me on the shoulder. Without irony, he said, "Hey, good luck." Other voices also chimed, "Good luck," and someone said, "Rock on."

I stepped in over the raised sill and helped them close it behind me.

I stood with my back to the door, breathing bottled oxygen. I was in a tight passage through ceiling-high racks of electronics, enveloped in their soft refrigerator hum. The floor was dirt-concealing flecked beige tile. Those aisles would have been just the place to conceal lurking Xombies, too, but none appeared.

For a second I was leery about giving myself away by speaking into the radio, but as I made myself start walking it came naturally. Talking made me feel less alone.

"Nothing so far," I said, more loudly than necessary. "I'm passing rows of computer equipment . . . checking all the doors. Nope. Now I'm passing under an escape trunk— it's closed. I'm looking into a room full of TV monitors and consoles—hello? Nobody there. Now a smaller room . . . the ceiling's getting low . . ."

I was at the end. This last room had the cramped, utilitarian look of a place behind the scenes—the front of the sub, I supposed. It was festooned with thick skeins of insulated cable that clung to the bulkhead like fossilized muscle and sinew. Fax machines and other communications gear were stuffed wherever they could fit amid gray-painted guts of ducts, pipes, wiring. Teletype paper had been dumped on the floor, but otherwise there was nothing there.

Feeling let off the hook, I dawdled to peer in every cranny. I still had fifteen minutes. What interested me was that I could see part of the actual hull here—that curved ceiling was all that kept the sea out. I noticed that the inner walls and floor did not actually contact the hull, but seemed to float within it, creating a crawlspace on all sides, as if the living and work areas of the sub were a clunky, angular structure shoehorned inside the ringed shell—a ship in a bottle. It dawned on me that I had seen all this in pieces back at that great hangar. It had been a submarine factory. *Duh,* as the boys would say.

Crawlspace. A chunky yellow flashlight hung from a hook in the corner; I took it and performed a few contortions with the tank on my back, struggling to peer into the narrow crevice along the hull.

Faces looked back at me.

I flinched, nearly dropping the flashlight. I must have cried out, too, because Mr. Cowper would later tell me that he and the other fellows in the control room thought I had "bought it." But the faces didn't move. They had stopped like clocks.

Years ago, when Mummy and I were still living in our old house in Oxnard, California, I had wormed my way through a mysterious trapdoor above the closet into a tiny neglected attic. Crouched on the ledge, I flicked on my flashlight and found myself surrounded by basketball-sized hornets' nests, papery-dry and long dead. This was much the same.

Mesmerized by something gleaming in the dark, I finally sighed and banged the radio against my mask, forgetting it was there. I said, "It worked." Then I turned off the flashlight so I could no longer see the boy's gold tooth.

t e n

NO MATTER HOW squeamish you are, getting rid of bodies breaks down to a job of heavy lifting. The novelty of cool rigid flesh wears off and you realize how awkward they are to move, how darn heavy. After a dozen or so, they're no more fearsome than the baggy old futons my mother always made us drag from apartment to apartment. "Come on, lazypants," she would cry as I buckled under my half. "Nearly home!"

Finding every Xombie was a grotesque Easter egg hunt, made more difficult by our breathing equipment in the tight spaces. To throw up would have been instant death. Since operating the boat took precedence, corpse-gathering was relegated to the boys and myself, under the supervision of a whiskery old character named Vic Noteiro. He knew every possible place to check, and was perfectly happy to let us do the checking while he made himself comfortable and told anecdotes about his days painting submarines. "Guys kept sayin' I should retire," he said. "Retire from what? Sittin' on my ass all night listening to da radio? Makin' twenny bucks an hour? Whenever ya feel like it, ya slap on a coat a Mare Island? Pure titty."

Then the question was how to dump them overboard. No one knew if exposure to air would cause them to revive, but we didn't want to find out, even if it meant we had to "suck rubber" a while longer. In the meantime, the bodies were weighted, bagged, and trussed like mummies. That was awful because they had lost their blue pallor and looked vibrantly alive—much more rosy-cheeked than any of us. "It's da cahbon monoxide is all," Vic told us dismissively. "Dey're stone dead."

A skeptical-faced boy asked, "How can the carbon monoxide affect them if they don't breathe?"

"Who said dey don't breathe? Dey breathe. Ya don't see it, but dey absorb air. Respiration stops just long enough for Agent X to infect 'em—dey gotta be dead foist. Afta dat dey staht breathin' again, only a lot slowa, like dem yogis in India. For all we know, dey're in Nirvana now."

There were fourteen of them altogether—ten from the crew (actually twelve crew members had been lost, but two conveniently fell into the sea), the two Marine guards, and two from our crowd. When we had them all lined up in the big mess hall, Kranuski and Mr. Cowper came down to look. Vic had identified each one with a Magic Marker, and Kraus ticked them off one by one: "Boggs, supply officer; Lester, weps; Gunderson, the nav; Montoya, communications; Lee, sonar chief; Baker, cob; Henderson, quartermaster; Selby, machinist's mate; O'Grady, torpedo-man—" He faltered, clearing his throat. "Shit."

"I know," said Cowper. "When you've worked with a man, it's hahd."

Kranuski snapped, "It's not that. What about the tubes?"

Cowper nodded carefully, as if treading on shaky ground. "I was thinkin' a that. Will your people accept it?"

"It's burial at sea. Better than dumping them down the TDU."

"Okay. I'll make an announcement—"

"No announcement. Sorry, *sir,* but you're the one who told me not to get hung up on ceremony. Let's just get this over with."

Cowper agreed, and they went back upstairs.

Not sure what we were doing, I helped carry all the corpses down another level to the torpedo room. This was frustrating because we had just dragged three bodies up from there, plus our oxygen, and it was hard not to brain yourself with those masks on. Shiny forest-green torpedoes with blue caps were stacked in cradles on either side of the aisle. Straight ahead were four elaborate chrome hatches with dangling tags that read, TUBE EMPTY. Mr. Noteiro yanked off the tags and opened the round doors.

"Slide 'em in there," he said, raspy-voiced. "Move it!"

We managed to pack three bodies in each tube. There was a huge piston that helped ram them in. Since I thought torpedoes ran on their own power, I wasn't sure how these were going to be launched, and I watched closely as Vic shut the tubes and went to a wall console with a padded stool in front of it. Headsets of different colors hung from a bar under the lights; he put on a pair and adjusted the controls. There was a hollow sound of water rushing through pipes.

"Flooding tubes one . . . two . . . tree . . . and four," he said. "Tubes one tru four ready in all respects." A moment later there was an explosive whoosh, unnervingly powerful, then three more hair-raising blasts in close succession. This was something even the boys had never seen. A bit shaken, we loaded the last bodies into one tube for a final firing. Then it was done. I couldn't say what I was thinking: *Like flushing goldfish.*

THE NEXT THING that happened nearly made us forget our exhaustion and all the night's ugliness: the diesel engine rumbled to life again, this time sucking fresh, cold air into the sub. Boys were so happy they hugged each other; they even forgot themselves and hugged *me*. Unfortunately, though most of the poison was gone in minutes, we were told to leave our masks on until every compartment could be ventilated and inspected for residual pockets of gas. This put a damper on things.

Since the boys and I were not trusted with this duty, we were left to wait in the crew's mess, our breathing gear plugged into jacks on the floor. We sat nodding off in the blue, upholstered booths like winos at an all-night diner.

"I've had it," said a maniacal freckle-faced guy with Creamsicle-orange hair and white eyelashes. "I'm not wearing this mask another second!" Then he went right back to sleep.

Ignoring him, chipmunk-boy asked me, "What's your name?"

"Lulu. Louise. Louise Pangloss."

"I'm Hector Albemarle." He offered me his furry mit and I shook it, feeling silly. Pointing at the others, he said, "That's Tyrell Banks, Jake—"

"Bartholomew," moaned the sleeping guy.

"—Jake Bartholomew, Julian Noteiro, uh, Shawn Dickey, Sal DeLuca, Lemuel Sanchez, Ray Despineau, and Cole Hayes."

Most of the boys acknowledged me in some way as they were introduced, nodding or at least glancing over. They were quite a mixed bag. You get to know someone pretty fast when sharing a chore as miserable as body-snatching, and I had formed distinct impressions of all their personalities:

In spite of the costume, Hector was mature for his age, brave, a peacemaker, and yet considered something of a nerd. I already liked him a lot, though I was afraid of his stepfather, Ed Albemarle, with whom he had a prickly relationship.

Tyrell was a goofy, streetwise guy, but also a hard worker, who brightened up the job with his incessant funny griping. He joked about fusing country-western and hip-hop to create a musical opus called *Westward Ho*. This was some kind of running jibe at Shawn, who aspired to preach New Age mysticism through the medium of rap.

Jake, too, considered himself a comic, dropping silly non sequiturs ("When I meet someone, I just like to know if they identify more with the Trix rabbit or with the kids. There's no right or wrong answer—take your time") that the others made no attempt to acknowledge, as if they thought he was a bore. He was sort of a spaz—I felt a little protective of him.

Julian was all business, a straight-edger who acted like he knew the sub better than anybody, and resented being the one to have to correct us. It was he whose suggestion about "piloting by scope" had been rebuffed by Mr. Albemarle up top. Julian was the grandson of old Vic, who derived a sly amusement from seeing the boy steam.

Shawn was a laid-back skate-punk and frequenter of poetry slams, sexy in a Madison Avenue–exploitation-of-youth kind of way; a walking hipness barometer with piercings like chrome acne, who seemed fascinated by everything that was going on. Upon seeing the first of the bodies he had said, "Smoked." Unfazed by Tyrell's jokes, he carried around a notepad at all times, scribbling down lyrical thunderbolts as they occurred. He had been the deejay back at the factory.

The other four were quiet and withdrawn, more obviously in shock: Sal was angry and said nothing that wasn't bitterly sarcastic—not that he said much. Ray was his best friend—I first assumed they were brothers—who spoke with a long-suffering weariness that reminded me of Eeyore in *Winnie the Pooh*. They both worked listlessly and had to be prodded to help.

Lemuel was the huge kid I had noticed on deck. I thought he was Samoan or some other Pacific islander because he had that tanned Buddha look, but I found out he was actually Native American of Narragansett ancestry. His mother had worked the buffet at Foxwoods Casino. He was very shy, perhaps distrustful, though his size and physical strength made him conspicuous among us. He kept stealing glances at me.

Cole Hayes was in his own world and barely took notice of us or anything else. It was like he was watching a movie only he could see. He did what was expected, but he was a tall kid and kept bumping his head on hangers and lights, reacting to the pain with an incomprehension that reminded me of King Kong getting strafed. I would find out there was a very good reason for this: He had been a high school track star who had risen from the projects in South Providence to be courted by the best colleges in the country. His future was a vision of paradise like no one in his family had ever imagined. Then Agent X came along.

I returned their nods, hoping they were starting to overcome their suspicion. "Nice to meet you," I said in general. To Hector, I asked, "How long have you all known each other?"

"Some of us went to Cranston East together, and I've known Julian and Tyrell a long time because our dads were friends. The rest I met up with for the first time at the plant, but we've all gotten to know each other pretty good since then."

"How long ago was that?"

" 'Bout a month."

"And you know everyone by name?" I was terrible with names.

"You learn it doing roll call twice a day. Plus it was kind of my job to get to know everyone—I was floor safety monitor."

"Narc!" snorted Jake, the orange-haired kid, still feigning sleep.

"Safety Squirrel," I said.

"Yeah."

"How did you wind up in that factory?"

"It was really weird. Right before Agent X took off, we all got brought in under police escort. It was Christmas break, and this big bus convoy goes to all our houses, picking everyone up like for camp or something, except it was the middle of the night. My mother and sister were freaking out thinking I was being arrested for something, until the security men told them my stepdad had authorized it—that there was something very important going on at the plant, and I was to take part. I think they gave her a note from him, too. We could see a lot of other guys already in the buses, so I started to think it might be some kind of lame father-son bonding thing sponsored by the company. As soon as they knew I was the guy on their list, they kind of raided my room, stuffed everything into dufflebags, and put it all on the bus with me. Sheila and my mom were standing out on the step in their nighties—I remember wishing they would go back inside, I was so embarrassed. That was the last time I ever saw them."

He stared down at the fake wood grain of the tabletop, tracing patterns with his finger.

He said, "A couple of weeks into the whole thing, there was a rumor at the plant that old women and little girls hadn't caught the disease, and a bunch of the men demanded to leave the compound so they could search for family members that might have survived. It got pretty hairy before Chairman Sandoval finally agreed to let them try. We all wanted to go along, but they chose up a couple hundred adults and said that was enough. My stepdad was crazy to go, but they said he was too important." Hector slowly shook his head, the mask blurring his features.

"They didn't find anyone," I said softly.

"They never came back at all." As if brushing these matters aside, he said, "What happened to you?"

"Um . . ." I was caught off guard. My mind had turned away from all that as from a stinging, cold wind, and I didn't know what would happen if I faced it. "I'm from California," I said noncommittally. "We came out here to find Mr. Cowper."

"That old guy who's in command? Is he your grandfather?"

"I think he's my father. My mother was after him for child-support. I never really knew him."

The boy named Tyrell piped up, "Yo, that was cold, way he turned you out to be bait for them Xombies."

"Yeah," Hector told me, "but he brought you here. Don't count that out. I never got along with my stepdad, but he probably saved my life bringing me here." Avoiding my eyes, he added, "Anyway, I, I just wanted to apologize for before . . . the way some of those guys were treating you. That wasn't too cool; I should've done something sooner. I'm sorry."

Why did he have to keep apologizing for everything? "That's all right," I said in confusion. Changing the subject, I asked, "How do you guys know so much about the sub?"

The severe one, Julian, replied, "They don't know shit, but you live in a submarine factory for two months, it kind of seeps in by osmosis."

Tyrell laughed, "Why you say that, man? He fuckin' with you—they drilled us hard on that shit. Told us we couldn't go on the boat 'less we passed BESS."

"Bess?"

"Basic Enlisted Submarine School," explained Hector. "Of course it was all crap—the boat was never for us. They were just jerking us off to keep their workforce on the job until the refit was done and they could ditch our asses. Almost worked, too . . . if you and that Cowper hadn't come along." There was a long, drowsy pause, as if everyone was digesting this point. I couldn't tell if they were grateful or blamed me for prolonging their agony. Then, as my attention seeped away, I realized that their feelings were exactly like my own:

They didn't care at all.

EVERYONE AWOKE TO Mr. Cowper's amplified voice ringing in our ears: "Attention all hands. Remove and stow EAB equipment—the air has been deemed fit ta breathe. All non-useful bodies—that's you kids—report ta Mr. Noteiro in Stores. He'll show ya how ta whip up a great big batch a hot cocoa."

The clock on the wall showed 3:45 a.m. It was blissful pain to rip off those masks and smell the sea air circulating through the sub. I was very thirsty.

"Cocoa," sighed Jake Bartholomew reverently. There was a cherry-red imprint around his face from the respirator.

"Dat cocoa's not fa you," Mr. Noteiro said gleefully, appearing in the galley. "You'll be soivin' it up top. Chop-chop!"

It was almost worth lugging a boiling-hot plastic drum up two flights of stairs and a ladder to see the reaction it drew. People had been huddled together for warmth most of the night, and no one had gotten any sleep. Sandoval—the man who had hurt his leg jumping across—had moaned in agony the whole time, and apparently there had been serious talk of ditching him over the side. When they heard shots fired up the sail, then felt the diesel, there were surges of excitement; but as the night wore on their hopes dimmed. Those of us who had gone below were written off as dead. The rest, lingering in that moonless vacuum like shipwreck survivors on a bare atoll, didn't expect to last much longer.

When the forward hatch popped open, it was light none of them had ever expected to see again. Then to have us come up bearing hot cocoa, cookies, and blankets—we were treated like heroes, like some kind of miracle. Grown men wept and thanked God for their deliverance. The deck became a party.

I say "we" were treated—actually the crush of congratulations centered on Hector and other guys, but he held them off and pointed at me. "She's the one you should thank," he said. "Without her we wouldn't have nailed the Xombies."

"No, it was obvious," I said demurely, and people were happy enough to take me at my word, thanking me only for filling their cups. Maybe they thought Hector was being facetious. Not that I expected thanks, even if the rest were feted like conquerers. A little help would have been good—since I was the only one not swamped with admirers, I succumbed to the insatiable demands of the crowd, doling out seconds and thirds. There was never a break until the spigot trickled its final sludgy dregs. "That's it! All gone!" I announced, sorry I hadn't set aside a cup for myself.

"Dude!" exclaimed a stringy-haired character with many tattoos. "You're bringing up more, right?"

"Not that I know of." I knew *I* wasn't—I could barely stand up.

He jabbed his bony finger into my chest. "Well you better! What are you doin' here, anyway? Who is this bitch? I thought women were supposed to be off-limits—disease-ridden fucking vampires—and here you are in charge of the cocoa. What, are we supposed to be grateful for any crumb you decide to give us? We're cold and hungry and tired, and we're not gonna sit still for this bullshit."

Now others were pressing in on me, among them the boy in the hairnet who had harrassed me before. "Little bitch thinks she all that," he said. "She thinks we gonna forget how she come bustin' in here like she own the place, takin' up room that shoulda gone to our families. The price a that space ain't nothin' to her! Now she gonna ration out the supplies for us? We gonna have to beg her for what's ours? It ain't happenin', uh-uh." He shoved the empty barrel into my arms, nearly knocking me into the sea.

The last frayed thread of my composure broke with a loud mental *twang* and I launched myself at the lead cretin.

"Hey!" A frail-looking man in a suit and a porkpie hat caught me from behind, gently taking the barrel from my arms and putting it down like a stool for me to sit on. His eyes were large and intense, glowing in a face like dark-stained wood. Completely ignoring the boys all around, he said, "Your name is Lulu?" His voice had a mild Caribbean lilt.

I nodded.

"I wanted to t'ank you."

"Thank me?" My brain was spinning.

"For what you did below. I'm Hercule Banks, Tyrell's father. He told me what hoppened." Solemnly he said, "You saved my son's life. I believe you saved all our lives."

I wavered stupidly, mumbling, "No, I mean . . . um . . . thanks . . . you're welcome."

He kissed his fingertips and pressed them to my icy cheek, then cast a baleful look at the boys. They shrank back, parting to make a path for him. As he ambled through, he tipped his hat at me, saying, "Praise Jesus."

None of the boys would look at me after that, and soon they all melted away like wraiths into the dark. The feeling of that warm touch stayed with me much longer.

SHLEPPING THE EMPTY drum down to the galley, I ran into Mr. Robles and was told to report to the command center. I just wanted to collapse somewhere and sleep, so having to climb two decks back up was a really dreary prospect. Who would have expected stairs to be such an issue on a submarine?

The boat looked stripped. Everywhere I went there were raw-looking spaces where banks of computers and other equipment had been pulled out, leaving haphazardly bundled wires and bare struts. The third level was especially naked. I was to learn that most of the controls related to the vessel's function as a nuclear missile platform had been there, removed many months before as part of some plan to keep the Cold War–era titan strategically relevant. When that all fell apart after Agent X, the sub was up for grabs.

I still couldn't get over the size of it. The submarine was divided into three segments, each nearly two hundred feet long and forty feet high. Farthest aft was the propulsion unit—the massive steam turbines that drove the screw, and the 60,000 horsepower General Electric S8G nuclear reactor that created the steam; then the hollowed-out missile room; and finally the CCSM deck—the five-story command and control module beneath the fairwater that extended to the sonar dome in the bow. It was a large underwater building.

Mr. Cowper met me at the top of the companionway. Staving off my embrace, he handed over a big leather pouch and said, "Take good care a this dittybag—I've put a few things in there might come in handy. Don't let that Kranuski see it, whatever you do. Come on." Before I could reply, he began leading me aft, saying, "The natives a getting restless. I need ya to communicate ta them what I plan ta do. Here."

We were standing before one of the watertight doors to the missile room. He leaned his arm on the gleaming valve wheel and said in the nasal voice of an old-time elevator operator, "First floor: missile compahtment. Ladies lingerie, sporting goods, household appliances, and otha picture postcahds." He pulled the door open, revealing that cavernous tunnel of cargo. "Be it eva so jumbled, there's no place like home. Whattaya think? Can we fit everybody in there?"

I didn't see how. "It's going to be hard with all that stuff in the way."

"Yeah, they turned her into a vault. A giant safe for all their crap. Anything they couldn't stand ta leave ungahded when they closed up shop, and anything they thought they might need in the future. It's like a do-it-yourself kit for restahting America from scratch. They probably have the formula fa Coke down there somewhere. It's a damn shame fa the kids."

"So what do we do?"

Mr. Cowper either grinned or gritted his teeth, I couldn't tell. He looked incredibly old.

"Heard a the Boston Tea Pahty?" he asked.

eleven

THE SUN RISING over the bay was like hot lemon and honey to the sickly cold multitudes laboring on deck. From a distance we would have looked like termites at work on a floating log, vanishing into holes and emerging with bits of stuff, then dropping it into the water. Closer up we felt more like slaves of the pharoah, dismantling a tomb rather than building one.

In spite of Mr. Kranuski's and Mr. Sandoval's strenuous objections, a bearer-brigade had been organized to clear the missile room. It happened before the crew could stop it—we were ten times their number and simply piled in; there was no fighting, and they didn't dare shoot anyone for fear of making Xombies.

All the next week we remained anchored off the north shore of Conanicut Island, painstakingly passing things up the three logistics hatches one at a time. There was great incentive to work fast, because as soon as floor space was

cleared it became living space, which in turn reduced topside crowding. The only problem was that much of the stuff
was too big to fit through the hatches, and could only be re-
arranged below.

"How did they ever get all this in here?" I asked Julian on
the second day. I couldn't believe how much had been done
while I was sleeping.

"In port you can use a crane to lift out the entire escape
trunk. Makes a much bigger opening."

"There's no way to do it now?"

"Well, we might be able to rig a scaffold and winch, but
it's not something I'd want to try at sea."

"Why not?"

"Just feel. This thing rocks like a bastard. Swell kicks up,
you could lose the escape trunk over the side. Then you're
left with a seven-foot-wide hole in the deck, which isn't too
good on a submarine."

"I guess not."

The boat itself was a breathtaking sight by day: a black
peninsula almost six hundred feet long—longer, I was told,
than the Washington Monument. We were conspicuous in
the channel, and a number of boats examined us from a dis-
creet distance. They did not approach, but as the days went
by we saw more and more of them, gathering like seagulls
around a dying whale. A lot of boys were thrilled at the
sight and desperate to join forces with other refugees, but
word came down that we were to make no attempt to signal
or in any way communicate with outsiders. Many were un-
happy with this, and we didn't even get an explanation because the command center was off-limits to all but "essential
personnel."

After that first night, a division had sprung up between
the working adults and the "nubs"—non-useful bodies. In
practical terms it meant that everything forward or aft of
the missile bay was off-limits. We had free run of that huge
chamber and free topside access, but I felt vulnerable without Mr. Cowper and hoped he would make contact soon.

I had been through the bag he gave me, and was incredibly grateful for the basic items he had packed: a wool blanket and knit cap, a windbreaker, a pair of blue coveralls (men's small but still too large for me), sneakers, and a waterproof survival kit with tissues, antiseptic wipes, bandages, tape, aspirin, eating utensils, small tools, flint, needle and thread, soap, penlight, and a compass. There was also an official-looking padded envelope, sealed with string, on which he had written, *To be opened in PRIVATE!*

Privacy was a rare phenomenon; the only time it was really possible was in the "head," and even then only if I could get someone to stand guard. Many already thought I used far more than my share of bathroom time; that my refusal to pee in public like a dog was some kind of finicky affectation. Ignoring their looks, I smuggled in the envelope and wasted no time ripping it open.

Inside was a heart-shaped locket on a chain and a set of pictures. They were well-worn, as if they'd spent ages in a wallet. In the locket was a trimmed photo of a prune-faced newborn. Was that me? Had Mr. Cowper, proud papa, taken the photo? I picked it out and on the back someone had written, *Terminal Island Nav. Shipyard, CA.* On the margin was a meaningless notation: *4 ABL S FR 13.* At first glance I thought it was some cutesy Valentine candy sentiment— *4EVER 2GETHER* or something—then I tried deciphering it, but couldn't come up with any initials or abbreviations that fit. Something something *Friday the 13th?* I gave up for now.

The other photos had nothing to do with me . . . and everything. They were older than the first, faded, and showed polyester artifacts from the '60s and '70s. They were of a younger Mr. Cowper with his family: a wife who was not my mother, a daughter who was not me. All of them aging through several jumps in time, the last one showing the pretty blond daughter in cap and gown. Years and years of happiness.

No wonder: *this* had been his life. He had lived his

whole life before I was ever born, and by that time it must
have seemed like such a bother. Been there, done that. And
my mother? Had she come in at the end and brought it all
down—the Other Woman? Well, no wonder. Could I honestly say I was surprised? Wasn't this exactly what I suspected all these years? I wanted to kick myself for the
dumb animal hurt I was feeling. No wonder. I fumbled
the pictures back into the envelope and could barely hear
the people talking to me as I left the head, suddenly desperate for fresh air. All the time I just kept nodding and
thinking, *Yup. No wonder.*

AS THE MISSILE room was gradually cleared, I found it
astounding to gaze up from the lead-bricked bilge into
those soaring cathedral heights. For twenty years it had
contained a forest of twenty-four Trident missile silos,
each one seven feet wide, extending through every deck.
It's crews had been accustomed to jogging laps around its
perimeter—nineteen to the mile. Now the "trees" were gone,
the steel-grated decks perforated like a colossal Swiss cheese
or ripped out altogether, leaving airy chasms surrounded
by red caution tape. Fanciful assemblies of scaffolding and
plywood rose like primitive cliff dwellings to the upper
tiers, and it was up these we ported the endless tons of
freight. Even though we worked in twenty-minute relays
and labor-saving pulley systems were in place, it was the
most exercise I'd ever known. I worried about getting a
repetitive-stress injury, but said nothing.

   Perhaps because those first days were so uncomfortable,
so full of head bumps, stairclimbing, and sleeping on hard
floors, the awesome vessel quickly lost its mystique and
became the "fuckin' torture chamber of Jacques Cousteau,"
as Tyrell put it. But everyone took care not to grumble in
the presence of the Navy people, who were understandably
touchy and more than willing—in fact eager—to send anyone ashore who wanted to go.

   This was illustrated during one of our meager meals,

when a group of kids began clamoring for seconds. They were the ones my mother would have called MABs—More Attitude than Brains. Now, it had already been explained to everyone that provisions were low and never intended to feed so many, but accepting this in the abstract and being faced with half a cup of grits, a slice of bacon, and a spoonful of fruit cocktail as the big meal of the day were two different things. Their complaints ignored, the boys started throwing the extremely short supply of dishes and silverware overboard.

As the strike began to spread, the volunteer cooks (of whom I was one), were told to clear an area of deck, then stood by while Mr. Robles and a gorilla-chested officer named Alton Webb quickly inflated a large rubber boat. The vandalism subsided as this strange activity progressed. Then Webb took long-handled prongs and gleefully began stalking the crowd. "Who's going?" he challenged. "Come on! Who's not happy? Speak up!"

This went on for an agonizing twenty minutes, as he singled out the ringleaders and made them beg to stay aboard. By the end I thought he had carried it a bit too far—they were groveling worms, puking in fear. I even felt sorry for the hairnet boy, Mitch, who got clobbered for mouthing off.

At last they were put to work stowing the raft, cleaning the deck, and washing the remaining dishes in buckets of seawater. They were very careful.

As the days went by, the number of people above dwindled, beginning with those who were ill or otherwise thought to be at risk from exposure. After sleeping both indoors and out, I actually found camping on deck to be preferable, not least because it was softer—the hull was slightly padded with rubber to make the boat stealthy—but also because by the fourth night it was a regular jamboree, with strings of Christmas lights, makeshift tents, hot-water showers, outhouses, and plenty of headroom.

A semblance of privacy finally became possible. The

top secret bales and boxes going over the side were raided for building supplies: cardboard and plastic for shelters; mattresses of bubblewrap or foam-rubber; Styrofoam hobo furniture. Stacks of blast-hardened laptop computers were passed around like party favors.

I did feel kind of bad about all this, as if we were doing something that could never be undone, but that was like saying our survival mattered less than a lot of blueprints and widgets and technical manuals.

And the view up top was better. Looking at the serene shores of Narragansett Bay, I did not feel so encroached upon by the apocalypse. There was no sign of Xombies, just the ever-changing panorama of water, sky, and house-dotted landscape as the tides lazily swung the boat on its anchor chain. Gulls were always present, but we also saw cormorants and even fat white swans. Life seemed to be going on.

I was not exactly "one of the guys," but Hector and Julian made me welcome in their clique, though it was obvious that my presence cramped their style—I'm sure it was a relief to them that I spent most of my free time catching up on Submarines 101, using materials Mr. Robles made available to me. Such technical material had never interested me before; perhaps I'd simply never had the incentive. Suddenly it was fiction I couldn't bear. There were DVDs for everything, and that terabyte-chomping military laptop was a welcome change from my old funky Packard Bell, still loaded with Windows 95. When I wasn't learning acronyms, I was helping Mr. Noteiro or Mr. Monte prepare and serve the twice-daily civilian ration.

At night there was a lot of prayer, hymn-singing, and purging of grief. Just about everyone on board was either Catholic or Baptist. As an agnostic, I refrained from joining in these sessions, though at times I went along with it to avoid drawing attention to myself. In the presence of religion or sports I've always felt like an anthropologist observing headhunters—best to keep a low profile. My mother had a religious side that I never found very attractive. Despite my care, it still became an issue.

Five days in I was approached to lead the group in prayer. It was a welcoming gesture, their way of saying I was okay, but it was a little much for me and I begged off, citing stage fright. They wouldn't let it go, countering my every excuse until finally there was nothing left but to concede that I was a heathen. Now I was mad.

They asked me, "Don't it matter to you that you're going to Hell?"

"I'm used to it by now."

"Don't act like it's a joke! For all you know, maybe this *is* Hell. Maybe we're here 'cause the Lord be giving a preview to all the nonbelievers. Maybe he's testin' you, like Eve! Maybe it's atheists like you brought this down upon us."

"I'm not an atheist, though."

"Do you believe in God?"

"I don't believe or disbelieve. I don't think it's possible to know, but I'm open-minded about it."

"You're straddlin' the fence. Jesus don't abide no fence-sitters. Don't you know He even prefers a pure unbeliever to someone who can't make up their mind? The Lord spits you from His mouth like lukewarm water."

"Spitting spreads disease."

"You think you can have it both ways. God won't be fooled. You can fool me, you can fool all of us here, you can even fool yourself, but Jehovah will not be fooled. It's the folly of your sex to think He can."

"Jesus, now it's my sex."

"Thy name is Vanity an' you just proved it takin' the Lord's name in vain."

This pointless back-and-forth went on and on until I finally pretended to start crying and did my whole little waif act. Then they backed off and let me sleep.

* * *

LATE THAT NIGHT I awoke in the grip of death.

"You unclean bitch. You little whore," rasped a hooded face inches from mine. "You act so fuckin' innocent, like you're some kinda Girl Scout, but you got it all figured out. Think you got all us guys twisted around your little pinkie. Well I ain't fooled. I see you parading your ass around like it's made a milk and honey. You're here to tempt us." Spittle flecked my cheek. "Well you know what? You succeeded."

It was the stringy-haired man who wanted more cocoa. He was straddling my chest, pinning my arms under the tarpaulin with his knees. His hands were clamped over my mouth and nose, suffocating me. Someone else was on my legs. It was all very silent and methodical—the rest of the deck beyond my low curtain was fast asleep. Almost as soon as I knew what was happening I began to fade, losing myself in a throbbing red buzz.

"Stop struggling or you die," he hissed in my ear. "You hear me? Hold still."

"Bust that fucking bitch, Adam," said the other from below, stripping off my panties. It was Mitch. "She playin' you."

"Come on, you cunt. Give it up."

I disappeared for a second then came back, fighting the deep willingness to do just as he was saying. Some part of me was grateful for the chance to go away for good. My body was a nest of agonies, but its troubles already seemed like someone else's problem.

All at once there was a commotion and the weight was gone. I could taste blood—the inside of my lip was cut from being mashed into my teeth. Gulping air, I looked up to see the wizened black face of Mr. Banks leaning over me. "You okay, bebby?" he asked.

"She okay, pop?" asked Tyrell, kneeling close by. There were a lot of other alarmed, sleepy people clustered around, men and boys all talking at once and ogling me. Big Lemuel was in tears. It was like the scene of a fire.

Afraid of them all, I nodded, eyes wide.

"Psh, she gone be fine," said the old man. "That's the first time I've had occasion to thank the lord for givin' me a weak bladder. Hallelujah!" He was holding one of the big hammers that had been standard equipment at the factory. There was a tuft of hair on it, beaded red.

Getting my breath back, I noticed someone lying motionless beside me. It was the tattooed one named Adam. A second body, that of Mitch, was draped partly over my leg and I could feel it moving. Trying to push it off, my hand encountered hot slimy hair covered with nylon netting. Blood. I cried out, squirming away.

"*Tch tch tch!* You're safe. Hey." Hands gently pressed my shoulders, trying to be reassuring. Mr. Banks soothed, "It's all over now—you're okay."

"Are they dead?" I choked.

"Might be. Don't you worry none about them. They was bad."

Wired, Tyrell said, "You clocked 'em good, pop. Sorry-ass mothafuckas."

Breathless, I moaned, "No, you have to check! Check them fast, because—"

With one swift motion Adam was on his feet in a feral crouch. His face was stained dark as wine, darker than the sky overhead, and eyes still blacker—glass marbles with centers yawning wide as collapsed stars, sucking everything in. His tongue lolled out, a glistening blue-gray slug tasting the air. *Rapture*—there was nothing else to call it. It was an obscene resurrection; he was born again.

I hardly saw what happened next as I quailed beneath the monstrous thing, trying to shrink into the deck. Boxed in on three sides by walls of recoiling onlookers, the Xombie took a leisurely survey of the situation, then seized hairnet-boy's living body by the collarbone as if it was a handle—Mitch awoke in agony—and lunged with him over the windscreen I had erected. It was just cardboard fastened to the safety cable; what appeared to be open space beyond was actually the port side of the boat. There was a skidding sound, then a splash as they both fell into the sea.

We shined flashlights down after them, but there was no movement in the milky green water.

"Boy had the devil in him," said Mr. Banks.

WHEN THE DAY of departure finally came and everyone had to break camp, I was deeply depressed. I didn't have the energy to deal with whatever plan they had for us or look ahead to the future, and I dreaded being cooped up with people who loathed me. On a purely aesthetic level, it was like moving from an airy patio to a windowless cellar . . . though the lights and warmth would be nice. But if it weren't for the weather turning bad, I could have stayed up there forever.

In the aftermath of the incident, most people avoided my eyes as if I were Medusa. Even the ones who took an interest in my welfare wouldn't look at me, but were suddenly fanatical about guarding me at night. There were a lot of fake-earnest expressions of sympathy; a stream of invitations to "just talk." All this got on my nerves because I didn't want them putting my trauma in a special category above their own—we were in this together. Others pretended nothing had happened, and I actually preferred this . . . except in the case of Mr. Cowper. It would have helped to talk to him.

The line to go below was forming, a lot of hustle and bustle. I lagged back to have a last long look over the water. It was choppy, and wind-torn pennants of red, green, and gold colored the dawn sky. The boat glistened with frost. Above her silo-like sail, the last stars were also taking their sweet time to go. How many people in the world were still around to see those stars? To feel what I felt?

"Red sky at morning, sailor take warning," someone said up front, and "Who's got Dramamine?" I wiped my eyes and headed down.

twelve

WE RAISED ANCHOR and sailed for the open ocean the morning of Sunday, February 5th. The rolling belowdecks told us a storm was brewing—a submarine's famed ability to ride out gales is all about its ability to submerge; since we were running on the surface we had no such immunity. In fact we were less stable than a surface ship would have been.

The effect of this irony was a plague of seasickness in the missile room. There was no adequate provision for this, no way to hurl over the side, and only one available rest-room for over four hundred people. It was like a painting by Bruegel in there. Five-gallon buckets were lashed down all over the compartment, and whenever they were full someone had to pour them into the three toilets, a terrible job in a rocking ship. Everyone took turns doing it, but not everyone was as surefooted as they might have been—I know I had a few spills of my own. Even with the air being constantly refreshed, it was impossible to escape the smell of vomit.

Knock wood, I was one of the few who never got sick.

Nobody knew where we were going, and the conscripted adults passing through the missile room did not stop to answer questions, so there was a certain envy when word came over the loudspeaker that I was to report to the command center.

"Lucky you, getting a pass out of steerage," Hector said, half-mocking. He and the other guys could barely drag themselves from their cardboard igloo on the fourth level. "Make sure to tell them we appreciate the accomodations."

"And make 'em tell you what's up with this secrecy shit," Tyrell said. "Brotha got a right to know what kinda plans they makin' for us. I ain't *doin'* no more tired-ass refugee-camp bullshit. Give me a island. We livin' in a democracy, dog—I say we vote on where we goin', be kickin' back in the Bahamas."

Doing a Jamaican-sounding falsetto, Jake sang, *"Sail away to Block Island . . . leave all your troubles behind . . ."* Then he retched.

Pausing dramatically at the forward bulkhead, I intoned, "I shall return."

I still hadn't seen or heard from Mr. Cowper since our first night on the water, six days before. I attributed this to the urgent demands put on him, as well as the need to avoid any appearance of favoritism—he couldn't afford to lavish attention on any one person. The crew had their limited sphere, the passengers our own. Being granted the largest open space on board, we were expected to make the best of it, which meant not bothering anyone forward amidships. It was an unavoidable apartheid; there was simply not enough room to let so many people roam free. But I didn't like it.

The luckiest among us were the adults who were permitted to use the enlisted berthing on the missile room's third level: nine bunks to a room, with doors that could be shut against the squalor. Everyone envied them.

Arriving at main control, I was told by Mr. Kranuski to report to the commander on the bridge. It reassured me to see that no one here seemed disturbed by the deck's motion. It didn't smell.

"Come right fifteen degrees," Kranuski said, and Robles replied, "Right fifteen, aye." The men at the steering yokes casually complied. Most of the people in the room were men who had come from the factory, but it was hard to tell them apart from the official crew now. A number of them were wearing the same blue "poopie suits" as the one Mr. Cowper gave me.

As I went up the hatch that had been such a dreadful source of terror before, I was grateful for this scene of quiet professionalism—only XO Kranuski so much as spared me a glance. "Just grab a harness and go all the way up," he said.

Climbing up through three dank chambers, I emerged into a tiny, pitching cockpit already full of Mr. Coombs. He had a bulky neck brace, and a big pair of binoculars slung from it. The wind was fierce.

"Coming through, sir!" I shouted, disappointed at not finding Mr. Cowper.

Coombs made room for me beside him while a burly man scanned the seas to my right—it was Albemarle. We were high above the waves, the sub's blunt nose plowing them into ridges of whitewater that doused us with spray. It was also sleeting. The toy windshield, on which cryptic figures and notations had been scribbled in grease pencil, offered no protection.

Turning stiffly toward me, Coombs shouted, "Why don't you have a coat?"

"Sorry sir. I didn't know."

He made me drop back down and put on a hooded rain slicker and a life vest—thank goodness, because I was freezing cold. When I returned to the top he clipped me to a safety cable, then handed me binoculars and bellowed, "Tell me if you see anything!"

There was nothing to see but gray. Feeling very nervous, I searched a wide swath of whitecaps but found no horizon or anything else. Spume misted the lenses. Looking astern I thought I saw something: a faint light that blinked and vanished. I waited for it and caught it blinking again.

"There," I said. "A light. It keeps going on and off."

"I should hope so," he said gruffly. "It's the Beaver Tail Light. You should be able to see that without the damn binoculars. On a clear day you'd see the cliffs at Newport. If you look about twenty degrees to the left you can probably find the automated light at Point Judith, too. It's operational."

I had been to the Point Judith Light. It was only a couple of miles from Jerusalem. Living there felt like a long, long time ago. That we could still be so close made my stomach muscles clench up. "I see it," I said.

"Now look forward again a little more carefully. See the compass? We're heading due east, following the mainland toward the Cape. Track ahead along the coast."

"But I can't even see the coast."

"Doesn't matter—the SVS-1200 says its there, see?"

He showed me a map displayed on a small glowing screen, and I nodded as if I could read it. I returned to scanning, trying to keep my balance in the swinging loft. "Wait—there it is. That one?"

"Sakonnet Point. Congratulations." He turned robotically and shook my hand.

"Thanks," I said, sheepishly handing back the binoculars.

"I'm not congratulating you for seeing the lighthouse. I'm congratulating you for being selected as the boat's official Youth Liaison Officer."

"Oh . . . the what, sir?"

"You'll be responsible for making sure all command directives are understood and followed to the letter by the other minors on board. You will also be the spokesperson for said minors, addressing their questions and concerns in whatever way you see fit, so long as it doesn't interfere

with the official duties of the crew or the rules and regulations of this vessel. Finally, you will be my eyes and ears in
the missile bay, and will be expected to furnish a daily report describing any problems you may be having with civilian order or morale. Anyone gives you trouble, report them
to me. Think you can handle the job?"

"I'm not sure, sir. I've never—"

"Am I to understand that you are the young woman who
came up with the carbon monoxide solution to the Xombies?"

"I guess so, yes, but—"

"Well, I'm sure that if you bring as much initiative to
your duties as Youth Liaison Officer as you did to the Xombie problem, you'll have 'em eating out of your hand. The
youths, that is. Now, these duties are not to be taken lightly.
All it takes is one bad apple to spoil the whole bunch,
girl—our lives and the success of our objective could once
again come down to your powers of observation. We've already compromised far too much of this mission . . . we
have to salvage what we can. May I count on you?"

It was not a question. "Yes, sir," I said dismally.

"Good. Mr. Monte will get you started on one of the
UNIX workstations. He'll also arrange for you to have a
private snack in the wardroom every day—but I advise you
to keep that to yourself. Welcome to the team. That's all."

"Mr. Coombs, sir?"

"You should call me commander or captain. Skipper is
all right too."

"Yes, sir. Uh, captain? Where can I find Mr. Cowper,
sir?"

He turned heavily away. "You wouldn't want to do that."

"Why not?"

"Fred Cowper is under arrest, pending charges of con-
spiracy, mutiny, sedition, and theft and destruction of classified government property. That's just the beginning. I
don't know what your relationship to him is, but I do know
that his personnel file specifies that he is widowed with no

dependents. All the times I've worked with him over the years, he never mentioned you. Don't you think it's about time you returned the favor?"

I shook my head no, tears blowing away.

"Lulu, Uncle Sam is your daddy now. He won't let you down."

Ice-cold, I descended.

I WAS USED to being shunned—kids had been shunning me all my life, as they will anyone who dares to use reason and four-syllable words—but under these circumstances it was bothersome beyond belief. As Youth Liaison Officer I was given scheduled times when I could roam beyond the missile compartment, and these outings became more and more necessary as my tolerance for being sniped at decreased—the decks were gauntlets of whispered asides, to which I responded in kind: "Bitch." "Jerk." "Bitch." "Creep." "Skank." "Pig." "Bitch." "Trash." No one cared that I had neither asked for nor desired my new title; any fledgling public sympathy just evaporated overnight. Word had gotten out about Mr. Cowper's arrest and confinement, and a lot of guys acted like he had been asking for it all along. *"Oh yeah,"* they muttered together. *"What did he expect?"* I couldn't believe it. He and I were even made the subject of outrageous graffiti—cartoons that portrayed me as a Nazi kewpie doll putting a noose around the old man's neck.

All my fears about sharing a cave with these troglodytes seemed to be coming true. I took to carrying my possessions everywhere I went for fear of vandalism. The boys blamed me for everything. When I had to announce that the laptops were being confiscated, they blamed me. When I couldn't increase the measly ration, or couldn't answer questions about our destination, they blamed me. For anything they could think up I was blamed, so that I began to feel like a sacrificial effigy: Coombs's stand-in. Fortunately there were no more psychos among them, or if there were they knew better than to try anything. But when animals are crowded together in unhealthy conditions they eventually start killing one another, and I think Coombs knew exactly what he was doing, letting me take the heat. I was expendable.

Rather than murdering me, however, the boys vented their testosterone on one another, fighting over any slight— I mean real fist-fights—and forming belligerent gangs. I tried to channel these passions in a positive direction, enlisting Shawn to help me organize a makeshift poetry slam, and even contributed a short piece in the style of my idol, Emily Dickinson: "Trapped in this armpit omnibus/The river feeds its source/We've traded in our Pegasus/And bought a rocking horse." But in spite of the captive audience, the reading was a bust; at best an unruly class assembly.

"Cut 'em some slack," Shawn said afterward, unfazed. "It's too soon. They'll rhyme when they're ready to rhyme. Right now it ain't real to 'em; everybody needs to feel safe first." He shrugged, not looking at me. "You just don't inspire that much confidence, Lulu. It's not your fault."

The ship's crew didn't like me any better than the passengers did, resenting my presence in "officer country" and taking full advantage of their option to bounce me out of any area deemed too sensitive. This was completely at their discretion, and depended on the whim or temperment of the individual officer. Robles and Noteiro were liberal; Kranuski and Webb not so nice. But at least I wasn't the only one receiving this treatment: there were over a hundred of our people—men and proficient older boys, Julian among them—who had been engaged to assist and relieve the burned-out crew. What made my position unique was that I only answered to the captain, and I didn't have to take on any old job that came up.

I should say here I did have my supporters, however reluctant. Hector, Julian, Jake, Tyrell, and a handful of others never treated me like a stooge; in fact they sheltered me as best they could from the bullying, though they were obviously terrified of being isolated themselves. It was due to their civility and encouragement that I was able to fulfill any part of my duties, not to mention sleep in peace. I really depended on them.

"You okay?"

It was late in the night, and the weight of woe had driven me to tears. I tried to be quiet about it, huddled in my corner, but Julian overheard me and crawled over. Back turned, I nodded, tried to hold it in, then blurted, "I'm sick of everybody hating me. I can't stand this anymore. I didn't do anything!"

"No they don't. Hey."

"What the hell are you talking about?" I retorted.

"Okay they do, but it's nothing personal."

"That's just it; it *is* personal. It's about me! It's always been about me. Either people think I'm stuck-up, or I'm some kind of mutant whiz kid—a sideshow freak. Now I get to be an evil she-devil on top of it all? Give me a break!" I turned and looked at him through brimming tears. "What the hell am I supposed to *do*? Kill myself?"

"Listen, everybody's just scared. We're all alone out here. Nobody knows what's going on, and right now they're taking it out on you, trying to do anything they can to bond together."

"Great."

"I know it sucks, but it's not something you're going to overcome by appealing to their sense of logic. Believe me, I've tried. You're going to have to aim lower."

"I'm not about to be the ship's slut, if that's what you mean."

"Not that low. I'm talking about the heart, the gut. Give them something to rally around."

"Like what?"

"I don't know. You're the whiz kid. Think of something."

* * *

EVERY DAY A hastily typed memo would appear in my file, describing in the vaguest possible terms the submarine's itinerary, and part of my job was to brighten this bland text with cheerful adjectives and patriotic platitudes, then read it out loudly from atop one of the big box girders that spanned the missile bay. This was part of what Coombs called "Building Team Spirit." I cranked out the fluff as he asked, though the thought of reading it made me cringe. I put it off and put it off. But when I finally got up the nerve, the response was nothing like I expected.

Here was the first such memo: SURFACE CRUISING 17 NAUT. MI. SOUTH OF CAPE COD—NANTUCKET SOUND—NORTHEASTERLY TRACK—MODERATE TO HEAVY SWELLS—PLANNED NORTHERLY COURSE CHANGE 1900 HRS—SHIP'S STATUS CONTINUED ALERT.

My read-aloud version went like this:

"It is only through adversity that we know our mettle. We follow the track of the fabled Nor'easter and charge through the burgeoning swells like Eros on his dolphin. The bayberry and beach-plum dunes of Cape Cod, only seventeen miles north, do not beckon us the way they did the scurvied whalemen of old Nantucket, returning to their Sound from mythic hunts in southern seas. Our hunt lies north, as tonight at the hour of seven we round the curling eyelash of the Cape and emulate the cool and forward-thrust brow of America. *America:* She looks to the North Atlantic as the source of her strength, first as the stream that brought her peoples—as the infant Moses was borne upon the Nile—then as the rich fishing grounds that sustained them. Her beating heart urges us this way . . . and as proud Americans we are bound to go."

Coombs liked this so much he had me broadcast it all over the boat. I have to say that with the "Star Spangled Banner" playing in the background it sounded pretty good, but what really surprised me was the effect it had on everyone: There wasn't a dry eye in the house. Best of all, after a few of these performances, kids stopped being so mean to me.

"WHAT ARE YOU gonna do, now that they've arrested your old man?" asked Hector after dinner.

"What is there to do?" I said.

"How can you keep working for them?"

"I'm not working *for* them. The idea is that we're all supposed to be working together."

"Yeah, right."

"Really, I consider myself your representative up there. Anything anybody asks about, I forward it to Coombs, just like I bring back any information he gives me."

"Which is bogus."

"Maybe, but without it we wouldn't know anything at all."

"I get more scuttlebutt just listening to my stepdad complain."

"Yeah, but that's just a lot of rumors and gossip," I said. "That's not real information sharing. The only people who really know anything are the senior officers."

"Like they're *sharing* with you, give me a break. You're a tool."

"Thanks."

"A *propaganda* tool, come on. They're using you."

"It goes both ways."

"Oh yeah? So what are they planning for us? Tell me that."

"You heard the message," I said. "We're going up north to find the 'environmental survivability threshold of Agent X'—"

"Whatever that means."

"—where Maenad activity might be less intense—"

"Where they're all frozen solid, in other words."

"Xombiesicles," Jake smirked.

"—and where we can presumably be dropped off safely." I shook my head. "God, you guys."

"Where? Like the North Pole? I don't believe in Santa Claus, Lulu," Hector said. "Spring is on its way, you know? And it ain't just flowers that are gonna be in bloom. Maybe it's cold now, but there's not gonna be anyplace cold enough to make ice in July—not anyplace we can live. And what are we supposed to eat in the meantime? What are we supposed to wear? None of us brought clothes for a damn Antarctic expedition."

"Arctic. Look, there's no point in talking about this, because we don't know what they have in mind."

"All I'm saying is we're starving already, and it's only gonna get worse."

A little shrilly, I snapped, "What do you expect me to do about it?"

Hector backed off, looking beat. "Nothing. Nothing man, I'm sorry." I suddenly realized I could see the beginnings of gauntness in his features. After three days trapped belowdecks, seasickness and the starvation diet were undermining his robust Boy Scout face. All of them—all their eyes were haunted. I felt terrible—my own belly was full of canned ham, biscuits, and three-bean salad, which I had wolfed down in the grizzled, jolly presence of Mess Officer Emilio Monte, who had prepared it for me in the wardroom pantry. Away from prying eyes.

"Eat up, girlie," he had said. *"Mmm-mm! Goes down good, does it? That's what good little children get. Bad little children go to the goat locker."*

"No, *I'm* sorry," I said to them now. "I'll have to try harder to be useful up there. Fish for more concrete information."

"Be better to fish for fish," Tyrell said. "They gone starve us till we don't care what they do. Make us weak as baby chicks, then they can kill us, leave us on a iceberg, don't matta. *Sub-mission*—ain't that the name a the game? We ain't nothin' but a drain on 'em."

"I just think we have to be patient."

"Being patient is a crock," Hector said. "But I know

you're doing everything you can, Lulu. You're a stand-up girl."

From that point on, I began abusing my privileges, creeping on cat feet around the forward compartments in the hope of finding Mr. Cowper or overhearing anything that might be helpful to the guys. I loitered just around the corner from every conversation I could, but though I did manage to learn that a dive was being planned, there was no clue to Cowper's whereabouts. Furthermore, my memos detailing the rotten conditions in the missile room (which was now being called simply the "Big Room") were going unacknowledged, if not unread, by the captain. Since I had been specifically told to address him only by electronic posting, I was afraid of what might happen if I broached the subject personally. My instinct—and my hungry belly—told me not to.

I did, though, begin to gravitate toward him. Whereas previously I had sought out the least-attended workstations on board for my assignments, now I began using consoles in the control center, hoping opportunities to speak with him would come up.

With all the training going on, it was a busy place, and on my second day there I was pleased to see Julian working too—we exchanged aloof nods like initiates to some inner sanctum. Julian didn't look well, and I wondered if he was getting the extra food I was. I had assumed it came with our duties, like pay.

"Lulu," Coombs said over my shoulder.

I jumped. "Sorry, sir, you snuck up on me."

"That's all right. Listen, I read your proposal about starting a Youth Corps on the boat. I've actually been thinking about something along those lines myself, internships for kids who show aptitude. Hey, what about 'Internships for Aptitude'? That's good. We're still critically undermanned; we could use more bright kids like you working on qual cards."

This was funny to me. They hadn't trained me for anything, but Coombs seemed to take a peculiar interest in promoting the fiction that I was a vital member of the team. A "qual card" was a card you got when qualifying for specialized jobs—Julian had one, I knew, as did most of the adults. But Youth Liaison Officer was not a recognized specialty. I knew nothing, and Coombs seemed to like it that way.

He said, "This skeleton crew has been working for ten days with not much relief, and they're doing a lot of jobs a trained monkey could handle, while those kids back there are twiddling their thumbs and getting into mischief. I say let's give 'em some responsibility; a crash course in seamanship. What do you think?"

"Yes, sir. I think it would be great." I couldn't wait to tell the boys. "They'll be thrilled."

"Good. Get on it right away—I want seventy-five non-puking candidates by oh-nine-thirty. Oh, one other thing," he lowered his voice, "you haven't told anyone about our arrangement, have you?"

"Sir . . .?"

"Because that little extra something is still a special deal between you and us. It's not for everybody and his brother-in-law. There isn't enough chow to go around, and we don't want everyone to get all up in arms about it, do we?"

A sickening feeling wrung my stomach. "But the ones who are working, who I nominate for training, they'll get it, won't they?"

Coombs smiled sadly, resting his hand on my arm. "Honey, I wish they could."

thirteen

AFTER FOUR DAYS of slowly pounding along the surface, we finally submerged. The weather had slowly improved every day, and now the sea was dead calm. I had learned from my furtive snooping that we were off Newfoundland, in the vicinity of a place called Hibernia, and that there was a lot of ice in the sea. It was the hazard posed by icebergs that prompted the dive, though with each passing day the crew was also becoming noticeably paranoid about hostile ships.

Although I knew about the maneuver (and shared the information with my small circle of confidants), I wasn't prepared for when it would occur. As it turned out, it was the middle of the "night"—that is, the agreed-upon time when everyone in the Big Room was trying to sleep. It really was night outside, but we just as easily could have been somewhere on the planet where it was high noon—the clocks weren't changed for different time zones. All that signified night on board was darkroom-red lighting in some areas, which was more creepy than restful. It was never truly dark. The crew berths had curtains, but we in our ever-bright dungeon slept fitfully, like stranded holiday travellers at an airport.

At least the noise didn't bother me. There was always some noise in the boat; however, it was not the distressing engine room variety that I would have expected. Billions had been spent to muffle the vessel; its overriding design theme—a fugue, really—was stealth. Literally, no two pieces of metal touched without the intercession of a rubber grommet, and the entire place was padded like an asylum. Every pipe and duct hung from a shock-absorbing strut, and the decks themselves floated on cushions within the hull. The net result of all this was that in the upper crawlspaces it was possible to hear the slosh of the sea, and, depending on where you went, you might hear muted office sounds of cooling, heating, plumbing, electronics, ventilation, the deeper hum of powerful forces hidden aft, and the occasional bell or loudspeaker, but generally it was the kind of noise that becomes subliminal. That was why the captain's midnight announcement barely registered:

"All hands, we are at dive status. Commence dive."

An earsplitting alarm sounded, and everyone was awake at once.

"The hell's that?" someone shouted.

"Oh my God—what is it?" cried someone else.

The worst possible sounds on a submarine—plunging waterfalls and blasts of escaping air—drowned my voice as I called, "We're diving! We're just diving!" My heart was fluttering like a panicky finch in a cage.

There was a fearful sense of waves closing above us, of going down a well into a subterranean river. Long minutes passed while word of what was happening got around, then people just sat in anxious silence, eyes wide and turned upward like saints in religious paintings.

Rather than a giddy headlong plummet to the depths,

there was instead a strange settling sensation, as of things becoming very heavy and still.

"Is it over?" I asked.

Julian said, "Wait . . ."

Torturous haunted house sounds reverberated through the hull.

"Still going down," he said.

"Oh my God."

"Just wait . . ."

The awful noises began to die down. As quiet descended, there was a collective awakening, as if the last few days had been spent in the throes of some hellish delirium; addicts in withdrawal suddenly clean. People too seasick to drink or move, and who had become dangerously dehydrated, were standing up in wonder like pilgrims to Lourdes. The floor was steady. We looked around at each other with growing euphoria: Whatever it was we had been riding, it wasn't a submarine. *This* was a submarine!

Coombs came on the loudspeaker:

"Ladies and gentlemen, we are now at our cruising depth of three hundred feet. I apologize for any turbulence you may have experienced. In case you're wondering, we have submerged because of sea ice around the Island of New-foundland. The easternmost Canadian city of St. John's is just fourteen miles off our port bow, and it appears to be in-habited; that is, we observed lights in that direction just be-fore diving. I'd like all civilian passengers to know that I have been well apprised of your difficult situation, and what I'd like to do is offer anyone who's interested the chance to go ashore."

The crowd thrilled to this bombshell; some began sob-bing.

"There's a good chance that this part of Canada has not been heavily affected by Agent X—it's an island, it's re-mote, it's very cold, and there won't have been a lot of refugees by sea because the port is iced in. They may be amenable to a few guests. I should tell you that for security reasons we will be surfacing under cover of darkness less than two hours from now, and won't stay long. We don't know how Canadian defense forces will react to having a nuclear sub on their doorstep, but I don't intend to find out. Since none of you is really prepared for the weather, those going ashore may take the Navy blankets they've been issued—these should be sufficient to keep the wind off until you get to shelter. Any child disembarking without parent or guardian must notify the Youth Liaison Officer so she can assign you a number. This number will determine the order in which you exit the hatch, so remember it."

Boys fell clamoring upon me. I had to make up a roster on the spot, unprepared.

Finally, Coombs said, "For those of you who may choose to remain aboard, I can't promise you anything. With fewer people the food may stretch a little longer, but it will still be carefully rationed. I can't tell you our destination, but I can tell you it may not be as inviting as this. For that reason I leave the decision to you. That's all."

It seemed that everyone wanted out. In twenty minutes I had assigned numbers to over three hundred boys—three-quarters of the boy population. Many of them had been sick the whole time and were so eager to go they were gibbering with delight: "I'm *outta* here, man!" Their excitement smothered whatever doubts others may have had, making us feel like fools for hesitating.

Signing up Tyrell, I joked, "Oh no! But it was just getting fun!"

"Yeah, we gone miss out on drawin' straws for who gets to be stew. Damn!"

The elder Banks, standing beside his son, asked, "You will be coming with us, won't you?" I was touched by his worried look. He said, "You must, of course."

"I don't know . . . it's different for me," I said.

"Come with us," he persisted. "Please. This is a ship of death—it's no place for children."

"I'm thinking about it. I have to think about it." Wilting

before the old man's pleading intensity, I said thickly, "I promise."

Tyrell lost me in some kind of soul-brother handshake and said, "Stay bad, yo. And watch out for that Hector, man—he a freak."

"How's that?"

"He got that fur jones; think he a animal."

"Oh yeah," I said, laughing.

"No shit, he was in a support group for it back in the day—now his fetish be runnin' wild." As they walked away, he called out, "Don't ack surprised when he want to get all fuzzy-wuzzy, yo." He said this in his usual jocular way; a final bit of shtick. It was more like one of the off-the-wall things Jake would say, but I was too busy to think about it.

After the heaviest of the rush was over, Hector came up to me. I had grown so used to the sight of that costume it hardly seemed odd anymore. He was trying to act cheerful, but his expression was something propped up by tooth-picks. "Are you going?" he asked.

"I don't know," I said honestly. "At first I wanted to, just because I couldn't stand being cooped up with all these guys, but now . . ." I held up the list of names. "Anyway, I can't really leave without Mr. Cowper."

"I hear you." He was all jittery.

"Why? What are you going to do?"

"I'm not sure. I mean, when I heard it I was psyched to go, 'cause that was kinda the whole *point,* right? I mean, it seems stupid not to. But my stepdad just told me he's staying on because the boat needs crew, and now Julian's staying . . . a bunch of the guys you picked for apprenticeships are stay-ing, too. Mr. Robles and a couple of other officers are going around quietly talking it up. It's weird—I thought they couldn't wait to get rid of us." He looked at me forlornly. "I guess I kind of hoped you were getting off . . . so I'd have a reason to."

I could feel my skin flush. I didn't know he felt that way

about me—certainly no boy ever had before. It pained me
to have to shoot him down.

"Hector, I really want to. But as long as Mr. Cowper is
on this boat I can't just leave. If I thought Coombs would
cut him loose I'd go in a second, but you know that's not
going to happen." Seeing his distress, I said gently, "You
should just go ashore if you want to."

"No," he said, withdrawing. "With these assholes? Nah,
I'll stick around."

"But why should you, just because—"

"No, it's cool, Lulu, really. I'll catch you later." He disappeared into the crowd.

In the control room it was like an unusually attentive
field trip: every seat was taken, and two or three boys
watched over the shoulder of each crewmember. There had
to be fifty people in there. Except for Tyrell, all the guys I'd
gone corpse-gathering with were present, not surprising
since it was mostly their relatives at the stations. Hector
pointedly ignored me from over by the trim and drain
panel. The room was darker than usual, its glowing buttons
and displays vivid as a Christmas tree, and there was a
sense of great anticipation. I gave my list to Mr. Coombs,
then dallied listening to Kranuski lecture everyone on the
fine points of surfacing under ice:

"—The fathometer is your best buddy here, but as the
ceiling gets low you also need to watch it closely on this
monitor. It's not only to avoid a collision, but to find a lead,
or *polynya,* between the ice sheets. Once you find one, you
want to position the boat under it, come to a full stop, and
do a periscope sighting. Be very careful with this, because
a chunk of ice you can barely see will still kill a periscope,
and then you're screwed. After establishing there are no
hazards above, make sure all masts are retracted, orient the
sail planes for vertical ascent, and come up dead slow
through the opening. Takes a little practice getting the trim
right. It's a matter of using the boat's buoyancy to just delicately nudge the floes apart. The fairwater is actually

hardened to withstand a forced ascent through solid ice, but that's like busting a girl's cherry—it's kind of violent, and you don't want to get hooked on it. Better to just rise up slowly underneath, push them apart like a gentle lover, and then slide in between—" The captain managed to alert him to the fact that I was present, and without missing a beat Kranuski said, "—with utmost courtesy and respect. Someone give the lady a chair."

Jake's heavy-bearded uncle, Henry Bartholomew, stood up from the pri-mate console and insisted I take his seat; I only did so because I felt too awkward to say no. I didn't hear much of what happened for a while—I was too busy wishing I was invisible—but then things became tense in the room and I noticed that we were actually doing what Kranuski had described. There was a lot of strained back and forth maneuvering that reminded me of my first attempt at parallel parking, then a slow countdown as we ascended: "One-nine-zero feet . . . one-eight-zero feet . . . one-seven-zero feet . . ."

It seemed to go on forever, but at about eighty feet Robles said, "Scope's breaking surface," and the boat stopped. He walked the periscope around in a fast circle, then stood in place studying something. "No threatening activity," he said. "I've got the waterfront less than a thousand yards to port. Looks snowed in. There are functional streetlights, but no other signs of life that I can see. The buildings are dark."

"That doesn't mean anything," said Coombs, having a look. "It's sleepy time, and they're probably on power restrictions. But those streetlights are good—they'll make us harder to see from shore. Secure the periscope, we're going up."

Now the countdown began again. Old Vic Noteiro stood at the ballast controls, saying, ". . . thirty-five feet . . . thirty feet . . . twenty-five feet . . . twenty feet . . . fifteen feet . . . ten feet . . . five feet . . . sail's clear . . ."

The boys started applauding and giving high fives until a loud, grinding bump sounded from above. Everyone ducked instinctively.

"Don't forget," Kranuski explained, "just because the sail comes up in a hole doesn't mean the rest of the deck will. We picked up a little ice, that's all. Nothing to pee your pants about." He was smirking at me as he said this.

Commander Coombs took a look around with the periscope and said, "Flight deck looks clear enough. Rich, is Mr. Webb standing by in a dry suit to assist in off-loading passengers? Good." He skimmed my list. "They'll be playing hopscotch until they get to the shelf, but the floes are packed pretty tight—I don't think a raft will help them much. Just make sure they each have a life-preserver and some rope in case anyone slips."

On the PA system, he announced, "Anyone intending to disembark, form a single-file line under the center logistics hatch, beginning with numbers one through twenty. Twenty-one through forty should be ready to immediately follow. Depending on circumstances, we may close the hatch and dive at any time, so your best chance of going is to be ready when your number is called. Anyone crowding or cutting in line will be sent to the back."

Hanging up the mike, he looked at me and said, "Louise, I'll need your vocabulary on the bridge—supervise the operation and report anything out of the ordinary. Be alert! Danger can come from anywhere, any time. Mr. Robles will see to it that you are properly outfitted to stand watch, but he's not there to babysit; I need him for that here. Once you're on station, you're on your own."

I was stunned. "Why me?" I asked.

"Because I can't spare anyone else, and I think you can handle it. You do have a history of saving the boat. Now go with Dan—he'll show you what to do."

REPORT ANYTHING OUT of the ordinary? As I returned to the little perch atop the sail, I suspected that order might be a bit broad.

The view was something out of Salvador Dali: a queasily elastic mosaic of broken shards, white on black, with the submarine rising from it like a cairn. Land was close by, the tiled sea cutting inland between high wooded hills, forming a harbor. Behind me the warping chessboard stretched to infinity. With the night sky looming so large, I felt like I was on the surface of Pluto, except that the face of the nearest hill was covered with buildings and lights—a friendly yellow constellation in dreamspace.

"I'm here," I said, fumbling the receiver. The gloves I'd been given were huge, as were the *mukluks* and the hooded parka, which for me was like wearing a teepee. There were also supposed to be stiff, insulated pants, but they had been like putting on a zeppelin—Robles settled for neoprene wetsuit pants under my poopie suit. I felt like Nanook of the North. "Uh, the city is just to the left, to port, and there are definitely lights showing. Mostly streetlights, from what I can see." *They already know that, you idiot.*

"Any movement?" someone quacked.

"No, but it's hard to tell—it's kind of far away. Hold on." I kicked myself, remembering the monster binoculars around my neck: *Stupid.* Hurriedly adjusting the focus, I scanned the waterfront. Immediately, snowbound streets and whipped cream–mounded rooftops sprang into view, quaint in a closed-for-the-season kind of way. A number of ships and smaller boats were frozen at dockside and all but buried under scalloped white dunes. The haloed streetlamps offered snapshots of winter desolation. "I don't know," I said. "It's quarter to three in the morning—I guess they could all be in bed."

Our people began emerging from the second hatch, midway down the boat. I couldn't see them well from my position at the front of the sail, but I could hear them complaining about the cold, as anyone in their right mind would at minus twelve degrees. I know my bare face was stinging. As inadequately dressed as they were, I wondered if they would really go through with it and tempt that forbidding ice field, pieces of which were strewn on deck like thick marble slabs. Nearer to shore, the ice was fused into a solid jumbled mass, but to get there everybody would first have to negotiate open water on these stepping-stones. It seemed impossible.

Perhaps it was less so from their perspective, or Mr. Webb's powers of persuasion convinced them, because before long I could see a tethered line of people stretching like a tentative feeler out over the floes.

"They're actually going," I reported. "This is crazy."

They were wearing capes and weird bulky armor made from packing materials—cardboard conquistadors groping for an icy Cibola. I held my breath as they advanced, but the footing appeared to be surprisingly stable, the big plates hardly budging as guys stepped from one to the next or bridged wider gaps with wooden planks. Before long I let out my breath: this was nothing at all. It was literally a cake-walk.

Suddenly I wished I were with them—*God!* They were getting away, and here I was a prisoner for heaven knew how much longer. The yellow lights of St. John's looked homy and warm, much more real than the nightmare I'd been living. The force of my yearning overwhelmed me: the thought of rugs and sofas and soft beds; windows and wooden doors. Walking outside. Most of all I yearned for the sight of other women.

The human chain became longer and longer, snaking around difficult places, occasionally backtracking, until it connected at last with the thick crust inshore.

"They made it!" I cried. "They made it!"

A line was now made fast, connecting the submarine to the ice shelf, and people were stationed at all the crossings to give a hand. As the trek became more ordered, the pace quickened. Everyone began to move more confidently, less like they were feeling their way across a minefield than like revelers on a volksmarch. I shook my head in wonder and envy to see the last of them close the distance.

Meanwhile, the first ones on the wharf were beating a path inland through deep snow. Their movements seemed rushed—I got the impression they were freezing. By the time the last of the helpers trickled ashore, most of the crowd had already disappeared from view. I had glimpses of them between wharf buildings, wallowing through snow-drifts as if on the trail of something, and waited for the flare that would tell us they were safe.

"They look like they know where they're going," I said. "They're all going the same way, to the right. Maybe they've seen something."

Just then a bright flickering caught my eye, as of multiple flashbulbs going off. That was actually my first half-formed notion: that our people were being swarmed by the media. It carried with it a rush of desperate annoyance—I was missing the big reception! This split-second thought process was interrupted by a metallic eruption of delayed noise, like faraway jackhammers pummeling asphalt. Now I could see puffs of smoke.

Sorting my frazzled impressions, I babbled, *"Shooting! There's shooting!"*

The radio crackled, "Clear the bridge."

"Someone's shooting at them! Didn't you hear what I said? Call them back, omigod!" I was frantic. The tiny figures appeared to be trapped in a horrible crossfire, trying to scatter but hampered by deep drifts and blind panic. From my narrow vantage I could see them falling like sheaves.

Something touched my leg, nearly causing me to jump overboard. It was Mr. Robles, down on the ladder. "Come below," he said urgently. "We're diving."

"We can't! They're shooting out there! Can't you hear it?" The mechanical clatter was not all—I could hear something else, shrill as the wind: Screams.

"Captain's orders! Come on!" He grabbed my clothes and practically yanked me down, stepping aside into the uppermost chamber of the sail so that I could pass, then slamming shut the square hatch to the bridge.

In tears, I begged, "Why? Why?"

He said nothing, hustling me down to the control room

and closing the second hatch behind us. "Bridge secure!" he shouted, causing a disorganized flurry of activity. No one even noticed my trauma. Every man's face was a mask of sick despair; they operated their instruments as if compelled to against their will, not by Coombs but by some higher mandate. Their misery said it all: *There is no other way.*

During my absence, the boys must have been sent aft, so I didn't know how they felt about this, but for me it was unreal, unfathomable. My reaction must have seemed like a reproach, for Mr. Albemarle and some of the others cast hateful looks, as if to snarl, *Shut up—you think you're the only one?* They knew what was going on and guiltily accepted the sacrifice, like Abraham. They had been prepared for this possibility all along.

"How can you do this?" I whimpered, as the dive alarm drilled into my head. "We're their only hope! We can't just leave!"

Robles said gently, "Shhhh—go to the equipment locker and get changed. It's all over. Nothing we can do. It's done." His eyes were watery and red, staring like a frightened horse's.

"It's *not* done! What if some of them make it back?"

"They've given us away—we're sitting ducks here."

"But—"

He took me by the shoulders, said softly, "Calm down. Nobody can help them. It was their choice. Ain't no safe bets anymore—all that's left are hard choices. You made one too, by staying, whether you know it or not. Let it go."

"But—"

"It's done, Lulu." He stared me down. "Now you have to decide what you're going to tell the others."

I flinched. "What? What do you mean?"

"The boys don't know about this. It's up to you whether or not to tell 'em—captain's orders."

I broke down. "*No . . .* why me?"

"They're your responsibility."

"No . . . I can't. I can't tell them that. How can I tell

them? Can't we just wait and see if anyone comes back? *Please!*"

Robles shook his head with genuine sorrow, saying, "Come on, Lulu. It's all over."

He led me away as we sank beneath the ice.

fourteen

WE CONTINUED NORTH all that next week, the second week of February, skirting pack-ice as we traversed the Labrador Sea. It was a strange time for me. The boat seemed haunted by all those missing boys—not literally, but in the sense that their absence created a merciless silence, a void I peopled with unforgiving spirits. I felt personally responsible for what had happened. Perhaps if I had not bombarded Coombs with all those memos about hunger and horrid conditions, he wouldn't have found it necessary to drop anyone off. He didn't seem to blame me, though; none of the adults did. They and I wandered the decks like ghosts ourselves, keepers of that awful secret. It was so hard—the boys talked of nothing but what a good time their friends must be having ashore.

The submarine was a different place now; more like a gloomy undersea boarding school than a Naval vessel. There was much to do, more to learn, and not nearly enough time in the day to do it all. It was too much, really. I knew because I wasn't the only one who couldn't keep up: Trainees followed their tutors around like befuddled apostles trying to understand obscure teachings, and critical members of the crew slept at their duty stations so the guys who were supposed to be their relief couldn't flub up too badly.

Otherwise, living conditions had improved, it pained me to admit. With only a hundred and eighty-six people aboard, there were now plenty of berths for those who wanted them, as well as enough space to satisfy those who thought berths too confining. In either case I had discretion over youth sleeping arrangements (Coombs had granted it to me so that I could ensure my own safety), which made me instantly popular—everyone had their own wish list of cozy nooks they wanted first dibs on. I assigned myself and the boys I trusted most to one whole enlisted cabin, which for me was like living in a boys' locker room. To their chagrin it became known as "the henhouse."

And the civilian meal ration was doubled. This surprising concession by the senior staff made more work for me and Mr. Monte, but it was the answer to my prayers. Those boys needed it so badly, and I think some of them were getting suspicious about my peach-cheeked vigor. I glowed among them like a disgustingly hale wood nymph. It didn't look good.

Apart from galley work and my daily pep talk, I was now also training on how to use the "Bridge Suitcase"— the portable command console used by the officer of the watch during surface maneuvers. It required technical knowledge of the boat itself, as well as all kinds of navigational expertise, including astronomy, meteorology, and whole volumes of nautical arcana passed down from the days of sailing ships. For what was the bridge of a submarine but a modern-day crow's nest?

Since the officers were secretive about their charts, giving only the barest details about our position or headi

I became very interested in the maps I had to study. Using a little deductive reasoning and the compass Mr. Cowper had given me, I found I could extrapolate our course with some reliability—to a point. Of course everyone else was doing this too, making for lots of lively discussion at night about where we were going.

We never surfaced, but on occasion we would come up to periscope depth and the commander would broadcast the bleak view over TV monitors in the enlisted mess: rows of giant molars jutting from a lead-colored sea; forbidding plains of drift ice. There was nothing to use for perspective, and I found the lonely vistas depressing. Everything depressed me. It wasn't until February 13th that something finally happened to brighten my spirits:

I found Mr. Cowper.

IT BEGAN WITH me having my usual mid-morning snack in the wardroom pantry. Even in my worst moments of depression, I still had the energy to stuff my face, having consoled myself with food for years. That was how I rationalized it, by telling myself it was the only thing keeping me sane.

The wardroom was a small, fancy dining room for the ship's officers, situated just forward of the cafeteria-like enlisted mess where the boys took their meals. Mr. Monte and I always had it to ourselves, and I believe it was declared off-limits to all others while we were in there. I chalked this up to secrecy, but also to the same nutty chivalry that I credited for getting me extra food in the first place.

Mr. Monte was sitting having a cigarette while I fixed us a couple of green chile omelettes on the hotplate. After a few of his bland meals, I had made the mistake of mentioning that I loved to cook, and he said, "Knock yaself
_w_ he no longer even offered to help. Actually, I
—this way I could make the spicy things I craved,
ot a break from being a "galley slave." But I could

tell he was grooming me to run the galley alone (he wanted to work in the far aft engineering spaces where he'd be left alone), and I wasn't crazy about that idea.

"Come on," he encouraged me. "All them punks are your friends. Why should I be the one taking their abuse? Try some of your yuppie nouvelle cuisine on 'em and see what happens."

Emilio Monte was a leathery, cruel-looking man with deep acne scars and a ridged skull like an upturned dinghy. The fringe of white hair over his ears and around the back of his head made me think of a cartoon buzzard. I had been frightened of him at first, but I came to find him charmingly crusty, if not lovable. I wouldn't care to know what he thought of me. He was not at all talkative, though as days went by I gathered that in antiquity he had served on submarines, until some incident forced him out of the Navy and he got a job as a lathe operator in the submarine factory. This job he had done for sixteen years, right up until our big escape. Many of the civilian men had similar stories.

When I asked Mr. Monte if he had any family aboard, he had replied, "Nah. Thank the good Lord for that. Wouldn't want 'em, the way things are."

I had been beating around the bush for days, hoping to get word of Mr. Cowper, but nobody would talk. Working up my nerve, I set Mr. Monte's omelette before him and finally asked point-blank, "Sir, do you know where my father is?"

He made a show of stubbing out his cigarette and scrutinizing the food. Digging in, he said, "If I was to tell you that, they might send me to the goat locker."

"Sorry. I just . . . I'm getting really worried. How do I know he's even still on board?"

He barked a sharp little laugh, said, "Where else would he be?"

"I don't know . . . do you?"

He kept eating as if he hadn't heard me. I poured myself

half a glass of the heinously sweet red drink the sailors called "bug juice," topping it off with water. That was one thing about the boat—there was always plenty of water: the distillation plant made ten thousand gallons a day.

Acting nonchalant, eating my omelette out of the pan, I said, "It's not like they'd throw him overboard or anything . . . right?"

Emilio grunted, mouth full.

We ate in silence for a few minutes. Even with canned green chiles and reconstituted milk and eggs, the food tasted good: fluffy, cheesy, and spicy. My nervous stomach wasn't handling it well, though. Changing tack, I asked, "How much longer are the provisions going to last?"

"You've seen what we got. Ya must have some idea."

I knew that the boat was normally provisioned with seventy-five thousand pounds of food for a three-month voyage, and that we had started with about five thousand pounds. There was a lot less now. "Well, there are fewer people, even if they're eating twice as much. I don't know," I said. "Two more weeks?"

Intently mopping his oily plate with a slice of bread, he said, "One. Maybe less."

"What is a goat locker, anyway?"

"It's the lounge where the chiefs hang out, if there were any chiefs." He put his dishes in the sink and said, "That about does it. *Adios, muchacha.*"

I finished my meal and cleaned up, drying and stowing the dishes the way Mr. Monte had shown me. The sub was like a stainless steel Shaker house—everything fit together with elegant precision and economy of space. Sometimes this was carried too far, as with the cramped shower/toilets, but in general it was one aspect of submarine living that appealed to me.

I loitered a bit before heading back to the galley, examining the plaques, portraits, and trophy cases in the wardroom. It was all dull Navy bric-a-brac. The only interesting thing was a small framed drawing of Homer Simpson in a flooded room, dreamily saying, "Mmmm—chicken switch." I knew the "chicken switches" were emergency levers for surfacing the boat.

Pausing at the forward door, I peeked down the narrow passageway, lined like a train with sleeper compartments. I had been through this area just once—when I and the boys had hunted corpses in the company of Mr. Noteiro. After that it had been one of the many places declared off-limits to civilians. I knew there was a sitting room with comfy couches and chairs at the far end, and I supposed that had to be the "goat locker." The aluminum door was always closed and had been posted with a Day-Glo orange notice.

Nervously stepping past the dormitories, I listened for snoring, but all the berths were deserted. Mr. Monte said there were no chiefs, meaning no chief petty officers (everyone in the tiny crew had a battlefield commission), but it seemed incredible to me that they would let these bunks sit empty because of an obsolete regulation.

Approaching the closed door, I read the sign. Under a skull-and-crossbones, it said: WARNING—RESTRICTED AREA—IT IS UNLAWFUL TO ENTER THIS AREA WITHOUT PERMISSION OF THE COMMANDER (SEC. 21, INTERNAL SECURITY ACT OF 1950, 50 USC 797)—USE OF DEADLY FORCE AUTHORIZED—CMDR HARVEY A. COOMBS, USN. His bouncy signature was at the bottom.

Heart thumping, I delicately tried the knob, but it was locked. I pressed my ear to the brushed aluminum—not a whisper. I didn't want to give myself away by knocking or calling out. Making extra sure the coast was clear, I got down on my hands and knees until my face was level with the air vent at the bottom of the door. There was no way of seeing through it, but maybe . . .

"Mr. Cowper," I hissed. "Psst! Mr. Cowper, are you there?"

There was a muffled clunk, then heavy limping footsteps. They sounded sinister to me. Losing my nerve, I scrambled away as silently as possible, cursing my stupidity. Now I'd done it! As I fled for the wardroom, I realized there was no pursuit. No one was yelling after me; no alarm being raised. As far as I could tell, nothing at all was happening and the door remained shut.

I hesitated, every nerve in my body tensed for flight. *What am I afraid of?* I thought. *I haven't done anything . . . yet.* The sign didn't say it was illegal to stand in front of the door. With extreme care I began creeping back, freon pulsing in my veins.

As I leaned up against the metal once more, I was startled by a voice just on the other side. It snapped, "Someone playing games?" It was not Mr. Cowper, but it was vaguely familiar: a supercilious, annoyed rumble. Where had I heard that before? The man made no attempt to come out.

"Sorry," I said squeakily, holding my ground. "Who is this?"

"Who is *this*?"

"I'm, uh . . . I'm looking for the goat locker?"

Silence, then: "What are you doing here? Is someone with you?"

"No, I'm alone," I said. "Are you?"

The man puffed with impatience. "This is ridiculous. Why don't you just open the door?"

"I don't have a key. Can't you open it?"

"Don't be an idiot. What the hell's going on out there? Who's with you?"

"Nobody. I'm here by myself." Voice cracking, I said, "I'm, um . . . looking for someone?"

Intensely wary, the voice asked, "Who?"

"Fred Cowper . . . my father."

The man limped away from the door, making angry-sounding grunts of discomfort. It wasn't a friendly exit—I expected to be arrested any second. Fidgeting, looking down the corridor for signs of approaching doom, I reminded myself how little anything mattered at this point. They couldn't do anything to me.

Someone wearing slippers shuffled up to the door, heels slapping. It made me think of a hospital. Then a warbling, phlegmy voice said, "That you, Lulu?"

It was Mr. Cowper.

"YES, IT'S ME," I said. I was breathless. "Are you all right?"

"I'm doin' fine. Don't let 'em catch ya out there, hear me? You run right along." He sounded a little woozy, as if he had been dragged out of bed.

"What's wrong? Are you sick?"

"Ah, it's just the usual crap—my angina actin' up. It'll pass."

"What have they done to you?"

"Nothin'. Coombs seems ta think I have somethin' he's lookin' for, but I keep tellin' 'im it musta went over the side. He just won't let up—it's all I can do ta catch forty winks around here. Have they asked you about it?"

"No. Why would they?"

"I got the impression they think we're in cahoots. Maybe that was just somethin' they said ta rattle me— don't worry about it. They been treatin' you okay?"

"Fine," I said, embarrassed to admit the coddling I received. "I'm good. Who else is in there with you?"

"Just the two of us: Jim Sandoval an' me." *Sandoval*— the man who had hurt his leg jumping across. The unpopular company boss. Mr. Cowper perked up with irritation, saying, "Why? Is that some kinda secret?"

"It hasn't exactly been announced. I only figured out just now where you were—stupid of me, since Mr. Monte's been dropping hints for days."

"Yeah, Emilio's a good man. Too good. That's why he got drummed outa the service."

From deeper in the room, I heard Sandoval's muffled voice say, "Ask her where we are, for Christ's sake. How much longer?"

"How's Mr. Sandoval's leg?" I asked.

"She wants to know how your leg is."

"Tell her swell. Jim-dandy."

"He'll be laid up awhile. Phil Tran has him high as a kite on Percodan, but he needs decent medical attention. There's a couple a prescriptions I could stand ta have filled, too. That's why anything you can tell us about our future would be appreciated."

"I'm probably the least knowledgeable person you could ask."

"Try me. We ain't exactly networkin' down here—Kranuski and that bastid Webb have made sure that nobody tells us a damn thing. A course there's some things they can't hide, like when the boat dives or surfaces. What was all that noise when we came up? Ice?"

"Yes."

"Where?"

"St. John's, Newfoundland." Shame welled up out of me in the form of burning tears. "A bunch of people got off there—over three hundred."

"What's the matta? Were they forced?"

"No, they wanted to go. Mr. Coombs gave us the choice." I could hardly speak.

"Lulu, what happened?"

Taking a shuddering breath, I said stonily, "There was shooting . . . so we left them there. We just left them there to die."

In the background I could hear Sandoval saying, "I told you! Deadwood, I said! All that son of a bitch can think of is how he's going to prune the deadwood. I'll be damned."

"That's fine, comin' from you," Mr. Cowper told him. "He just finished what you stahted."

Sandoval acted stung: "That's not fair. That's an unfair assessment. I may have been guilty of over-optimism and misled those people into thinking the Navy would follow through, but that's the extent of it. My hand was forced."

"Yeah, an' if I hadn't led them folks down ta the slip,

you'd a just sailed away without us. Just sailed away, and you an' Coombs would be best buddies."

"Ah, but we're not, are we? He's upstairs and I'm down here. That should tell you something. 'Best buddies' indeed. Ask her if before he gave those kids the 'choice' to go ashore, Coombs informed them that in January we bombarded Canada with EMPs to hobble them until Agent X could spread there. That we crippled their communications infrastructure so no one would know how weak we were. Ask her if they knew *that* before they went."

"No," I said, shocked.

"'Best buddies,'" Sandoval scoffed again, deeply offended. "That'll be the day."

"Is that *true*?" I asked.

"Ah, shit." Furious at Sandoval, Mr. Cowper replied, "I'm sorry, honey. He shouldn't a told you that."

I flew off the handle: "Why not? To protect me? Is that it? For my own good? Keeping secrets from people doesn't make them safe . . . *daddy*."

"I guess not," he sighed. "I haven't always told you what's in my heart, Lulu, but you hafta know it's all fa you." With grim intensity, he insisted, "Ask any a the old-timers and they'll tell ya. Now I'm tired, so you'll hafta excuse me. Go! Get the hell outta here before someone catches ya." Even as he said this he was shuffling away.

fifteen

WE CROSSED THE Arctic Circle on the twentieth of February, in an area of the sea called the Davis Strait, between Baffin Island and Greenland, inadvertently following Amundsen's route of a century before. At some point the ice closed tight above us, ending surface sightings. There was a high-powered light on the sail, however, which allowed the periscope to function as an underwater camera. The video could be shown on any monitor in the sub, but Coombs had found a way to improve on this: While taking inventory of the remaining artifacts in the Big Room, Robles had turned up a number of 80" high-definition flat plasma displays. These were intended for supercomputer simulations (the computer itself—an experimental Cray— was still in the box), but Coombs didn't think there would be any harm in setting a few up around the control room and linking them to the periscope. The first time they were turned on, they elicited gasps. These were not just pictures on TV; they were vivid undersea windows, through which we could watch the milky jade ice-scape passing above, and every glowing mite streaming by. Some of the guys had a claustrophobic reaction to it, but for me in my ignorance it was too abstract to be really scary, just amazing.

As we followed the converging lines of longitude to the top of the world, gossip and speculation ran rampant: What was our objective? The unofficial consensus seemed to be that we were heading for Alaska via the Arctic Ocean, and this quickly became such an accepted matter of common knowledge (or wishful thinking) that people spoke of it openly, as in, "When we get to Alaska—" or "I can't wait 'til we get to Alaska so I can—."

The minute this reached the ears of Coombs, he took me aside and said, "You know what the 'butt' on a ship is?"

"The stern?"

"No. On old sailing ships they called the drinking-water cask the 'butt'. It was kind of like the water cooler—sailors would stand around it and gossip, just like people in offices do today. Used to do, I mean. Understand?"

I nodded sagely.

He said, "Sometimes the talk would be out of order, even mutinous. The kind of thing that could lead to the scuttling of the ship. You know what they called that kind of talk?"

"Scuttlebutt?"

He deflated a little. "Yes, scuttlebutt. Maybe you also know the expression, 'Loose Lips Sink Ships.' Okay, you let those kids know I won't have it. Not in my control room, not anywhere. Our destination is classified, and it'll remain classified until such time as I find it prudent to reveal it. Is that understood?"

"Yes, sir."

"I don't want to have to make an example of anyone."

"No, sir."

"Dismissed."

When I told Julian about the directive, he acted as though it confirmed his Alaska hypothesis.

"How can you be so sure?" I asked.

"Come on, it's obvious. It's America, it's frozen solid, it's geographically isolated, there's a strong military presence, and we can use the Arctic Ocean as a shortcut. There's even a huge Trident submarine base just south of there in Bangor, Washington. Do I have to go on?"

"Have you heard anything about this from Mr. Robles?" I knew Julian was understudying for the quartermaster position presently filled by Robles.

"Of course not, but he's got us learning the sextant, the NAVSAT, the Loran, the radar, the fathometer, the SINS, the gyrocompass and the accelerometer—if I can't estimate where we're going it'd be pretty sad."

"You said it, not me." I nudged him playfully, but he wouldn't crack a smile. For some reason it had become imperative for me to get this serious guy to smile, but he just wouldn't do it.

Julian Noteiro was interesting; an anomolous combination of strength, intelligence, character, and good looks. I had never liked people who were too competent because they made me feel inadequate, yet Julian was not stuck up. You couldn't call him humble, but he was not self-obsessed. Order was his way of coping. Having come from a troubled working-class family with alcohol issues, anything irrational galled him, and in this need for control I saw something of myself. Perhaps I felt that if he would smile . . . it would mean I could, too.

Ignoring my nudge, he said, "You'll know I'm right when we make a ninety-degree course change into Lancaster Sound. Wait and see."

MR. COWPER HAD another opinion.

"Alaska, ya say?" he asked from behind the door.

"That's the scuttlebutt."

"That don't make sense. Not *west* of Greenland. Our approach would have to be up the eastern side, where there's some depth to work with."

"Wouldn't that take longer, though?"

"Sure, but you're not gonna save time if you get hung up in the shallows. That ice is gonna be thick as a bastid this time a year, and this beast needs a lotta elbow room, especially at these latitudes. The nearer ya get ta magnetic north, the hahder it is ta navigate." He conferred with Sandoval out of earshot. After a moment he said, "Sandoval thinks Alaska is impossible. He says the last he heard there was a war going on there between coastal defenses and an armada of refugee ships. Food supplies from the lower forty-eight had been cut off, so ya had stahvation, ya had cold, ya had panic—"

"Not to mention Xombies," I said.

"Sure. Anchorage is a big city—hadda be pretty bad. Doesn't sound like much of a haven. Not to mention there's a good chance the Russians may have mined the approaches to the Arctic Ocean. I know *we* did—while I was in command I found active mine coordinates in the safe. Coombs knows that."

"Then what's he up to?"

"Give us a while ta think on it. And Lulu?"

"Yes?"

"Neitha one of us is doin' too well in here, but me with my ticka . . . ya never can tell. And if I go, he's gonna go right afta, if you know what I mean. Just in case, I wanted to tell ya again what's in my haht. Ya still got that baby picture?"

"Yes."

"Well, look at it when I'm gone. Don't think badly a me—it's what's in my haht that counts."

I wanted to reply, *Easy for you to say,* but I held my tongue—this was obviously important to him. Frustrated as I felt, I couldn't hurt his feelings, and the thought that he might die, after everything we'd survived so far, it was unthinkable. He was all I had.

ON SCREEN I could see an immense black object suspended in pale ice, like a seedpod in dirty cotton. It was fat at the sides and ridged down the center, narrowing to a wedge just above us. It looked ready to split along that seam and spill its contents on our heads. There was a hush in the control room, making me feel even more conspicuous than usual as I found a place to sit.

"What's that?" I whispered.

"It's a ship," Julian said impatiently. "The hull of an ocean liner, trapped in the ice. She's about nine hundred feet long."

Kranuski was speaking to Coombs: "She's not doing too well, sir. About a ten-degree list to port, heavy at the bow. You can see where the ice is staving her in, there's a flooded compartment in there."

"So she's sinking?" Albemarle asked, listening in. "Why the hell are we underneath her?"

Ignoring the civilian, Kranuski went on, "We're not picking up any sounds, so the flooding must have stopped for now. They build these babies with a lot of redundancy; she can survive a few flooded baffles. But you never know. If we're going to have a look at her topside we better do it quick."

Coombs asked, "Is that your recommendation?"

"Yes, sir. We can't afford to pass up any potential windfall, and this is a big one."

"What about you, Mr. Robles?"

Without taking his heavy-lidded eyes off the screen, Robles said, "Why not?"

WE MADE A wide circle around the stranded liner, searching for openings, and almost immediately lucked into what we were looking for: a thinly frozen-over polynya winding like a river through the ice. It was miles long, and we had actually already crossed beneath it several times that morning. Now we deliberately followed it as near to the ship as possible, about fourteen hundred yards west, and surfaced well clear of any floes. The sun was dim and low in the sky, but at least it was daylight. Topside relays were organized so everyone could get a taste of the outdoors, but most didn't use their alotted five minutes. It was too cold.

The captain accompanied me up to the bridge, and from there I had a good view of the slushy lead and high banks of ice that just went on and on. But there was one peculiar feature in the emptiness, a tall white shape like a wedding cake.

Coombs was letting me report, so I said, "The ship is directly ahead. It's definitely a cruise ship. It doesn't look damaged, but . . . I can't see any signs of life. No fire or smoke, or movement of any kind."

"What about lifeboats?" Coombs prompted me.

"Uh, yeah, most of the lifeboats are gone—on this side anyway. Looks like they must have abandoned ship."

"Exactly," Coombs said. "So you want to take a walk out there?"

"Yeah right," I said, shocked to think he was being funny.

"We're organizing a boarding party. We're well beyond the survivability threshold, and that ship is stone cold. I'm asking if you'd like to go along."

Alarm bells went off in my head. "Um . . . I'm fine here."

"Your reluctance wouldn't have anything to do with St. John's, would it?"

"Yes, sir."

"What if I were to tell you I need you out there to get medicine for someone? Someone you know, who might die without it?"

"Mr. Cowper."

"What do you say?"

I looked off at that lonely white spire, trapped like a bug in amber. "Who else is going?"

"Well, we can't afford to spare any Navy personnel, but your Mr. Monte has agreed to go, as well as Mr. Noteiro, Mr. DeLuca, and Mr. Albemarle. These men are essential to the boat, so I don't send them lightly. I'll also expect you to assemble a team of thirty of your brightest volunteers. You'll be responsible for them on the ice, so make sure they can handle the hike."

"Commander Coombs, sir?"

"Yes?"

"Can I have your word as an officer and a gentleman that you won't leave us out there?"

There was a long, tense pause, then a sigh. "Miss Pangloss, I cannot give you that assurance."

I blinked, dumbfounded.

He went on, "But let me say this: *In the absence of any perceived threat to this vessel,* I will not submerge. Is that good enough?"

"Based on whose perception, though?"

"I'm not going to bargain with you about what constitutes a threat. Any radar contact, any sonar contact, anything odd whatsoever, and we dive. That's the mission."

"But not just to get rid of us?"

"Now you're hurting my feelings."

IN THE TIME it took to gather and outfit the boarding party, the sun fell below the horizon, leaving only a greenish glow.

"This is all the daylight you're gonna see," Albemarle said, giving us a final once-over as we lined up on deck. "Let's not waste it."

We were all wearing the same winter gear I'd become accustomed to, and I helped a few people snug their fastenings.

"I know how to do it," Hector said irritably.

"Shut ya trap," his stepfather, Albemarle, told him. "Let the little girl show ya how before you freeze your ass off."

"Sorry," I whispered to Hector, cinching in his hood. He ignored me, staring straight ahead.

"Aww, look what a good boy he's being," Jake said. "Give mamma a kiss."

"Oh, be quiet," I said, blushing.

We left the submarine. Her hull had drifted up against the ice-shelf, and it was a small matter to lay a plank across and simply walk down. The crunchy surface was as stable as solid ground and less slippery than the deck. Those thirty boys could hardly contain themselves, being away from the sub for the first time in weeks—it was like a snow day. Cole had finally gotten over his shock, and Julian was actually smiling. They had no inkling of the anxieties of myself and the men, waiting to see if Coombs would ditch us here. Why had we all agreed to this? Guilt, maybe. In short order we were trooping toward the ship.

The ship.

It was a floating luxury hotel, an unearthly resort planted in the middle of nowhere, with vertical tiers of balconies and fanciful space-age architecture. Her winged funnel was swept back, a sleeker, flimsier version of our fairwater, and the curving banks of windows at her bridge were like wraparound sunglasses on a friendly shark. I could make out her name through a layer of frost: *Northern Queen*. She looked very top-heavy. Coombs had said she could carry over three thousand people.

"Ya hafta wonda why dey abandoned ship," said Mr. Noteiro, short of breath.

"Yeah," agreed Mr. Monte. "They musta really been under the gun if they thought setting out in a lifeboat was preferable to staying high and dry on this mother."

"Maybe dey thought she was gonna sink. Dey didn't wanna chance bein' stranded out on de ice."

"I don't know. Wouldn't they a taken all the boats, then? Why'd they leave that big motor launch? It all looks rushed and half-assed to me. Look how the lines are fucked up."

"Maybe they were in a hurry," said Albemarle.

"Or maybe they went day sailin'," Mr. DeLuca said, irritated at the empty speculation. "These cruise ships are always getting cited for something—toxic dumping, bad emergency procedures, inoperative davits. They probably didn't know what the fuck they were doing. What the hell difference does it make, long as they're gone?"

"Gus is right. We should all be focusing on the really important things, like finding him a smoke."

"Damn straight."

As we neared the thing, we began to appreciate the amount of snow and ice on it. I had assumed the ship was simply painted white, but it could have been any color beneath the thick, knobby glaze that coated everything. Ice festooned the railings like grotesque roots, and lines that had lowered lifeboats were stiff with congealed drippings—it reminded me of the weird formations my mother and I had seen at Carlsbad Caverns. That ship could have been here forever, encased in its mantle of solitude. I kept glancing back to make sure I could still see the sub.

"Jesus! It's a wonder she ain't capsized, carrying all that extra tonnage."

"Sea-ice must be all that's keepin' her from rollin' over."

"We shouldn't get any closer if there's a chance she'll flip."

Gustave DeLuca erupted, "Will you guys shut up? Can't you see she's been here for ages? She's solid as a damn rock. Let's do what we came here to do and have a little less fantasyland, can we please?"

We crossed beneath the anchors and the long-snouted bow to the vessel's port side. Here most of the lifeboats were in place and only a few ropes plumbed the surface like candle wicks. It wasn't easy to approach the hull because of buckled and refrozen ice, but there was a gangway, a covered stair that climbed the sheer wall of the ship to a large open doorway.

"Well that's convenient," said Mr. DeLuca.

Noteiro said, "Dem stairs been down awhile."

"Shouldn't we try to hail her again?" Albemarle said.

"If they couldn't hear the boat's whistle they'll never hear us."

"They might." He pulled a megaphone out of a bag and said, "ATTENTION CRUISE SHIP. ATTENTION CRUISE SHIP—IS THERE ANYONE ABOARD? REPEAT: IS THERE ANYONE ABOARD?" We waited, straining for any sound, but there was no reply. Albemarle said, "Try firing a couple of rounds in the air."

DeLuca shrugged the shotgun off his shoulder, aimed it out at the void, and squeezed off a shot. The bang rippled away skittishly to the horizon. Pumping the smoking shell out, he said, "Waste of good ammunition, you ask me."

"We didn't ask ya," said Monte.

DeLuca fired again.

"ATTENTION CRUISE SHIP—IS ANYONE THERE? WE COME IN PEACE."

The acres of frosted-over windows remained blank. I didn't like standing there with that dead colossus leaning over us.

"Take us to your leader," Jake muttered.

"ALL RIGHT, THEN. WE'RE COMING ABOARD." Ed Albemarle put away the bullhorn and took out his faithful hammer. "Let's go," he said.

SMASHING ICE OFF each step, Albemarle led the way up, followed by the other three men, myself, and the boys. The stairs were not quite level; it was a little disturbing to climb that overhanging cliff with nothing more than a slippery handrail between you and a bone-shattering fall. The higher we went, the more steeply the ship seemed to lean out. About thirty feet up I suddenly realized there was no one behind me. Hector had stopped, blocking the line.

"I have to go back," he said firmly. "I'm going back down."

"What's wrong?" I asked.

"Nothing—I just can't . . ." He shook his head, paralyzed with fear. "This isn't safe."

From behind him, Julian Noteiro said, "C'mon, we're almost there!"

Hector snapped, "Shut up! Go around if you want to!"

"There's no room to pass," Julian said. "Come *on,* dude. It's cold."

"Don't push me!"

I went down to him. "Hey, it's okay," I said. "Just don't look down."

"Where the hell am I supposed to look? Everything looks like it's falling. I keep feeling like we're starting to tip over." He had a point.

"What's wrong back there?" Mr. Albemarle said from above. "Get a move on, son!"

"Ignore them," I told Hector. "Listen, you know what they do to keep horses from panicking on steep trails? They lead them along blindfolded."

"Screw that!"

"Just take my hand, then. Here." I took my giant glove off and stuffed it in my pocket. "Take my hand before it freezes."

"No way." He was starting to tremble violently.

"Please—I'm going to get frostbite if you don't hold my hand."

He stared at my dainty fingers for a second, then he ripped off his left glove with his teeth and grabbed me. He was so scared he nearly dragged me down on top of him.

"Good!" I grunted. "That's good! Awesome! Don't pull—you're okay! Now just look at me. Just focus on me, nothing else. Try taking a step."

"I cah. I cah ooob." I took the glove from his mouth and he said, "I can't move."

"You can do it. Just take a deep breath and relax. This is just like the stairs on the boat, no different."

He closed his eyes, clutching me hard, and took a wild step.

"That's the way! Now you're doing it," I urged gently. "Don't stop—keep it up. We're just walkin' upstairs, yessiree . . ."

"Is he coming or isn't he?" I heard Mr. DeLuca growl from above.

"Do you mind?" I shot back.

Hector was relaxing a little, creeping faster bit by bit. Then he let go of my hand. "I got it," he said, eyes still closed. "You go on—I got it under control."

"Seriously?"

"I just don't want to trip over you. Go! I'm right behind you." Hunched and groping the rail like a blind man, he followed me the rest of the way up.

The doorway opened onto a broad enclosed deck with high windows. In ordinary daylight it would have been a sunny place, but in this iced-over twilight it was a cave. A mini-glacier had formed inside the door, fanning across the teak promenade like an octopus, and the men had considerately chopped a path through it. Now they wielded flashlights and a device called a thermograph, probing for spots of warmth amid the pitch-black restaurants and shops opposite the windows. Mr. DeLuca had his shotgun at the ready, but the place looked more than deserted: It looked fossilized.

Once we were all gathered inside, Mr. Albemarle said, "All right. Everybody listening? Here's the plan: We're going to divide into five squads, seven to a squad. Four of the squads will be led by myself and the other three men; the fifth will be led by Officer Lulu, unless she thinks one of you is better suited for the job. That's up to her.

"Each squad has a specific objective, which they are to fulfill as fast as possible before regrouping back here. Vic's squad is to go up top and flash Coombs that we're aboard, and that the ship is clear. Then they are to proceed to the bridge and find out what's functional and what's not, check the PA system, and make an announcement to the rest of us about the status of this barge. Vic knows what to do.

"Gus DeLuca's group is to find the radio shack and see if we can call out. Since the sub can't reveal its position by sending radio signals, it may be possible for some of us to be rescued from here by sending a mayday. At the very least we may be able to contact someone who can catch us up on current events.

"My squad is heading belowdecks to inspect the power plant and the pumps. See if it's possible to stabilize her some. Emilio will be taking his people on a tour of ship's stores. The rest will accompany Officer Lulu to the infirmary, where they will be expected to stock up on a few medical necessities." He handed me a flashlight and a printed list. "Any questions?"

There were too many to ask.

"Good. Here are your squads."

He held up a roster and we gathered around his light. Under my name I read: Hector Albemarle, Jacob Bartholomew, Julian Noteiro, Shawn Dickey, Lemuel Sanchez, and Cole Hayes—all of them boys in my crib. Coombs had thought of everything. It hurt my feelings that they seemed disappointed to be going with me instead of with the men. I heard Julian muttering about how he didn't come here to "raid a damn drugstore." Hector was still sour-faced from before.

Albemarle said, "I'll expect you all back here within ninety minutes. Ninety minutes! Anyone not back here in an hour and a half may find themselves left behind. Get moving."

IT WAS A pretty disorganized scavenger hunt. Since the first thing we all needed was a map, everyone ran up and down the promenade looking for an information booth or a large diagram saying YOU ARE HERE. As it happened, there were touch-screen computers for just this purpose, but they were all dead.

While we were rifling the check-in desk at the lobby, Julian called us back out to the promenade and said, "I don't think we need a map." Handing out souvenir flashlights, he led us to a sign next door to the gift shop. Above a green cross were the words, FIRST-AID STATION.

"Oh man," said Hector.

I was giddy with relief. What I had thought would be a trying ordeal was over before it had begun—no fumbling through dark mazes, no getting lost or left behind. No humiliation. I gave silent thanks for Coombs's mercy.

"You know what this means, don't you?" Julian said.

"Hell yeah," Cole replied. "Means we home free."

"It means we got the pussy assignment. They don't trust us with a real job."

"That sucks," said Shawn. "I wanted to scope out the Galleria."

"Give me a break," I said, though what Julian said was

certainly true. I didn't care. Except for him and Shawn, the others were on my side, grateful for the reprieve.

We filed into a waiting room with magazine racks and a block of yellowish ice that had been a fish tank. Our first indication that things would not be so simple was the shattered glass in the reception window. The second was black spatters of dried blood everywhere we shined our flashlights.

"Dude, is that blood?" Shawn asked.

"Where?" asked Cole, whipping his light around. "Oh shit."

Hector said, "Not good, man, not good. Let's get out of here."

"Hey," said Julian calmly. "It's a *first aid* station? So somebody was bleeding, big deal. Attempt to chill."

"I'm plenty chilled, thanks," said Jake.

Pushing through a swinging door to the interior rooms, we entered a real mess. The place had been ransacked. Filing cabinets were overturned, spilling paper everywhere; furniture was broken; latex gloves, cotton swabs, and other medical supplies were scattered about; and anything locked had been broken open—there were loose pills frozen to the floor in a pebbly mosaic. Nothing I could identify from my list.

"Whoa, this place been jacked up," said Cole.

Julian nodded. "Somebody beat us to it."

"Totally," said Shawn. "Yo, check it out: Prednisone. Cool." He pocketed it.

Searching smashed drawers, I said, "*They* were here." I couldn't bring myself to speak the word.

Lemuel piped up from the rear, "Xombies." His voice was soft and high-pitched for such a big guy, and perhaps because he didn't talk much it always caught our attention.

"Yes," I said. "We need to tell Mr. Albemarle and the others."

"I think they're gone," said Lemuel at the doorway.

"Then we better go after them," I said.

Julian held up his hands. "Can we just not panic? Seriously."

"Nobody's panicking," I said with annoyance. "But we have to let them know."

"Let them know what? That the clinic's been looted? I mean come on! What the hell difference does it make? It's still a dead ship, and besides it's twenty below in here—unless those Xombies have antifreeze in their veins they're rock-solid." He seemed energized by this turn of events. "Environmental survivability threshold, remember?"

"You're right, man," said Hector. "So what should we do?"

I didn't like him directing this question to Julian. "Okay," I said quickly, "so as far as you guys are concerned we should proceed with the mission? You're cool with that?"

They all looked at each other in the wavering flashlight beams. There were hesitant nods and nervous shrugging, but the gist of it seemed to be a wary willingness to go. Julian said, "Like I give a crap about 'the mission.' Let's just *do* something."

"Why did you even volunteer to come?" I asked irritably.

"Same as everyone else—to stretch my legs. Why? Why did you come? To get in good with *Harv?*" Here it was, their suspicion that I was the commander's toady.

I hadn't told anyone I'd found Mr. Cowper, or about the drugs he needed. It suddenly occurred to me that we were all waiting for someone to tell us what to do, that every second I dithered a pressure of anxiety and resentment was building against me. Trying not to be bossy and waiting for a clear signal from them was not the polite, respectful, and humble leadership I intended. It was an abdication of responsibility, and they rightfully despised me for confirming their low expectations. *Wake up, girlfriend,* cried my mother's Oprah-fortified voice in my head.

"Listen," I said, "there's still an hour and twelve minutes. Here's what we're going to do . . ."

sixteen

WE HAD MAPS and information handbooks from the front desk; using these we were able to determine that there was another first-aid station on the ship, as well as a twenty-bed infirmary and a chain drugstore.

"I think the pharmacy is our best bet," I said, huddled over the deck plan. "Considering what happened to the first-aid station, I don't think we should go anywhere sick people would've gone." No arguments there. "The pharmacy is in the Galleria—there you go, Shawn—so it shouldn't be too difficult to find. Just a straight shot forward, up the companionway, and then cut across the upper promenade to the casino."

"Oooh, casino," Jake said. "Lemuel's all about that."

Lemuel thought he'd missed something. "Huh? All about what?"

"Casino? Indian gaming? Didn't your tribe want to open

a casino?" Sensing his joke had fallen flat, Jake said, "Never mind."

Without warning, Lemuel suddenly slammed Jake up against the bulkhead. "Don't fuckin' joke like that about my *tribe,* man," he said softly, as the other boy squirmed in his grip. "I may *be* my whole tribe now. Last of the fuckin' Mohicans, you know? It ain't a fuckin' joke."

"Sorry," Jake said, shocked.

"Nobody I know ever got rich off a fucking casino—they were the hired help. The real gambling tycoons are the same white guys who own everything else, so don't make jokes about Indians running casinos. I hate that shit."

"All *right,* I'm *sorry.*"

"Come on, Lemuel," I said. "He didn't know. He goofed, that's all."

Lemuel released him, not meeting any of our eyes.

"Good," said Julian impatiently. "Let's go before we get hypothermia."

Right away, my plan fizzled. The companionway was choked with a massive trunk of ice.

"Obviously we can't go up that way," Julian said.

"Obviously," said Hector.

"It opens onto exposed deck up there," I said. "I should've realized it would be plugged, darn it. We'll have to try another way."

"Do, or do not," said Jake in a croaking voice. "There is no try."

Cole asked, "What now?"

"We have no choice but to stick to all interior passages. I was hoping for more light than that, but if the other teams can handle it, so can we." Trying to rub feeling back in my nose, I said, "Okay, we can cut across right here through the second-class staterooms. Then we'll hit third class and turn left on Broadway, which will take us directly to the bottom floor of the Galleria."

Jake tapped my hood. "Teacher, I have to pee."

"Shut up."

We made our way down a passage between administrative offices and recreation rooms, catching a glimpse of ping-pong tables in the dark. Side corridors were lined with numbered doors as far as our lights would penetrate, and it was disturbing to see women's shoes littering the floor. There was a fur of hoarfrost on every surface.

"Hey look," Lemuel said. He was shining his plastic penlight on the floor just ahead of us. The ice on the carpet was trampled. Sounding reassured, he said, "Another team musta come this way."

I won't deny the absurd relief I felt looking at those tracks, knowing we weren't alone in this catacomb. But I played it cool, saying, "So they did. Let's keep moving."

We came to an elevator foyer and the companionway we were seeking. The elevators were useless, the companionway blocked. The sight of what it was blocked with made us all gasp and rear up like spooked ponies:

There was a gate across the stairwell, and sprouting through the metal bars was a thicket of grasping blue arms, frozen solid. It was a tree of hands. They were so tightly packed it was difficult to see the bodies to which they were attached, and their combined force had caused the padlocked gate to bulge outward. Hyperventilating, I stepped forward and tapped my flashlight against one frosty hand. It made a ceramic *clink*.

"Mothuh*fuck*," said Cole.

"Holy shit," said Jake.

Seizing the initiative, I said, "Well, at least this proves we're not in any danger. Come on—there must be another way up." The boys looked at me like I was insane. "Come *on*," I insisted. They followed, Shawn giggling nervously.

I found an alcove marked, SHIP'S PERSONNEL ONLY. It opened on an uncarpeted utility tunnel full of pipes and wiring, reminiscent of the submarine. The side doors were all locked, and we were afraid to penetrate too deeply because none of this was shown on our deck plan.

Just as we thought we were going to have to backtrack

out again and start over, Lemuel called, "Hey guys? I found where the tracks end." He was shining his light up a dark hatch in the ceiling. Steel rungs ran from it down into another hatch below, this one covered with a locked grate. Above, the shaft seemed to go up quite a long way—even with my flashlight I couldn't see the top.

"Oh shit," Cole said. "Where the fuck does that go?"

"Only one way to find out," I said, and started climbing.

Before my initiation by sub, these restricted crawlspaces would have been unthinkable, but there was no stopping me now. Experience had shown that my size and my sex were great advantages in such places—I was more limber and agile than the most able seaman, and had learned to plunge into dark holes like a ferret. It had earned me some admirers among the crew. The boys by comparison were bumbling oafs.

We only climbed as far as the next level, emerging in an electrical substation just off Broadway, and followed that spacious avenue forward to the Galleria. We knew when we had arrived by the echo. Suddenly we were in a huge hollow place, a soaring atrium within the ship's superstructure. Only my high-powered lantern could begin to penetrate it, and the pinprick flashlights of the others made me think of ducklings following their mother.

Here was a movie theater, a casino, a ballroom, a disco, several theme bars and clubs, a video arcade, a hair salon, many duty-free shops, and ATMs on every level. It was a seagoing shopping mall. It was a towering crypt.

"Oh, that's dope, dude," said Shawn. "That's fuckin' awesome."

Cole said, "My boy Shawn be feelin' right at home. All he need is a Orange Julius."

We had picked up the trail of our predecessors once again, and began following it up dead escalators as we searched for the drugstore. I announced our elapsed time at five-minute intervals. We were approaching the halfway point—forty-five minutes—when it would be sensible to turn back. But since I counted on it being easier to return than it had been to get there, I wasn't going to be a stickler about it. Not when we were so close.

"Hey, Lulu," Lemuel said, huffing and puffing. "How could that other team have covered so much ground? Have you noticed that these footprints go in and out of every doorway? I mean, they're everywhere! We didn't take *that* long to get here."

As soon as Lemuel spoke, I knew what he said was incontrovertible; in fact it was gnawing at me, too, and I had been rationalizing it away.

Julian said, "Not only that, but a lot of them go in the wrong direction." He pointed out a very clear set of boot prints facing us. "And these soles are different than ours, look."

"Holy crap," said Hector. "It's true."

Suddenly the echoing void seemed very haunted. Several of the guys began babbling at once: "I *knew* it!" "Let's get the fuck *outta* here, then!" "I fuckin' knew this would happen."

"Hold on," said Julian, clinging to his composure. "We don't know how old those footprints are. They could've been here for weeks. Months. Maybe a rescue party came through, anything! All I know is, *there's nothing to be afraid of*." I loved him just then.

"I don't know, dude," said Shawn Dickey. "Does anybody else smell smoke?"

"I don't smell anything," said Jake, all jumpy.

"I do," said Lemuel. "It's stronger the higher we climb."

"Shut up, man, there's no smoke!" Jake was on the verge of panic.

But I could smell it, too, the faintest tang of burnt wood. Shushing the boys, I called out, "Hello? Is anybody there?" We waited.

Julian broke the silence. "Come on, we're wasting time. If you think about it, the frost in here probably condensed out of the air as soon as the heating plant shut down. Those tracks were probably made before the ship was even abandoned . . ." He trailed off, listening hard.

We all flinched as somewhere above us a door was thrown open. Hectic footsteps pattered a short distance and stopped. I leaned out over the glass-and-chrome balustrade, shining my beam up at the higher galleries. *It's just the other guys,* I thought.

For a second I saw nothing, until I turned the light straight up. Then I froze as if electrocuted. Staring directly at me from the top floor were four horrific creatures—I only had a glimpse before they vanished, leaving a red afterimage of gleaming saucer eyes burned in my retinas—but I knew I had seen something like giant black birds with vicious beaks. Monstrous hooded crows. *It can't be,* I thought, scalp prickling.

Now we could hear them moving again, and ghastly croaking sounds as they scuttled heedless of the dark down toward us. The boys were practically jumping out of their skins, knowing I had seen something terrible. They were desperate for a signal.

I couldn't think of what else to do. "They're coming!" I said sharply. "Move!"

We fled, tripping over one another as we chased my spot of light down the concourse. Knowing the guys were all but blind, I tried to keep up a running patter that they could follow: "This way, this way! Keep up! No, left, left! Watch the ash stand! Now down! Keep going! Careful! Watch it! Don't let anybody fall behind! *Ow!* Wait up!" I had no idea where I was going.

The sound of our pursuers was lost in the tumult, but I imagined those wicked beaks jabbing at the back of my neck.

"Where are we going?" Hector panted on the escalator.

"I don't know," I said. "Just go."

"Lemuel is falling behind," he said urgently. "We can't keep running like this!"

"In here!" I shouted, lunging through the next open

doorway I came to. It was a bank, with a glassed-in counter and currency exchange rates posted on a board. I had to stop short to keep from tripping over velvet ropes, but someone piled into me from behind and I went flying into a pile of scattered money. If not for my thick winter padding I might have been seriously hurt, but as it was the only thing damaged by contact with the parquet floor was my flashlight. Slammed down with the force of several bodies behind it, the bulb winked out.

Now I was the blindest of all, seeing nothing but the light's residual dazzle. "Is everyone here?" I shouted.

"Yeah, we're here," said Hector, waving his flashlight. Soon I could see them all, six fireflies in the night.

"The door!" I yelled. "Somebody shut the door!"

"There is no door," said Julian.

"What?"

"It's an electric gate—it won't budge."

This unbelievable bit of bad luck left me stunned. With no way to shut ourselves in and no back door, we were cornered, and if we tried to run with only those feeble reading lights to guide us we would break our necks. I tried to remember if on our way up we had passed any possible escape routes, but nothing came to mind. There was no time anyway. A crust of frozen sweat fringed my hood as if the ice was closing around me.

Hector called, "Lulu, we need your light!"

"It broke."

"It *broke?*"

"Damn!" said Cole. "What the fuck we gonna do?"

"I . . . don't know," I said.

"Oh God, oh God . . ." moaned Jake.

Icy-calm, Julian said, "We better do *something*. They'll be here any second."

Coming to a hopeless decision, I said, "Everyone be quiet! Turn off your flashlights and don't move!"

"Dude, you're fuckin' crazy!" Shawn said. "We have to book it outta here!"

Grimly, I said, "There's no place to go, and no time. All we can do is hide."

"Then we're fucked! No way!"

"She's right, man," Julian told him, disgusted to have been left with this poorest of options. "If we just sit tight in here they might lose us in the dark. It's a big place. Everybody come in from the doorway! Line up against the wall."

I didn't care that Julian was giving orders. "Hurry, do what he says," I whispered.

"This is nuts," Hector muttered, brushing past me.

"Shhh. Quiet."

There was no sound outside. Without even the toy flashlights it was an absolute abyss.

"Listen," Hector whispered. "If they come through that door, two of us rush 'em with the rope stretched between us and drive 'em back to the railing. Then we all dump them over."

"Why the hell not?" said Julian.

"I've wrestled before," offered Lemuel. "I'll take one end."

"Aw, fuck. Gimme the other," said Cole.

Touched by their futile machismo, I said, "Good idea. Now hush up."

Silence settled in our bones like the cold, freezing time itself. I would have given anything to be able to run in place and get my blood going. My hood was cinched to a tiny peephole and my face still ached. Gradually I became aware that I was looking out the peephole. It wasn't light exactly, more like shades of black, but I could *see* it: a snow-strained gloom filtering through the atrium skylights. Moonrise.

My concentration was broken by shuffling footsteps on the landing, coming our way.

"How much time left?" Hector whispered, startling me.

The time! I had forgotten. Checking my watch, I said, "We're due back in less than twenty minutes." My voice shivered apart. "I'm sorry you guys." The glowing watch face was like a beacon—Julian hissed at me to kill it.

All of a sudden Hector blurted, "I love you, Lulu."

The words just dangled there for what seemed like ages. I was glad he couldn't see how they hurt me; how I couldn't bear to hear this now. There was enough to mourn without that.

Then I heard Lemuel say, "So do I."

Shawn protested, "Since when, dude? I've loved her from day one."

"Oh, great," said Jake. "Take a number. While we're at it, she might as well know I love her, too."

Cole started to speak, and Julian cut him off, snarling, "Will you assholes shut up?"

The steps neared, loud as hoofbeats in the silence. As they reached a crescendo, I wanted to scream . . . then they stopped. We could hear snuffling breaths right outside the door. What *were* they? Their clothes rustled stiffly as they shifted in place, peering in, and I realized I could *smell* them: an oily, burnt odor like smoked mackerel. I found Hector's hand in the dark and gripped it.

The bird-men came in.

The silence blew up.

All the boys rushed the invaders, sobbing and screaming their lungs out as they attacked. At most I could see a dim scuffle, but I could tell that Hector's plan to drive the creatures over the balcony had failed—the fight remained in the bank lobby. Staying well clear, I backed into a corner and waited for death to find me. I wasn't frightened anymore; what I felt was a great sense of pity for my poor boys.

Something happened—I was blind again. Not because of darkness, but because of too-bright light. I jerked back as if I'd been punched, squinting in pain. The ceiling lights were on! Shielding my eyes, I said, "Hey!"

Cries of surprise were coming from the stalled combatants as well. My team-mates found themselves entwined with four of the filthiest, most unkempt men I had ever seen. They were black with grease and soot, bearded like

Rasputin, and dressed in heaping layers of mismatched leisurewear. Strapped to their faces were cones they had improvised from some insulating material, and goggles. They looked medieval, pagan, but not exactly dangerous. In fact they looked terrified.

"What the fuck, man," said Julian, getting to his feet. "Where did you guys come from?"

One of the men said, "I might ask you the same question." He had an English accent.

We all went stock-still as Mr. Noteiro's voice boomed over the ship's PA system: "RETURN TO THE LOWER PROMENADE, LADIES AND GENTS. DON'T MAKE US COME LOOKIN' FOR YA."

Shaky with gratitude, I happened to glance behind me and only then cried out.

On the other side of the bank's frosty security glass was a mass of bodies, perhaps a hundred or more, slumped together under a mantle of crystal fur like the ash-smothered victims of Pompeii. Their curdled eyeballs seemed to stare right through me.

"Well, Phil," said one of the bird-men, his voice a muffled squawk behind the mask. "I told you they was bloomin' kids."

s e v e n t e e n

"WHY DIDN'T YOU guys tell us who you were?" I asked. "You scared us to death!"

The one named Wally said, "We tried to, but you just ran away."

"You lads 'ad us 'alf believing in ghosts," said another, Reggie. "The mind plays tricks in a place like this."

"We didn't know what to think," said Wally.

"We felt the same way!" I said.

A third man, Dick, now spoke up. "But we'd have more cause to be suspicious, wouldn't we? You might expect to find poor sods like ourselves on a derelict ship, but who, I ask you, would ever dream of findin' a group of choirboys on bleedin' 'oliday, much less a wee moppet like yourself?"

"We thought we'd gone mad," said Reggie.

"Didn't you hear us hail you?" asked Julian a little belligerently.

Dick replied, "We live in a right fortress of mattresses up there, so we wouldn't, would we?"

"I guess not."

"Warmth has been a rather abiding concern, I'm afraid."

Hector asked, "How do you get around in the dark like that?"

The one named Phil said, "We've come to know this bloody scow like the backs of our 'ands, son. In the beginning we used torches, same as you. Still and all, you took us by surprise with that ambush." He swiveled his sore neck. "Nice scrimmage, that."

"What a way to break the ice," said Wally.

As they showed us their shortcut to the promenade, we briefly explained our situation (which must have seemed nonsensical to them—they offered no comment) and they told us what had happened to them.

They were a singing group—The Blackpudlians—a Beatles tribute band from England that had been booked to play twelve days of Christmas gigs as the ship steamed from the British Isles to New Brunswick and back again, skirting the arctic ice-cap. The on-board festivities were to have culminated in a New Year's Eve party the last night of the voyage. But it turned out to be a different kind of carnival.

"Blue meanies," said Wally, laughing unsteadily—it was almost a sob.

"Blue meanies," agreed Dick. "While we were 'aving tea with Mr. Coffey in the Lido Lounge."

"I remember I was in the middle of spreading clotted cream on a perfectly toasted currant scone, when there was an alarm and Mr. Coffey 'ad to excuse 'imself. 'What's this, then?' says I. 'We've not 'it an iceberg, I 'ope.' An' 'ee laughs back, 'I'll remember that when I'm 'andin' out loif-jackets.'" Wally shook his head.

"Weren't no iceberg," said Reggie gravely.

"Course it weren't no iceberg, you sod," Wally said. "After a few minutes we hear crockery breaking and see a brawl at another table—"

"This madwoman's attacking 'er 'usband—"

"Now, we don't know it was 'er 'usband, Dick."

"—an she's got the poor bloke in a clutch like a bleedin' boa constrictor—"

"Looks like she's off her bloody nut."

"—*Kisses* the man—"

"No bloomin' peck on the cheek, I can tell you."

"—Whole place goes mad. Chaps at the next table try to intervene, she drops 'er 'usband and pounces like a leopard—this is a high-class woman dressed for a proper tea, mind you. *Second* man goes down—"

"Sturdy-looking chap, too."

"—Now the stewards arrive, and there must be a dozen stout fellows pitching in to restrain the woman, who looks the very devil: blue as a coot, slippery with blood and jam, but she's holding her own! At last they seem to gain the upper hand—"

"We're all standing about with our mouths 'angin' open like bloody carp."

"—People are administering CPR to the two men on the floor, kicking biscuits this way and that, when suddenly *another* woman joins the fray!—"

"Frightful, really."

"—My first thought was that she was simply hysterical—"

"People were, you know. I was a bit cracked meself."

"Not something you see every day."

"—but it was plain as day this woman was as daft as the first, strangling the life out of some poor steward while the rest of us were still in shock from the previous bit. Then things became really queer: The body of the first man—and I say body because he was plainly as dead as a haddock, in spite of their attempts at resuscitation—unexpectedly lunged up and seized hold of a good samaritan who had been attempting mouth-to-mouth on 'im! Grabbed the fellow's head in the middle of a breath an' held on tight while the other man thrashed about like a hooked fish, trying to break off the unholy kiss—"

"I'll never forget the look in their eyes, mate. It was bloody rape."

"—So then Phil says to us, 'I must go, lads,' and that like breaks the spell, and we all bolt for the exit. But as you may imagine that was only the beginning. Out in the corridor we can hear the whole bloody ship going mad. Through the windows we can see a full-fledged melee on the lido deck, a whole crowd of men stampeding like antelopes and being picked off by nasty devils that had only just been society dames—"

"Sheer bedlam . . ."

"—Some a the men were lowering lifeboats, but I could tell we didn't 'ave a hope in 'ell a pushin' through that lot—"

"Dante's bloomin' *Inferno*."

"—so I figured we'd best get to our lodgings and shut ourselves in good an' tight. Just hold out until the cavalry arrived."

"Problem was getting there."

"Yeh, there was no way down. Every stair was full a people flockin' up, slaughtering an' being slaughtered, and for the moment the slaughterees, such as ourselves, were still sufficiently numerous that the four of us were able, *just for that brief moment,* to stand apart from it all and consider. But the window of opportunity was closing even as we watched."

"The blue meanies were multiplying."

"Quick as a wink, those monstrous women and murdered men were taking over the ship, like some . . . chemical reaction spreading outward, some elemental change. Soon we'd 'ave the whole nest after us."

"Dick said, 'We have to get off this concourse,' and it made perfect sense: the public areas were the killing fields. So we found a staff-only door and slipped inside. It was a short corridor piled with racks of empty bottles, leading to the lounge scullery. There was no one about, and we didn't think it likely that anyone from the crew would return to ordinary duty, but of course it wasn't the crew that we feared—"

"God, the fear! Miracle that alone didn't kill us."

"—so we ducked into the first available foxhole: the wine closet."

"Brilliant. Really brilliant."

"It couldn't have been better suited to our purpose. A small room, yes, but stout as a keep to protect the really expensive vintages; well insulated, and with its own humidity and temperature controls. Even a spy hole to view the kitchen."

"Not to mention floor-to-ceiling shelves of the finest grape."

"All it lacked, in fact, was a means of locking ourselves inside, and Dick made short work o' that."

"Dick knows fuck-all about drums, but 'ee's a right genius when it comes to bending a handle." I gathered that this was a private joke among them. "Isn't that right, Dick?"

"Sod off. It was simple: Once we broke the outside door handle nothing could get in. There was a mallet and chisel for opening crates—it was easily done."

"But you puzzled it out, lad," said Phil. "Credit where credit is due."

"Hear hear," said Reggie.

Ignoring them, Dick continued, "An' that's where we stayed, dashing out now and again for the niceties, but never losing sight o' that door. You can be sure we took every bleeding precaution not to lock ourselves out. Twenty-two days we lived like that."

"Didn't you ever wonder what was happening in the rest of the ship?" asked Hector.

"Course we did. But let me tell you something, lad: When you've seen what we 'ad, and every so often you 'ear a figment from your worst nightmare scratching at the door, it tempers your curiosity. I think we'd be there still if it hadn't been for the cold."

"Bloody 'ell, that was torment."

"The ship's power failed not long after the meanies came. Day by day we watched the thermometer drop. Not as fast where we were as outside, but too fast for comfort. I don't know why we thought it would stop at zero C, but it was a blow when it didn't."

"Meanwhile we was tucked under dirty aprons and sacking, with bags of flour heaped around us—we were a sorry sight, mate. The warmth from our bodies caused moisture to condense on the walls, so that after a few days it began to look like a bloody icebox in there. We 'ad to chip it off the peephole to look out. An' that was nothing compared to what it was like outside."

"Bottles, tins, everything froze solid. The sink taps went dry. There was still plenty to eat and drink, but we 'ad to use Sterno to melt it. Once the lights went out, all we 'ad to see by was Sterno, too. I think it was our silly gobs pressed around that anemic flame, with a bottle of Chateau Lafite Rothschild melting above it, that finally pushed us over the edge."

"We couldn't take it no more."

"We came out, found a torch, and used the kitchen's big gas cooker to make a proper joint of beef, hardly taking notice of how much bangin' about it required. The heat and the smell of roasting meat almost drove us mad with pleasure—"

"We ate it before it was barely done."

"Blimey that was good."

"Best bit o' beef I ever ate."

"—and while it cooked we thawed cases of porter on the stove, so that for once there was no shortage of drink. We lived in that kitchen for eight days, making up for lost time. When no meanies set upon us, the range of our forays increased, until eventually we deemed the ship safe."

"That's how we've been living ever since. Robinson Crusoe times four."

"Until you lot came along."

"Which begs a question . . ." said Dick.

"Yes?" I asked.

"We heard a few things on the wireless. We thought the women had all . . ."

"Become Xombies? No. It has something to do with

menstruation. Since I don't, uh, menstruate, I didn't catch it." They looked at me askance and I added, "I have a medical condition that keeps me from ever menstruating."

"Ah." They seemed to accept this without further question.

During the walk back, Jake came up next to me and said, *sotto voce,* "Did that guy call you a muppet?"

We arrived at the lower promenade a few minutes late, but no one was much upset. They were too busy. Most of the sub's crew was there, including Commander Coombs, and a major operation appeared to be underway. Our new companions did attract a great deal of attention, however. I tried to politely introduce them, but Coombs and the other officers rudely brushed me aside, subjecting the overwhelmed quartet to an extensive "debriefing."

"Not cool," said Hector, watching the interrogation.

"I mean, this has been their home for months," I said. "And we just barge in and take over? What are they supposed to think?"

Julian said, "Hey, survival of the fittest."

I was disappointed in him. "That's not right," I said. "We have to come together, especially now."

"Dream on."

Approaching Mr. Robles, who looked miserably cold, I asked, "What's going on? Why is everybody here?"

"We're salvaging whatever we can off this ship."

"Really?" My heart sank. Mr. Cowper's medicine was one thing, but . . . "That's a long way to carry stuff," I said.

"We'll rig up something. Maybe open a loading bay. Don't worry." Trying to cheer himself up, he asked, "So how is it in there?"

I thought about the cold, the bodies, the dark. He wasn't asking about that. Looking at his beaming expression, I replied, "It's a fucking extravaganza."

The next few days were full of hard physical work, but I can't say it wasn't interesting. Using the sub's massive sail-planes as levers, a crane was improvised to hoist the forward escape trunk out of its bed, leaving the bathysphere-like pod dangling in midair above a large well in the deck. Now objects up to seven feet wide could be taken aboard. While the men were handling this delicate operation, the boys and I were given long lists of provisions and sent off to scour the liner.

It was decided—wisely, I think—to leave the ship in its deep-freeze, with only a small back-up generator running to provide light. Whether or not Xombies could revive after being frozen was unknown, and we wanted it to remain unknown. Apart from that, there were concerns about heat or vibration destabilizing the ice mass on the ship's superstructure.

Mr. DeLuca had managed to activate the liner's communications suite, though there was nothing coming over the airwaves that the sub's array couldn't already pick up. As civilians, we weren't allowed to listen in, but by all accounts it was a weird and troubling international chorus of despair, the last struggling pockets of humanity. If we did send a mayday, it would only join that hopeless din, but anyone who wanted to could try it—they just had to wait for the submarine to leave the area first. It was a gamble Coombs knew no one would take.

Using the Englishmen as guides, pack routes were established throughout the ship, and I organized parties to loot the various regions. It bothered me to be doing this without seeking the Blackpudlians' consent, but I kept reminding myself that it was not really *their* ship.

They looked a lot different once they had gotten cleaned up and trimmed their beards and hair. First, they were quite young, all under thirty. Second, though they were third- and fourth-generation citizens of the UK, all were ethnic Pakistanis—Reggie, for instance, was actually Rajeev Jinnah. Two of them were practicing Muslims. Much as he loved the Beatles, Commander Coombs was not pleased to have these aliens aboard.

Large cargo sledges were cobbled together from lifeboats and heaped high with goods. The mountains of booty included food and drink, bedding, towels, toilet paper (probably the most eagerly anticipated item), furniture, appliances, plumbing, electronics, building supplies, sporting goods (including a brace of shotguns for skeet), cookware, silver, fine china, clothing, bulk fabric, laundry supplies (also much awaited), freezer components to expand our cold-storage capacity, and medical supplies—including Mr. Cowper's Lanoxin. Diesel fuel, oil, and various other substances usable by the sub were also tapped, though our reactor, of course, required nothing.

Then the task was dragging this treasure trove to the boat and finding room for it belowdecks. The Big Room became something of a warehouse again, but at least this time with the promise of greater comforts to come.

The cold was our bitter taskmaster. With the sub wide open and tons of subzero groceries being stowed, heat was retained only in certain sections, and these were not the sections most frequented by civilians. A couple of barely adequate warming stations, heated tents, were set up for us, but my requests for more were answered with, *The sooner you're done, the sooner we can close the hatch.* The officers hated leaving the boat open like this—it was too vulnerable to attack. They wouldn't let us relax until we finished.

The only ones who did not seem uncomfortable were the four Brits. They actually requested to stay in the more familiar environs of their ship until it was time to leave, and they could be glimpsed from time to time following their own routines like backwoods trappers encroached upon by modernity.

As it turned out, we left a bit sooner than expected. Four days after our first sight of the *Northern Queen,* and just as we were dragging our umpteenth sledge-load through a deep groove in the ice, the boys and I were shocked to hear the sub's deafening horn. We could see the crew up top rushing to replace the escape trunk.

"Holy shit!" said Julian. "We're under attack!" We dropped the lines and ran.

But it was not an attack, it was a leak. There was serious flooding on the liner—the boys stripping the carpentry shop had noticed it and flashed a signal to the officer on watch. The ship was sinking. It was not happening so quickly that there was any danger, but Coombs wanted to be sure the sub was in one piece and we were all on board in case of any ice upheaval.

The Blackpudlians were the last to come below, lugging their instruments.

"Well, that's it then," sighed Wally, taking a final look at the ship.

"That's it, mate," said Dick.

"Feels like a lifetime we been on 'er."

"It does at that."

Turning to Officer Robles, Phil asked, "How much longer d'you reckon she'll last?"

"A little while," Robles said. "Few hours, maybe. Strange how she popped all her gaskets at once."

"Bloody mysterious," said Dick.

Robles shook his head. "I guess it's a miracle she's lasted this long."

"Hear that, Reg?" said Phil. "A miracle."

"Auld girl did right by us."

"And we by 'er."

We left the awesome, ghostly sight, shutting ourselves once more in the confines of the submarine. There was something melancholy about it, about turning our backs on that lost ship, and I was reminded of a time when my mother and I had taken walks along a pasture, bringing slices of Wonderbread to a huge old horse that lived there. I was four or five, and the animal was wonderful and terrifying. My mother was always the one who did the feeding, holding each slice on her wide-open palm in such a way that the horse could nibble it off with its giant lips. She made it look easy, and the day came when I begged her to let me feed the horse. *Are you sure?* she asked. I swore I was, and she showed me just how to do it, palm flat. But

when the great animal came at me I panicked, clutching the
bread in my outstretched fingers so that the horse acciden-
tally bit them. I screamed. My mother tried to soothe me,
saying, *Honey, look—your fingers are fine,* but I was child-
ishly hurt and petulant, crying, *I never want to see that
horse again! Promise me, Mummy! Promise me we'll never
come here again!* And as I said it, part of me prayed she
wouldn't hold me to it, that she'd see me through the
tantrum and give me a chance to make up with the horse.
But she never took us back there.

"SIR?" IT WAS sonarman Gus DeLuca. "I'm picking up
sounds from the ship."

Coombs was impatient. "What kind of sounds?"

"She's foundering, sir."

"All stop."

"All stop, aye."

I sat back from my workstation, cocking an ear toward
the sonar room. Everyone became very quiet. Coombs put
on the earphones, tilting his head in concentration. Then he
straightened up and gave the headset back. Crossing very
deliberately to his station, he announced, "Gentlemen, I
need a periscope sighting if you please." He seemed to be
gritting his teeth.

We maneuvered around until we located a small
polynya, just big enough to raise the periscope. Coombs
broadcast the view over every monitor in the boat.

There was the *Northern Queen,* blue in the twilight and
looking much as I remembered her. It hadn't been that
long; we were barely underway. She was several miles
south, but at full magnification she filled the screen.

"Attention all hands," Coombs said over the loudspeaker. "I advise you to look at your handiwork."

A subterranean popping sound reverberated through the
hull. It had been going on for some time and I just didn't
register it, dismissing it as pack-ice movement. Ice made a
lot of peculiar noises, and this was similar: a groan like

rope creaking under a great and increasing strain. Coombs put the hydrophones on the PA, turning the volume way up, and now we could hear a harsh metallic grinding, like a freight train screaming to a stop, and roaring water.

His voice muffled by the racket, Coombs said, "The tub's overflowing."

Perhaps the liner was listing at a more extreme angle than I remembered.

"Omigod, look!" Shawn said as the sleek whale's-tail funnel atop the ship buckled and crashed down her side. An instant later we heard sheet-metal thunder. Icy clouds bloomed in the night, white as stage smoke. "Whoa," said Shawn, delighted.

The vast ship began to roll over.

Again the noise was very much like an approaching train, triggering a primordial instinct to flee. Feeling it in our marrow, we watched the many-tiered superstructure tip over with gathering force until it struck the patch of sea-ice so recently occupied by ourselves. The sledges we had built were no more, lost in that tumultuous junkyard crash that went on and on until the ship was completely upside down . . . and even then it continued: dual cacophanies of ruptured steel and surging rapids that provided an awful accompaniment to the visible death throes we could see on screen. The gargantuan hull moved as if alive; a sea-monster sloshing in a pond, rolling this way and that, spouting geysers high into the air, until at last it reared up accusingly and plunged out of sight.

I thought it was over. My hands were clinging, white knuckled, to the console. No—Coombs, like a demonic maestro, let us hear the whole ghastly works all the way to the bottom. It was like he was saying, *This could be you.*

When it was finished, he lowered the periscope and said, "See, that's the thing about a submarine, boys and girls. It's not just about what's on the surface."

eighteen

THERE WAS NO course change as Julius had predicted, no Lancaster Sound, just that continual northward push. We passed latitude seventy-five, only fifteen degrees short of the North Pole, yet continued up toward the encroaching glaciers of Greenland and Ellesmere Island. It looked to me like a dead end, at least on the map. There was only one narrow cut threading those land masses, a permanently frozen-over passage called the Kennedy Channel, and I dearly hoped we were not going to attempt that. The frustrated atmosphere in the sub told me I was not alone—everyone was confused. But our fears turned out to be groundless: on February twenty-fifth, Commander Coombs ordered a course correction that put us on a direct heading for the Greenland ice-cap.

"Thule!"

"Toolie?"

"Thule!" Cowper triumphantly said. He seemed to be feeling better. "T-H-U-L-E! Thule Air Base!"

"Where's that?"

"Just where we're headin', on the west coast of Greenland. It's a dead giveaway."

"I didn't see any air base on my atlas."

"They don't advertise it. Look again—it's probably just listed as Thule, or maybe even Qaanaaq." He spelled it for me. "Seventy-six north by sixty-eight west. It hasn't been a fully functioning air base since the Eighties, but it has an airstrip and a permanent Air Force contingent of about a hundred and thirty: the Air Force Space Command. There's also Air National Guard, some Canadians, Danes, even native Greenlanders—about a thousand people all told."

"A thousand people way up here?"

"That's nothin'—it used ta be a city of ten thousand, back durin' the height of the Cold War. The Ballistic Missile Warning System. It's practically a ghost town these days, but they still monitor space launches for NASA . . . or did. No tellin' what they're up to now."

"Why would we be going there?"

"Who knows? Ask Coombs."

"Maybe I will."

AS IT TURNED out, Coombs came to me.

He approached me as I was "cranking"—doing chores—and told me that when I was through with the lunch dishes there was a small job of relagging he needed done. Relagging was one of the few menial jobs nobody complained about. Except for stainless steel, all exposed metal on the sub was covered with something, whether it was perforated foam paneling on bulkheads, hard rubbery tiles on tanks and stanchions, or cloth wrapping around air ducts. This last was called lagging. Being fairly flimsy, it frayed over time like an old leg cast, eventually becoming so dirty and ragged it had to be re-applied like plaster of Paris—an arts-and-craftsy activity I found soothing. Relagging was a nev-erending job, but for me it was break time . . . usually.

This time the duct was in Coombs' cabin, which would have been interesting except that he hung around while I prepared the materials. It made me very uncomfortable.

"So I guess the boys must be enjoying the new provisions," he said, sitting at his small desk. He had his own compact command console in there, and a fold-up sink which was kind of cool, but the place was papered with fake wood paneling like so many of the cheap motel rooms my mother and I had stayed in. Up at eye level there was a safe that must have once held secret launch codes. It looked like someone had burned through the lock—it was the heat from this that had scorched the lagging above.

Working on it, I said, "Oh, my God—yes, sir. They're calling it 'Barbie's Dream Sub.' "

"They are, huh?" I could feel him staring at me.

"Oh, yeah. They're turning the Big Room into their own Galleria, and the British guys have made a private little den—I think they're feeling a little overwhelmed. But the boys are fine. I guess this is the first time they've had enough to eat in weeks."

"No doubt. I'm glad to hear it. Must make your job easier."

"Yeah, morale's good . . . except for one thing, I guess."

"What's that?"

"Just the uncertainty. Same old thing."

"Hm." He had suddenly become disinterested, checking figures on his computer screen.

I couldn't stand it. Hesitantly I said, "Sir, I was wondering . . . about Thule . . ."

He looked sharply at me. "What about it?"

"Are we going there?"

He turned back to his screen. "Of course we're going to Thule. Where else would we be going?"

Surprised by his frankness, I said, "Well, there was talk of Alaska."

"Remember what I told you about scuttlebutt?"

"Why Thule?" I was scrambling for follow-up questions; he had caught me off guard.

"The military installation, of course. Right now it's the most secure facility in this hemisphere, except maybe for Alert up on Cape Sheridan. Thule has been designated a federal SPAM depot. With nobody watching the store, the Fed has been moving anything critical to national security up here."

"Sensitive Personnel and Materials."

"Yes. Of which we are still a vital part, in spite of the serious breaches that have occurred."

"Why didn't you tell anyone about this earlier?" I was freshly outraged. "How could you let all those people get off, when you knew—"

"Knew what? Yes, I *let* them—I did not *make* them. What did I have to offer them if they had stayed aboard? I haven't been in contact with Thule—they're restricting their emissions just as we are. For all we know, they may be no more amenable to refugees than St. John's. It's a harsh place to survive."

"But at least you could have told them—"

"Miss Pangloss, I am under no obligation to share any information whatsoever with you or any other civilian, especially in regards to a highly classified operation such as SPAM. Thule's SPAM status is probably the most closely guarded secret in the world at this time. If a bunch of civilians with that knowledge were to land on a foreign shore, do you have any idea how fatally that could impact the mission? One well-placed bomb—boom! No more SPAM. And SPAM is the key to rebuilding America."

"So . . . what are we supposed to do if Thule doesn't want us?"

"Cross that bridge when we come to it. Don't worry—you're one of us now."

I was not in the control room at the time, but Julian would later describe to me how we surfaced through twenty feet of solid ice. The black water off the western Greenland shore offered very little clearance, being only about a hundred feet deep from bottom to frozen ceiling. Since the boat was some seventy feet high this did not allow for much "wiggle room," but Coombs got as close as he dared—around two miles offshore. Once he found a good spot, he backed a thousand yards away from it and fired two Mark 48 ADCAP torpedoes. They were wire-guided, and Mr. Noteiro (who had been some kind of torpedo specialist in ages past) wove them over shoals and around hanging ice-masses to the precise spot Coombs had chosen. Julian said everyone in the control room held their breath as the "fish" unspooled.

Then Vic detonated them.

This, no one on board failed to appreciate. The torpedoes seemed to hatch two howling leviathans of liquid force that descended on the sub and swallowed it whole, causing the rock-steady floor to bounce like a trampoline. For a minute the stealthy ship was a rattletrap jalopy, all squeaks and bangs and rattling cutlery, but in short order things settled down, replaced by more reassuring sounds of cheering and applause from the control center. Apparently we were all right.

We made our way back to the site of the explosion, penetrating a cloud of silt to find a wide, shallow crater in the seabed. Above was all loose floating rubble, broken in a spiderweb pattern outward from the blast. Even shattered, the volume of ice was so massive that Coombs did not try surfacing the entire boat, but only raised the fairwater like a gopher peering from its hole.

This was the true arctic winter. This was darkness at noon. I ascended to my lookout on the bridge and for a moment could only stare at the lunar desolation: black and white, yin and yang. By comparison, the snowy landscape of St. John's had been a ski resort, with its buildings and lights and forested hills. The sea there was still a liquid presence, just as it had been around the cruise ship, where the liner itself had been a constant reminder that we were in fact *at sea*. But here . . .

Here there was nothing. Nothing moving. Nothing to render scale. The deep ice and deeper snow gave no intimation of water beneath, any more than sand dunes in the Sahara give hints of a hidden aquifer. And this did look like fine sand, a vast rippled plain of it. More oppressive still was the fact that I was not towering above the way I usually did, but was only about eight feet high—that was how much of the sail protruded from the ice. I could have easily jumped from the bridge down onto that buckled white heap. The great blocks pushed up by the dive-planes actually rose higher than my head.

Officer Robles came up and rigged the spotlight, flashing a Morse code signal out across the nothingness. Snowflakes caught in the beam were as brilliant as welding sparks.

"Can't we just call them on the phone?" I asked. I had learned to leave no flesh exposed, but the cold still penetrated. The thermometer read minus thirty-four.

"And reveal our position?"

"Isn't that exactly what you're doing?"

"Reveal our position to someone other than that guy, I mean."

Slow on the uptake, I hesitated before following his line of sight. "Oh," I said. "Wow!" Far away in the murk there were answering flashes. A live human being! Thrilled, I babbled into the mike, "Contact! We've established contact! What's he saying?"

Robles said, "He's just acknowledging us. Wait. Repeat after me: 'Welcome USS No-Name . . . official escort en route . . . ETA five minutes.' "

I duly reported every word. Then Robles checked my safety line and boosted me over into a little rumble seat behind the main cockpit to make room for the exiting shore party. A folding ladder was passed up the hatch; Robles planted it on the ice, then swung himself over the edge and climbed down, testing the upheaved surface for stability. It was utterly dry and solid.

As he did this, men began emerging from the hatch. The first was Phil Tran from the navigation center, then there were three seldom-seen officers from the propulsion spaces aft—one of them was the bland Reactor Control Operator, Mr. Fisk, who the boys hated because he was always torturing them with tutorials on nuclear physics and thermodynamics and all kinds of specialized engineering and chemistry. They just wanted to know which buttons to push. The fifth man out I wouldn't have recognized if he hadn't spoken, but he was gruffly complaining about his stiff leg and had to be helped off the sail.

"Mr. Sandoval?" I called, amazed. "You're Mr. Sandoval, right?"

He was facing me, starting down the ladder. "Oh. You," he said.

"Is Mr. Cowper out, too?" I asked, heart beating wildly.

He hesitated, then brusquely continued down to the ice. I didn't know what to think.

The last man out was Commander Coombs. When I saw him I threw caution to the wind, saying, "Captain! I just saw Mr. Sandoval! Does that mean you've let them out? Please, if I could just see him . . ."

Coombs had a look of grim urgency. Shaking his head no, he turned off my microphone and said, "Lulu, shut up and listen. This is very important—probably the most important thing you'll ever hear. Don't tell anyone what I'm about to tell you. I know you can be entrusted with a secret, and this is a doozy.

"I don't know what's going to happen here, or who is in charge, but I am not going to just turn this submarine over to the Air Force. If they give me sealed orders from CINCLANT, or I can talk to some Navy brass, fine. That's how it should be. But in the event that there's no Navy presence and no direct line of communication to some pertinent senior authority, I have no intention of relinquishing control of this vessel. She's too important to waste as a back-up generator to light Air Force barracks. In that case, I deliver the SPAM and head to Norfolk. But the Base Commander may think differently. That's where you come in.

"I've watched you for weeks now, and you're a very

smart girl. I haven't given you any guidance, yet you have taken a fictitious job title and the most cursory instructions and created an efficient program for managing the other kids on this boat. You have never come to me with an excuse, or failed to execute an assignment. You've never even asked me for clarification, yet your solutions exceed my expectations at every turn. You know when to keep your mouth shut, and when to dole out a few crumbs of information to keep your peers' trust. You're not mindlessly loyal, but you also don't bear a grudge—you home in on what *works,* because *you* like it that way.

"When we put Fred Cowper under lock and key, he told me about you. I thought he just wanted me to look out for you, and half the reason I gave you that Youth Liaison title was so I could keep tabs. But you've been very dependable . . . much more so than some people I've counted on."

Disturbed by his praise, which I thought made me sound like a rat, I said, "What did Mr. Cowper say about me?"

"He called you a tough cookie. 'Ya wouldn't know it to look at her, but she's a tough cookie,' he said. He doesn't think you should suffer for his crimes, and I agree."

"Oh . . ."

"And he *has* committed serious crimes; crimes against the future of this nation. That's not just right-wing ranting, Lulu—for all we know, the information and technology that he wantonly ordered destroyed could be the difference between America rising to prominence again or being swept into the dustbin of history."

Trying to defend Mr. Cowper, I said, "But sir . . . I don't quite understand what 'America' means now. I mean, what's left of it?"

"There's no way of knowing. But that's why protecting what we still have is so desperately important."

"But that includes *us,* doesn't it? Don't people have to be preserved, ultimately?"

"Yes, but not individually. Not at the cost of national security."

"Security for whom, then?"

"Oh boy. 'For ourselves and our posterity,' to quote a document that for all I know was made into a paper airplane and tossed overboard by one of the beneficiaries of Cowper's humanitarian zeal! Now that's enough; we don't have time for this. All you need to know is that a few officers and I are going to go ashore. In case somebody other than me should try to take command—" he leaned across and pressed a fat silver key into my oven mitt "—you know what to do."

I watched him climb down and join the others. They were a strange, anachronistic sight in their bulky arctic gear—all they needed was sled dogs and a flag. I put the key in my pocket, shuddering involuntarily. *You know what to do.* The men began laying down a row of chemical glow-wands in the snow.

I heard a far-off whine and saw headlights following the contours of an unseen hill. "Vehicles approaching," I said with chattering teeth. Then I remembered to switch the mike back on and repeated more clearly, "Vehicles approaching."

As the lights neared, wreathed in swirling powder, the sound of turbines became so loud it turned the ice into a vibrating drum. These were not ordinary vehicles. They were gigantic saucers gliding on fat rubber bumpers, their topsides bristling with antennae and weapons.

"*Hovercraft,*" I said in disbelief. "Three of them, coming in fast. Big ones."

Now Coombs and the others were waving flashlights as if directing taxiing aircraft. The imposing vehicles stopped well short, pulling up side-by-side in a howling blizzard of their own making, then powered down the rotors. Their blinding headlights turned ridges of upthrust ice translucent blue, brighter than the glow-wands, and when they lowered their boarding ramps it was like an alien visitation.

"There are ten or twelve men coming out," I said. "They are approaching our group."

Barely audible under the idling engines, I could hear the lead stranger shout, "Colonel Brad Lowenthal, Commander

Twelfth Space Warning Squadron! Welcome to Thule!"

"Thank you, Commander!" replied Coombs. They shook hands. "I'm Admiral Harvey Coombs, and these are my senior officers! Are there any Navy personnel with you?" It was the first time I had heard Coombs call himself Admiral.

"Everything is being arranged through SAC! First let's get your people out of this wet sub and into a dry martini!"

"The rest of my crew will be staying aboard for now!"

"That's not necessary, Admiral! We have a team ready to take charge of your cargo and watch the ship! You're under our security umbrella now!"

"Thank you, Commander, but I need confirmation from NavSea before I can . . ."

They were moving toward the hovercraft and I couldn't hear any more. It looked like an affable enough disagreement. Soon they were boarding the lead craft, which thundered to life and sideslipped away, trailed by the others. As the big vehicles turned in formation, I was sandblasted by their rotor-wash. Seconds later they were practically out of sight, and the heavy curtain of snow and space drew shut again.

Half deaf, I said, "They're gone!"

MR. ALBEMARLE WAS the OOW—the officer of the watch—and he erected a clear canopy over the cockpit to permit a normal six-hour duty shift. After an hour or so he was called below to attend to some minor crisis, and I volunteered to stand watch. He didn't like me, but he trusted me enough to leave me alone up there, keeping in radio contact from the control room. From time to time he or someone else would sneak up underneath, trying to catch me napping. They didn't do this to be funny— falling asleep on watch was considered a heinous crime. That was why standing watch topside wasn't considered a very desirable posting, because it was not just the boredom and the cold you had to contend with, it was also Navy guys threatening you with the whippings, hangings, and keel-haulings traditionally meted out to errant sentries.

They didn't scare me; I wasn't there to sleep. I was grateful for the chance to be alone. Never having been a tremendously sociable person, the daily strain of being in close quarters with so many people was taking a toll on me. Just after St. John's, the boat had seemed incredibly roomy, but now its limitations were starting to sink in again and I was glad the end was in sight . . . if in fact it was. I was shaken by what Coombs had said. I didn't want that responsibility, or even that key. Now *I* was Mr. Cowper's jailer! Every second I had that key it was killing me.

As the midmorning darkness wore on, I started thinking about my mother and what I had been through because of Mr. Cowper. The memories were intensely vivid, a trance-like dislocation that was common to everyone on the sub, weighed upon as we all were by the unfinished business of our lives. It was hardly surprising that our subconscious should come on so strong—what is a submarine but a giant sensory-deprivation tank?

I remembered singing in a church at Christmas time. It was the only time I ever went to church, except for a brief enrollment at Sunday school. This was a Southern California Lutheran church, airy as a basketball court, with honeyed sunlight beaming down on the lustrous blond wood and congregation; above it all an understated, minimalist cross.

My mother was beside me, gripping my hand. We were all holding hands and singing carols, but from my mother's glazed look and sweaty palm I suspected an agenda.

She had been working part-time in the church office as a secretary, and I knew she liked the pastor. When I had asked her if he was married, she said, *Oh, it's not like that, honey. We're just friends. He's a nice man, that's all.* She had even arranged for me to have a private talk with him in his study, under the pretense that the two of them had discussed my bookish ways, and he was "fascinated." But meeting the man was only awkward; I knew at once that Pastor Lund and I had both been duped—each of us kept waiting for the other to evince any sign of interest. In desperation I scanned his bookshelf for anything familiar. Seizing upon *Alive—The Story of the Andes Survivors,* I asked, "What do you think of the proposition that survival cannibalism is a form of Communion?" He became very uncomfortable and recommended I read C.S. Lewis.

Now Mummy was singing in German; singing *O Tannenbaum* while everyone else was singing *Oh Christmas Tree,* and doing it in loud tones of righteous indignation. People craned their necks to see what was going on.

"Mom," I hissed. "What are you doing?"

She sang right over me. No one had any idea how to deal with it, paralyzed by the hard-to-define offense. When the song ended, a man in our pew leaned over and pleasantly asked her, "Was that German?"

She remained rigid as a wooden Indian.

It wasn't over. When *Silent Night* began, she belted out the German version of that, too—*Stille Nacht*—while Pastor Lund duelled with her from the pulpit, directing his organist and choir to pour it on. Elderly ladies got up to leave, covering their ears.

Once again I had been brought along as a prop. I was boiling. When it was finally over (I believe the service was cut short) and Mummy and I were outside in that opulent residential neighborhood heading back to our roach motel, I turned on her furiously. "This is it," I stormed. "This is the last time I trust you."

She put on her innocent face, twitching nervously. "What? Why?" she asked.

"Don't give me that! How could you do that?"

"Because I love him! Can I help it if I love the man?"

"But why do you have to drag me into it?"

"Because you're my child!"

"Oh please. So it's my duty to let you humiliate me like this? Uh-uh, this is the last time. No more."

She faltered a little in her haughtiness. "Lulu, have a heart. What do you mean, 'no more'?"

"I mean that's the last time I ever let myself be taken advantage of. I should have just got up and left, but I sat there and let you use me. Well no more, no more."

I WAS YANKED back to the present by the appearance of a string of fairy lights in the distance. Their blue twinkle revealed higher elevations in the dark, creating the illusion of a floating island.

"Lights—I see lights," I said. "They just came on to the east, running in a straight line. It looks like a runway or something—" Just as I said this, I could hear the whistle of approaching jet engines. "—omigod, a plane! A big jet is flying in from the south! It's flying right over us! It looks like it's coming in for a landing!"

"It is an *air* base, after all," said Albemarle dryly in my ear. "We've been tracking it. Kranuski is going to try to make a sighting."

Behind me the periscope rose up from its shaft.

"C-5A Galaxy," Albemarle said as I watched the plane set down. "That's a big mother. It's for cargo; nothing to worry about."

The lights went out again. The magic island vanished.

WHEN MY SHIFT was over I was supposed to go directly to the galley and help make lunch. I did go down there intending to do just that, but when I arrived on the third deck I didn't see Mr. Monte. I loitered around for awhile, feeling tense and fidgity, then found myself walking straight through the enlisted mess and the wardroom to the deserted CPO quarters. It was not a conscious decision so much as a deliberately *un*conscious one. With the blood pounding in my head, I strode at that orange warning sign and stabbed the key into the lock. It went in smoothly. I turned the knob and opened the door.

"Mr. Cowper," I said. "Mr. Cowper!"

The goat locker was empty.

nineteen

I STOOD IN the room for a few minutes, staring blankly around at the brown Naugahyde couches, the TV and VCR, the coffeemaker.

"I told him he couldn't trust you," said Mr. Kranuski from the corridor. "You just won me fifty bucks."

I turned around, not even surprised. The burly Alton Webb was with him, holding a flashlight. "Why not a million?" I asked. "It's all Monopoly money now. Where's Mr. Cowper?"

Webb roughly grabbed me by the arm, saying, "Come on, we'll take you to him." When I broke his grip and tried to use some of the other techniques I'd learned in self-defense class, he caught me much harder and grunted, "Keep it up and I'll break it."

"Why are you doing this?" I cried in pain. I couldn't believe they were laying hands on me.

"There's been enough child's play on this boat."

Webb dragged me forward to a small round hatch and held me tight while Kranuski opened it up. I knew from my studies that this was the terminal end of the CCSM deck—beyond was hydraulic machinery and then the great sonar dome at the bow. It was cold and dark in there.

"I'll be goddamned if I'm gonna keep up this goddamn charade," Kranuski said. "This vessel is not fit to be at sea, and never was. We dodged a bullet, but it's high time we submitted to military authority instead of trying to train a bunch of jackasses who couldn't get a learner's permit, much less master basic seamanship. Air Force, Navy—what the hell difference does it make at this point? We're here, we made it, it's over."

"Good! I agree with you! So let me go!"

He paid no attention, shoving me through the hole. It opened into a crevasse full of mammoth pumps and the forward main ballast tanks. Above, I could make out the access tunnel to the enclosed sonar sphere. I was standing on a grate above a twenty-foot drop to the bilge, and down there, hog-tied and handcuffed to a pipe in the shadows, was Mr. Cowper.

"Oh my *God*," I said, tears springing to my eyes. "Mr. Cowper!" As Kranuski came in behind me, I yelled, "What are you *doing* to him?"

The old man could see me clearly enough up on my lit perch, but he was gagged and couldn't speak. There was no way to tell if he was hurt. Kranuski left Webb guarding the door and stood next to me, gazing down at Mr. Cowper with a nasty look of disdain. I couldn't believe I had ever found him handsome.

"This is what *happens* when order breaks down," he said. "I'm a Navy officer—this doesn't come easy to me. But I know that once order breaks down it's sometimes necessary to use harsh measures to restore it. Read Clausewitz. I haven't been able to make the commander understand that, and the result has been this ridiculous stalemate."

Without warning, he slapped me so hard I collapsed on

the grating and would have bounced over the edge if he hadn't snatched me back. I was a rag doll, my mind spinning with hurt and confusion. The skin of my cheek felt flayed.

"I don't like this any more than you do," Kranuski said, breathing hard. Was he talking to me or Mr. Cowper? "But I'm not just going to curl up and die. For what? Chivalry? I'm thirty-four. I'm a young man, goddammit! Do you have any idea what it means for me to know this is the last piece of ass I may ever see? Try to look at it from my point of view. All the rules have changed, Cowper—everything's strictly cash and carry from here on out. I'm only human. You want to protect this girl, you have to make it worth my while. A trade. No more bullshit—I know you've got it stashed away somewhere. Even you wouldn't be stupid enough to let something like that be thrown overboard, not when you had to cut through the safe to get it. Just nod and we'll call it quits."

Mr. Cowper's face was turned away. He didn't nod.

Kranuski tore at my clothes, first yanking off the blue coveralls, then the thermal wetsuit pants I was wearing underneath, and finally my T-shirt. It was so cold in there I could see my breath. As he stripped me to gooseflesh he said, "You see this? Look at her! Look what she has to go through because of your stupid power trip. You think you're holding something over our heads? You're crazy! Look!" He ran his free hand down my white torso, kneading my belly. "What is all this leverage buying you? Is it worth it?"

"Stop," I said.

"She says to stop," Kranuski yelled down. To me he said, "It's his own stubbornness, honey-bun. Tell *him* to stop." He couldn't look me in the eye.

"What is it you want?"

"Ask *him*."

He bent me forward over a cold steel bar and smacked my behind. "This is your last chance," he said, voice quaking. "Tell me and it ends now." I heard him open his zipper.

All I could see, bent double, was my pink knees and the clothes around my ankles.

I grimaced in preparation for what was to come, unable to imagine whatever pain it might bring . . . to both me and the helpless old man below. Strangely enough, it was Mr. Cowper I was more worried about. What in the world did they think he had done? Kranuski was taking a long time, really milking the suspense for all it was worth, and somehow this seemed the ultimate cruelty.

"C'mon, pig. If you're going to do it, just do it," I said. "Prove what a big man you are."

The XO wavered another few seconds, then let out his breath and snarled, "God *damn* it!" He closed his pants and clambered away through the hatch. It became very quiet. When nothing happened for a moment, I hurriedly pulled up my clothes and looked out after them, but Kranuski and Webb were nowhere to be seen.

Like a shot, I was down by Mr. Cowper, peeling dark green duct tape off his mouth and trying to lift him out of the freezing bilge water. "Mr. Cowper!" I cried. "Are you okay?"

His skin was colder than mine, and he looked half dead, but he was laughing—a dry husk of a laugh. "Sons a bitches couldn't find Joe Louis in a bowl a rice," he mumbled. "Too afraid a gettin' their feet wet." His eyes lit with a dull flame of recognition. "Lulu, don't show 'em. Use it . . . use it ta save yaself . . ." His voice trailed off.

They had done an incredible job tying him up—I couldn't undo a single knot. *Well duh,* I thought frantically. *Sailors.* And even if I did get the nylon cords off, there were still the handcuffs to contend with.

"Mr. Cowper," I said, "I have to go get help. Just hang on a little longer and I'll be right back!" I pressed his icy, limp hand and started up. My mind was skittering like a pinball thinking of how to free him. The galley seemed like the best bet: all those heavy-duty kitchen tools and Mr. Monte to lend a hand, plus it was closer than—

The lights went out. A velvet cushion of blackness pressed to my face and I groped in limbo for something to cling to. Fortunately I had just cleared the hatch to the goat locker. "Mr. Cowper!" I called down behind me. "The lights just went out up here, but I'm all right. I'm still on my way!" His reply was unintelligible.

Feeling my way forward, I found the wardroom and then the mess. It was strange that there wasn't a soul around. People should have been in full cry about the blackout, but there wasn't a peep from anywhere. I couldn't even smell food cooking, as I should have by this time, and Mr. Monte was not banging around in the galley. "Mr. Monte?" I ventured. "Is there anyone in here?"

From back behind the galley, in the vicinity of the cold storage lockers, I heard something moving. It was an animal sound, furtive and fast, loping forward in a stop-and-go pattern as if searching every inch. As the sounds drew near I could tell there were others behind the leader . . . all hunting.

Not knowing what else to do, I querulously said, "Hello?"

There was no answer. Now I became very unnerved, feeling a queasy sense of déjà vu. Having needlessly panicked once before, I was holding myself in check, but all my instincts screamed, *Xombies!* It was the only possible explanation—Xombies were loose on the boat. And if that was true, I was a goner.

They came through the galley and into the big enlisted mess, padding silently between tables toward me. I held absolutely still, waiting for them to charge. Several of them skirted right by me, so close I could feel the breeze, but they didn't pounce. Instead they heedlessly continued on into the wardroom as if they had missed me in the dark. I found this hard to believe—they should have tripped over me at the very least. Maybe I *was* immune! Then the last one stopped in front of me, panting.

An arm's length away, a man's voice said, "You're not

a Xombie." He flicked on a flashlight just long enough for me to see that he was some kind of commando, with infrared goggles, a catcher's mask over a black ski mask, body armor, and more artillery than Pancho Villa. He also had a dog by his side, a big wolf-like animal with its own night-vision rig and little booties.

"Who are you?" I burst out. "What's going on? Where is everyone?"

"We're just here to secure the boat. Your friends are being looked after up top, which is where you should be. Where are the Xombies?"

"I don't know! What Xombies?"

"I was told we'd be plastering a couple of Xombies down here, but the dogs aren't picking up a thing."

"There's only me and an old man forward who needs help."

The man paused, listening to something from his earpiece. He nodded, visibly relaxing. "Roger that." To me he said, "Okay, don't worry. False alarm. Here, take my arm."

I felt for his sleeve and he gently led me up to the next level, where a group of men were standing around a table in red half-light. They were not our people, but Webb was there, quietly going over diagrams of the ship with them. They all had the same ninja getup as the one who brought me. When Webb spotted me emerging from the companionway he said, "She's the one." He looked disgusted to see me alive.

"Put her with the others," ordered one of the strangers.

"What's going on?" I demanded.

The man with me said, "Just a security sweep. It's for your protection."

"There's a man tied up down there who needs medical attention," I shouted accusingly. "They've been torturing him!"

"We'll take care of it," said my escort. None of them was perturbed in the slightest, or even paid attention to me.

As I was led upstairs, all I could think was, *For our protection, huh? That must be why I feel so safe.*

Everyone from the sub was gathered on the first level, either in crisp Navy dress or looking festive in fashions plundered from the cruise ship. They had bags and suitcases, and were filing up the sail with the eagerness of disembarking tourists, as if being rousted by armed men with dogs was the most natural thing in the world; a welcome taste of civilization. It was not a melancholy leave-taking by any means. I suppose I would have felt the same way if not for what had just happened. My jaw ached.

Hector waved me over. He was wearing a full-length fur coat and looked like a hepcat from the Roaring '20s. "Lulu!" he called. "Where have you been?" Then, studying my swelling cheek, "Holy crap, what happened?"

"Nothing." It wasn't the time; there was too much else going on, and too much I didn't understand . . . yet. "I bumped it. I'm fine. What's everybody doing?"

Unable to take his eyes off my cheek, he said, "We're going ashore! I guess it's over. I can't even believe it."

"Since when? Did Captain Coombs authorize this?"

"Well *yeah,* I guess. Be pretty funny if Kranuski was doing all this on his own initiative."

"Hilarious."

He looked at my poopie suit. "Why aren't you dressed? You can't go out in that."

"I haven't had a chance."

"Here—take this." He opened his dufflebag and pulled out a hooded fur cape. I never liked fur, but this was a dazzling thing: glossy reddish-gold, absurdly luxuriant. It drew appreciative glances from the guys standing nearby—except for Julian, who smirked and looked away.

I had to shake my head. "Where'd you get this?"

"Where do you think? Put it on."

"Don't you know fur is murder?" But I slipped it on, wrapping myself in its plush folds and hugging it against me. It soothed my aching jaw. "Oh my gosh," I said. "Hector, this is ridiculous."

"Keep it," he said, grinning.

As we emerged from the sail, we were helped down onto the ice by briskly smiling greeters, men who handed us blankets and hot coffee off a truck, then loaded us aboard several old blue Air Force buses. A tanklike vehicle with a massive roller had made a smooth white highway to shore. The three hovercraft had also returned, but these were apparently reserved for our officers and the Thule people themselves, who were clearly shocked to see so many civilians and minors—the more of us that poured forth, the more their smiles assumed a drawn-on falsity. I heard one say, "Where's the crew?"

Taking our seats, we could see them bringing out Mr. Cowper on a stretcher and hustling him to a hovercraft. Everyone on the bus was very interested, trying to figure out who it might be.

"It's Fred Cowper," I said. They all looked at me.

Mr. Albemarle broke the hush, patting me on the shoulder and saying, "He's in good hands now, I'm sure." It was the first kind thing he had ever said to me.

A few rows back, I heard Mr. Noteiro squawk, "Say, look." He was directing our attention to an approaching truck that was laying electric cable off a huge spool. "Dey ain't wastin' no time. Dey're awready gonna tap da boat's power."

Someone said, "So?"

"So why buy da cow when you can get da milk fa free?"

We didn't see the whole operation. When we pulled out, most of the Navy crew were out on the ice trying to supervise the swelling ranks of unidentified shore personnel tramping into their vessel. Executive Officer Kranuski was there—the creep—vainly struggling to keep order, but as we pulled away it became impossible to tell our people from theirs. All were hooded silhouettes puffing phosphor—ice-age hunters quarreling over a carcass.

"Hey," shouted Jake from up front. "One hundred bottles of beer on the wall, one hundred bottles of beer—"

Groaning at first, we all sang along. It was sort of nice.

THERE WAS A twenty-minute uphill drive to our new quarters. I don't know what kind of reception we were expecting, but it was a bit strange how we were ushered off the buses and simply left standing before a cluster of empty buildings in the middle of nowhere. We couldn't even ask the drivers anything, because they didn't speak English— all were stony-faced Inuit, intent mainly on leaving.

The buildings themselves were unremarkable in the worst sense of the word: three-story cinderblock structures resembling bad public housing, as deserted and forlorn on that midnight tundra as sacrificial structures erected for A-bomb testing.

"Welcome to Siberia," someone said.

"All right, this way!" shouted Albemarle, taking charge. "This way, people!" He led us up a freshly plowed walk to the front door of the nearest unit. The door was ajar, and looked like it had been kicked in.

Beside me, Shawn Dickey said sourly, "Slammin', dude. It's a crackhouse."

"Long as it's warm," said Cole. "I ain't handlin' this cold."

"How can it be warm when the door's wide open?"

"They probably just left it open while they're getting it ready for us," ventured Julian. "There's probably guys working in there."

"Yeah, they're restocking the minibar," said Jake.

Mr. Albemarle found the light switch, and we all piled in. Julian was wrong; there was no one here, and hadn't been in a long time. In the unwholesome light of buzzing fluorescents, we trooped down a corridor between rows of seedy, decrepit hotel rooms, ugly as a skid row flophouse, saturated with the stink of ancient cigarettes and mildew. The communal bathrooms, kitchen, and TV room were all badly in need of painting and repairs, not to mention a good cleaning. The pipes were frozen, so there was no water.

"This *sucks,* man," said Shawn.

Jake replied, "Oh, you never like anything."

"Shut up, all of you," said Albemarle. "Now here's the thing: Obviously there's a lot that needs to be done to make this place livable, but at least it's shelter. I'm sure our hosts will be arriving shortly to address all our concerns. In the meantime, there's plenty we can do to make ourselves more comfortable, starting with finding the heat, but we can't do it if you're blocking the hall like this. I want you to go to the upper floors and set up quarters for yourselves while the men and I establish a base of operations here. Don't fool with anything mechanical until we know it won't cause a fire or a flood. Other than that, get cracking."

Since we were under the impression that all would soon be sorted out, we gave ourselves over to exploring the building and staking out beds. Combing the place for useful items, we found a lot of moldy bedding and aluminum cookware, but nothing in the way of food. A few people braved the vicious cold, going from building to building in deep snow, but every door was padlocked and appeared condemned; there was nothing to be found. After all our work loading the submarine with months of supplies, it was disheartening to find ourselves in such a state.

"They better be letting us loose in the commissary," said Julian.

"Hey, survival of the fittest," I told him.

One thing that helped keep our spirits up was the casual competence and cheer of the four Blackpudlians. The routines they had developed on the ocean liner seemed particularly well-suited to our present predicament, and it wasn't long before they had ice melting in a pot for tea, which they had brought in quantity. When we praised their foresight, they shrugged, and the one named Phil said, "Knowin' you blokes, we couldn't be sure of a good cuppa, could we?"

"Just isn't the same, coffee," said Wally.

"Oh, coffee wouldn't do," said Reggie. "Wouldn't do at all."

"Unless it was Irish coffee," Dick said, and they all laughed.

Thus we were kept busy for several hours, doing our best to create decent quarters as rusty electric heaters slowly took the sting from the air. Eventually there was nothing more to do and we settled in to wait.

No one came.

ONE BY ONE and room by room we all fell asleep. Late into the night I woke up under the excruciating fluorescents and had to go to the bathroom. The toilets weren't defrosted, but there were buckets and a window to dump them from. My pee steamed as if boiling hot. Finishing up as quickly as possible, I went to leave and found Hector waiting at the restroom door.

"Oh. Hi," I said, startled.

"Hi," he whispered. He looked very sad. "Can I talk to you?"

"Sure. Come in here so we don't disturb anybody." I stepped aside for him and closed the door, muting the snores beyond. "Are you all right?"

"No."

"What's wrong?"

"I've been thinking too much . . . about everything. On the boat I didn't really think, and for some reason I thought that meant I was okay. But I'm not okay, Lulu. I can't go on like this. There's nothing left, and I don't think I can keep pretending there is."

"But there is," I said. "There's life. You're alive."

"I don't feel alive. I feel like one of those *things* we left behind, like I'm walking around dead and just don't know it." He sat against the sink and began to cry, saying, "God, I'm so lonely."

I reached out and stroked his hair. "Hey, hey," I said. "It's okay. We all feel that way, which means none of us is alone."

He wept for a little while, holding the edge of my fur cape. "It's so soft," he sniffed.

"Yours, too," I said, touching his coat. Its metallic black fur shimmered in the light. "I never really handled real fur before."

"No?" He seemed to brighten a little. "Oh my God, I love fur. I always wanted to have a costume made out of real fur."

I had to laugh. "Like Safety Squirrel?"

"Yeah, except the real thing." He caressed my shoulder. "You're not going to believe this, but that's what I used to do when I was depressed: put on a furry costume and pretend I was something else. When my real dad died last year it was the only thing that took me out of my grief. It's hard to describe, and maybe it sounds funny, but it's not a joke. It's a release I don't know if I can live without. Especially now."

"Hector," I said, suddenly sad for him, "we've all had to give up a lot. But we're going to survive."

He hung his head, unmoved by my platitudes. I put my arms around him and crushed him against me, drowning us both in fur. For a second he recoiled, then he clutched me to him, convulsing with emotion. I cried, too. After a moment we relaxed, heaving, and he looked at me searchingly. "God, you're beautiful," he said.

"No, I'm not. If anything I'm weird looking."

He chuckled softly. "No you're not. Here, I'll show you." He took something from his pocket: a stub of grease pencil.

"What are you doing?" I said, leaning away.

"Don't worry," he said, backing off. "I won't bite."

"What's that for?"

"Just a little touch-up. It'll come right off." He made a curlicue in the air. "I wouldn't do anything to embarrass you, Lulu. Ever."

"Okay . . . just watch the cheek." I submitted while he made some marks on my face. It felt strange to have his face right in mine as he drew, so that I could study the tortoiseshell brown of his eyes, his every tiny mole. The pressure of the pencil and his baked-bread smell caused a ticklish heat to spread through my body. Without thinking about it, I leaned that extra few inches and kissed him.

He broke off before I did, leaning back with a grin to inspect his handiwork. Then he got up off the sink and stood me in front of the mirror. In the smeared reflection I could see a striking cat-girl, oval face framed in a fur hood, with black-tipped nose and whiskers. It was not a tragic face. It was a face that belonged to a whimsical world free of the shitty buckets and cold that defined this one. I nodded, eyes welling with tears again.

"I like it," I said.

twenty

"THIS IS BULLSHIT," said Mr. Monte the next day. It had been twenty hours since we'd been dropped off. "We don't have a clue when they're comin' back, and they've stranded us out here with nothin'. Meanwhile we've left them a boatload of supplies fit for a king. It ain't right."

Everyone was awake now, though it was as dark as ever. We had shared out whatever candy and snacks people had brought, and once more the Brits had made tea, but once this meager breakfast was over we were all restless. We weren't accustomed to having free time. There was nothing to do except listen to the men argue downstairs.

Albemarle was trying to remain positive: "Hey, we have heat, we have lights. We have water. If you think about it, it hasn't really been that long—"

"Those friggin' utilities are electric-powered," said Monte. "They're only givin' us back a little bit of what they're gettin' in spades from the boat's reactor. It's our own juice! They ain't doin' us no favors."

"And where's the CO? Where's Coombs?" demanded Gus DeLuca. "What the hell are they thinking, cutting us off like this? Now we're just fuckin' civilians again, is that it? After we been covering their asses all this time? I'm sorry, but we've earned the right to *at least* know what's goin' on. At *least*. I'll tell you what: I'm about ready to go and ask. They don't want to come to us? Fuck 'em, we'll go to them."

Mr. DeLuca's idea resonated with the frustrated men, and soon snowballed into a plan: if four more hours went by with no word, a mini-expedition would be sent out to find Thule's headquarters. It wasn't expected to be far away, just a matter of following the packed-down road taken by the buses. At the very least we could walk back to the sub.

I say "we" because I was part of the plan. When I heard what was being discussed, I piped up, "Excuse me, but I'd like to volunteer to go." Before they could dismiss me out of hand, I said, "It'll be harder for them to turn you away if you have suffering children with you. Believe me, I know— my mother used me as a weapon all the time. People get self-conscious about their behavior when kids are around. They're afraid of looking cruel."

"Lulu," Albemarle sighed, "you don't know what you're talking about. This is a military base on highest alert. They're not going to give a shit. Go back upstairs."

I didn't budge. "Well what chance do you think you guys have, then?" I asked.

"Probably nil, but at least they'll have to take notice of us. Even getting arrested would be better than nothing."

"But that's just it," I said. "They can't arrest kids. They're not *prepared* for kids. We're your ace in the hole. Send in a children's crusade and all the bureaucracy falls apart."

"What horseshit," scoffed Albemarle.

"Oh really? Well it got me in the gates of your factory,

Mr. Albemarle. It got me past *you*. Why am I here among you now, when everyone knows women are a plague on mankind?" Suddenly I clasped my hands together and gave them my most yearning, guileless eyes. "Please, sir," I begged weepily. "My daddy is in there. Please let me go see my daddy."

The men looked at me like I was a monster. But they knew I was right.

COLD OR NOT, it was good to be out doing something. There were nine of us: Mr. DeLuca, Mr. Albemarle, me, and all the boys I knew best—Hector, Julian, Jake, Shawn, Cole, and Lemuel. This time they wanted to go with me. We followed the road across broad snowfields, with dark blue hills on one side and an endless sloping plain on the other. Somewhere down there it became the frozen sea, but it was impossible to tell where.

As we walked, the two men traded furtive glugs from a pint bottle—part of the swag from the cruise ship—and when we noticed they told us it was "cold medicine."

At one point Lemuel said, "Hey, is that the boat?"

He was right. Far away across the flats we could see specks of light. I felt a strange twinge of loss to see it, and the feeling surprised me. When had I become attached to that submarine? Or maybe it was only the sense of forward motion I was attached to. We all felt something, because the boys stopped heckling each other and became very somber. Shawn recited a strange little poem:

"One bright day in the middle of the night,
Two dead boys got up to fight.
Back to back, they faced each other,
Drew their swords and shot each other.
When the deaf policeman heard this noise,
He came out and shot the two dead boys."

We came up on more empty barracks, dustbowl home-steads rising from the plains, and then gradually other shuttered structures, one labeled BX and another labeled

USO. Except for a few radio towers and radomes it could have been a deserted frontier town. Wind whistled through the wires.

"What the hell's going on here?" Mr. DeLuca said. "Is this the goddamn base or isn't it?"

Albemarle replied, "They're around here somewhere. Look!" He pointed out a thin curl of smoke rising from one of the buildings set back from the main street. There were two snowmobiles with little trailers parked by the entrance. "Now we're getting somewhere."

"Those LCACs we saw didn't come from there, Ed. We're missing something."

"One thing at a time."

We wallowed through the snow to the glass doors and went inside. There was a kind of airlock to preserve warmth, and on the other side of that a pile of broken furniture heaped to the ceiling. It was warm in there, and the woodsmoke was so thick it was almost overpowering. Yellow firelight flickered through hundreds of tiny windows that covered the inner walls—they were mailboxes. There was muted conversation coming from behind them.

"It's the APO," whispered Albemarle. "The base post office."

"No shit," said DeLuca.

A sooty canvas flap covered the opening to the sorting area. Very cautiously, Albemarle lifted it and we all peeked inside. "Jesus," he whispered.

In the middle of the floor there was a makeshift stove fashioned from heating ducts, and a group of Inuit men camped around it. In the firelight they looked incredibly primitive; hunter-gatherers from some prehistoric age. They were toasting Pop-Tarts. When they saw us, I felt a thrill of fear, not knowing what they might do.

It was not much. Most of them glanced our way and went back to their own business. Only one got to his feet and came over, looking us up and down with a jaded air. It wasn't that we weren't strange—it was that he had seen it all.

"Do you speak English?" asked Albemarle. "Any of you?"

The man said something using the word "English," but he clearly didn't speak it. His consonant-rich native language—every other syllable ending in *uk* or *ak* or *ik*—was impenetrable. He was trying to incorporate foreign words for our benefit, but none of them were English. Several times he repeated, *"Hvor kommer du fra?"*

"Is that Danish?" Albemarle asked.

"I wouldn't know," replied DeLuca. "Now if it was Italian."

Enunciating clearly, Albemarle asked the man, "Where air base? Air base—Thule? Where white men?" He flew his hand through the air like a little plane, with sound effects.

"Smoke-um peace pipe," Jake said in my ear. Lemuel slugged him.

One of the men at the fire said something that sounded like *kapluna,* and all the Inuit laughed. The one who was speaking to us led us outside and pointed in the direction we'd been heading.

"Valhalla," he said. *"Air base."*

"The base is that way?" said Albemarle. "How far?" He waggled his fingers like tiny legs. "Close enough to walk?"

The man made a chopping motion with his arm and repeated, *"Valhalla."* It seemed to suggest that we were coming to the end.

"That's good enough for me," said Mr. DeLuca. "Let's go. I gotta get my blood circulating."

We thanked the man as best we could and went on our way. Shawn complained, "Shoulda taken those snowmobiles."

"Oh, that'd be good," I replied. "Let's see if we can get ourselves killed by the natives."

"What do you mean 'we,' paleface?" said Lemuel.

It wasn't far. Looming up before us at the far edge of town was a wall of plowed snow at least twenty feet high. Its crest mimicked the horizon in the dark, or we would have noticed it much sooner. There was no telling where it ended on either side—it snaked across the land like the Great Wall of China—but straight ahead of us we could see a fenced gap where the road passed through.

"That's one big-ass pile of snow," remarked Cole.

We ventured up to the base of the thing, abashed by our relative puniness. There were no sentries at the gate, no signs, but also no way through. We could see cleared ground on the other side, but nothing beyond that because of an inner mound blocking the view. We could hear something, though: faint sounds of machinery—churning diesels and the high silvery whine of turbines. It sounded like an airport, and a moment later it looked like one as the sound reached a high pitch and we practically had to duck for a chunky gray cargo plane that climbed screaming into the sky right over us, fat wheels dangling like curled talons.

"That's it," said DeLuca, eagerly rubbing his hands. "That's definitely it. Now we just need to let them know we're here."

Albemarle pulled out the megaphone he had used at the ship. Instead of using it himself, however, he handed it to me, saying, "Let 'er rip, Little Orphan Annie."

"Oh," I said. The scarf covering my face was a frozen caul, and I had to peel it off. "Okay . . . uh: GREETINGS, THULE AIR BASE. UM, I'M LOUISE PANGLOSS— FROM THE BIG SUBMARINE?—AND I'M HERE BE-CAUSE WE'VE BEEN LEFT ALONE SO LONG WE GOT SCARED YOU MIGHT HAVE FORGOTTEN ABOUT US. WE'RE COLD AND HUNGRY AND ARE WONDERING WHAT IS HAPPENING WITH THE CREW AND COMMANDER COOMBS . . . AND ALSO MY FATHER, FRED COWPER. HE WAS VERY SICK WHEN I LAST SAW HIM. WE HAVE WALKED A LONG WAY AND ARE VERY, VERY TIRED. PLEASE LET US IN. PLEASE HELP."

Mr. Albemarle looked at me approvingly. "Well, if that don't do it, nothing will."

We waited a long time, but there was no sign of activity. They directed me to try again, and keep trying every few minutes, but halfway through my second plea the megaphone died.

"Batteries maybe," Albemarle said after examining the thing. "Or maybe the cold. We can try to warm it up a little and see."

DeLuca erupted, "Fuck that. I'd like to get noticed before my toes turn black and fall off, if it's okay with you. They obviously can't hear that thing. What I propose to do is scale the wall and have a look-see, maybe signal them by flashlight. Shoulda done that in the first place." Without waiting for approval, he climbed the roadside embankment and plunged into deep snow, making for the barrier.

Albemarle watched him for a minute, then shrugged and said to us, "What are you waitin' for? You heard the man." We all followed behind.

It was hard going. The snow was tart-like, its icy crust just barely too weak to support a person's full weight, so that every step ended in a plunge and a battle to break free. I kept losing my boots. In the time it took us to slog over, Mr. DeLuca was halfway to the top, working his way up a heap of rubble at the base of the wall. The bottom was steep, imprinted with a bulldozer's curved blade, but it had collapsed in places and windblown snow had formed deep drifts that rose high up the sides. He was using one of these as an awkward ramp.

"Could stand to have . . . some snowshoes," he grunted.

"You're okay," said Albemarle from below. "You're almost there." He was heftier and less agile than DeLuca, and he was treading the snow as if stomping grapes, trying to beat down a path. Suddenly he struck something underfoot and absently aimed his flashlight there. He stopped moving.

"What?" said Hector.

Albemarle slowly bent down and prized a large crooked object from the snow, holding it before the light.

It was a human arm gripping a .45 automatic pistol.

Rock-solid and perfectly preserved in its stiff glove and fur-lined sleeve, it looked like a limb from a mannequin. As we approached in sickly wonderment, Albemarle handed off the disturbing relic to his stepson and hunkered back down in the glowing scrape, his underlit face ghoulish as a grave robber's. Hector took the arm as a matter of pure reflex, then didn't know what to do with it.

The snow was full of bodies . . . or rather parts of bodies, tangled and bound together in the ice like freezer leftovers. Crablike hands and hairy heads and torsos and boot soles and pink-boned stumps all glistened underfoot. Everywhere we stepped there was more. I suppose I shouldn't have been surprised at how calm we all were, considering how much we'd been through already.

"Gus!" Albemarle called, holding a tiny silver leaf pin up to the light. "Get down here!"

Mr. DeLuca had reached the top and was oblivious to what was happening with us—something on the far side of the berm had his complete attention. "Sweet Jesus," he said in awe.

"Gus! Gus, you gotta see this!"

Shaking his head, Deluca said, "No, Ed, you gotta see *this*."

"There's a bunch of dead airmen down here."

"What?"

"A bunch of dead men under the snow!" He took the arm back from Hector and waved it in the air. "Look!"

DeLuca switched on his flashlight and shined it down. At that second there was a loud *ZAP!* and the flashlight tumbled down the slope, its bulb gone red. Other, larger objects were also tumbling, but Gus DeLuca himself was nowhere to be seen. I blinked, not sure what had just happened.

Mr. Albemarle flicked his beam up the wall, then immediately turned it off and shouted, "Everyone back! Back the way we came, fast! *Run!*" We all saw what he had seen, what was left of Mr. DeLuca, and we did not hesitate.

Running in that deep snow was exactly the same as trying to run in a dream. You lunge forward as hard as you
can, but your feet have no purchase and a maddening, dull
force holds you back. It seems as if you are actually going
slower than you would by walking. Our short sprint back to
the road was a Sisyphean ordeal, and just as we were reaching its hard-frozen shoulder, we realized it was no use anyway. The fence flew open and a blue schoolbus rolled out,
wheezing to a stop before our frozen noses. They had us.

"Everyone get behind me," Albemarle said, out of
breath.

The door opened on a jolly Inuit waving us in. He was
wearing a top hat. There was no one else on board.

"What the fuck, man?" wailed Shawn. "Why'd you assholes have to kill him? You didn't have to kill him!" The
driver's bronze Asiatic face was cheerily befuddled, un-
comprehending. He seemed to have no idea what was going on.

Mr. Albemarle raggedly told us to get on the bus, and
what else was there to do? We trooped in like a work-gang
fresh from the gulag, collapsing into the front rows. I think
we were more resigned than horrified. Personally, I was
grateful for the ride, even if we were just going to be returned to our doomed ghetto. And as the bus began to
move, it did take us back the way we had come . . . for a
moment. Then the driver found a wide enough spot in the
road to turn around. Shortly we returned to the gate and
passed through with impunity, not that we cared.

In a low, cracked voice, Jake sang, "Eighty-eight bottles
of beer on the wall . . ." then trailed off.

Out the windows we could see what Mr. DeLuca saw.

twenty-one

IT WAS AN airplane city, a City of the Planes, so crowded it was more rookery than airport, with hundreds of jumbo and lesser jets making up a dense belt—a great thorny briar of silver fins and fuselages—surrounding a many-lobed dome complex of such incredible size that at first glance I thought it was a glacier.

"Mr. Albemarle," I said as we hurtled toward it, "have you ever seen anything like this?"

He spoke as if roused from a trance. "No. No . . . I don't know what this is. Whatever it is, it's not what's supposed to be here. It's not like any kind of air base I've ever seen. I don't know what the hell it is."

"Mr. Cowper said it would be a ghost town."

"Well . . . it's a boom town now."

"Looks like an aviation junkyard," said Julian. "You know, a graveyard, like where elephants go to die."

"Graveyard my ass," said Cole. "These motherfuckers are livin' large."

He was right—as tangled up as they appeared, all the jets were draped like racehorses, warm and well cared for. We rolled down a boulevard surrounded by pristine aircraft of every type, from hulking 747s to sleek baby Lears, each one a giant aluminum flower in a precise arrangement. Far from being abandoned to the elements, these aircraft were *occupied*. Like RVs in a trailer park, they were hooked up to utilities, their bright oval windows aglow with toasty domesticity. Watching us pass from those windows were carefree men in bathrobes!

"Goddamn Happy Acres," said Mr. Albemarle.

Amid the cozy fleet was a network of tent workshops and support equipment that was a village unto itself, populated by the breed of men who still had to labor in the cold. This was the essence of civilization, the haves and the have-nots, and it made me realize I'd been such a fool. Such a stupid little girl—what had I been thinking? That we had inherited the world? That we could demand some kind of justice? It was funny, really, my pathetic disappointment at having to accept a smaller role in the scheme of things. I had never seen it coming. Stupid me.

Alongside the trucks and tractors, I could see a number of dogsleds, and for some reason this was comforting to me. The dogs didn't care. I looked at those contented huskies curled up in the snow and thought, *It's just the way it is.*

THE BUS PULLED into a covered area full of other vehicles. Hot-air blowers were running, and it was slightly less freezing than outside. Our bearlike Inuit driver got out and waved us after him, sauntering down an aisle between repair bays. There weren't any other people around, and I had the feeling they had scattered like mice at our approach.

We came to the edge of the motor pool and paused. This

was the inner circle of the compound. Only a bare strip of no-man's land separated us from the gigantic domes in the middle, which rose from the permafrost like an archipelago made up of thousand-foot-wide fungi, with smaller polyps branching off. But if its outward structure was organic, its skeleton was geometric: visible through the milky surface membrane was a hexagonal web of supporting members, fine as capillaries in the human eye, at least from a distance.

"Valhalla," grunted the driver, pointing. "You go."

This was apparently the closest he dared approach.

"I don't like this," said Jake, looking skittish.

"Take it easy. You're okay," said Mr. Albemarle.

Shawn, standing apart, turned on him. "Dude, I *wish* you would stop saying that. Every time you say that, somebody gets wasted."

"Cut it out," said Hector.

"Hey, all I'm sayin' is we're all fucked, and I don't need somebody telling me I'm okay! Unless there's the rave of the century in there, I'm not okay! Unless there's a poetry slam going on under there and they're calling for entries, I'm not okay! Unless there's a phone in there and my moms is on the line telling me my spoken-word CD is in heavy rotation on college stations across the country, I'm not okay! None of us is okay! The only person I know who's probably okay is Tyrell, and that's because he's in fucking Canada! Which is where we should all be!"

"Cut it out," I said miserably. "This isn't helping."

"I'm okay," said Jake.

We left the driver and ventured into the open, heading for a large portal directly across the way. Our perception of distance was off—it took us longer to get there than we expected, and the nearer we got, the more peculiar the whole thing appeared. It was a colossal brood sow with prefabricated structures around its base like feeding piglets.

"What *is* this?" I wondered aloud.

"It's an inflatable building," said Albemarle. "I've heard

of something like this. It's supported by air pressure, so there's no limit to how big it can be."

The entrance we were approaching was certainly a huge thing, a raised loading dock wide enough inside for a dozen semi trailers. It had a modular, impermanent look. As we climbed to the platform and pushed through clear insulating flaps, we could hear elevator music coming from inside: the noodlings of a generic saxophone. It was such a perversely ordinary sound that we were rapt, listening. Then a prerecorded voice-over cut in:

"Welcome to Valhalla. You are now entering a wholly owned subsidiary of the Mogul Cooperative, a transnational partnership dedicated to preserving and restoring the benefits of civilization. But we can't do it without you. When you give your allegiance to MoCo, you are protected by the largest coherent military power in the world today; you are cared for by a Medical Research Division with all the resources of a major hospital—and which alone pursues a cure for Agent X—and you join an organization with branches in over thirty countries, where a network of export professionals tirelessly combs the Earth in search of the Things You Need. Isn't this reason enough to say, 'MoCo Is My Future'?"

Albemarle said, "You've gotta be shittin' me."

Now the tape was turned off and a testy male voice came on, flat as the order-taker at a drive-thru. It said, "We've been informed that one of you was killed at the perimeter wall, and I'd like to offer our very sincere condolences. I'm *afraid* we operate within a very strictly enforced *boundary* here, and our defense system does not distinguish between friend or foe. Without being *forewarned* of your arrival, we had no way of preventing what happened."

"Well, what was the idea of stranding us out there in the goddamn boondocks?" Albemarle shouted to the air.

As if correcting a petulant child, the voice said, "Your people at Thule are being briefed right now, as a matter of fact. If you had only waited at billeting, the tragedy would have been avoided. We were getting to you as quickly as we could. Since you were *provided* with the basic necessities of survival, we didn't think a one-day wait was excessive, certainly not by ordinary bureaucratic standards, and *particularly* in light of the fact that we are dealing here with a worldwide disaster of such *extreme* proportions that the only previous event it can be compared to is the extinction of the *dinosaurs.*"

I have to say this speech made me feel very small, but Albemarle was unfazed. "And what about the remains we found outside?" he said. "Were they impatient, too?"

There was silence from above.

"Oh *man*," muttered Cole. "What'd you have to say that for, man? That shit was not necessary."

Tentatively, the voice said, "If you are *speaking* of the bodies at the perimeter, I can only reiterate that survival dictates everything we do. Those men chose to be billeted outside this compound because they objected to a *legal* transfer of authority that was taking place. They were informed of the risk. At some point the contagion must have appeared among them and they rushed the automatic defenses. It was over before anyone here even knew what was happening. Could you enter the airlock, please?"

There was a pneumatic hiss, and a big door rumbled aside. Inside was a brightly lit room that reminded me of a racquetball court. High in the ceiling was a glass booth, and behind its windows we could make out the man speaking. He was young, clean-shaven, and wore a dark baseball cap. He waved.

"Legal transfer of authority my ass," Albemarle muttered.

"Come on, Ed," Hector hissed at his stepfather. "You're drunk. Save the complaints for later."

"Listen, smart-ass, once we go through that door there may *be* no later. We don't know what they've got waiting for us in there."

"It can't be any worse than what's waiting for us out here."

Annoyed by our hesitation, the man in the booth said, "There's no *danger,* if that's what you're worried about."

"What happens if the building gets a hole in it?" Mr. Albemarle asked. "Does it all go flat?"

"No, but it won't have what we call 'optimal rigidity.' There are helium cells and heated air to provide back-up suspension. A hole would be unlikely anyway. The envelope is an *extremely* robust Vectran composite developed by NASA. But if there was one, it would trigger sensors in the fabric and we'd be right on it. Step inside, please."

"Beautiful," Albemarle grumbled as we went in. The door thundered shut and rubber valves wheezed tight around the frame.

The man said, "You may experience a little discomfort as the pressure equalizes."

Warm air came rushing in through vents as if blow-drying us. It pressed on our ears and sinuses, some more than others. Hector and Lemuel winced, but for me it was no worse than being stuffed up from a cold. The breeze slackened . . . then stopped. We waited for the inner door to open, but it remained sealed.

Albemarle asked, "What now?"

"Now comes the trickiest part." Electric motors came on, driving a grappling system that ran on tracks in the ceiling. I realized the glass booth was the crane cockpit. Suspended from cables was a metal box, a freight car, and this now began slowly descending to the floor. When it touched down the man said, "Go inside and leave your clothes in the container to be sterilized."

"What are we gonna wear in the meantime?"

"Nothing, until you go through decon. It's standard procedure for all newcomers: decontamination, health screening, and civic preparation. Nothing too *complicated,* I assure you."

Albemarle opened the sliding door. Inside was a chamber

containing a large empty bin with a biohazard symbol stenciled on it, then a narrow tunnel to a second chamber at the opposite end. There were cartoon instructions all along the way. "Nothing like a little privacy," he said. "What's *she* s'posed to do?"

"I'm all right," I said. "It's no big deal." I had survived so much already it just seemed absurd to quibble about nudity. This was a first for me, because I had always been so paranoid about my body.

As long as they knew I was all right with it, no one else had any objections. We went in and stripped off all our soaked clothes, everyone doing their best not to look at anything or even say anything. The door had closed on its own and we discovered that it didn't open from the inside.

"Well, we're locked in," said Julian, covering his privates.

Mr. Albemarle stepped into the tunnel. Without warning, a torrent of hot spray blasted him from all sides. "It's all right!" he shouted back. "Come on!"

Single file, we all followed, whooping like baboons at the force and heat of the spray, as well as the strong chemical smell. But it wasn't exactly unpleasant. In fact, once our bodies adjusted to the pain it became cathartic ecstasy, scouring our grief away along with whatever hapless microbes we carried. Foam and billowing steam made it hard to move forward without bumping into other slippery bodies, but after a few minutes we stopped troubling over it and just gave in to the stinging peace.

The shower went on for a long time, or maybe just seemed to compared with the half-minute spritzes I'd become accustomed to on the boat. There were several stages in the process, including a final one in which we donned dark goggles and were baked with bright light. By that point I was almost serene, though without the noise and lashing spray it was a little bit awkward to be standing there nude with all those boys and hairy old Mr. Albemarle.

There was a jarring vibration and we all had to steady ourselves as the whole room rose in the air.

Amid alarmed complaints, Jake said, "Elevator goin' up."

It stopped, then began gliding sideways. After a few seconds it shut down and stayed still. We could hear sounds of a heavy door being unlatched and thrown back, but it wasn't our door.

"Is it safe to come out?" Albemarle bellowed. He tried the door and found it unlocked. Instead of a thirty-foot drop to the floor, there was a room on the other side. "Well whattaya know," he said.

It was a dressing room lined with racks of clothing and towels. All the clothes were like hospital scrubs: loose drawstring pants and baggy blouses, with only cloth booties to wear on our feet. Everything was white or off-white. It was very comfortable stuff, and I was especially glad to put it on because I kept catching the guys sneaking tortured looks at me through the mirrors. A couple of them—Lemuel and, of all people, Julian—were having trouble controlling their bodily reactions, and were at great pains to conceal it. I wished I could have told them it was all right, but thought that would only make things worse.

When the eight of us were dressed, Cole said, "Look like a damn karate class."

"Or kendo," Jake said, smirking at Lemuel and Julian. "What was that about 'optimal rigidity'?"

There were four doorways off the changing room: The first opened onto a gleaming-clean institutional bathroom, of which we all availed ourselves; the second was locked; and the third led to a large dormitory with forty or fifty freshly made-up cots—a paradise of crisp cotton sheets and soft pillows. The motherly smell of clean linen actually brought tears to my eyes.

Albemarle interrupted the bliss. "Don't anybody get any ideas. Nobody hits the sack until I get some answers."

We dragged ourselves away, checking out the fourth door. It opened onto a sight even more welcome than a bedroom: a banquet hall. Dozens of tables stood folded against the walls, leaving the floor empty except for a single table and eight chairs. There were also eight glasses of orange juice, eight huge cheeseburgers with french fries, eight bowls of vegetable soup, eight bars of Swiss chocolate, and eight plastic binders.

Each binder had a note on it which said, *Welcome, new Citizen of Valhalla, Official Headquarters of MoCo. Our regulations require a 24-hour period of observation and quarantine before you may begin the orientation phase of your citizenship. Enjoy the opportunity to relax and begin familiarizing yourself with the duties and privileges afforded you as a Citizen of Valhalla MoCo. Thank you!* The binders contained handbooks full of propaganda and corporate jargon.

"Listen to this," Julian said as we sat down. " 'Company History: Mogul Cooperative was founded over twenty years ago by an international group of visionary business leaders from many different fields who shared a single goal: to provide safe haven from worldly cycles of boom and bust. These men's investment in the future has made possible the comfort and security—perhaps the very existence—that you now enjoy. Since its humble beginnings as a gerontology institute led by Nobel Laureate Dr. Uri Miska, MoCo has become a country unto itself; a borderless nation-state with no single language, culture, or religion, but with an unswerving commitment to long-term prosperity and growth. MoCo employs corporate principles of efficiency to meet the ever-changing demands of today's world . . . and tomorrow's.' "

"What crap," Albemarle said, mouth full.

"What's gerontology?" asked Cole.

"Aging," I said. "The science of aging."

None of us could be bothered to think about it just now—we were too busy digging in.

"Mr. Albemarle," I said, as we drowsily contemplated our full bellies. "One thing is bugging me. I was on the bridge when Captain Coombs and the rest of the shore party met the representatives from the base. There was some Air Force colonel there, or at least that's what he said he was. Lowenthal. He didn't say anything about Valhalla or this corporate-sounding deal they've got going here."

"Yeah, I don't know," replied Albemarle. "There's definitely been a major regime-change around here since the commander got his orders. The old bait-and-switch. They got the boat and we get hamburgers."

Julian asked, "But why keep us on at all? What good are we to them?"

"I think manpower has become the second most valuable commodity in the world today," said Albemarle. "Think about it: You can't be a ruler without subjects to rule. To keep a show like this running you need workers, lots of 'em, and we're in short supply."

"What's the first most valuable?" I asked.

"Women," he said.

Ouch. Why it should have been a rude awakening, I don't know. You would think it was so obvious. But I suddenly realized we weren't all sitting at the same table. It wasn't the same table at all. Theirs was cozy and safe—a complacent Boy Scout luncheon—while I was seated off by myself in the bitter cold, segregated, awaiting male whims. It wasn't their fault, but it made me mad. Before any of them could offer some threadbare reassurance, I snapped, "Yeah right," and kept eating.

As we sat there digesting, we all began to droop. It was so quiet and warm, and it had been a long day—a long month. Almost falling out of my seat at one point, I asked permission to go to bed. Albemarle nodded and made a groggy announcement to the effect that we were all badly in need of rest and should turn in. He himself would stand watch for a few hours, and then awaken some of us to take over. I felt terrible for him—he looked half asleep already—but I was too tired to argue. That cool, cool pillow beckoned. I don't even remember falling into it.

We were drugged, of course. It made for a long, peculiar sleep, full of strange aches and proddings, as if someone wouldn't leave me alone to rest but kept pecking at my face, giving me a headache. At first I fled the intrusive glare of consciousness, then began fighting toward it, painstakingly clawing upward through the dense narcotic membrane like a baby turtle hatching from its buried shell until finally I could feel my body twisting against cloth restraints. I was tied to a wheelchair.

"Hey, shhh," someone said gently. "Just relax, Louise."

It was a woman's voice.

twenty-two

"WHO ARE YOU?" I asked plaintively, trying to focus. I had the strange sensation that we were outdoors. "Untie me . . ."

"I'm Doctor Langhorne—Alice. I'm supervising your treatment. The restraints are only so you wouldn't hurt yourself, *shhh*. When you're completely alert we'll take them right off."

Her voice was cool and smart, with a slight rasp from hard use. She was out of my view; all I could see was a colorful blur like a city on a summer night. I knew this couldn't be, but as my vision sharpened, it only seemed more and more like a city.

"Where are the others? Where am I?"

"You're in a place we call 'The Global Village.' "

It all gelled. I really was on a platform overlooking a city, or rather a theme-park replica of a city; a sprawling assemblage of all the world's great capitals, identified by their dominant icons: the Eiffel Tower, Big Ben, the Coliseum, the Statue of Liberty, and many more. All the world under one roof. And it *was* a roof, an inflatable dome, in spite of the sparkles and cobalt-blue lighting that suggested sky. The buildings, too, were balloons, not solid masonry at all but illuminated tapestries like enormous kites. Amid this elaborate stage setting I could see real people moving about with the cheerful deliberation of retirees at a swap-meet. There were women and little girls among them—only the old and young; nothing in-between. No one like me.

"What is this?" I asked, voice cracking.

"Isn't it *fabulous?*" There was sarcasm in her tone. "Welcome to the Vegas of the North."

"Vegas?"

"That's what it was intended to be: Nunavut International—the world's biggest casino. Commandeered and delivered here by the happy minions of MoCo."

"How did all these people survive?"

"They're friends, family, valued employees, and honored guests of Mogul."

"What does that mean?"

The doctor leaned down beside me so I could see her. She was a strikingly tall older woman with a pink complexion and a flaxen flat-top, an aging Amazon uncowed by time. Around her forehead was a hammered gold band with a silver bauble.

Her green eyes bored into mine as she said, "Mogul is an old-boy's club; a group of very powerful men who pooled their resources to bring all this here, and they call the shots—that's all there is to it. We couldn't exist without them. But most of them don't feel comfortable in here, rubbing elbows with the commoners, so they delegate from their planes outside. If they want something, we jump, but otherwise we're on our own. You do what's expected and nobody bothers you."

"But this is incredible. All these *people* . . ." I could see little kids playing jump-rope. For a minute I was too over-whelmed to speak.

"Yes, it looks like a carnival," said Langhorne, "but it isn't. Some folks think they've died and gone to Disneyland, but it's a far cry from that, I can assure you. It's survival of the fittest around here, and you have to be very careful whose toes you step on. Mogul executives and family members are top of the heap; below that it's a free-for-all for power and privilege. I should tell you that as a teenage girl you already have enemies here. You're a threat."

"But I can't get Agent X. I have a problem with my—"

She cut me off. "That's not what I mean. You're a *sexual* threat. A lot of power here comes from sexual patronage, and some of these dames can be very jealous of the attention of their Mogul patrons, especially if they're married to them. They've gotten to like being queen of the roost, and won't appreciate competing against a teeny bopper like you—not again. They thought those days were over."

"I would never—"

"And *speaking* of Agent X, you *can* get it, I'm sorry to have to tell you. That's what I really need to talk to you about, Louise. We have been able to eliminate the risk of infection in here only through some very stringent safety protocols. It can be startling to a newcomer, but it is essential to our survival—and yours." She unclasped her headband. The gold part came away, leaving the teardrop-shaped metal knob stuck in the middle of her forehead. It had tiny rivets in it.

"What's that?" I said, recoiling.

"Don't let it scare you. It may look weird, but it's nothing more than a simple electrode and a GPS transceiver. It monitors basic life signs and triggers a security alert if your blood-oxygen level takes a dive. It's only because of these little devices that we can live together here without fear."

I suddenly noticed that everyone below had the same shiny amulet on their foreheads, including the double-dutch girls. "Oh my God," I said.

"It's so everyone can be sure of everyone else at a glance. This is too important to leave up to individual choice. One bad apple can spoil the whole bunch. That's also why they're fixed in place permanently, so they can't be tampered with or removed."

"Permanently? How?"

"They're seated on surgical steel posts that penetrate the scalp and are actually drilled into the cranium. I know that sounds bad, but it's actually a very safe office procedure. A few days on painkillers and you'll never know it's there."

"I don't care! I don't want it!"

The doctor nodded understandingly. "That's a perfectly normal reaction," she said. "But you'll get used to it." She unfastened my right wrist, and I slowly brought my hand up to my brow.

Stomach whirlpooling, I thought, *No way . . .*

But it was. It was there already, a foreign lump as smooth and hard as horn. The flesh around it felt novocained. "No," I said, struggling to clear my head of lingering haze. This had to be a nightmare. "Get it off!" The thing held fast; wouldn't budge. "Get it the hell off, *now!*"

"Hey, just think of it as a body piercing," Dr. Langhorne said, restraining me. "Some people think it's kind of cool: a tribal accessory."

"Where are the others? Hector! Julian!" I cried.

"Your friends have been moved to their orientation sites, where they'll each eventually be assigned a 'guardian.' They're going through the same period of adjustment you are. We all have. And speaking of periods—"

"Can't I stay with them? Please!"

"No. You're different. They're just drones, but you are something special. We know about you, Lulu. We've been told some very interesting things, and would like to find out if they're true."

"You mean like I'm immune to Xombies? That's just junk Mr. Cowper made up!"

"Oh, I know. We examined you thoroughly. There's

nothing physically extraordinary about you. In fact, I seriously doubt you have chromosomal primary amenorrhea, as has been reported to me."

"Of course I do! Why do you think I don't have a period?"

"I'll tell you. The reason you don't have a period is that you are suffering from prolonged malnutrition. It's affected your physical development."

"That's because we've been starving for a month!"

"Not you. You've been eating well, and thank goodness. I'm not talking about the last month, but the years before that. I'm talking about your old life. You're obviously in recovery now, but there are lasting effects of an extended bout of anorexic behavior—possibly going back to puberty. I suspect that the shock treatment of Agent X saved your life. You were a terminal case, I think."

"That's not true!" I couldn't believe what I was hearing—the bitch was out of her mind!

"I think it is. I think Agent X is the best thing that ever happened to you. That's all right—you're not alone. It's been my experience that many Agent X survivors are people who felt alienated in their previous life, and found a new sense of purpose afterward. Anyone too attached to the past doesn't make it."

"That's sick! You're sick!"

"I'm not sick, and neither are you. In fact I think you're well enough to take a little trip with me. There's someone in our clinic here you might be interested to see. I know he's very interested in seeing *you*."

"Mr. Cowper? Oh my God, please—" I almost toppled the chair over.

"Whoa! Cool your jets, kid. Just sit back and leave the driving to us."

LEAVING MY RESTRAINTS on, Dr. Langhorne rolled me down a ramp to the stadium floor. I was dizzy at first, nauseated, but as we moved things settled down. I ached to pry that metal knot off my head.

Beneath the Oz-like psuedo-city was a real tent-city, several thousand people bivouacked on nonskid rubber matting amid soaring backdrops of the Pyramids and Alps. What was funny was that the different nationalities seemed to have segregated themselves according to their cultural symbols: French was being spoken under the fake Eiffel Tower, and Japanese under Mount Fuji. I didn't get the feeling there was a lot of mingling going on, and there certainly seemed to be a concerted effort by everyone to ignore me. The older women especially looked snooty and unfriendly. One thing I found reassuring was that there were no guns in sight; no soldiers.

Speaking into my ear as she pushed, the doctor said, "Lulu, I'm going to confide something to you now that you're going to find hard to believe, but which I think will help you understand your role here. Would it surprise you to hear that Agent X was man-made?"

I couldn't honestly say I was surprised. We had talked about it often enough on the boat—that the whole thing was probably the result of germ warfare or bioterrorism or some stupid lab accident. *So what?* I thought bitterly. What the hell difference did it make now?

"I told you before that Mogul was a boys' club," she said. "An extremely exclusive boys' club. Its purpose was to preserve the perquisites of great wealth for its members. What do you suppose is the biggest obstacle to their continued wealth and power; the thing that galls them above everything else?"

"Agent X, obviously."

"No. This is something that's been around much longer. Caesars and pharoahs have tried to get around it since the beginning of time, creating religious empires and anointing themselves gods, but in this matter there's never been any real difference between a king and the average jerk in the street."

"Death?" I scoffed.

"Yes, death, of course. Death and taxes. Doesn't it make

sense that these tycoons would do what they could to erect a tax shelter? That's what Mogul is. It was discreetly founded to pursue so-called 'life-extension technologies.' "

I would have laughed if I wasn't so miserable. "Oh, right."

"It's true."

"When did all this begin?"

"Back in the Eighties."

"And somehow this never made the news?"

"It wasn't a publicly traded company. Just an obscure private research foundation doing longevity studies. They were a dime a dozen."

"So Agent X was supposed to be some kind of Fountain of Youth?"

"We've always tried to avoid the stigma of putting it in quite those words, but yes."

"And you were part of it, I suppose?"

"Every doctor here was part of it. I had been doing proteome work for Brown University when I was approached by a man named Uri Miska. He was a Nobel laureate for his work on the AIDS vaccine, and he came to me with a very interesting proposal involving synthetic DNA. Have you ever heard of something called the Mandelbrot Set?" I shrugged, and she said, "It's a simple mathematical equation—z equals z squared plus c—which produces a fractal structure of infinite complexity. Here, this is what it looks like . . ."

She showed me her laminated ID card, which hung by an alligator clamp from her smock. On the reverse side was an outline of a kidney shape fused to a sphere, with crystalline fronds sprouting from all sides. It resembled a weird snowflake or a fuzzy seated Buddha.

She said, "You can't tell from this, but if you could zoom in on any part of this structure, you would find that it expands into an endless series of organic patterns, seemingly random, but all incorporating smaller and smaller versions of this same basic shape, literally to infinity. Do you know what it is you're looking at, Lulu?"

"Not really."

"It's the face of God."

"What's that supposed to mean?"

"This is how nature stores information. This is how DNA molecules with only four basic nucleotides—adenine, cytosine, guanine, and thymine—can contain all the incredible diversity of life. Not just human life, but all life. Miska realized that if we could harness this information-carrying capacity, we could revolutionize . . . well, you name it. An infinitely small computer with infinitely large storage capacity? Can you imagine? So we started creating our own Mandelbrot Set, our own self-perpetuating equation, not with figures but with organic molecules. In effect, blank DNA. *Writable* DNA."

We were approaching an archway in the dome wall. It funneled down to an airlock door like the one we had encountered outside. Dr. Langhorne rolled me in, and as the pressure equalized very slightly, I asked, "Are you telling me that was Agent X?"

"Not quite. But we used it to create a very interesting thing: a rudimentary organism with some of the desirable properties of a stem cell, only far more robust, like a prion. We called it our 'Magic Bean.' It could replicate itself and incorporate its genetic matrix into other cells."

"A virus, you mean."

"Kind of, except that instead of killing the cells, it streamlined them, radically simplifying the metabolic processes and turning each cell into an independent unit within the whole. The body as colony organism; analogous, I suppose, to a jellyfish. Strictly speaking, the host was no longer human, or even life as we know it, but it was far more efficient and resilient. The organic structure remained, but it was arbitrary—a bag of obsolete parts governed by a solid-state master. Think analog to digital."

Listening to her talk, I wondered if this woman had ever seen a Xombie. Had she ever run for dear life, with blue hands clawing at her back? Had she ever seen a loved one transformed into a demonic predator? "You make it sound like an upgrade," I said.

"It was supposed to be. You have to look objectively at what we accomplished—don't think of them as monsters, but as an interim stage of our evolution. Because that's what it is: an evolutionary leap, a transformation to another state of being, just as when Neanderthals and Cro-Magnons shared the Earth. Change is always scary, but our fear comes from ignorance. We can outgrow it and learn to understand."

Understand what? I thought. "Didn't Neanderthals go extinct?"

We passed through the airlock and she wheeled me into a separate dome, one that was smaller, emptier, and far less colorful than the first, but just as impressive in its own right, being all unobstructed open space. They could have held a monster truck rally in there. It looked like it was still under construction, with aluminum catwalks crisscrossing a treadmarked field of gray mud, and prefabricated sheds clustered among boulders in a fenced compound in the center. All around the periphery a deep trench had been excavated to drain the thawing permafrost, and we paused at the edge of the moat.

"Why are you telling me all this?" I asked.

"Because you're going to be challenged to overcome your prejudice and see this for what it is."

"I've seen it. I've been out there. Have *you?*"

"What you've seen is only half the picture . . . it's more complex than that."

"Oh, well, I'm glad there's more to it than just the human race being wiped out. What the hell *happened?*"

"There were fail-safes to prevent the lab strains from being infectious, even if they got loose. We had configured them to form a chemical bond with anoxic hemoglobin, but it was much, much weaker than the normal oxygen bond, so that they would be neutralized in the presence of air. Pure oxygen swept it away like a magic wand. What we failed to anticipate was how long the inert organism could remain infectious, its longer-term mutagenic properties, and that it could colonize iron, forming a fast-spreading blue anaerobic rust. These x-factors allowed our 'Magic Bean' to take root and multiply in all kinds of hard-to-reach places, away from the air—inside vacuum-sealed containers and liquid-filled tanks, in plumbing and wiring and soil—eventually saturating the environment. It went worldwide before anyone even noticed."

"Hard-to-reach places. Oh my God." I winced as a million-watt lightbulb exploded in my brain. "You mean like the uterus. That's how it got into women—through the uterus. During their cycle."

"Yes," she said, studying me. "Boy, they weren't lying about you. The uterus was an ideal incubator, I'm sorry to say."

Across the trench, an erector-set drawbridge jerked to life, spanning the mucky green water.

I watched it move, suddenly conscious of how real it was. The grinding motor, the stadium lights, the mud. This was all *real*. But it *couldn't* be, it *couldn't* be! Lightheaded, I tried to ground myself by asking, "What caused all the women to go at once?"

"The organism reached the end of its shelf life. That was another safeguard: a biological timer that expired on midnight of the new year. Beyond that, its governing proteins were expected to become unstable and break down. Instead it . . . did something else, and the rest is history. Okay, go on across—they'll meet you on the other side." She ripped the Velcro bands off my wrists.

It took me a second to grasp that she was telling me to get up. "Oh. By myself?"

"Yup. This is where we part company, kiddo. I have a house call to make."

I hesitantly stood up out of the wheelchair. She must have given me a shot of something to bring me around: my legs were steady, my head clearer by the second. But I still felt vulnerable emotionally. Much as I resented what they had done to me, I dreaded being left alone. I called back, "What am I supposed to do?"

"Just try to keep an open mind," she said.

twenty-three

I CROSSED THE bridge and made my way down a metal pier. It ended short of the fence, so that I had to walk in freezing-cold mud with only thin booties on. A door opened somewhere in the complex and I could hear the hyperventilating approach of a dog . . . or what I thought was a dog. It came charging around a corner and leaped high up the fence, its great frizzy mane bouncing like an oversized afro. At first I took it for a hideous giant poodle, and even when I realized what it was I couldn't believe it: an exotic beast I had only seen on TV or at the zoo, though I couldn't recall ever having seen one this big.

It was a baboon, the gorgeously colored type known as a mandrill, with curved fangs as long as my pinky and malevolent golden eyes that peered at me out of a face like a witchdoctor's mask. It was berserk with blood-lust—lust for *my* blood. I froze well back from the gate, hoping that whoever had released the animal would get control of it before it realized it could easily scale the fence.

With a buzz, the gate rolled open.

I backpedaled frantically, searching for anything to climb or hide behind, but my only prayer of shelter on that bulldozed wasteland was the deep watery drainage ditch, and there was no chance of reaching that. Still, I ran for it.

"Yo!" a man's voice shouted. "Little girl! Stop!"

Sensing the baboon at my heels, I dove to earth and shielded my head with my arms in the classic "duck and cover" position. The mandrill trampled up and leapfrogged over me, my back muscles jerking involuntarily at the touch of its hard little hands.

"Don't worry, he won't bite," said the approaching voice.

"People always say that," I whimpered.

"You're too young to be so cynical. C'mon, try standing up. Don won't bother you—he only attacks Xombies. He's just excited."

"That's what worries me." I slowly got to my feet. The baboon watched closely, sitting on its haunches with a magisterial air. He really was a frightening creature, but now I could tell he didn't mean to kill me. Still, I was afraid to talk too loud. "You call him Don?"

"That's his name: Don Ameche. Mine's Rudy." He offered me his clean hand and with some reluctance I gave him my dirty one. He was middle aged and had the wan look of a graveyard-shift motel clerk; albeit one with a cultish amulet on his head. "You must be Louise," he said, flicking a bit of mud off my nose.

"Lulu."

"Lulu. Well, Lulu, I'm sorry to have scared you. Don doesn't usually come on so strong. You put quite a scare into me, too, running toward the ditch like that. Lotta stuff has gone in there and never been heard from again."

"Why do you have a baboon?"

"This is a research facility. We use animals for tests."

"I mean why is he running around loose?"

"Oh come on! Don't you think he's a charming fellow?" He smiled at my expression. "We got the idea from the Egyptians. Don ensures we don't get a lot of casual visitors disrupting our work. There aren't enough security personnel to go around, and you'd be surprised at how many people are interested in what we do here. Privacy is at a high premium these days."

We strolled to the enclosure, Don loping ahead. Inside the fence it felt like a concentration camp, with longhouses jacked up on planks and muddy runs in-between. Power cables drooped overhead like clotheslines, and dirty lawn furniture was scattered about on atolls of cigarette butts. One of the sheds had an open door, and inside I could see lab-coated people laughing and drinking coffee under fluorescent lighting. They all had the implant. A genial-looking older woman with hair like steel wool saw me and leaned out, cackling, "Well if it isn't Little Bo Peep! I see you've met the foul brute that stalks this compound. The other one we call Don."

"Charming," sighed Rudy.

"Hi," I said.

"Wow, that's a fresh one." She brazenly examined my forehead. "Let's splash a little hydrogen peroxide on this before it goes septic, whattaya think? You gotta keep that stud *clean*."

Rudy said, "Lulu, this is Dr. Chandra Stevens, Assistant Chief of Experimental Gerontology under Dr. Langhorne. Did you meet Dr. Langhorne?"

I nodded. "She brought me here." .

"And she didn't come in?" Dr. Stevens was mock-outraged. "What a brat—ever since her ex showed up, we never see her anymore. Don! Outside! Outside!" The baboon snorted indignantly and vanished down the alley, flashing his barstool-red behind.

They gave me a pair of plastic sandals and took me into their cluttered office. It looked like a third-world medical clinic, except that the cots were for the doctors' own use. There was also a small kitchen, so that they could presumably work, sleep, and eat in the same room. It didn't look like they got out much.

"May I see my father now, please?" I asked.

"Sure thing, hon," said Dr. Stevens sympathetically, dabbing my head. "It's just that there's a little formality we have to go through before we can admit you to the ward."

My heart fell. "What kind of formality?"

The woman lost some of her twinkle. With the ham-handed compassion of a grief counselor, she said, "I am so sorry. It's a little complicated. Not everybody gets the grand tour—it's to help you better understand what to expect . . . and why you are here."

"Is he dead? Just tell me if he's dead, please."

"No, he's not dead, but—"

"Are you sure? Because this sounds an awful lot like you're trying to break it to me, it really does."

She glanced at her colleagues, who were fiddling with their coffee cups. "Of course I'm sure. Although we did have to intervene quite aggressively to save his life. Ordinarily we would not take measures like that. If someone is close to death in here, they are euthanized and immediately cremated for safety's sake. But we were instructed in this case to keep him alive for questioning. Do you have any idea what that might be about?"

"Not really." I tried to calm myself down. "There was something about him having stolen something from the submarine. They had him tied up and were trying to force him to tell them where it was. They even assaulted me in front of him, but he still didn't say anything. I think they made a mistake, or one of *them* took it! Mr. Cowper was just trying to save our lives!"

Dr. Stevens nodded thoughtfully, arranging her pens. "Did Dr. Langhorne tell you the nature of our work here?"

"I guess so. The 'Magic Bean.' "

"Yes. Pretty terrible, wouldn't you say?"

Feeling like she was testing me, I warily nodded.

"What if I told you there were people lining up for it? Lining up for a dose of Agent X?"

"Why?"

"The same reason people used to have their ashes shot into space, or had themselves cryogenically preserved: a shot at immortality. Agent X stops time. It stops the aging process."

"But . . . you're not *human* anymore." The deeply buried memory of my ravening mother flickered in my mind and I had to wrench my thoughts away. "There's nothing left of you. Just a horrible *thing*."

"Insomuch as you have seen."

"Duh, because I've seen it! God! Are you people all crazy in here?"

"Louise, Lulu, I'm sorry. We know you've been through a lot, and we're not trying to make it harder for you. Believe it or not, we're trying to make it easier." They were all looking at me like I was an unstable psycho.

"Then let me see Mr. Cowper!"

"Of course. But in order to do that, you're going to have to help us question him. He won't speak to us, and we very much need to know what he knows. We think he might talk to you."

"About what?"

"About the 'Tonic.' The corrective to Agent X. Come this way."

SHE LED ME through the office and into a dark doorway, flicking on the lights. It was a storage room filled with oblong metal boxes, all propped upright. They could have been sturdy lockers, but somehow I just knew they were caskets. It was not cold enough in there to preserve a body, so my immediate thought was that these were empty, being held in reserve for the men whose names were inscribed on them: Klaus Manfred Van Oort, Roger Danforth Eakins, Marcus Hugh Sudbury-Wainwright. There were hundreds of them, many with foreign lettering—Russian, Chinese, Arabic names.

"What is this?" I asked nervously, scanning for the words *Fred Cowper*. It occurred to me I didn't even know his middle name.

In the sunny tones of a real estate agent, Stevens said, "This is our little morgue."

"You told me he wasn't dead!"

"I'm sorry—no one's dead in here. We've just cemented their status as Moguls."

Dr. Stevens went to a random coffin belonging to one Charles Wesley Cox, unlocked it with a key, and opened the burnished door. My hackles raised up, but inside was a body encased in some hardened resin; a plastic mummy with a metal pipe protruding from its mouth, inert as a fossil. Then I heard a thin wheezing sound bubbling up the tube.

"Mr. Cox here passed away last October, but he is exactly as he was when we administered the morphocyte, thank you very much."

"He's a Xombie," I said, aghast. "But you said—oh my God. Mr. Cowper is one too, isn't he? They're *all* Xombies!"

"We don't use that term here. And they're not Xombies in the sense you may be familiar with. Listen." Ignoring my hysterics, she leaned over the pipe and said, "Mr. Cox? Can you hear me?"

I was flipping out to think that Mr. Cowper was gone, a ghoul like my mother and all the rest, but then my skin crawled to hear a muffled voice reply, *"I hear you Dr. Stevens. Who's that with you?"* The words scuttled quick as a cockroach in a paper bag.

"Oh my God," I said.

"Just a visitor, Charles. I thought you might reassure her that you're quite comfortable."

"Stop!" I cried.

"Comfortable," crackled the paper-dry voice, tasting each syllable. It kept weirdly changing in pitch, weaving in and out of clarity. *"Comfort is how you cope, I know you*

make a womb out of trash and huddle there for comfort, I remember. Time is a cancer you can't cut off, heavier and heavier it shrivels you to nothing and you take refuge in hollow comfort." He made a grotesque sucking noise. *"My only discomfort is that I can't save you, doomed pups fighting over a dead teat and I can't help you. Not from here. Not with talk."*

Dr. Stevens shut the lid and locked it. "Wow, he's on a roll."

"God," I said, quaking. "You just *keep* them in there?"

"We have no choice. One thing Agent X confers, along with everlasting life, is a powerful 'evangelical impulse.' They will do anything to 'convert' us, if you know what I mean, and they are tremendously slippery. You've seen it. This is the only practical way of handling them, long term."

"But he can talk! He's intelligent!"

"Yes, we've about perfected that part. It's a matter of controlling the brain damage caused by oxygen starvation while the microbe colonizes the body. It's only a few minutes of clinical death, but without precautions it leaves cognitive deficiencies—the 'Xombie' behavior you're so familiar with. The morphocyte eventually repairs the cerebral damage, but it can't restore personality. Keeping the mind intact is as simple as lowering brain temperature until full inoculation takes hold. About twelve minutes, on average."

"Why do they keep wanting to attack us?"

"Strangely enough, it seems to be an altruistic thing. They're just spreading the gospel."

"What's the kissing all about?"

"Ah, you've noticed that. Yes, we call that 'Downloading' or 'X-piration.' In a way, it's the opposite of the 'breath of life' used in CPR. Instead of delivering air to a person who has stopped breathing, it actively *prevents* the person from breathing while feeding them a dose of morphocyte-laden vapor. It guarantees a quick, successful transmission."

"And people *volunteer* for this?"

"These were all very old or dying men. They didn't have anything to lose. You know what they say: If you can't beat 'em, join 'em." She gave me a shrewd look. "But this is nobody's idea of heaven, I mean please. This is just a halfway measure. What these gentlemen went in there gambling on is that we would eventually *perfect* the treatment so they could come out some day and resume their lives as Moguls, only safe from disease, aging, and death. The ultimate golden parachute. But it didn't sit well with some people, including the head of the project, Dr. Uri Miska. He sabotaged everything."

"Sabotaged? How?"

"We think he might have been the one who let the morphocyte escape into the environment, and we know he stole the 'Tonic' when he destroyed his lab and records and everything pertaining to Agent X, so that our chance of making the Mogul dream come true was almost sunk. But Dr. Miska was in a hurry, and he didn't do a perfect job. A lot of material he tried to erase from his hard drive was salvaged, as well as a test sample mounted on a slide."

"And that's supposed to be the cure for Agent X?"

"Not so much a cure as a perfected strain, a kinder and gentler strain, one without the virulence and predatory mania conferred by this one. One that can be meted out to the righteous. It's the carrot to top all carrots, you see."

"Carrot top?"

"Carrot and stick, reward and punishment—those are the only ways you get people to do things, and nothing beats religion in both departments. The Moguls want that power so they can motivate people with something that until now has been an exercise of pure faith. It's better than a cure, you understand. It's literally the Holy Grail! That's what we were expecting to arrive on that submarine of yours, so you can see why everyone's pestering you so much."

"You think Mr. Cowper knows where it is."

"Honey, *somebody* knows, and if you know what's good for you, you'll do everything you can to bring that information to light. Our division has jurisdiction over you only so long as we can promise results. Once Mogul steps in it'll get ugly. That's not a threat, just a helpful hint."

I shrugged helplessly, miserably. Hate was pounding in me like a drum. "I'll try. Where is he?"

"Not in here. Follow me."

We left the building and crossed to a different longhouse. This one had a heavy black curtain for a door, and a second one just inside. It was pitch-dark between the drapes, but once past the inner flap we entered a long narrow hall running down a row of dimly lit viewing windows.

"Don't be nervous," said the doctor.

"I'm not."

Each window was a porthole into a metal tank, and each tank contained a naked blue Xombie, mounted like an insect on an exhibit stand. Steel rods had been driven through their limbs, torsos, and even heads to hold them in place. Some were immersed in water or other liquids, some were in a fog of caustic gas, and some were being frozen, sawed apart, burned, or otherwise mutilated in various creative ways. Despite these torments, they were weirdly resigned, even peaceful, their smooth brows free of woe or implants—paragons of yogism, unearthly fakirs.

I ran outside and threw up in the mud.

The doctor watched me from the curtain and said, "You know, your Mr. Cowper is depending on you. You're his only hope. That's what you have to get through to him."

"I can't," I said, gasping. "I can't see him like that."

"Then he'll be incinerated with all the others. That's what happens here when a test subject is no longer useful. They get incinerated and tossed in the ditch. His only chance lies in us finding those research materials—then he'll be first in line for the treatment."

"Don't lie to me! Stop lying to me! That's only for those rich guys!"

"Not until it's tested. It has to be screened on someone; why not him?"

There was nothing to do but force myself back inside, shielding my eyes from the gallery of ravaged flesh.

"This may seem cruel," Dr. Stevens said, "but Maenads have no consciousness of pain as we know it. The Agent X morphocyte was modeled on prokaryotes and archaea—primitive life forms that exist in highly adverse environments—so they're all but unkillable, however grisly this may appear. They regenerate in no time."

"But I killed some," I said. "On the submarine we killed a whole bunch."

"Ah yes, your carbon monoxide flush! We heard about that. That was good, but I hate to tell you, they were far from dead. They were simply dormant, and if they had been first-generation females or neurologically intact specimens like we have here, they wouldn't have fallen for it. Like Clinton, they wouldn't have inhaled. You got lucky."

Lucky, I thought, coming to the last window. At first I didn't see a thing, but as I reluctantly stepped closer I spotted him crouching in the bottom of the cell, squat as a toad, his lacquered-blue back turned to me. Mr. Cowper.

I clapped my hands to my mouth, moaning, "Oh no, oh no . . ." It was actually a subdued reaction, tempered by relief: at least he wasn't mangled or hung up like a gruesome marionette! I had seen worse, let's face it. Maybe there was even a chance he could be saved. I grasped that flimsy straw, thinking, *We'll get through this. Just hold on, Mr. Cowper. Hold on.*

"You wanna try to talk to him?" Dr. Stevens coaxed gently. A microphone was pressed into my hand. "Just push the button to speak."

"I know how it works." As if preparing to jump from a high-dive, I closed my eyes and took a deep breath. With as much calm as I could muster, I said, "Mr. Cowper? It's—"

There was a startling thud that caused me to open my eyes. Mr. Cowper's gargoyle leer was pressed to the glass only inches from me, his black eyes bugging out so hard they seemed about to pop like corks. He was horrible—a giant baby bird yearning for a worm. The shock made me trip backward and fall on my butt. *"Oof,"* I said.

"That's good," Dr. Stevens urged, thrilled. She helped me up. "Don't worry, he can't get out. He can't even see you."

I wished I didn't have to see him. He remained imprinted on the glass, waiting, his eyeballs rolling with the slow deliberation of a man cracking a safe. Those *eyes.* They made me think of our floating compasses that went haywire around magnetic north. They were my mother's eyes.

Shuddering, I swallowed and whispered, "It's me. Lulu."

Mr. Cowper spoke: *"Lulu . . ."* His voice was a bottomless silky rasp, savoring the word. The sound of it, especially over the crackly radio, was so freakish it curdled even the doctor's enthusiasm. Her wiry hair seemed to stand on end.

"Yes, it's me," I said tremulously. "Do you remember me?"

"A course. I hope I don't scare ya." His bulging eyes, undersides glistening, fixed on something above the window. He was looking at the intercom speaker, the source of my voice. Before I could reply, he asked, *"Ah ya still there?"*

"Yes, I'm still here."

"Good. They treatin' ya okay?"

"I'm . . . fine."

"Because it can get cold in here . . . very cold . . ."

"He's cold," I protested.

"Interesting," said the doctor. "I've never heard one complain before. It has to be some kind of ruse."

"Are you cold?" I asked him.

"Why? Ah my lips blue?"

Dr. Stevens and I glanced at each other. "I think that was a joke," she said.

I shook my head, eyes wide, and said to him, "I'm just concerned, that's all."

"I'm sorry to worry ya. There's nothin' you can do fa me . . . except trust me."

"Trust you?"

"Trust me ta help ya. That's all I want, Lulu, fa you and me ta have all that we neva had togetha, before ya turn ta dust an' slip through my fingas. Ya dust already an' don't know it, just waitin' for a breeze ta come along an' blow ya away. I'm not what ya think. You're in the shadow of that big grindin' wheel an' it's comin' around, it's comin' around, but I can make ya real so the bastid can't touch ya. I can take ya home."

It was awful to hear him say these things, these travesties of fatherly concern. Swallowing my grief, I forged ahead. "Mr. Cowper, I need your help."

"I'm here fa you, sweethaht."

"I need you to remember something. About the boat. When you were in command, did you take something from the captain's safe?"

"Lulu, why didn't you neva look inta my haht? All you hadda do was look inta my haht."

"What are you talking about?"

"I gave you my haht an' ya don't even give it a second glance. Smaht kid like you . . ."

Crumbling, I demanded, "How can you say that? I tried, but you were never there!"

Dr. Stevens put her hand over the mike and said, "Let's stay focused, shall we?"

I nodded, regrouping. Keeping my eyes fixed on her, I said to him, "This is important. I need to know if you took what was in the safe, and what you did with it. This can help both of us."

"Come with me. That's all the help we'll eva need, Lulu. That's all I want. I know you think I'm a monsta, but I've changed. I been blind, now I can see. I was scared like you, spittin' like a cat stuck in a drainpipe because a time eatin' away at me, but now I know that's not real. It's a movie, Lulu, only a movie. You're stuck on the screen and you

know it's gotta end, because every movie you've eva seen has a beginning and an end. But it doesn't hafta. Step outta the picture and join me."

"I . . . can't. I'm sorry."

"I know. There ain't words for it, and all you have to go by are words. That's the curse a the Xombie. But try ta rememba one last thing."

I was weeping. "What?"

"I loved ya, baby girl."

He fell away, folding down into a crouched homunculus once again. Nothing we could do would make him move. After a while it was hard to believe he ever had.

twenty-four

AS THE DOCTOR and I tried our best to re-animate Mr. Cowper, a few people came in through the flaps. All of them were wearing the crisp blue uniforms of Air Force officers, their head implants strangely in harmony with the other medals. They weren't armed.

"Colonel Lowenthal," said Dr. Stevens, sounding tense.

"Hello, doctor," said the leader. This was the man who had met Commander Coombs when we first arrived, but I hadn't had a very good look at him then. Seeing him close up, I thought he seemed very young to be a colonel—mid-twenties at most—and too wispy to be any kind of military officer. He looked more like a sullen supermarket bagger. "Still no luck?" he inquired.

"I wouldn't say that. She was able to elicit more information in five minutes than we were able to in three days."

"Yes, I saw, but I wouldn't call it useful information, would you?"

"Without reviewing it properly, I couldn't say."

Lowenthal smirked. Looking at me, he said, "So this is our little Lulu. You wouldn't be holding back on us, would you?"

"No, sir."

"Sir!" he repeated, amused. To the man next to him he joked, "You see that, Rusty? *Some* people respect my authority around here."

I suddenly realized where I had heard that effeminate drawl before: he was the twerp in the booth who had admitted us to the complex.

Sobering up, he said, "All right, let's give this one last shot. Lulu, you're in a very tough position. I realize you probably don't have a clue about what your dad did with our property, but I've been mandated to find out anything—*anything*—you may know that could help us. Anything at all, no matter how insignificant you may think it is. Something your father said to you, something you overheard and thought, 'Hmm, that's weird.' Anything."

I shook my head. "He gave me a survival kit when we first got on the boat," I said. "After that I never saw him until just before we were taken off, and he wasn't really conscious then. It's Mr. Kranuski and Mr. Webb you should be asking—they tortured him."

"Oh, we're *talking* to them, don't worry. And we've examined your belongings, too. The trouble is, it's a big ship and there are lots and lots of hiding places, especially for an old hand like Cowper. What makes it difficult is that we don't have a lot of subma*rine* experts available here to help us in our search. We don't dare let your people loose on the sub, and if we start picking it apart ourselves we're liable to wreck it. It's not exactly tied up to a wharf—anything could happen to it out there. Without your help, we don't have a whole lot of options."

Dr. Stevens said, "I'm still hopeful that we can reach Cowper again."

"Was I talking to you?" he said snidely. Turning back to

me, he confided, "These *doc*tors will tell you anything, but the truth is they don't know squat about what makes these Xombies tick. Xombies have their own agenda, and you can't push 'em an inch beyond it. Cowper's tapped out. I've seen it numerous times."

"What's going to happen to him?" I asked anxiously.

"You *should* be more worried about what's going to happen to *you*. I understand you've been made privy to all our secrets around here, and unless you can prove you're deserving of that trust, it puts you on pretty thin ice. See, the problem I have, Lulu, is that I don't think you're being entirely honest with me."

"But I am!"

"Oh, you may *think* you are, but I don't think you're completely honest with anyone. You're a natural spy, that's what I heard. In fact you're the perfect spy, because you even keep secrets from yourself. Coombs saw that, and used it. I think your dad may have as well. But ultimately, your inner spook exists to serve you, and maybe with the right incentive we can get at the truth."

"What are you talking about?"

"I'll show you. Come on."

They led me out of the building and into a remarkable gathering of people. The alleys of the research compound were suddenly full of well-dressed older men, clomping through the mud in fashionable gear and Wellingtons as if outfitted for a shooting party. Not a single one had the implant. They stared at me in fascinated silence, and I back at them.

"Just keep going," said the colonel, indicating a path through the crowd. "Go right out the gate. If you get any brainstorms you want to share, just cross your arms like this—" He made a big X over his head.

I looked for Dr. Stevens, but she was gone. None of the doctors were in evidence. Something red flashed across my eye, and I realized men were aiming laser pointers at me. They didn't care that I could see them doing it.

Feeling a nameless dread, I walked out of the compound and onto the surrounding mire. What now? The gate shut behind me, leaving me alone under that silvery quilted sky full of hot air. Not knowing what else to do, I picked my way over to the metal pier leading to the drawbridge. It was my hope that I was dismissed for the moment. Just then the electric winch activated, lowering the bridge for me. No, not for me. For a small group of people standing on the far side.

My heart leaped to see them. It was my posse—all six of them: Hector, Julian, Jake, Shawn, Lemuel, and Cole. They crossed at a run and we collided joyously on the catwalk.

"Ohmygodohmygod!" I screamed. The boys, too, were the most emotional I had ever seen them. We were all in tears, delirious with relief, yet stung by the sight of that gadget on each other's heads. "Where have you guys *been*?" I cried.

"There's no time to talk," Julian said, suddenly aware of the curious mob behind the fence. Lowering his voice and making a warning sign to the others, he said, "We're breaking out."

"Call us mint jelly, 'cause we're on the lam," said Jake.

This only made me cry harder. "You mean right now? How?"

Shawn said, "They were gonna punk us out to a bunch of old queers. I was like, 'No way, dude. See ya!' "

"What?"

"It's true," Hector said. "There aren't enough women to go around, so there's like a sex-slavery thing going on, like in prison. That's how we're expected to earn our keep! They have sugar daddies all picked out for us, and we're supposed to act all grateful or nobody will want us. It's either that or be guinea pigs for medical research."

"Fuck that shit," said Cole. "I didn't come here to marry no millionaire."

"How do you expect to escape?"

Julian said, "There's no security in here, no guns; everything's on the fucking honor system. Nobody even tried to stop us!" He was giddy. "They left us alone in this big tent and we just took off!"

"Shouldn't be any problem getting outside," said Hector. "Keeping people *in* is incidental; they let the arctic climate handle that."

And with good reason, I thought, but I wasn't about to nit-pick. If there was ever a time to march out into a freezing void, this was it. "How'd you find me?"

"That was the easiest part! They showed us the map program they have here that traces everybody's movements. Anybody can find anybody. It's a joke."

"Where's Mr. Albemarle?"

Hector answered brusquely, "He's not in the system. We couldn't find him. We couldn't find Mr. Cowper either. I'm sorry, Lulu. We were hoping you might know something."

I shook my head no, reluctant to speak. Mr. Cowper was beyond rescuing.

"The rest of the crew is at the boat," Julian said. "They're all still being held out there to keep it running, so we're going to try to free them and retake the ship. I know it sounds sketchy, but if we can just reach the motor pool we may be able to swipe a vehicle and crash the gate before anybody knows what's happening. From what I've heard, there may even be a few people who want to throw in with us."

Cole corrected him, "A *lotta* people. You heard how they hate that Mogul shit."

"Almost as much as they hate that colonel dude for selling out the Air Force and then acting like George fucking Washington," Shawn said.

"Colonel Lowenthal?" I asked.

"That's the one. He wasn't even a colonel until he hooked up with Mogul. The real colonel's dead. It's sorta like what happened with Coombs—Lowenthal was just a second lieutenant, but he was willing to play ball and they put him in charge of everything."

"They inflated a statue in his honor," said Jake.

"They definitely have problems in here," agreed Julian, "but we can't waste time trying to whip up a revolt. Main thing is to get our guys free and storm the boat." He was more and more worried by the spectators. "Let's get the hell out of here."

We had been moving toward the bridge. Now it was suddenly raised in our faces.

I whispered, "I'm so sorry, you guys."

No one heard me. They were all swearing and attacking the cable mechanism.

This had to be what Lowenthal was talking about—this was the "incentive." I had almost fooled myself into believing we could run. Now the scales fell from my eyes as I looked back at the men behind the fence. They were watching us like rapt bettors at the Kentucky Derby, waiting for the starting gun. There was even a zoom-lens camera on a crane to capture live video of our plight. *The revolution will be televised,* I thought.

"We need tools," Julian said, stepping back in disgust from the greasy, unyielding winch. He had hurt his hand.

"We have to go another way," said Lemuel.

Dreamily, I answered, "There is no other way. The moat goes all the way around."

"Then we'll swim it."

Shawn piped up, "No way! *Look* down there!" There seemed to be things moving under the slimy water. Glutinous, embryonic shapes.

"He's right," said Julian. "It's a deathtrap down there."

"Well what the fuck we gone do?" demanded Cole.

"I know what I'm gonna do," said Jake, looking across the field.

"What?"

"Pray."

Alerted by his tone, we turned to see what he was looking at. Someone was coming. Someone blue.

"Oh no, man," Hector said. "*Fuck* no."

It was Ed Albemarle.

HE CAME ON like a charging rhino, and we knew there would be no stopping him. There was no choice but to flee the onslaught.

"You run ahead of us," Hector said to me. "We'll try to hold him off."

"Run where?"

"That gate!" said Cole, gesticulating at the men in the compound. "They have to let us in!"

"They won't," I said. "They're only here to watch."

Julian barked, "Then we'll run in circles! Just go!"

I ran. My sandals flew off my feet, then my mud-caked booties. Barefoot I could run faster anyway, clay smooshing between my toes as I left a trail of perfect footprints. The five boys were following in close formation, and behind them the juggernaut. For all his bulk, Mr. Albemarle barely seemed to touch the ground, legs a pistoning blur and clods of mud rising in his wake. He was a flesh and bone torpedo homing in.

"We can take him down if we have to!" shouted Julian. "Two of us on each leg, two on each arm, one in the middle, and one around his neck! Be ready!"

Without panic or argument they arranged themselves into a loose flying wedge, chests heaving. Mr. Albemarle drew closer and closer, his thumping footfalls matching my racing heartbeat—I thought I could feel the ground shake. In the space of a few seconds, he went from being a barely believable threat in the distance to a drowned specter at our heels, scattering us like sheep. Hector overtook me now, singled out by his stepfather and frantic to keep his lead as the rest of us peeled off to either side and closed formation behind them.

They were getting away from us; it was now or never. "Go!" Julian shouted.

Cole and Lemuel put on a last burst of speed and closed

on Albemarle, trying to tackle him around the legs. At the same time, Julian, Jake, and Shawn swept in from either side. I held back, not wanting to be crushed in the fight, but there was no fight to speak of—they never touched him. The big man slipped through their grasp with animal fluidity, barely conscious of their clumsy grabs. Fumbling after him, the boys tripped over each other and fell in the dirt.

Hector knew he didn't have a chance. As a last resort he tried to feint and double back like a jackrabbit, but Albemarle was quicker: Simple as picking fruit from a vine, he snatched the boy off his feet, cutting him off mid-scream with a crushing embrace; the zealous affection of a feeding anaconda. Hector's pleading eyes went dull.

"No!" I cried. "You can't!"

Ed Albemarle opened his plum-colored lips wide and engulfed Hector's mouth and nose. As we scrambled up, he turned his back on us and moved off, hoarding his stepson's body the way a dog hoards a bone. It was not that he was intimidated by us, just that he was in the middle of something and could not be disturbed. Hector already looked dead, but I wasn't ready to believe it.

Echoing my thoughts, Julian yelled, "We have to catch him! Cut them off at the moat! C'mon!"

The other boys, muddy and wild-eyed, fanned out. Albemarle reached the edge of the ditch and cut left. We began to converge on him, and he trotted right toward us with Hector slack in his arms. I remembered a picture in one of my mother's art books that had given me nightmares when I was little, a hideous painting by Goya called *Saturn Devouring His Son,* and suddenly I knew what we had to do.

"Push them in!" I shouted on the run. "Hector's gone—we have to push them both in *now,* before it's too late!"

God help them, the boys were with me. I would have tried alone, but they were there at my side, all of us riding the same wave of shame and horror at what we were about to do. Albemarle hesitated as we closed in, then he abruptly dropped Hector's body and rushed us—rushed *me*. His big hand grabbed me like snatching up a barnyard chicken, and I was hauled before that dark Buddha face. Intelligence burned there, the inscrutable grin of a cannibal idol, and I imagined I heard a voice say *It's gonna be okay*. Then Lemuel head-butted him at full speed.

Lemuel had lost some weight on the boat, but he was still a hefty kid, and the force of his blow probably would have knocked a normal person cold. The only effect it had on Albemarle was to throw him off balance, so that the combined momentum of the other boys was enough to shove him in the deep trench.

Falling, Ed Albemarle sensibly dropped me and seized the two biggest boys, the two athletes, Lemuel and Cole, like a climber trading handholds, but even they weren't enough to offer purchase—the dynamics overwhelmingly favored gravity, and all three vanished under a heaving spout of muck. Julian yanked me back from the brink.

"Lulu! You okay? You okay?" He was frantic, tears streaking his muddy face, and the other two, Jake and Shawn, staring over the edge, shellshocked.

Coughing through my bruised windpipe, I tried to gather enough air to say *Hector,* but before I could do it there was an explosive movement to my left. Shawn shot bolt upright, neck arching backward in a volley of popping cartilage, and began gliding away as if on a dolly. His feet weren't touching the ground! But I could see footprints and a second pair of feet underneath—it was Hector. Hector had Shawn on his back like a side of beef, throttling him from behind as he capered away.

None of us had anything left, but we gave chase.

"Albemarle was one thing, but I can *take* Hector," Julian gasped. "I can take him . . ."

But it was obvious we were never going to catch them. It is exhausting to run through mud, and we were already beat: Jake's face was blotchy red, Julian seemed delirious, and the strain was aggravating my implant something fierce—it felt like a chisel in my head. The painkillers were wearing off. If theirs felt anything like mine, we were all going to be out of action soon. And every second poor Shawn was flopping farther and farther out of reach.

Watching them get away, I finally called it quits: "That's enough . . . we can't." I sounded like I had laryngitis.

"No!" Jake yelled, still plodding. "We have to catch them! Come on!"

Julian slumped in the mud. "It's all over, dude. Give it up."

"No!" But the strength seemed to go out of him and he slowed to an aimless, broken walk. "Don't you get it?" he whimpered. *"We're next."*

It was hard to think with my skull aching so bad. I tried to look at the whole thing methodically, rationally, in the way that always drove my mother crazy. *I'm not a robot like you!* she would scream during our fights. *I'm a human being! I have feelings!* I thought of Mr. Cowper saying, *Why didn't you look into my haht?* and of Lowenthal calling me a spy.

Maybe they were right. Maybe instead of the innocent victim of circumstances I always imagined myself to be, I was a selfish, scheming little creep. Was that the only reason I had made it this far, by conning everyone, including myself? If so, maybe it was justice that it ended now. I had gotten the boys into this—it was only right that I share their fate.

Crying a little, I fished the gold locket out of my shirt and looked at the baby picture. When had I ceased to be that child? When had I gone bad?

"Here they come," said Jake.

All you hadda do was look inta my haht. Why didn't ya look inta my haht?

Frowning, I picked open the clasp and took out the picture, looking again at the tiny chicken-scratching on the back: *4 ABL S FR 13*. A chill blew through me. I *recognized* this. I couldn't have understood when I first read it, but I did now. *4 ABL* was four feet Above Base Line—the lowest part of the submarine; *S* was Starboard; *FR 13* was Frame thirteen, as in one of the submarine's numbered ribs, up near the bow, perhaps inside one of the forward ballast-tanks. These were engineering abbreviations used on the diagrams I had been studying. Coordinates. Anyone who knew subs would know these things. I was holding a set of directions.

I looked up. Hector and Shawn were bearing down on us, full of demonic sunshine, so close I could see that the swelling around their implants had gone robin's egg blue. In a few seconds they would grab us and do the things they did. Jake and Julian weren't moving, impassively watching them come. The men behind the fence watched, too.

Standing up and making an X with my arms, I screeched, "Wait! I know where it is! Colonel Lowenthal! *I know where it's hidden!*"

Jake and Julian stared at me, startled.

"I know now! Oh God, help us! Please!" Suddenly I knew this hopeless, ragged plea would be the last sound I would ever make. It was just too late. Hector was coming for me, and nothing anyone could do would be fast enough to stop that. I sank to my knees before him and saw points of red dancing all over his body.

With a strobing, brilliant flash, he came apart. Just tumbled to pieces mid-stride, while the after-images of that searing light lingered in the air like childish squiggles. He and Shawn both.

The gate rolled open.

twenty-five

"COME ON, LULU," Julian said. "You did it. They're waving us in."

He and Jake were standing over me, dog-tired and dirty as losers at tug-o'-war. I couldn't seem to move or look them in the face. Everything was a hazy jumble of accusatory ghosts, an ever-growing population of those I had wronged, crowding my aching head. I was out of my mind. It's a strange thing to be mad and to know it.

"Tyrell's dead," I muttered.

Julian wasn't listening. "Come on, we gotta go."

"We left them there to die. I couldn't tell you."

"She's out of it, man," said Jake, crying.

"I lied about the rations, too. They were giving me extra the whole time."

"Lulu, it's okay."

"They're all *dead!* Don't you *get* it?"

"Lulu, it's okay, it's okay." Julian knelt beside me, trying to get me to look at him. "Whatever you're talking about, it doesn't matter. All that matters is that we're still here, and that's because of you. You saved us."

Resisting, wanting to shout, *Shut up! Shut up! You're so stupid!* I melted and sobbed, "No . . ."

"Lulu, what do you have? If we're gonna survive, you hafta tell us what's going on. Obviously you know something we don't. Quick, before they get here."

Angrily meeting his eyes, I said, "I have something these people want. Something Mr. Cowper gave me."

Jake exhaled harshly, head bobbing.

"What is it?" Julian asked me.

"Kind of a . . . Xombie vaccine. A miracle cure."

"For Agent X? Are you serious?"

"For everything. It's what Agent X was supposed to be: some kind of elixir of life for the fabulously wealthy." I couldn't stop a loony giggle from bursting out. "It's the gift that keeps on giving."

"Are you *serious?*" Julian took me roughly by the shoulders. "Where is it?"

"Hidden on the boat."

"Holy shit! Lulu! And you didn't *tell* anyone?" Horror and outrage were driving the initial disbelief from his voice. His hands were a pair of live wires. I could see he felt betrayed, not just for himself but for the whole human race.

"I didn't *know,*" I said. "I didn't realize where it was until just now!"

Julian was about to kill me or something, but Jake stepped in and said giddily, "She's fucking *bluffing,* dude. Can't you see that? She's *bluffing* the fuckers!"

Julian wavered, taken aback. "What?"

"Of course she's bluffing. She's buying us time; tricking them into letting us back on the boat. She's playing 'em!" Speaking in a fluted English accent, he said, " '*Their magic must be very powerful, or she wouldn't want them so badly.*' Remember in *The Wizard of Oz?*"

"Jake, shut up. Is that what's going on, Lulu? Because if

you're not bluffing and this shit is real, then you absolutely can *not* give it to them. It's our only leverage. If you hand it over we got nothing."

Jake said, "Don't you see? That's the beauty of it. It doesn't even matter if it's real or not. All that matters is that *they* think it's real! The Ruby Slippers! She's got it all worked out!"

"Do you, Lulu?"

I couldn't bring myself to answer. To let them down.

"Ice-cold, man," Jake marveled. "You think she's gonna tell you? Chick is ice-cold."

Don came galloping out the gate, ivory fangs gnashing. The sight of that red, white, and blue-daubed monster ripped us from our funk.

"Bad monkey!" Jake gibbered.

I held their sleeves and said, "Stay calm, he's tame, he's tame. Just wait."

"Are you sure?"

"He's friendly, you'll see."

"Are you *sure?*" There was no fight left in them, but they stood their ground, instinctively shielding me from the fantastic beast. Don raced around behind and menaced us toward the compound. Jake said, "If that thing bites me I'm gonna freak."

"Just walk. He's not going to bite you, trust me." As I said this I caught a peripheral look at the squirming remains of Hector and Shawn; a scalding rebuke to my continued prideful existence. *Trust me.* The peat fire that was my madness suddenly flared up and I ran to them, diving to my knees amid their loose parts and trying to piece them back together or something. I don't know what I was doing. Just before Julian dragged me away, I had picked up a small piece of Hector and swallowed it. Screwing my eyes shut, I pressed on the implant with the heel of my hand until pain routed everything else.

Laser dots swarmed us like persistent flies as we were shepherded through the gate.

"Any time, Lulu."

Colonel Lowenthal's weasely voice, amplified by the intercom, was piercingly loud in the confines of the cell, a brightly lit metal tank exactly like the ones I had seen holding Mr. Cowper and the other Xombies. Now I was on the mirrored side of the glass, sandwiched between Jake and Julian in a space about the size of a phone booth.

I looked at our scruffy reflection and summoned the words, "I want to make a trade." It was not me speaking, but it was so sane-sounding I said it again: "I want to make a trade."

"We've already made one. I fulfilled my end of the bargain, now it's your turn."

"I'm not going to tell you anything until you return our people to the boat."

"I see."

"Once we're all out there and Captain Coombs is back in charge, I will let him set the conditions under which we will hand over the materials. I don't think I can make that determination on my own."

"Really? You mean to say that's too much responsibility for an underdeveloped seventeen-year-old girl to handle? I'm shocked. And here I was all prepared to fold."

"Fuck you," said Julian.

"I'm sorry," Lowenthal said, anything but. *"I shouldn't joke. It's just funny to me that you think you're in a position to negotiate. You sound like some of the guys we had to deal with here, all polished brass, as if military protocol was some kind of natural law like gravity. They couldn't tell which way the wind was blowing until it blew them away. It was really sad. Lucky for me, I guess. But you're just like them—you think you're privileged to hold onto your illusions, exempt from anything that doesn't suit you. Haven't you learned anything by now? Maybe they let you get away with this on the sub, but if so, I don't know why you're demanding to have that dummy Coombs be put back in charge. Captain Lulu is more like it."*

"If you think you're intimidating me, you're wrong," I said. "I know how important what I have is to you. You and your *Moguls*. Well, tell them they'll never get it without me, not until you set us free."

"*Ooooh. Listen to her. Hey, it may be true we'll never find it, lady, but at this point I seriously doubt you know anything helpful. I personally think your papa destroyed it, if it ever really existed, but we'll keep searching every inch of that sub until we know for sure, even if it takes a year. Either way we're not cutting any more deals. All you're doing now is grasping at straws, trying to buy time. I respect that—it's what I would do in your position—but unless you have something real to offer, it has to end now.*"

"It is real. I could take you to it right now, right this second, but I guarantee you'll never find it if anything happens to us or anyone else from the boat."

"*You're such a baby. Even if that were true, don't you realize your best bet is to accept what you've been so generously offered? Full citizenship in MoCo, security, a halfway-decent future? Life, goddammit! It's the most anyone can hope for now, and you're throwing it away because somebody changed the rules on you and your feelings are hurt? I don't think so; you're not that dumb. And if you are . . . well, honey, we no longer have the luxury of being able to save people like you from themselves, I'm sorry.*"

Julian said, "It's you we need to be saved from, asshole."

Lowenthal suddenly seemed to lose all interest. "*I'm sure we're all in dire need of a savior. In the meantime, we have to manage as best we can. Without Miska's data we'll have to beef up our own research, which means we need a lot of test subjects. Fortunately, we've just received a big shipment by U-boat: You three will participate in the the first clinical trial, starting right now.*"

"Good!" yelled Jake, losing it. "Bring it on, motherfucker!"

"*I will.*"

"You do that!"

"I am."

"We don't give a shit!"

"You got it."

"Then *do* it, if you got the stones! Bust a move!"

"Jake, be quiet."

"It's done," said the Colonel. *"Just a few seconds now . . ."* There was a slithering noise outside the tank, getting louder. *"Well, it's been fun."*

"You're out of your mind," I said.

"That's what they said about Masters and Johnson."

From a row of chrome spouts high up the wall, ice–cold water began gushing in.

I THOUGHT I knew what cold water was. I had spent plenty of time mucking around in tidepools, foraging oysters, clams, and periwinkles in the dead of winter, with my numbed fingers getting all cut up by mussel shells as I dug. But this was colder. Cold was the wrong word for this. This *burned*. Burned like it was peeling off skin as it rose over feet, ankles, calves, knees, thighs, crotch, hips, waist, nipples, shoulders. The boys and I pressed together as tightly as we could, our shouts and moans lost in the deafening torrent:

"Oh my God, it's so cold!" "Turn it off!" "Hang on!" "Get closer!" "Away from the spray, right here!" "Let us out!"

As the lapping tide threatened to rise over my head, I had to swim, meaning I was forced to surrender my precious upraised arms to that searing flood; the last warmth I could give without going under completely.

Then the boys were lifting me from either side, boosting me above the swirling, green pool. My white flesh was as rubbery as a half-thawed turkey, but not so dead that I couldn't feel the vivid pleasure of warm air.

"No!" I shrieked, fighting the intense relief. "You can't!"

"Shut up, we're taller," said Julian.

"Pretend you're on *Girls Gone Wild*," Jake said.

I didn't try to resist as they propped me up on their shoulders, cradling my hips between their still-warm heads. My own head was jammed up against a caged light fixture in the ceiling, basking in its slight heat, while my submerged legs were sheathed in a fragile pocket of less-freezing water between the boys' bodies. If they moved at all, colder eddies swirled in like biting drafts. Violently shivering, I watched from my perch as Jake and Julian became immersed, standing on tiptoes and craning their necks until only their gulping, disembodied faces broke the surface like floating masks.

Pounding the intercom in front of my face, I screamed, "Stop! Stop it! Turn it off! Stop!"

The water stopped.

All of a sudden it was so quiet—the only sound was our teeth chattering in that shallow pocket of air, and I was miserably aware that the boys couldn't hear anything with their ears underwater. Nobody spoke. I searched their faces for some sign of what to do, but their eyes stared straight up, unblinking, all thoughts turned inward as warmth and life ebbed from their bodies. They hardly seemed aware of me.

She's bluffing, dude.

If you hand it over we got nothing.

Chick is ice-cold.

"I know where it is," I said.

"Where?" asked Lowenthal.

"Let us out first."

"No."

"Please!"

"No."

Sitting hunched there on the faltering shoulders of my friends was so precarious I expected it to be mercifully short, yet the moment stretched on and on like a detour in time, a missed off-ramp with no U-turn in sight, receding into eternity: all the loneliness, pointlessness, emptiness of it. The waiting. I realized it was not death but death's delay that was the ultimate cruelty.

To the intercom, I said, "D-d-don't you realize you're d-doing us a f-f-favor?" Lowenthal didn't reply.

As Jake and Julian succumbed, I begged them to hold on, not because I was afraid of the end, but because I was afraid of being left alone. I resented them going first. And yet I continued to struggle: As Jake went under, I clung to Julian, and even as Julian's upturned mouth filled with water, I tried to climb his sinking body to keep my own head above. In the end, I stood upon them both as the cold took its sweet time stealing over me.

Actually I wasn't getting colder. A deep warmth had started to bloom, and with it a dreamy calm. I knew what this was, this welcome, enfolding dark. I knew these were precursors to the end, and the gratitude I felt was indescribable. *Thank you thank you thank you thank you . . .*

But even as I slipped beneath the surface, trailing a string of mirrored bubbles, my alien hand found the necklace, snapped the chain, and held the locket up above the water. Up where the gold would catch the light.

I COULD FEEL cool grass against my cheek, and desert wind riffling my clothes. *Red sky at morning, sailor take warning.* I was heavy, immovable, a lizard sunning on a rock. In the hazy distance, I could see our old house in Oxnard, white as a milk carton on the grass, with the peeling eucalyptus trees and the laundry line. At first I sensed the presence of my mother inside and was overjoyed, wild to tell her something. Then I began to notice it wasn't right— the focus was peculiar—and as I reached my hand out the illusion collapsed: it was a miniature, a fake. A crummy little diorama. I was so frustrated I wanted to smash it! That's why I never liked miniatures and models, not even the good ones in museums, because the more real they are, the more daintily inviting, the more they put you at arm's length. But this one was the most crushing disappointment of all.

Maybe I was just too old for it. I remembered a time when it might have delighted me . . . like I was delighted by the toy circus set on my birthday cake when I was five: the plastic ferris wheel, the big top, the flags and trapeze, the clowns and camels. There was nothing realistic about it, nothing to scale. It was probably very cheap. But it was the only thing that interested me—the few other presents were so drab and functional I have no memory of them at all. But at the end of the party, the landlord and her daughter wrapped up what was left of the cake and disappeared with it.

Not sure what had just happened, I said, "Mummy, where did the circus go?"

"Oh, honey, those were just decorations. They belong to Mrs. Reese."

"But it's my birthday," I said, tears streaming. "I wanted them."

"Well, she made the cake, Lulu. I'm sorry. Come on now, be a big girl."

My mother's voice was growing faint. The house was empty, a cheap toy, and the more I pawed at it, the more unreal she became. My heart seized up with a terrible feeling of loss, and I called, "Mom!"

As I spoke, the dream shivered apart. I was in bed, naked as a baby, swaddled in flannel. It was no ordinary bed, but a fluffy giant pillow as rapturously soft and warm as a sheltering bosom—Mama Bear's bed. The room was dim, but the impression I got was something out of Ali Baba—a large carpeted tent with hanging swaths of colorful sheer fabric and pillows all over the place. Was I still dreaming? I squirmed deeper, away from bad thoughts and the ghostly hand petting my head.

"Welcome back, Lulu."

I scrunched up my face. It was that blond woman doctor—Dr. Langhorne. She was sitting cross-legged at the head of the bed. Her eyes were red and her face raw-scrubbed, as if fresh from a long crying jag.

"How are you feeling?" she asked.

"Alive," I murmured, heartsick.

"Oh yes. *You* were never in any danger. We made sure of that."

"*Why?*"

"Because you have a place here. You've earned a place here."

"Don't *say* that."

"Why not? It's a new day, Lulu. A brand-new life starts today."

"No . . ."

"Louise, I know this is hard, but from what I know about you, you're tough enough to take it. And starting tomorrow, things are going to get a whole lot easier."

Reluctantly, I asked, "How?"

"Tomorrow you'll get a guardian. Someone to take care of you."

"Oh."

"I know that doesn't mean much to you yet, but I think you'll find it exciting."

"Uh-huh."

"You're a princess around here. A rare bird. Important men are eager to meet you."

"You mean like they've been meeting the boys?"

She looked at me shrewdly, grateful to dispense with childish fictions. "Much more so," she said. "Boys are just a substitute born of necessity."

"Swell."

"You know, later on you'll have a chance to see some of your pals again, the ones who have been 'adopted.' You'll see that they're getting along just fine."

"Why not now?"

"They're still going through orientation."

"Why can't I go through orientation with them?"

She smiled and put her hand on my shoulder. "Honey, you don't need to."

I remained in bed all day, feeling leaden and ill. At intervals, my guts would seize up, bending me double and wringing out harsh silent tears, like juice from a frost-damaged lemon. As I used the bedpan, I wondered if there were any hidden cameras. Several Asian doctors dropped by to check my vitals, and I had the impression they had drawn straws for the privilege. They didn't speak English. Ridiculously sumptuous meals were brought on a cart—soft-boiled eggs, fresh fruit, a variety of breads and crackers with a basket of individual little spreads and cheeses, a pot of tea. At lunch there was an antipasto tray that could have fed six people, and at dinner a four-course meal with whole roasted game hens. I hardly ate any of it—I could tell it was from the boat.

Some time later, Dr. Langhorne returned, accompanied by a much older lady, a Miss Riggs, whose baggy face was plastered with makeup, and whose flaming copper wig looked about as natural as a coonskin cap. I couldn't believe they had given this poor old thing an implant! She dragged a huge rolling suitcase behind her like a homeless person.

"Lulu, Miss Riggs is going to help you get ready for tomorrow. She's a professional, so give her your full cooperation, okay?"

Professional what? I thought apprehensively.

"Oh, my achin' feet," said Miss Riggs, opening the suitcase and setting up a bright light on a stand. "Come on, honey. I ain't gettin' any younger." I hesitated because of my nakedness, but she didn't give a darn. "Let's go!" she squawked.

Half her suitcase was taken up by a big make-up kit with folding trays full of every conceivable grooming tool. I nearly swooned from the smell, which evoked the spicy-sweet aroma of numberless beauty parlors. The color palette had the worn look of long, expert use, and the tools and brushes were arranged as neatly as surgical instruments. The other half of the case contained a stack of carefully packed dresses, all plastic-wrapped as if fresh from the dry cleaner. On top I could see a baroque layered gown of jade silk and antique lace.

"Excuse me," Miss Riggs said to the doctor. "I can take it from here."

"I won't get in your way," said Langhorne.

"I can't stand people lookin' over my shoulder when I'm workin'! Beat it!"

Langhorne was shocked and furious, but she held her tongue. "All right," she said. "Let me know when you're done." To me, she said, "Your escort tomorrow will be a Mr. Utik. He'll be here at eleven, so be ready to go. He's conversant in Inuktitut, French, and Danish, but his English may leave something to be desired. I suggest you don't call him an Eskimo or he'll think you uncouth." She brusquely ducked out.

"Some people can't take a hint," the old lady said. "They don't understand the artistic temperment. You can't crowd talent. I learned that from Jayne Mansfield. You gotta stick up for yourself, or these bozos will walk all over ya." Measuring me, she said, "Honey, you sure ain't no Jayne Mansfield, I'll tell you that. How old are you?"

"Seventeen."

"That's a shame. You need some meat on your bones; you look like a plucked chicken. They treatin' you all right in here?"

I couldn't begin to answer; all I could do was cry.

"Aw honey, you're gonna be all right. You know how many fresh-faced young girls I worked with over the years? I seen 'em all go through it, even Marilyn Monroe. You ain't the first. Some became tramps, some became drunks and dope addicts, some made a career of getting knocked around by the wrong kind of men. There's always gonna be men who think having a pretty dame around will make them hate themselves less, and they take it out on the girl when it doesn't work. Ain't no different now. Hold still."

"What can I do?" I quavered. "What can I do?"

"Don't move." She was fastening the tiny hooks on a carapace-like bustier, her hands strong and nimble and utterly without hesitation or wasted movement, everything coming together with an accidental ease that suggested the opposite of entropy—order flowing from chaos. Despite her rheumy yellow eyes and cigarette-stained teeth, I sensed that nothing could shake her; she was solid. I wished she would stay with me and tell me what to do. I wanted to hide in her suitcase.

With effortless speed she threw clothes on me from that treasure chest of couture, one dazzling outfit after another, enough to stage the Oscars, all pristine and new. Obscenely plush designer gowns straight off a Paris runway; metallic silks and jewel-fruited filigree; blood-red taffeta and peach satin; cream lace studded with pearls; Versace, Gucci, Dior—annoying names that littered my consciousness with all the other obsolete pop-culture clutter, but which I had never seen on a label, suddenly delivered into my pauper's hands like so much pirate booty. Nothing fit me, but needles sprouted from Miss Riggs's withered lips, thread from her spiderlike hands, cinching in and hemming and pleating, filling out the tops with blubbery foam inserts so that for the first time in my life I looked like a woman. Amazed at my unfamiliar spangled self, I realized I was booty, too; part of the loot.

"You wanna know what to do?" she said through a mouthful of pins. "None of the above. That's the extent of my wisdom, hon: Do none of the above."

MISS RIGGS TOOK all the costumes with her to finish working on them—a whole lavish wardrobe, custom-fitted for me. I couldn't quite comprehend it. It had been such a bizarre flurry of activity that I almost believed I had imagined the whole thing, and it was a little bit of a shock the next morning to find all the completed dresses hanging in the tent, with a row of matching shoes lined up below. One of the outfits was set apart, and next to it was something I never expected to see again: the hooded fur cape Hector had given me. I wept to touch it. It had been cleaned and brushed to a high reddish gloss, matching perfectly with the teal-and-black ensemble I was to wear.

At exactly eleven (by the Tiffany watch that had appeared on my bedstand), a pair of Air Force men came in through the tent flap and escorted me down a sausage-like inflated tunnel. I sensed them taking great pains not to stare at me in my finery.

"What happens now?" I asked them.

"We're not at liberty to say, ma'am."

"What do you think of all this?" I tapped my forehead nodule.

One of them was annoyed by my questions, but the other one said, "Everybody's just coping. That's all you can do. Forget who you were and roll with it. Those who can't . . ." He shrugged.

Eyes swimming with tears, I said, "I'm not sure if I can live like that."

"You wouldn't be the first."

At the end, we came to a revolving door and they sent me through. Pushed by a gust of warm air, I emerged on an enclosed balcony in pale, subzero twilight. I was outside the dome!

There was someone else on the balcony. A large Inuit man in a long black overcoat with the collar turned up and a gleaming stovepipe hat. He had no implant, making me more aware than ever of mine.

"Oh," I said. "Are you Mr. Utik?"

Doffing the hat with a comical flourish, he said, "Herman." He opened a pneumatic outer door and gestured me through. I braced for the murderous cold, but he took his heavy coat off and wrapped it around me as we went. Underneath, he was wearing a striking charcoal uniform with jodhpurs, gold buttons, and highly polished leather boots. The outfit made him look like some kind of Prussian officer. His face was familiar, and then I realized he was the bus driver who had intercepted us at the perimeter wall.

I looked across the white divide to that motley armada of planes and suddenly made the connection—I was being taken out there. Mogul country. Mr. Utik hustled me down a short flight of stairs to a waiting armored truck, and two other equally decked-out native Greenlanders appeared to help me aboard. They all stared at me with frank curiosity.

Climbing into the truck, I had to laugh: From the outside it looked like some kind of tank or riot vehicle, replete with turret, but on the inside it was an outrageous Victorian carriage, roomy as a small RV, with velvet-upholstered walls, pastoral thumbnail portraits in gilded frames (by the likes of Sargent and Cassatt—if they were real), stained-glass lamps, a small mahogany bookcase with miniature editions of Herodotus and Thucydides, two antique divans, and curtains over the gun slits.

"Oh my God," I said, plopping down on one of the burgundy divans. It reminded me of a psychiatrist's couch. All I could think was, *If this van's a-rockin—*

Mr. Utik got me squared away as the others took their places in the cockpit, tucking high-tech hot-water bottles around my legs and showing me a cooler full of liquor.

"No thanks," I said. "I'm underage." This seemed to fluster him, and he gave the order for us to get going. "I'd give anything to know what you make of all this," I said in an undertone as the vehicle lumbered forward.

"Better than hunting seal," said Utik, sitting behind the drivers.

"What?"

"I said it's better than freezing your ass off out on the ice hunting seal. That's what these guys would be doing now if we weren't working for the *qallunaat*." He pointed to their backs in turn—"This is Nulialik, and this little runt is my brother, Qanatsiak."

"You speak English."

"Shhh—don't tell anyone."

"Why tell me, then?"

"You're not one of them."

"How do you know?"

"I'm a spy." He winked at me.

"Give me a break."

"I'm spying on you right now."

"I'd believe that."

"But I'm also spying on *them*."

"The Moguls?"

"Kapluna. Qallunaat."

"What for?"

"Something big is going on. Bigger than all this. We want to know what it is."

From his grin I couldn't tell if he was being serious or not. "Who's 'we'?" I asked.

"Ilagiit nangminariit—my extended family, and many others, led by an elder—the *inhumataq.* He believes we bear a special responsibility for all that is happening. We may be the only ones with the power to intervene."

"How so?"

"The indigenous peoples of the Arctic are now the dominant race on the planet. Our civilization is the most intact; the meek have inherited the Earth, just as Christ foretold. But this means nothing unless we can stop the *tunraq kigdloretto* that has been unleashed."

"The what?"

"The thing you call Agent X. We call it a *tunraq*—a spirit invoked by a shaman. Usually it's a helper spirit, but if it is invoked for evil purposes, *ilisiniq,* it can get out of control and even turn on its user. The *kigdloretto* is this kind of rogue spirit."

"Okay . . ."

"My Netsilik anscestors routinely practiced female infanticide, and many of us now believe that it is the ghosts of these girls that are coming back to possess the living. We think they were released by an *angotkok,* a powerful shaman, who is practicing witchcraft."

"Do you really believe that?"

"All the Seal People were converted to Catholicism long ago, so there aren't many who remember the old ways. Most of what we know comes from legends we heard as children. But a lot of the legends are relevant—it isn't superstition to see connections where they exist. Is it a coincidence that menstrual blood was one of the most powerful instruments of *ilisiniq?"*

"But how does that help you? What is it you think you can do about it? Cast a spell or something?"

"You're humoring me, but I do believe the answer lies somewhere in our tradition. It's a question of recognizing the signs when we see them and interpreting them correctly."

"Good luck."

"It's not a matter of luck, but of fate. Whatever is supposed to happen will happen. Is it luck that all our hunting parties were pinned down by a blizzard on the day the women turned? We came back after a week to find our houses cold, our families gone. The few men and old people who survived told what they saw, showed us the blue bodies of the ghost-ones, frozen while trying to break down the doors of the living. Many children, too. Whole towns were dead, and yet all the able-bodied men survived, far out on the sea-ice. Was that luck? Some thought we were cursed to have survived. I knew it was for a reason, and when I heard that the *qallunaat* were arriving in great numbers I realized it was connected to our purpose. We're here." He got up and threw the door open, admitting a blast of cold. Aircraft loomed around us like a forest.

I didn't want to move just yet. "How did you wind up working here?"

"I've worked for them a long time. I started by selling fossil ivory out of a kiosk in the BX, then I served for eight years as Native Liaison and Labor Coordinator for the Danish Interests Office, which used to broadcast Danish Radio off a transmitter at Thule."

"*Danish* radio?"

"Kalaallit Nunaat, what you call Greenland, is part of Denmark."

"No, I know, but you speak English."

"I grew up in western Canada, outside Yellowknife. Also, there were Canadians and Americans here at Thule. It was what they call a 'joint-use facility.' I remember once a guy from Siorapaluk was caught toking up, and he told them that's what he thought it meant. They let him off the hook!

We got along pretty well with the Air Force. I didn't like to see them slaughtered."

I thought of the frozen body parts at the perimeter wall. "What exactly happened?"

"Same as with my people. *Piblokto*. Madness. Starting with the women, the blue ones spread like lice, but the blizzard prevented them from getting far. There were not many women to begin with, mostly wives of officers. By the time it was over, the Base Commander's Office was being run by a small-fry like that Lowenthal, who kept issuing statements that help was coming, and the situation was 'well in hand.' When the first wave of planes landed, it seemed to be like he promised. The planes were full of important civilian men with a private army of their own.

"But no one was airlifted out; in fact, it was the other way around. More and more newcomers arrived, setting up a separate command post outside the base perimeter. The planes just kept coming in, bringing everything you see now. The Air Force and Air National Guard people who went along with it all got promoted and rewarded, while the ones who complained or resisted were left to rule the empty remains of their base, totally isolated like the Vikings that perished here long ago.

"Since native workers became the only interface between the two systems, we saw it all go down: the frustration of the banished ones as they had to beg for supplies, and the feudal society of the domes. We knew it couldn't last, and it didn't."

"They killed them."

"The second dome had just gone up, and all the military men decided enough was enough—they were gonna march in and demand their rights. So they put on their dress uniforms, loaded their sidearms, and tried a show of force. But those automatic COIL weapons were already in place; there were not even any MPs to appeal to or intimidate. It lasted about two seconds. Not many under the dome even knew it happened."

"*What* happened?"

"Same as with your friend."

I had a horrible flash of Mr. DeLuca on the snowbank, just before . . . "I didn't really see that. It was too fast."

"It's a laser beam, like *Star Wars*. COIL stands for Chemical Oxygen-Iodine Laser. It's an anti-ballistic missile system, but it works just as good against people." Sounding awkward, he said, "I'm sorry."

"You don't have to be sorry," I replied. "It's not your fault. It's nobody's fault. We're all just killing time until the end, I guess."

"No, I mean I'm sorry, but you have to get up. It's time to go."

"Oh."

Helping me out of the truck, he said, "You speak of killing time. We call winter the killing time. Just as summer follows winter, we believe there will be a new season for my people. For all people. We are chosen to be witnesses to the fall, so that we may tell the story—it's a great responsibility. This means you, too. You carry within you the story of your people, and you must pass it on."

"That's a little hokey, I'm sorry."

"Why? What do you think's gonna happen?"

"I think spring is going to come and the Xombies will finish taking over the world. The Moguls will either fight it out to the end, or turn themselves into a better class of Xombie. There won't be any more babies, and eventually it'll all just sputter out. That's fine. I don't even care anymore."

"What do you mean, turn themselves into Xombies?"

"They're all Xombie wannabes in there. Maybe it's the blue blood. They tried to make a race of supermen and got Xombies instead. They're still at it."

We entered a tented area between jumbo jets, and Mr. Utik led me through a series of insulating flaps to a security station humming with electric radiators. I was reminded of the sub; of its cheap power in the hands of these people. We had come cheap, too, I guess. Armed sentries dressed in commando garb stole lewd looks at me, but were outwardly respectful . . . if not outright nervous. I wondered if they saw me as some kind of a threat. Not as a potential Xombie, but as an elite sex slave; a concubine with royal privilege. It was strange to think about.

Utik left me there without a word, and I wondered if he had been mocking or testing me; but our conversation was already unreal and fading fast. I didn't have the capacity for worry that I once had; it just sloughed off. I felt slow and stupid, and liked it that way.

I climbed an enclosed ramp and boarded the plane. It was not a 747, but it was close—a seven-something-seven. After the fancy carriage ride, I was expecting the Palace of Versailles, but the interior of the jet was more low-key— not exactly understated, but of a more contemporary splen- dor: a wide-open seating area like a sleek hotel bar, with earth-toned carpeting and furniture, and aqua lighting from banks of TV monitors. At the back there was a softly lit hallway like a modern-art gallery, leading past smaller compartments. Out of this hall emerged a lithe-looking older man. He was dressed in a striped satin robe as shiny as those Christmas ribbon candies, and his bald head gleamed intermittently in the spotlights, implant-free. He looked like he had just stepped out of the shower.

My snap judgement was, *Well, could be worse*. I was shaking like a leaf.

As he approached, I could see that despite his age and slight limp he was quite handsome, with chiseled features and the unthreatening demeanor of a man sharing a laugh at his own expense. My hackles went up: *Pervert*. He looked at me in the eager, expectant way of some forgotten acquain- tance—an elementary-school teacher or distant uncle. But I *did* know him. Why was he so familiar?

"Hello, Lulu," he said, gravel-voiced. "Welcome."

It was Sandoval.

twenty-six

"DON'T YOU REMEMBER me? I know we were never properly introduced, but your father talked about you so much, I already feel like I know you. I'm Jim Sandoval."

"I remember you. Chairman Sandoval."

Actually, I was trying hard to remember; trying to imagine what it could mean that he was here. All I really remembered of him was a gruff voice in the goat locker and that long-ago leap to the sub. The last time I had seen him was when he snubbed me going ashore. But I also dimly recalled that first night out on the deck, when he was surrounded by angry men—Mr. Cowper chief among them—who seemed to think he was the reason we were locked out of the boat. He had betrayed them for SPAM. He *was* SPAM. I remember I had felt great empathy for Sandoval, not just because he was injured and helpless, but because at the time I was being harrassed by a hostile mob myself.

"I hope the ride wasn't too unpleasant," he said. "It's

what passes for limousine service around here. Are you cold?"

"No."

"Really? I'm glad. You look spectacular." When I didn't reply, he said, "Lulu, nothing's going to happen. You don't have to be afraid of me. I know it's been . . . incredibly difficult, but that's all over. You're safe now."

"I've heard that before." I refused to meet his eyes.

"I'm just making clear my intentions. I'm not your lord; you are not my chattel. You are part of my household, yes, but that's only so you can be spared the unpleasantness that some other men might have visited upon you. The world is poor enough without that. Wherever you go here, you are under my protection, which merely means you will be left alone. I'll certainly never lay a hand on you without your consent. All I ask is that you honor me with your company on such occasions as I may request it, purely as a friend."

I must have been radiating cynicism and contempt. Smiling a little, he said, "Your doubts prove your character. I hope you'll give me a chance to prove mine."

"Do I have a choice?"

"Lulu, you've seen the other side. You've tested the waters. It's because you made a choice that you are here today, and I very much want you to succeed. To stay." He reached for my hand.

I recoiled as if from a striking cobra, more violently than I intended.

He backed off. "I know you're still in shock, but you have to understand that I do this out of caring, not because I want to torture you."

"No, just my friends!"

"That was not my doing. The domes have their own hierarchy—we have a strict hands-off policy out here to keep the peace. Otherwise . . . too many cooks, you know?"

"You all stink."

"Maybe so, but I'm your ticket out of there." He lit a slim black cigarette and offered me one. I declined. Savoring the smoke, he said, "Would your friends want you to throw away your chance at life? Weren't they willing to give up their lives to save yours? I'm sure it's their wish that you should go on."

"Their *final* wish. Just shut up—we both know what this is about."

"You're wrong. You want to know what it's about? Talk. A little innocent talk."

"Baloney. Talk is cheap."

"That's where you're wrong. Talk is really all that matters; talk about real things. Believe me, I know. When you spend as much time in the realms of business and politics as I have, you learn the meaning of the term 'seats of power'—it's because they're full of the biggest asses on Earth! I'll tell you a secret: The Moguls? They're idiots."

"Yeah, and you're one of them."

"No, I'm not. I'm not. I didn't start out this way. I grew up in group homes and foster care, and I never even knew who my father was until I received notice from a legal firm in Zurich that he had died."

"Oh, boo hoo."

"I learned only then that he had been a silent partner in the global economy—one of these puppetmasters of capitalism you see all around us. I also learned I was a secret billionaire, with fortunes buried like dog bones in tax havens around the world, safe from prying eyes. But he had left me more than money—he left me a manifesto, a battle plan. The means of waging war against an enemy he himself had created."

"What enemy?" I sneered.

"All my father's interests: his corporations, his politicians, his offshore banks, his media holdings. Thousands of seemingly independent entities all owned by third parties under his invisible web of control. Except he felt he had lost control of it; it had all become corrupt and evil, an unstable kleptocracy that was dragging down mankind rather than bettering it. He had experienced some kind of epiphany, I guess, when he found out he had HIV. Before he died he wanted to overhaul everything, come clean, but he knew he was too compromised—the lawyers would bury him before he could scratch the surface. He needed someone spotless.

"Then he remembered some poor girl he had knocked up and abandoned back in his fraternity days. My dear mother. She was dead but I wasn't, and in me he saw the opportunity to reduce the amount of bullshit in the world, to forge a nobler purpose for mankind than 'shop 'til you drop.' This was my inheritance, this mission."

In spite of myself, I asked, "What did you do?"

"Nothing. Not a thing. I had been through hell because of that asshole, had seen my mother die in poverty and been bounced all over kingdom come—I didn't care about his stupid crusade. I had my own life. I wanted to be a jazz musician. Life as a plutocrat didn't interest me, and I didn't realize how right my instincts were until I met some of those people. They're peasants, Lulu. Greedy, witless provincials to whom global power is an extension of their golf game. Amoral louts who dismiss art, nature, the whole universe, as socialist propaganda. Anything they can't win at is for suckers. They have no imagination; no humor beyond dirty limericks. They're *boring*. But I'll say this for them: they're survivors. There's nothing they won't do to ensure their survival."

"So I've seen."

"I guess you have. To them you're nothing but a status symbol. I'm risking a lot taking you under my wing—it stirs up trouble for me to have something none of them has, especially since I'm a Johnny-come-lately to begin with. My people here thought I was dead, and were about to start trading my assets for new alliances when I showed up on that submarine. Now they all hate me. So you see, talk may be cheap, but you were expensive."

"I never asked to be bought."

"I know that. Come sit down. I won't touch you."

"I'm fine here. What happens now?"

"Nothing at all. I'm at your service. Anything you'd like, just ask. We have a tremendous library on disc, as well as music, movies, games, you name it. There's also a hot shower or a sauna if that would help you relax. Or a drink."

"No thanks."

"You're also free to return to your quarters in the bubble at any time. You're not a prisoner here."

"Quarters?" I had assumed I would be living in the plane with him.

"Yes, the private area you've just come from, that's yours. Of course, if you're not satisfied with that, other arrangements might be—"

"No, that's fine. I would like to head back, if it's okay with you."

If he was angry or disappointed, he didn't show it. "Absolutely. We'll talk again tomorrow. I have a little proposal I'd like to discuss with you. Purely business." Stubbing out his cigarette, he said, "We'll have lunch."

OVER THE FOLLOWING week, I found Sandoval to be as good as his word, though I didn't let my guard down for a second. His business proposal was exactly that: a request for my services as a copy editor. Somehow he had gotten hold of my UNIX files from the boat and was very impressed with my sense of "melodrama." He wanted me to vet some kind of speech he had to deliver, touting the accomplishments of the Mogul Research Division. Out of relief that the proposal didn't involve fellatio, I agreed to it.

Most of my time was my own, to be spent exploring the vast indoor facility of the domes or channel surfing the even more vast quantity of recorded entertainment. At first I laughed to see a TV in my quarters, thinking of it as a silly relic, until I turned it on and discovered the interactive bonanza available by cable. My mother and I had never had cable, except in motels. The Valhalla database was comprehensive to the point of absurdity—there seemed to be no book, magazine, movie, TV or radio program, videogame, music, or hard-to-define other that was not included in the listing. Apparently, this was what the elite did with their time here.

I wondered how they did it without becoming utterly depressed—there was something disturbing about all those images from the fallen world. Was this what we had to show for our civilization, this catalogue of trivia? Flintstones Chewables and *General Hospital?* It was. Like it or not, we were the new Essenes, and this mishmash of hype and nonsense and vanishingly rare beauty was our Dead Sea Scrolls.

I found myself dwelling on news coverage taped during the last days, everything I and my mother had missed, from Special Bulletins intruding on painful-to-watch sitcom jollity to the final technical glitches, gaps in the broadcast, and dead air that presaged the end. I saw a crudely edited compilation of police dashboard cams showing officers arriving at the scene and being ambushed by Xombies. I saw aerial footage of city streets overrun with Xombies, and Xombies storming the White House. I saw the president, unshaven, as he wearily addressed the nation:

"In all the hysteria, we must not forget that these unfortunates are victims as well, that they deserve compassion, not hate or fear; and treatment, not destruction. They are not she-devils, but afflicted human beings who, through no fault of their own, are caught up in this emergency along with the rest of us. Terms like 'Xombie' and 'Hellion' only lead to misunderstanding and needless violence. I think we can all agree that the last thing this nation needs now is more violence. Let us show that we can rise above our fear and approach this desperate situation as a public health issue, not as a witch hunt. We are not a nation of executioners, but a nation of mourners. We are a nation that will do the right thing. Goodbye, and God bless America." Then he shot himself in the head. Men jumped to tend him, and the camera remained on just long enough to capture their wild flurry of panic and gunfire as he revived.

In this way I witnessed it all for the first time, and really understood how strange I had become, because the simple, puerile old world seemed infinitely stranger to me than the dark one it had spawned.

Every day, Sandoval and I had a sumptuous lunch in the plane, and he would tell funny anecdotes about his early, fumbling encounters with great wealth, suggesting that he knew what I was going through. I was not much in the way of company, but he didn't seem to mind. He also told me about how he had founded the Mogul Cooperative:

"Originally it was meant to be a joke!" he said. "There was this crazy explosion of wealth during the Reagan years, and it just became obscene to me. Financial firms blatantly touting sleazy tax shelters and 'wealth preservation' at the same time I was exploring ways to redistribute my own dirty money. What was it all for? I wanted to do something to mock all that avarice, so I took it to its logical extreme: You *can* take it with you! Let me tell you how!

"Since one of my holdings was a reputable biochemical company, it was easy to make a classy prospectus, but all I really wanted to do was make a point. My mistake was letting that professor, Uri Miska, chair the foundation. He wasn't in on the prank, and he stole the show from day one. What a maniac! At first I thought he was the best snake-oil salesman of all time, and I couldn't believe the interest he was drumming up—elderly fat-cats were apparently all too happy to throw money at us rather than at their greedy heirs—but then the whole thing began taking on a life of its own. It was paying for itself and getting bigger year after year; I couldn't pull the plug. Eventually I just left it to Miska, not knowing if I had scored the biggest coup of all time or . . . done something else. Of course, now we know the answer to that, twenty years too late."

"So this whole thing is your doing." I said this with all the animation of a dead fish.

"Indirectly, I suppose. I started the ball rolling. But

what did I know? The one who really made it happen was Dr. Miska."

"What became of him?"

"He disappeared. When everything went down, he trashed the Providence lab and took off with his experimental 'Tonic.' We recovered what we could—some data and a small sample—and transferred it by helicopter to the submarine for safekeeping. This was all in the heat of the Agent X outbreak—you can imagine the difficulties. We lost hundreds of men on the ground. All of them, actually. Only the helicopter pilot and I made it back to the plant." He said this as if it made him shaky to think about it.

"Lucky you just happened to have a submarine lying around."

"Hey, what can I tell you? Submarines were my hobby ever since I was a kid. With some guys it's model trains. I just happened to be in a position to own my own submarine factory. If I'd known it would be such a headache, I would've unloaded it long ago."

"Poor little rich boy."

"No, but until you're faced with the kinds of choices I've had to make, you can't judge."

"You mean like choosing SPAM over people?"

This struck a nerve. "SPAM had nothing to do with it," he said. "I had to be sure that the Tonic would reach its destination. We couldn't predict what would happen with a lot of refugees on board—it was too much like letting the inmates run the asylum."

"But you *promised* them!"

"It was the only way to keep them on the job. That sub had to be seaworthy and ready to go. There was no other choice. Of course it was all moot after you and Cowper showed up."

"We were only trying to survive."

"I know. I don't blame you for almost getting me killed. That was *your* only choice. At that moment, you had the leverage and would have been stupid not to use it. Plus, stealing the Tonic ensured that we didn't dare throw you overboard. The most we could do was lock Cowper up and try to get him to talk."

"But . . . you were in there with him. You were arrested, too."

"No, I wasn't." His lips formed into a sly, rueful smile.

He had been *pretending* to be a prisoner. That whole time. "You lying creep," I said.

"Hey, it was all I could think of to get Cowper's confidence. It was rough, too. I was stuck in there with a ruptured kneecap, and Fred Cowper is not the most gentle nursemaid a person could ask for. I should have known he was too smart to open up—did you know he was my first choice to command the boat? I was very disappointed when he turned me down. I never liked that Coombs. He tolerates too much hanky-panky."

"You mean like giving me the run of the ship."

"No, that was actually deliberate. We thought Cowper might confide something to you through the door. You were slower on the uptake than we expected, though—it took you a week to find him."

"Thanks."

"*De nada*. More tea?"

EACH DAY WHEN I returned to my tent it was a little more furnished, more deluxe, though the one amenity I really wanted was a bathroom—I didn't like using a chamber pot, no matter how unobtrusively it was whisked away, and I would have liked to wash more often. I suspected that Sandoval was allowing me only so much comfort, so that visiting him would remain a welcome indulgence.

One thing that surprised me was how free I was to roam around. Valhalla was wide open to me, and I could even leave the bubble altogether via my private balcony if I could stand the cold, though I wouldn't get much farther than that. There was no Inuit taxi service except by Mogul appointment.

My tent was at the northwest side of the main bubble, close to the wall, in a thinly peopled region of giant helium tanks, compressors, and webs of anchor cable. The lines creaked eerily from the force of the wind outside—I gathered the dome would blow away without these robust moorings, which moaned like the tortured rigging of a great sailing ship. I could see why most people chose to live more toward the center, in the faux-cheery surroundings of the Global Village. But at least I could come and go as I pleased.

What I quickly discovered, however, was that there was nowhere I cared to go. My first act after leaving Sandoval was to try and find someone, anyone, from the sub. This did not require much of a search—I remembered what the boys had told me about being able to locate a person by their implant, and immediately found this monitoring system—the Valhalla Directory, or VD—on Channel 8 of my interactive television. All I had to do was type in a name, and the selected implantee would appear as a numbered dot on a map of the complex.

I could find myself, I could find Dr. Langhorne or Dr. Stevens or Rudy or Colonel Lowenthal or even Miss Riggs, but the people I really wanted to find were not there: all the surviving boys and men from the boat. They were either being detained outside the bubble . . . or they were gone altogether. I prayed it was the former, but either way they were out of reach. I was alone.

What made this worse was my isolation within the complex. Except for the doctors, no one would speak to me, no one would come anywhere near me, and when I ventured out of my area I felt like Typhoid Mary—word got around that I was coming, and people disappeared into their holes like timid rabbits. I could sometimes see stragglers clearing out as I approached, and it made me mad. Obviously they were following my movements, using the Directory to shun me, but why? I remembered what Dr. Langhorne had told me about sexual competition here, and wondered if that was it—did they hate me because they thought I was an interloper poaching on their territory? Were they scared of me because they thought I could bring Sandoval's might to bear? If that was so, it was worth thinking about. How much power did I wield? What could I get away with?

The more I considered, the more I began to feel a peculiar thrill of a kind I had never experienced before. Look at it objectively, I thought: If Sandoval was king, and he adopted me, that made me a princess. Even in less fanciful terms, he was certainly one of the most powerful men on Earth—and had been even before Agent X—whereas what had I been? A nothing, a nobody . . . yet it was me he wanted by his side. Furthermore, even at fifty-ish he wasn't exactly a broken-down old geezer. Again, looking objectively, he was handsome, charming, even boyish in a way— all the qualities prized by romance novelists. In my young girlhood I had been a secret reader of such tripe, and it must have been lying dormant—my Harlequin gene—waiting for the right moment to bust out. The fact that he didn't make me physically ill made anything possible.

Every now and then I was overwhelmed with the numb gratitude of a sweepstakes winner—maybe I was not going to have to suffer and die like the others . . . or even break much of a sweat. This kind of fantasizing began to occupy more and more of my thoughts, steering them away from uglier matters. Maybe I was *set for life!* Whatever became of the rest of these people, I was off the hook. I had a *man.*

Or did I? What about those who were resentful, who felt I had an unfair advantage? *You already have enemies here,* Dr Langhorne had said. *You're a threat.* What would they do to me? No, the question was, what would I be willing to do to hold onto my advantage? Some deep, grubbing part of me, I knew, would do just about anything. Paranoia and self-loathing added their flavors to my demented euphoria.

But why should I fear the worst, when Sandoval had all but promised me anything I wanted? I was getting way ahead of myself. This was my chance to take an active role in deciding how the future played out—if Sandoval was so interested in proving himself to me, then he would have to show some goodwill to my friends. Put them under my jurisdiction, maybe, as they had been on the sub. It was too late for Mr. Cowper and Hector and Julian and—no . . . I didn't dare think of them. Bang on the implant until they go away. But there were many more to save. And if my position was as secure as I hoped, I would work toward more humanitarian policies for the complex as a whole. We should all be working together!

A vast sense of responsibility and purpose welled up inside me. Utik was right—I was the Mother of the Future, *me*. Somehow all this fell to me. But I had to be careful; if I was going to flex my muscles, I would have to tread lightly; come up with a plan. Approach Sandoval. And most of all beware the jealous envy of the less-enlightened.

The next day, over our sixth lunch together, I made my case to him.

"No," he said.

I was caught short. The brevity of his dismissal was inappropriate to the well-reasoned, inspiring 12-point proposal I had spent all night drafting.

"Why not?" I asked.

"Why not?" The question seemed to amuse and disgust him. "Lulu, you're not Eleanor Roosevelt and I'm not FDR. You're a sweet girl, and I know you had to do this as a matter of conscience. I salute you, but that's about it. Now that you've done all you can, try to relax."

"But you—"

"No buts!" A trace of anger flashed across his face. Then he relented a bit and said, "Look, I know where you're coming from. I used to be a charitable man. When you have great wealth, it's easy to be generous, especially when it's tax-deductible. Humanitarian awards, honorary degrees, hospital wings, plaques—I could have had it all if I hadn't given anonymously. But I'm not here today because I was generous. None of us is, not even you. We survived out of pure selfishness, and must continue to do so. It may not

seem like it, but we're in a school of piranha here: at the
first sign of weakness they attack. Don't look so down in the
mouth—I know it sounds cruel, but once you accept the necessity of it, you will begin to see the higher purpose: hon-
oring the gift of life. We won't redress the world's wrongs
by sacrificing ourselves. We must *exalt* ourselves, or risk
being destroyed by others who do."

"I think that's called looking out for number one."

"No, you want to know what it's called? Here's what it's
called."

He picked up a remote control and programmed something into it, then struck a disco pose as the lights dimmed
and kaleidoscopic colors swirled around the plane's cabin.
The sound system began booming out *Stayin' Alive* by the
BeeGees. His silvery robe and pajamas flashed as he paraded
around.

When it was clear I was not going to get up and start
boogeying, he shut it all down and said, "Okay, look. You
want to see your friends? Here's what's going to happen. I
shouldn't be telling you this, but there's going to be a big
ceremony tomorrow night out at the submarine. Big doings.
All the Moguls are going to be there, and your people will
be with them. I had planned to tell you tomorrow, but those
big sad eyes are killing me—you could have made a fortune
for charity." He held out his hand to me. "Is it a date?"

Heart slugging like a prizefighter, I nodded and took it.

twenty-seven

THE NEXT NIGHT, Sandoval personally escorted me from my tent to Utik's armored carriage. We looked impossibly fabulous, me in my jade-and-parchment dress, and he in gleaming baronial black tie, as if we were going to some kind of fairy tale ball. But I felt grotesque; not well. Anxiety had been building and building all day, and now the prospect of seeing all those familiar faces again—people it had taken me so long to win over—was caning my stomach like a piñata. What did I have to offer them? What was there to say to each other? I felt like the Whore of Babylon.

Utik got us situated on the divans with brusque efficiency, paying no special attention to me. Refusing the hot-water bottles, Sandoval said to him, "That's fine, Herman. Let's go, we're running late." Utik nodded and took his seat, barking something to the drivers. The vehicle lurched into motion.

"Isn't this exciting?" Sandoval asked me, grinning like an idiot.

I nodded stiffly.

"Bet you thought you'd never see that submarine again."

"Are we going on board?"

"No."

"Then why aren't we dressed for the outdoors?"

"You'll see," he said with a mischievous twinkle.

We sped through the planes, across the airfield, and toward the barrier wall. Looking out a gunport at the arctic night, I had a brief twinge thinking about that COIL weapon. "They're not going to shoot us by accident are they?" I asked.

"No," Sandoval replied. "We have a radio beacon that protects us. You see this?" He produced a hefty pen from his sleeve—it was chained to his wrist—and pushed a button on it. A red spot of light appeared on the wall.

"Yeah, it's a laser pointer. What is it with those things?"

"It's more than a laser pointer. It's also sending out a radio signal to the defensive array. It not only protects us, but anything I point at, I can destroy at the touch of a button. One of the perks of Moguldom." He put the thing away, looking as pleased as a little kid.

"Where do you get all this stuff?"

"Off-the-shelf, mostly. This is just a cheap computer accessory that we adapted to the existing missile-defense system. That forehead implant is a slightly modified version of life-signs monitors used for years in animal testing."

"But where did it come from? How did it get here?"

"We fly it in."

"From where? Aren't there Xombies everywhere?"

"Not everywhere. We have a lot of remote bases from which we conduct foraging operations. I have one in Namibia that's fantastic—an abandoned diamond-mining town in the middle of the desert. It has this huge old opera house that you wouldn't believe."

"But if you have all that, why come here?"

"Because, my dear, the people we have running those places are not quite as *genteel* as you and me. In fact they're murderers and criminals—literally. They're all former prison inmates."

"What do you mean?"

"Male convicts represent the single largest proportion of Agent X survivors, especially those who were held in maximum security. The Maenads couldn't get at them. Some of our biggest Moguls are captains of the prison-industrial complex, and they organized the labor pool. It's the best-equipped army in the world today. The only one, as far as I know. About a million heavily armed thugs, all doing our shopping for us."

"What do they get out of it?"

"Peace of mind. Some semblance of order. Life. Without our administrative apparatus they would degenerate into squabbling factions and be picked off by Xombies. As it is, the attrition rate is . . ." He stopped himself. "Anyway, trust me, they need us as much as we need them."

We passed uneventfully through the barrier and continued down a long, gentle grade to the sea.

At one point in the drive, Sandoval asked, "Would you like to see where we're going?" When I gave a tentative nod, he directed me to a small window up in the vehicle's turret, resting his hand on my waist as I looked.

Out across the ice was another dome. A lone bubble, dimly glowing in the moonlight.

"You know, Lulu," he said, "without Agent X to bring us together, we might never have met." Then he kissed me.

AS WE PULLED up to the dome, men helped us out of the truck and hustled us inside. We passed through a drumlike revolving door, then a large antechamber full of parkas and boots, and then a heavy flap bleeding warm air. I could hear music. Our escorts parted the curtain, and my mouth fell open at the sight that greeted us.

It was green. Live green grass as far as the eye could see,

an achingly sweet-smelling park with sweet music filling the air and banks of stadium lights making the place look like a concert on a summer night. It *was* a concert. A silvery voice sang the refrain from a mellow Beatles song—*"Nothing's gonna change my world . . . nothing's gonna change my world . . . nothing's gonna change my world . . . nothing's gonna change my world . . ."*—and I got misty at the familiar melody.

"That's a lotta sod," said Sandoval, enjoying my reaction.

Rising like a monument from a flowered mound in the center of the grass was the submarine's fairwater, its dive-planes hung with bunting, and four musicians dressed in Sgt. Pepper regalia atop the starboard wing. It was the Blackpudlians! Their lurid purple and yellow stage lights shone hotly on the spectators below, turning them into violet cutouts limned in gold. The turf at the base of the mound was incised with a deep, emerald-lit hole—a bottomless spring with porcelain sides, cut as cleanly as if with a cookie cutter. Surrounding the pool and fanning out across the lawn in all directions was a crowd of exquisitely dressed men—and *women*. Beautiful young women . . . just like me.

Tuxedoed waiters with trays of cocktails circulated through the crowd, eager to please; and as one of them approached us with champagne, I noticed it was Dr. Langhorne.

"Jim! How nice to see you!" she said, not sounding at all sincere. "Care for something cold?"

"Why thank you, Alice. I just might do that." He picked up a glass.

"And your little friend?"

"She can speak for herself. Lulu, you two have met, haven't you?"

I nodded, unsure why Dr. Langhorne was so angry.

"Sure, we've met," she said. "We're just a couple of soul sisters, aren't we?"

Turning serious, Sandoval leaned toward her asked, "Everybody ready?"

"All is in readiness, sire." She gave a mocking curtsy.

"It better be. It's all or nothing now."

"You've always been able to trust *me*." Without offering me champagne, she smiled poisonously and said, "Well, I'll be trotting along. If you two need anything, just give me a ring."

Sandoval smiled sheepishly and said, "Already have, thanks." When she was gone, he said, "*Phew,* she's in rare form tonight."

"What's the matter?"

"She's my ex-wife." Seeing my dismay, he laughed, "Don't worry about it."

As we approached the fringes of the crowd and people began turning to acknowledge Sandoval, I had another unpleasant shock.

"Oh shit," I said under my breath.

The beautifully made-up girls that I had been so happy to see were entirely made-up. That is, they were not girls at all, but gleaming-coiffed boys. The boys from the submarine—*my* boys.

"Yep, a lotta sod," Sandoval repeated.

They wobbled on their sinking heels and miserably marked my approach, some arm-in-arm with their brazen guardians . . . as indeed I was myself. I recognized Rick and Henry and Sal, Sasha and Derrick, Andy and John, Dexter, Todd, Dan, Freddy, Bryce, Tony, Aram, Kyle, Gen, Lucas, Chuck, Nate, Bill, as well as all the dozens of others whose names I had never properly memorized. I recognized them in spite of the blonde falls and breast inserts and killer clothes and expertly applied foundation and lipstick and eyeliner I knew so well: They had Miss Riggs written all over them, every one.

Their dates, the Moguls, smirked with joshing camraderie, some more serious, more sneering, or more envious than others, but all completely in the game. This was their world.

It was as if a drain in my spine had become unplugged

and all my strength leaked out. I could barely stand. Sandoval felt me lean on him and took it for affection, giving me
a squeeze. A scream welled up and I forced it back, shuddering, admonishing myself to be as strong as the boys. But in
my mind I screamed: *We should have died! Why didn't we
all just die?* I wanted to just start running, run free until
someone put a dot on me and blew me to bits, but the solemn
faces of the boys, weirdly savage in that kabuki makeup,
held me back. They smoldered with the harsh desire to live,
and I was shamed by their hideous perseverence.

Sandoval whispered to me, "Now Lulu, I know you'll be
extremely sensitive to these men's feelings. They want to
feel that their companions are every bit as feminine as you."

I made an involuntary grunt of disgust.

"I understand," he said. "It's like a comedy, isn't it? But
unless you want to embarrass these men, you should be totally respectful. Otherwise they might take it out on your
friends."

"What does that mean?"

"I *mean,* these men are not homosexual. In fact, most of
them are about as hetero as you can get, and maybe funda-
mentalist to boot. This is a big compromise for them, maybe
nothing more than a status symbol. They might be sickened
by this—who do you think is going to suffer for it?"

"Why don't they just stop doing it, then?"

Sandoval chuckled, kissing the top of my head. "My innocent."

I stood back demurely, wanting to retch as Sandoval
was enveloped by his backslapping peers. The dolled-up
boys and I regarded each other amid the swells with an all-
knowing blankness, not saying a word.

More champagne came by on a cart, as well as iced
caviar and oysters, and I accepted some—not only to appear calm, but because it was too good to pass up. The boys
regarded me with loathing as I ate these delicacies. Apparently that was where they drew the line.

I began to notice that all the wait-staff were doctors

from the research compound, including Dr. Stevens and even Rudy, who was standing off on his own next to a large pet carrier emblazoned RUFF RIDER. Their eagerness to please reminded me of teachers during Open House. In some way they were on trial tonight, and they were doing everything they could to make a favorable impression.

No one spoke to me, but Sandoval was congratulated again and again on his 'coup'—the right to throw this party and get all these VIPs under one roof. Apparently it was an unprecedented feat of influence. The snide tone of these compliments suggested that he had forfeited a lot for the privilege . . . perhaps too much.

"You're a romantic, James," said an olive-skinned man with several chins erupting from his cravat. "A bloody dreamer! The extraordinary concessions you have made and the expectations you have raised—it is shocking to a conservative man like myself. It's like the risk you take by claiming this little one." He gestured at me as if I were a pet. "You have two women when others have none—it shows a lack of delicacy. Ah! But you are a romantic, what can one do? You lead with your heart."

"Not my head, eh, Ibn?"

"I hope not. It is your recklessness that is keeping the other egos in check. You are the lion tamer, James. They are afraid to cross you. But if you fail to impress them to-night, it will be every man for himself. Very bad."

"That sounds like an ultimatum."

"I said 'if.' But it sends a confusing signal when tremendous capital is expended for no apparent tactical advantage." The fat man indicated the spectacle around us. "It smacks of desperation."

"Then I've confused you."

"Not at all! As a descendent of Shah Jahan, I admire great passion . . . as well as great folly. But either way, use plenty of raw force to back it up, yes?"

"I'll try to remember that."

We reached the pool. It seemed hazardous to me, that

deep well in the ice; the arctic ocean depths right there in front of us. It was about the size of a large swimming pool, but it was bottomless. My skin crawled as I realized I could see part of the boat's gigantic hull down there in the emerald dark.

Turning away, I asked Sandoval, "Why don't I recognize any of these men? I've read *Forbes,* but I don't see anybody familiar in here. Bill Gates or whatever."

"That's because those people were not the true arbiters of power, but only the front men. Wealth is not power—rich men are just cash cows; they generate capital, but those assets are not really theirs. It's these men who control them, from within, just as they do political power. And they can use them at will. They hold the keys to the kingdom; the secret passwords that open backdoors into every significant enterprise on Earth."

"How did they get them?"

"Birthright, for the most part. They wouldn't be here otherwise, and they know it. That's why publicity is not something a truly powerful man seeks, because it only reveals what an obnoxious parasite he is. But anonymity is a commodity like everything else, and he can buy all he needs. He operates through many layers of intermediaries in order to accomplish what he wants to in complete privacy and freedom. If his full range of interests were to be known, barriers would rise, so he makes sure he can attack from many different angles, using his pawns in business, government, religion, whatever, to do his bidding for him."

"Why do they do it?"

"It's their only purpose."

"The corrupt ones."

"Corrupt is a misleading word. It makes more sense to say conservative, because they're only doing what they've always done. Familiarity and tradition are much more effective tools of manipulation than money."

Wilting, I asked, "Is that why the world was so messed up? With wars and everything? Because of you people?"

"Oh boy. Lulu, we're not God. We can't change human nature—all we can do is cash in on it. Just kidding. I'll tell you one thing: Nothing purifies a corrupt or stagnant system better than all-out war. Total destruction can be healthy."

"Would you say we're healthy now?"

"Hey, at least the Arabs and Jews aren't fighting anymore."

Nearing the front of the crowd, Sandoval and I paused to appreciate the music. The Blackpudlians were wrapping up a blistering version of *Come Together*—they looked like they were singing for their lives up there, drenched in sweat. It was hard not to climb the flowerbed and touch the sail. It was so unreal. I wanted to ask Sandoval what this evening was all about—what was the big mystery?—but it was too loud for conversation. Some of the Moguls were weeping nostalgic tears, eyes closed in reverent appreciation.

The song ended, leaving a residue of applause like silt in a bucket after the amplified music, and the band took a bow. As they did so, a couple of them saw me and nudged the others. Their eyes seemed to say, *Look out.* I nodded back. Then they sardonically addressed the crowd, in character as John, Paul, George, and Ringo:

"Thanks. Thank you very much. It's been grand—how often do you get to fiddle while Rome burns?"

"And without a fiddle, at that."

"That's a myth, John. The fiddle 'adn't been invented in Nero's time. Only the lyre."

"I hate bloody liars."

"No, the *instrument*. Like what they play in 'eaven."

"What do they play in 'ell, then?"

"Apparently, old Beatles songs." Rim-shot.

"And now we'd like to introduce a man who needs no introduction. The magnetic magnate who has made all this possible: Mr. James Sandoval!"

I was startled, though I don't know why I should have been. Obviously they had all been waiting for him to arrive. As applause rose and vanished into cavernous heights,

Sandoval mounted the "stage" and accepted the microphone, saying, "Weren't they great? Gee, what a treat." He clapped for the band as they took another bow.

Someone touched my elbow and I turned to find Dr. Langhorne standing at my side. Her eyes were intent on Sandoval, but she spoke to me:

"Enjoying the party?"

I didn't know what to say.

"You should be," she said grimly. "You're the guest of honor."

"I didn't have any choice," I pleaded. "I didn't *know*. What was I supposed to do?"

"Shh. Listen."

Without a trace of irony, Sandoval said, "Ladies and gentlemen, the Mogul Research Division and I are so pleased to welcome you all to this little shindig, which would not have been possible without your generous support. I do not exaggerate when I say that you gentlemen are carrying the world on your shoulders, or that your noble efforts to keep the flame of civilization alive will some day be the stuff of legend."

This was the speech that he had asked me to punch up. Now he gave a subtle signal and the Blackpudlians began softly harmonizing—an undertone at first so soft as to be almost inaudible, accompanied by mournful-sweet strains of the electric organ, but rising.

"Am I presumptuous to speak of future events?" he continued. "You may wonder who will be alive to read of these glorious endeavors. You men are realists. You don't believe in fairy tales. Since the earliest beginnings of the Mogul Project, you have expressed again and again your skepticism about our ultimate goal, preferring to focus on the less-sensational milestones along the way. Yet what milestones! Cracking the proteome. Creating the means of designing life, and programming it to serve our interests. The Autonomous Self-Replicator. These things were not narcissistic pipe dreams. They were about AIDS and Alzheimer's and Parkinson's. They were about ending human suffering.

"Perhaps that all seems very quaint now. Naïve. My colleagues in the Research Division—" He indicated Dr. Langhorne "—harbor no illusions about your opinion of them: freeloaders, charlatans, crackpots. Fools and hucksters who have left us in this quagmire with no means of escape, all the while filling our heads with schemes and nonsense. You worry it's all been a confidence game, the scam of all time, and you the suckers who bought it. I myself have even acquired a funny little nickname—we've all heard it: Ponzi de Leon. But in your hearts, you're sick. Sick at the cost of it all. The *ruin*. The loved ones you've lost. You think nothing can ever make up for it . . . and perhaps you're right." He stooped, slowly shaking his bowed head, letting the microphone dangle at his side.

An awful silence settled on the crowd, a gulf of dead air that grew wider and wider until the offended Moguls began filling it in with grumpy asides and throat-clearing. Some of them were gloating feverishly over Sandoval's capitulation. They thought he was throwing himself at their mercy.

Then Sandoval lifted his head and put the mike to his lips: "But . . . we . . . *did* it."

The band erupted in a blaze of guitars and screaming—the opening of *Sgt. Pepper's Lonely Hearts Club Band: "It was twenty years ago today, Sgt. Pepper taught the band to play . . ."* When they got to *"—so let me introduce to you—"* Dr. Langhorne left me and climbed up to join Sandoval. They embraced in the spotlight like Hollywood royalty, and he said, "Dr. Alice Langhorne, ladies and gentlemen!" It was getting crowded up there.

When the music died down to an expectant hum again, she said, "Thank you, Jim. Gosh. You know, when you sift through the hysteria about Maenad Cytosis—Agent X—what you find is that in many ways the Mogul Poject was an unqualified success. We did achieve what we set out to, and if it wasn't for one bad apple we would have been heralded as the saviors of the human race. Has this epidemic made us lose sight of that basic truth? It has, hasn't it? When the emphasis is all on developing a cure, a return to the status quo, that means we have failed. All a cure means is that you are back to where you started: doomed. Succeeding at that is nothing but a death sentence. So what I have to say is this: Who needs a cure? What does a cure avail us, other than a few paltry extra years in our aging carcasses? No. I say no. Why settle for the consolation prize when you can have it all?"

A heckler in the crowd yelled, "Have what?"

"What you paid for in the first place. What the faithful have been promised from time immemorial." She descended from the sail, taking the mike with her. Sandoval followed, and then the rest of us. She didn't go far, only to a low wall of ice on the far side of the sub, where the grass ended. The crowd spread out along the barrier, looking across.

There, behind the fairwater, in the half of the dome that had been deserted and dark until now, a single spotlight shone. We could see a man standing in its harsh beam, perhaps thirty feet away. He was a Xombie, or at least had that familiar blue cast to his skin, but he was not grotesque—though at first sight of him the crowd gasped and drew their laser pointers in alarm. He was wearing a white robe, and it gave him the bearing of a Greek god. Sea-green light webbed across him from a polynya at his feet—it was all that separated us from the striking, unearthly creature. As he stared back, I had the feeling of being watched by some vast dispassionate intelligence. I couldn't believe how different he looked from the homunculus I had seen in the tank.

In a hushed voice, Langhorne said, "Everyone, I'd like you to meet *Homo Perrenius*."

It was Mr. Cowper.

twenty-eight

"YOU HAVE SEEN them die, and you have seen them rise," said Langhorne. "But you ain't seen nothin' yet. Gentlemen, I direct your attention to the man on the conning tower."

Sandoval had climbed stairs up to the port sail-plane, the one opposite the band, and was picking up an elaborate compound bow. It was camouflage-colored, with day-glo arrows attached to it, and with practiced grace he removed one, nocked it, and cranked back the string. His posture with the bow was heroic; Olympian.

Unbelieving, I mouthed the words, "What is he . . .?"

Without the slightest hesitation, Sandoval let fly. The arrow flitted across the water, too fast to follow, but then as if by magic it was planted in Mr. Cowper's chest, its wicked point sticking out his back as if to indicate something. The old man barely reacted except to steady himself from the impact. Easy as plucking off a piece of lint, he removed the arrow and dropped it on the ice. It came out perfectly clean.

Sandoval called out, "Anybody else want to take a turn?" He held up an armload of bows.

The Moguls were suddenly animated with surprise and delight. They had not been expecting party favors this interesting. Sandoval passed down the bows, and men lined up along the wall to try their luck.

"This is sick," I said.

"It's a guy thing," Langhorne replied over her shoulder.

The row of archers tested the feel of their bows, some more awkwardly than others, twelve in all. They were so close to Cowper they could scarcely miss, but the first two who fired did, sending their arrows skittering far across the ice. Friendly ribbing and encouragement emanated from their less-adventurous fellows: "Hey, Chauncy, got your game permit?" Then several men shot almost simultaneously, and three arrows struck Cowper's upper body—one so deeply that its gaudy quills resembled a pink boutonniere. I flinched. He didn't bother removing these.

Everything became very quiet as the men methodically fired and reloaded. I was reminded of the boys' grisly revenge on the fallen Xombie in the sub, so long ago. The men's catharsis continued until the supply of arrows was exhausted. I made myself turn away, more out of protest than horror. I knew Mr. Cowper couldn't be hurt, though he was the picture of martyrdom with all those spines sticking out of him. When they were done he looked exactly like what he was: an archery target. There were even arrows in his face! For a long moment he stood there in the water-dappled light, literally transfixed.

After a span of awed silence, the Moguls began to applaud. The bows were tossed aside and the archers welcomed back into the crowd.

Langhorne asked, "Do we all agree he can't be harmed?"

The spectators scoffed, "Of course! He's a Xombie!" Fun over, they were more annoyed than impressed. They were convinced now that this was all a cheap stunt. While they were grumbling, Sandoval gave a signal and several doctors began maneuvering a light pontoon bridge across the water. This caused pandemonium:

"Are you out of your mind? Stop! He's a killer!"

Langhorne replied, "Strictly speaking, Xombies don't kill; they share. But I understand your anxiety. Be assured you are in no danger whatsoever."

While Dr. Langhorne was trying to calm them, Sandoval nudged me, smiling benignly. "Go to your father," he said.

"What?"

"Go to your father, Lulu. This is it: the reunion you've been waiting for. It's why you're here. It's why we're all here. Don't be afraid."

"I'm not."

My instinct was to resist, but then I realized I *wanted* to go to him, no matter what happened. I really wasn't afraid. Sandoval saw the change, the tears, and nodded in encouragement. The bastard. I slapped him and jumped over the wall and onto the wobbly platform, making my way across. The crowd buzz doubled, and I could hear boys entreating me to stop.

Mr. Cowper waited for me as patiently as he had borne the arrows. Something was different, I knew, or he would have been all over me. I was almost disappointed. Red speckles danced on him, and on my back as well, I'm sure. Freezer-cold air wafted off the water—I tried not to look into the depths.

As I mounted the far ice bank, I began to be anxious, thinking of the wolfish faces of Xombies I had known, including his. But this new Cowper had the tragic bearing of a Claudius, regarding my approach with world-weary compassion rather than animal lust. Looking out from that thicket of feathered shafts, his marble-black eyes were full of pity.

I wasn't sure he knew me, and ventured, "Mr. Cowper?"

He didn't respond.

Now we were about ten feet apart, and as I cautiously closed the distance he turned his face away, showing all those embedded spines in profile. They looked strangely ceremonial; shamanistic. He was looking across the ice to the dark side of the dome. Someone there was running out of the shadows toward us—another Xombie.

I was saddened to see that it was Julian. He was not placid like Cowper, but of the more familiar type, monstrous and vulpine, with all the rapturous fury of an avenging angel.

He came straight for me, ignoring Cowper. From the crowd, boys' voices were entreating me to swim for it, run, hurry, but there was not a thing I could do to escape, and I didn't try. As Julian got close, Cowper suddenly darted between us, snagging the boy by one leg, whirling with it, and slamming him down on his face. Julian was bigger and younger, but he seemed clumsy next to Cowper—or maybe it was just that he wasn't fighting back at all. While Cowper attacked, he behaved as if the old man was some kind of baffling invisible obstacle, like a high wind. In a flurry of blue limbs, Julian tried to break free and get at me, but Cowper was tenacious as a pit bull dragging down a great dane. He wrestled Julian to the edge of the ice and finally flipped him into the water. With a pleading cry of, *"Lulu!"* Julian scrabbled at the slick ice, then sank like a stone.

The wind was knocked out of me, seeing Julian just vanish like that, but I slowly became aware of the sensation this caused among the spectators on the opposite shore. It was fizzing in me as well—*what just happened?* Could it be true that those doctors had done what they promised? Had they cured Mr. Cowper? No. He wasn't a horrible Xombie, but he wasn't human. What had they turned him into?

The show was not over. As I stood there mourning Julian, something else stirred in the darkness: many people this time. A whole host of men came shuffling out, and from the way they walked I knew at once they were human.

There were about a hundred of them. Even before they were fully in the light, I began frantically slipping and sliding my way over, because it was obvious from their clothes that they were the men from the sub. Commander Coombs was in front! Flanking him were Mr. Robles and Mr. Monte, with Noteiro and Fisk and all the others streaming after. Kranuski and Webb were there, too.

They all looked haggard and suspicious, and the sight of me in my get-up didn't seem to alleviate their fears. I couldn't blame them; I was just part of the whole appalling circus and apparently in collaboration with it, if they had witnessed what happened to Julian. For Mr. Noteiro's sake, I hoped not. My own relief was short-lived. Before I could reach the men, there was more commotion from another direction, a line of dark figures that unmercifully resolved itself into Xombies. Scores of Xombies, swarming in to intercept the men.

A collective moan of dread arose from the everyone. As the rampaging creatures skittered into the light, I could make out the warped features of Albemarle and Jake and Cole and Lemuel, as well as some from the tanks in the research compound and many others I had never seen before—forty or fifty, all told. But there was something unusually awkward about them, and, as they swept forward like a bizarre chorus line, I realized what it was: They were connected together by a wire that had been threaded through their bodies, like fish on a loop.

Coombs and the others reacted as if they had been expecting something like this, bracing themselves for the Xombie attack. They were doomed, and knew it. Nothing would protect any of us from that host. Not even Mr. Cowper.

Just before the two groups could collide, however, the tethered Xombies were abruptly jerked up short as if they had reached the end of their leash. Thrashing wildly, they began to be dragged backward and then, one after another, hoisted *upward,* until the whole string of them flailed in the air, dangling from the boom of a high crane.

"Ooooh," went the crowd.

Jim Sandoval's amplified voice rang out: "This is to all the new citizens of Valhalla: Congratulations, your period of orientation is finished. We welcome you to this ceremony ushering in a new age of mankind, and we invite you to join our community, to share in our fortune, and to enter a world where the Xombie threat has been lifted."

Relieved laughter and grudging applause from the Moguls met this pronouncement. The rest of us looked on stonily.

Sandoval continued, "Today we bury the past, not just symbolically, but in our hearts. We bury it and put flowers on it and stand before its gravestone to say our final good-byes. This applies to us no less than to yourselves. Today we renounce the past and are baptized anew. There can be no doubters, no one left dangling. Lulu, will you please come forward?"

The float-bridge had been put back in place, and at the end of it stood Sandoval, reaching out to me with a big phony smile. I hesitated, reluctant to leave Mr. Cowper and the other men. I was suddenly very self-conscious about participating in whatever this was they were doing. Having cast my lot with the undead, I couldn't bear to set foot back on that deceiving turf. What would happen if I refused? As if reading my thoughts, Sandoval flicked his eyes warningly upward at the flailing Xombies. The sword of Damocles. There was no choice—I went.

"Don't be nervous," Sandoval said, helping me across. Before anyone else could follow, Rudy brought Don over on a chain to police the bridge, barely restraining the beast from charging across and attacking Mr. Cowper. The baboon either had an innate hatred of Xombies or was trained to go after them, because he was really champing at the bit while Rudy and I exchanged an anguished look. Dr. Langhorne came up and took my arm.

"What's going on?" I asked her.

"Cheer up," she said. "You're about to be saved."

They walked me around to the garden side of the fairwater and stopped before the brilliant ocean pool sunk in the grass. The crowd moved with us. Several doctors, including wire-haired Chandra Stevens, were waiting there with medical instruments and an aluminum stretcher of the type used for helicopter evacuations.

"Now just relax," Langhorne said, and ripped my dress off.

There was a minor uproar among some of the boys, shouts of "Leave her alone!" But Sandoval, who was standing back from the whole thing, quashed it by saying, "Now now—these are doctors. Professionals." The Blackpudlians, who had been softly singing the whole time, went dead. As Langhorne strapped me naked to the stretcher, I asked, "Why are you doing this?"

"Because it's the only thing to do. My daughter was about your age, so don't think this is easy for me. But there's no cure, no future—nowadays little girls grow up to be Xombies. This is all that's left." She put her lips to my ear, whispered, "None of this would be happening if you'd done what you were supposed to."

"What?"

"I expected your cycle to have kicked in by now, honey. A surprise package for that bum I was married to. Why do you think I let him have you? But I guess he gets the last laugh after all, the bastard. Now he gets to be Christ Almighty." She strapped an oxygen mask to my face and turned on the flow. Cold air hissed through. It seemed thin—I couldn't get enough and began hyperventilating.

While Dr. Langhorne was ministering to me, Sandoval addressed the Moguls. As unctuously as a TV evangelist, he said, "There is no salvation without baptism. Cold-water immersion—not as a superstitious rite, mind you, but as a means of preserving higher brain function while the morphocyte conquers the body—is the key to resurrection." He shook his head despairingly. "But what kind of resurrection? Resurrection as an intelligent monster, anathema to all that's human? That's not my idea of a quality afterlife. *Quality* resurrection requires something more. Alice, can you hand me the inhalant?" A small glass tube was produced and he held it up for all to see. "This is it. The chalice. The sacrament. It doesn't look like much, does it? But it is body, mind, and spirit. It is freedom and safety from the ravages of time."

The Moguls became fiercely intrigued, their competing babble resembling the trading floor of a stock exchange. Questions rang out: Is it really the lost formula? Is there enough to go around? How much are you asking for it? Is it safe? Does it have to make you blue? Many of them were concerned with the disposition of their wealth and power—would they still have use for these things, and the ability to manage their affairs? Above all, they wanted to remain themselves, or what was the point?

Sandoval grinned, holding up his hands. "Gentlemen, please. In answer to your questions, let me just explain that this is indeed the end product of Dr. Uri Miska's research: the famous non–infectious, behavior–stabilized strain of the ASR morphocyte, which I promised you we had recovered. New, improved Agent X, now Xombie–free!" (Laughter all around.) "It's not a myth. You've just seen for yourselves how well it works in that unscripted demonstration of paternal love—a father very clearly recognizing his daughter and rescuing her from a marauding ghoul! It was a beautiful moment, wasn't it? Is that the ugly behavior we have all come to associate with life after death? Of course not. Aside from the minor cosmetic alteration, it's perfect, and as far as we know this is all there is of it in the whole world. A single, last dose is all that remains."

This sobered the crowd. Someone said, "That's all? Just what's in that little bottle?"

"Yes." He paused a moment to let them stew, then said, "But we can make more. Oh, yes. We can make quite a bit more, as I will demonstrate. Because just as wine is changed into *Sangre de Cristo* by the miracle of transubstantiation, so does the morphocyte multiply in the fecund female body, changing it into a wellspring of eternal life. Gentlemen, I hold before you your future . . ." He handed the ampule back to Langhorne, who loaded it into a pneumatic gun resembling a cordless drill. ". . . Synthesized in the consecrated body of a virgin, and extracted and distilled for your everlasting benefit by myself and the dedicated staff of Mogul Research Division. But, as a famous man once said, 'You must act now.'"

A tumultuous clamor of bidding and protest erupted from the crowd.

Sounding a little hysterical, Langhorne babbled in my ear, "Just relax and you won't feel a thing. Just go to sleep, baby. I won't give you the dose until you're good and chilled down—you won't even know it's happening. It won't hurt a bit, I promise . . . and then you'll never have to suffer again." Suppressing a sob, she kissed my cheek.

The doctors tipped me upright and quickly began lowering me by ropes into the pool. Struggling for breath, I couldn't scream as my feet dipped in. It was deep and cold, and so clear—I could see all the way to the bottom of the ice ridge, ten or fifteen feet below the surface, to the yawning black gulf beneath. Tiny fish swirled down there in spears of olive light.

The stretcher banged against the enamel-white sides, then lurched violently, swinging me around. Someone plunged into the water at my feet, a doctor, and the freezing splash interrupted my yelling like a slap, so that I could hear other shouts from above:

"Allah ackbar! Allah ackbar!"

With a jerk the stretcher rose up and landed hard on the grass. Someone yanked off my oxygen mask and unfastened my restraints. It was Wally, of the Black-pudlians, wearing a big fake John Lennon mustache and gold epaulets. "'Ave you out in a second, luv," he said breathlessly.

Over his shoulder I could see Phil and Reggie in a wild-eyed defensive stance, brandishing their electric guitars by the necks like war clubs, strings twanging, and Dick up on the dive-plane hurling equipment at the doctors from above.

"Dance, you sorry sods!" Dick bellowed, swinging an amplifier by its cord and letting it fly. "It's the British invasion!"

twenty-nine

FROM THIS POINT on, everything happened very quickly.

As the four Englishmen swarmed Sandoval and the doctors, clouting them down, bedlam broke out in the crowd. All the boys set upon their Mogul overlords with a ferocity that belied their slinky eveningwear, tearing into the fat cats like demonic bimbos on *Jerry Springer*.

The riot didn't last long. There was a strange discontinuity, a break in time, during which I somehow peed myself and bit my tongue so hard it bled. But it wasn't the pain or taste of blood that told me something had happened . . . it was the silence. All those howling boys and Beatles were suddenly silenced, and now I could see them crumpled on the grass, slowly coming to their senses like me. Even the doctors had collapsed. Only the Moguls remained standing amid the groaning masses, looking smug and barely ruffled. Sandoval was unconscious, having been pithed by Reggie's blue-fleck Fender Stratocaster, but his fellow bigwigs were in tip-top form.

It was the implants. The darn implants. There had never been any chance that we could rebel—they could strike us down at any time with a jolt of electricity to the brain. Shock treatment.

"Stay calm!" Moguls were yelling to one another. "Microwave pulse! Everything's under control! If any of them act up, nuke them again!"

"Hit the little bastards again! Teach 'em a lesson!"

"Fry their fuckin' brains until they know their place!"

"How do you like that, you little shits?"

In the middle of this triumphant gloating, there came a strange, unholy grunt from the left side of the dome, and an awesome geyser of sod and ice erupted from the field. Debris shot high in the air, some of it getting sucked out a huge rip that mysteriously appeared in the canopy, frayed edges whipping outward into the arctic void. A stiff breeze suddenly kicked up and the whole dome billowed like an inverted sea.

As the Moguls all turned in bewilderment and alarm, a familiar armored vehicle barreled out of the debris plume.

"Utik!" I cried.

Hurtling toward us, the vehicle braked, going into a spin and piling up sod beneath its wheels the way a skidding dog bunches up a rug, revealing raw ice beneath. The Moguls scattered, but the tank stopped well short. Its turret moved as if looking around, then spit lightning with an ear-splitting *GRONK!*—the same goliath pig-grunt as before. Fleeing VIPs dove for cover as a curtain of chipped ice rose between them and the exit. Disregarding the gunfire, the boys recovered their senses enough to break from their masters in the pandemonium and race for the sub, converging there with the liberated crew, who were crossing the pontoon bridge as Rudy restrained Don and waved them across. Mr. Cowper was out of my view behind the sail.

A couple of Moguls were returning fire. They crouched

behind the ice wall, aiming their laser pointers like wizards with magic wands to summon down all the might of the COIL weapon. Its beam originated from hidden points around the base of the canopy, each shot a blinding strobe that left pinprick ghosts in my eyes—its sound that unnerving, familiar *ZAPZAPZAP!* Wherever the thing touched the truck it flared up intensely, leaving scorched, glowing pits in the armor, though it wasn't as instantly devastating on steel as it was on flesh. The men inside seemed well aware of this, driving evasively to present a moving target and doing what they could to keep the Moguls pinned down in a curtain of stinging debris. But it was only a matter of time.

Sandoval was lying on the grass near me with a cut in his bald scalp. I crawled over to him. He was out cold, but I was as careful as could be as I gingerly took his laser pen from its wrist clip. It was an elegantly simple thing with two buttons, one marked PROPOSE and the other, DISPOSE. The chain was only a few inches long, so I lifted his arm on my lap to aim. It was trickier than I would have expected, the tiny red dot darting all over the place, but finally I got it settled on one of the Moguls who was directing fire and pressed the trigger.

Nothing.

In frustration I tried clicking on other Moguls. Nothing. Nothing, nothing, nothing! Of course not—Sandoval had *told* me they were exempt from the thing! I hunted around for something to shoot, and as a last resort aimed it at the crane that was holding the Xombies.

This time it worked—a hydraulic piston exploded, toppling the crane's boom like a tree on the firing Moguls. Then I had to make sure no Xombies interfered with the guys boarding the boat. As I picked a few off, I felt the secret god-like glee of a kid zapping ants with a magnifying glass.

While I was so intent on this, a brutal hand closed on my wrist, and a furious, bloody face pressed into mine.

"What do you think you're doing?" Sandoval demanded.

"Just what the *hell* do you think you're doing?"

"Nothing!"

"That's right you're doing nothing! You're doing nothing ever again!" He savagely swung me by the arm over the edge of the pool, so that my bare body slammed against the ice shelf and my feet touched the water. He tried to let go, but I was still holding the laser pen, actually hanging from it, as he made every effort to pull away.

"Get off!" he bellowed.

"No!"

The bitterly cold ice quaked against my body, and something massive lumbered toward us. It was the armored truck. Sandoval tried frantically to withdraw his arm or haul me out, but before he could do either the vehicle ran over his legs. He didn't scream so much as make an explosive moan, a sound like a maimed animal. But he wasn't dead yet, just pinned; and as the door on the tank was thrown open, he weakly gasped, "Find . . . Miska." Then a combat boot stepped on him and wiry arms seized mine, lifting me into the vehicle.

"Well, well, what have we here?" crowed a high-pitched munchkin voice. It was so freakish my heart skipped a beat, but the person speaking was altogether more mundane, if terrible to see.

It was Colonel Lowenthal.

"LOOK WHAT I caught, Rusty," Lowenthal quacked to a helmeted man sitting in the turret. I couldn't reconcile his bizarre new voice with everything else that was going on, and I didn't have the energy to try. This was the same truck I had been in before, but the men driving it now were Lowenthal's people, not Inuits, and all the trappings of Mogul luxury had been crudely ripped out. Now it was undisguised pure function: gray bench seating and a huge Gatling-type gun with an articulated ammunition-feeder like a crocodile's tail. It smelled like hot iron in there. "A mermaid! Does that mean I get a wish?"

In a voice just as squeaky, the driver replied, "Strap yourself in before they get a bead on us!" The two of them sounded like Donald Duck's nephews.

"What are you waiting for?" Lowenthal screamed shrilly. As the vehicle roared into motion, he handed me a heavy flak jacket and a pair of headphones. "Put these on," he shouted. "When he fires that cannon, it'll blow your ears out!" He patted the weapon affectionately. "Thirty millimeter Avenger! Forty-two hundred rounds a minute! Depleted uranium shells! You know who makes it?"

Dull with cold and shock, I didn't realize he was still talking to me.

He poked me. "Guess!" When I shook my head, he said, "General Electric!" The way he said it, I could tell he was expecting a reaction of some kind.

I shrugged.

"Depleted uranium? Come on!"

"I don't *know*."

"Same company that made your submarine's reactor!"

"Oh."

"Uranium goes in one and out the other—never mind."

There was a loud, searing crackle, accompanied by flashes of light from outside. It was that COIL weapon stabbing at us. I drew the jacket up around my head.

Lowenthal saw my dread and said, "Don't worry! That laser is designed to cut through the thin skin of a missile, not the armor of this APC." Just as he said this, a brilliant green flare appeared in the ceiling, raining white-hot sparks on us and filling the cabin with smoke. A spot on the floor burst briefly into flame. Then the truck lurched evasively and the glare disappeared, leaving a molten orange peephole to the outside. "Whoops!" he laughed.

I suddenly noticed he had a bloody bandage where his implant had been. Had he gouged it out?

"What's wrong with your voice?" I asked.

"Helium! We drove through a bunch of helium on the way in! Sounds like Alvin and the Chipmunks, doesn't it?"

"What do you want with me?"

"We're taking back the base; the whole shebang," Lowenthal said. "The Moguls are through! We've been waiting for a chance to catch them all together! Now it's *our* turn!"

I felt a thin stirring of hope. "The Air Force?"

"There is no Air Force any more. We know that. But we sure as hell aren't going to fetch and carry while they suck down piña coladas and hog all the women. Schneider, hose down those fuckers, we're getting out of here!"

There was a tremendous roar that buffeted the vehicle, deafening even with the headphones. What Schneider hit I don't know, but there were no more laser blasts. A few seconds later I felt a big bump and all at once the ride became quiet and smooth, as if we had emerged from a tunnel. There was no light through the viewports. This could only mean one thing: we were outside the bubble and racing across the sea. I could hear distant-sounding concussions, like fireworks.

Saying, "You must be freezing," Lowenthal handed me a hot-water bottle and went forward. I took the opportunity to peer out the nearest viewport. Falling away to our rear was the dome, partially caved in like a rotten pumpkin, and within it the submarine. I prayed for its escape, weeping a little for myself, but so grateful for the boys' sake.

All around us, explosions lit up the winter night—the ice was a battlefield. Giant hovercraft were colliding like bumper cars, and the sky was full of airplanes and tracer bullets. Flaming ice fountains shot to the heavens. Other vehicles were in formation behind us as if we were part of a convoy . . . then I noticed they were shooting at us. A volley of rockets slashed through the air overhead. The force of their detonations rattled the tank like a garbage can.

Up front, Lowenthal shouted, "Goddammit, where are those UCAVs? Does Boyleston know we're out here? Tell him we need air cover!" Facing forward, he pounded the gunner's leg. "Schneider! Return fire, dammit!" Then he looked back.

What he saw was as astonishing to him as it was to me. Schneider was dead, with my blue hands around his neck. I looked at those hands, then at the plum-colored menstrual blood running down my legs—*my* blood—as if they belonged to someone else. Like Mummy had always said, I was a late bloomer.

"Aw shit," Lowenthal said, as a blinding light shone in the front windshield.

Then the wave hit: the cockpit blew in, and glass and smoke billowed toward me, enveloping everything. I was weightless, the floor underfoot burst upward like the flaps of a cardboard box—it was so sudden there was no fear or pain or surprise—and in the peculiar lull that followed, I and every other loose object in the tank whirled in space, a dirty blitz of crushed ice, hamburger, and hot metal, all ricocheting off each other and flying apart in a perfect illustration of atomic fission. Gravity returned with a wallop as the armored truck landed upside down and plunged into the fractured sea. Gray icewater rushed in, covering the mess and driving out the smoke. We sank to the bottom.

thirty

IT WAS TAKING an awful long time to die. I wasn't in any discomfort, but I worried about the grievous pain to come, not to mention that awful death by drowning. Twice in one week! But it was different this time. For one thing, I seemed to acclimate quicker to the temperature. The water was cold, yes, but the effect was not so torturous as vividly sensual . . . and not all bad. I was surrounded by a flowing corona of warmth, with tendrils of incoming cold twining around and through me like a time-lapse film of roots growing. The cold had a calming, grounding effect, which I was grateful for.

My eyes idly roamed the flooded interior of the over-turned tank. It was like a shaken snowglobe, full of drifting particles. Everything was so totally smashed I was amazed to be in one piece. The gunner, Schneider, was inextricably tangled with the cannon works, having been stuffed up into the turret by the force of the blast. Lowenthal and the

other men I couldn't see at all, the whole cockpit area being lost behind peeled-back flooring and machinery.

Soft light filtered down from the gaping hole. Forcing
my creaky joints to bend, I reached out and carefully took
hold of a buckled sheet of steel, leery of jagged edges, and
eased partway through the opening.

The sea. I was buried in depths of silty green dusk,
looking through paler heights to a weblike membrane far
above. Streamers of bubbles and lava-lamp blobs of oil
rose to that circle of light, but my body felt anything but
buoyant—it was stiff and heavy as a rusting Tin Man.

With molasses-thick bewilderment, I realized I hadn't
caught a breath in . . . how long? Minutes. Ten minutes at
least. Longer than I'd ever held my breath before, that was
for sure, and I didn't feel a thing. Come to think of it, I was
not actually even holding my breath—my mouth and nose
had been open to the sea the whole time, slowly cycling
frigid, salty, diesel-tainted water in and out. Was I *breathing* water? I consciously stopped doing it, but it didn't
seem to make any difference.

Hovering there at the bottom of the ocean, half in and
half out of the tank, I felt a pang of intense loneliness: I
was dead, but I lived. I was a Xombie. *Duh.*

I let myself sink languorously back inside the vehicle,
pondering this, wondering what would happen to me in this
cold, cold water. Things were gradually ticking down to
some kind of stop; not death, but a cessation of motion
in which the glowing ember of my consciousness would
remain, dreaming, as the tissues and fluids of my body
congealed at the freezing point. This was what I had read
about black holes in space, that to be sucked into one was
to have time stretched to infinity at the "event horizon."
That's where I was now—nearing the event horizon, never
to escape.

And I was not alone. Someone else had awakened in the
confines of the vehicle: the upside-down gunner, Schneider. Unlike me, he was squirming around, his gloved hands

slowly clenching and unclenching, releasing trapped puffs of blood from his clothing; his head and torso compressed into the squat bell of the tank's cupola by the upthrust seat platform.

As I looked down in fascination, his limbs stretched out like probing feelers, each seeming to have an inquisitive life of its own. The right hand located a belt-tool—an oversized pocketknife in a leather holster—and both hands speedily extended the blade. With quick, violent chops, Schneider used the knife to first cut through the seat harness, then any offending bone or joint that was pinned in place, tailoring himself to squeeze out. I thought of trapped animals gnawing their own limbs off, but Schneider did it completely mechanically, with the same cool deliberation as myself.

Even so, the cold was working on him as well—he was ebbing—and when he finally jerked free it was only to lie writhing in place, black eyes staring, mouth working silently. Looking at him, I felt nothing. *He* was nothing. Nothingness was the main impression I had of everything; a never-changing infinite void in four dimensions, stretching out before me with no possibility of relief, because I too was nothing.

Now something long, white, and slender, an enormous skeletal finger, reached in from the blocked cockpit. Tapping along the junkpile, it found an opening and began to emerge, one great finger after another until the entire monstrous hag's hand was visible, larger than my body—a giant spider crab: a king crab. Its basketball-sized carapace moved over Schneider's twisting form, its claws seizing and picking at the ragged edges of his wounds. As it ate, its eye-stalks remained fixed on me, not warily but brazenly. Then a second crab came through to join the feast. Soon the opening was all pointed legs, as crabs crowded the narrow space. I was bait in a crab trap.

Schneider wasn't finished. As the creatures covered him, he pushed against them, fended off their claws, trying to get out from under, but they were strong and blandly determined, clamping tight and digging in. Soon I could barely see him. When there was no more elbow room at the table, the next crab came for me.

It was a challenge to move—I was almost completely inert, and could forgive the crabs for mistaking me for a drowned corpse. Propped stiffly in the far corner of the compartment, hair swaying like moss, I was even in the semi-fetal posture of the dead.

The crab's extraordinarily long, bony pincers, each one a grasping six-foot tong as thick as my arm, stretched out and took hold of my hair and left hand. It pinched as hard as tin-snips, but I felt no pain. Nor was I numb—my body registered every nuance of the injury, yet it was a clinical, detached analysis. It did not "hurt." There is no way to describe it except perhaps to say my body was a country under seige, and I its queen. I felt a certain stewardship, but that was it. The stolid-faced crustacean began pulling me toward its mouth to feed. Others were coming as well.

With glacial speed, I began to move. Far more agile than me, the crab anchored its legs and improved its grip—I wasn't going anywhere. Reaching for a place to lodge the deadwood of my right hand, I encountered one of the hot-water bottles and clutched it to me like a toddler with a security blanket. It was still warm, the chemical heating element still circulating. By taking it, I surrendered to the crab, and was drawn head first to its bristly mandibles.

Taking the bag's drain valve in my teeth, I tore it open and squeezed with all the strength I could still muster, gulping the hot water. There was no conscious plan in this, but rather some sort of physical compulsion, like an infant sucking milk—what had been my mind was subsumed to a larger but less-civilized intelligence spreading throughout my body. Though the water was scalding, the little of me that was left had no veto power over this ruthless new

master, which registered it, Martha Stewart–like, as a Good
Thing. I did not stop drinking even when I felt organs rup-
turing inside me.

I was Gumby. That's what this was about. This freakish
world was my toyland; my flesh, mutable clay. If it didn't
hurt, why not play?

As I kept drinking, I could feel the heat circulating. My
belly became distended in a way that would have been
agonizing to a living person, but I could feel myself soft-
ening up, growing more limber every second. My mind
quickened.

The crab was fussily chewing a snipped-off hank of my
hair with some scalp attached. I had only felt it as a tug and
a cold spot behind my ear. With an abrupt jerk, I broke
free, inadvertently taking one of its claws with me. The
crab didn't seem at all troubled by the damage or disappointed by my escape, and I felt a rush of mutual understanding: We were both privy to a perfect peace unknown
to higher forms of life.

Fully aware that the cold would soon immobilize me
again, I arthritically clambered out and atop the vehicle. A
number of crabs were in the way, but I jabbed at them with
the severed claw to drive them back.

Standing on that overturned hulk with its wheels car-
toonishly splayed outward, I stopped and stared at the surrounding seabed, my flight arrested.

It was solid crabs, covering every square foot of ocean
floor, their legions receding into the murk. Surrounding the
tank were layers, drifts of them, piling up ten deep. Around
the front, two heaps seemed particularly busy—as I
watched, a face surged up from the living mass, crab claws
dragging down lips and eyelids in a caricature of facelift-
ing, giving the features an exaggerated expression of gaping terror. It was Lowenthal. His one remaining eye looked
at me and I had an electric sense of contact; of his voice
saying, *Go.* Then a claw penetrated his mouth and wrenched
at his tongue. They pulled him down.

Shedding the heavy bulletproof vest, I kicked off for the surface.

THERE WERE FIRES above, casting the broken ice in fluorescent candy colors, but the heat did not radiate through the water. Coming up underneath the floating wrack, I found it already frozen together. I had no bouyancy, no air in my lungs, and had to keep treading water every second or I would drop to the bottom. The crabs were content to wait, I knew.

Working my way up between jumbled slabs, I punched through glassy new ice, shattering my knuckles but opening a sharp-edged hole I could cling to. My hair and face froze instantly upon contact with the air—the temperature was seventy or eighty degrees colder than the water. Not far away I could see flames and smoke coiling into the midnight sky. I boosted myself up on the ice and ran for it.

Water drained from my every orifice and flash-froze as I moved, so that I shed icicles with every step. My flesh was crystallizing, cracking, splitting open at the joints. As I ran I encountered bits of scrap and a charred torso, finally coming in range of the fire's warmth. Its source was the blackened shell of a hovercraft, a giant crucible guttering in a pool of meltwater, and I sloshed up to it with arms outspread.

I don't know how long I stood there. It might have been minutes or it might have been hours. Eyes closed against the withering heat, I could feel my ice glaze dissolve and the tissues of my body become pliable; alive. Not alive in the ordinary sense—which was as a mysterious entity separate from my mind, with its hidden anatomy and dimly recognized processes—but alive like a very familiar landscape whose every feature was known to me and whose every part I could not only inspect from afar, but also inhabit at will with my mind's eye.

In the full flower of Xombie womanhood, I could ply the rivers and tributaries of my body, and explore the deep meandering wounds made by schrapnel. I could close the wounds and seal them, just as easily as sealing my lips. I could even pucker my tissues around bits of scrap, squeezing them from one muscle to another until they emerged from bloodless slits in my side and plopped in the water.

I reached up and touched the implant, sunk in rigid bone. I could actually taste the metal screws and test the grip of their threads in my skull. The distant echo of my old sense of wonder wafted by like music in a passing car. Then I flexed my forehead. With a crack the implant popped loose into my hand. It gleamed in the firelight, and I let it fall.

The sea was littered with wreckage. Here and there, Xombies wandered like lost children at a fairground, fast succumbing to the cold. I was neither afraid nor empathetic, and they were equally indifferent to me. But something did stir me—a riotous sound far across the ice. It rang in my head like the voices of long-dead loved ones, nearly forgotten. It was unbearably sweet and sad. Beckoning.

It was people. Miles away, Utik's people were leaving Thule, a caravan of buses, snowmobiles and dogsleds streaming north as Valhalla burned. The ones left behind were too busy fighting to stop them, and I could sense both the eager flight of the Inuit and the hatred and misery of those in the domes. This knowledge came through all my pores, as if my entire body had become an antenna attuned to the signals of fragile humanity. I could feel them, and they were all I could feel: a heartbreaking symphony in the vacuum, a kaleidoscopic concert of destruction, and I ached to liberate every one of them from the hideous threat that hung over them—the parasite of time. I had no choice: they were all that was left of me, each one a jarringly vivid light in the vast emptiness of eternity, yet here they were at the whims of dismal mortality like candles set afloat in the night sea, left to drift and fizzle out. No. They had to be saved. I had the power to save them. To preserve them, as I used to preserve delicate flowers in my memory-book.

Lulu.

I stopped.

Lulu. Hurry.

It was the sound of the wind, playing my name. I couldn't tell if it was one voice or many, but it reverberated in the sinews of my dead blue heart like a benevolent God. It *knew* me; knew me in a way I no longer knew myself, reminding me of what I most desperately wanted to remember: who I was. The Voice was not calling me to Thule, but back in the direction of the boat.

The boat—I had almost forgotten about it. Not to mention the guys in it. "Out of sight, out of mind" seemed to be the way of things now. Remembering those men was a shock, as finding valuables long thought lost; living heirlooms held in hock. They were mine!

Torn, I looked off toward the flickering chaos of Valhalla, miles away. The complex was so large that the distance was deceiving—some part of me knew I could never even make it that far, that I would set like concrete before I was even halfway there, but it was very difficult to sever my attention from those warring throngs and run the opposite way. Equivocation was foreign to my new nature. It wanted to just go. Running against the current, I went for the sub.

Following serpentine power cables across the ice, I felt myself freezing again, but found I could hoard more heat than before—my skin had swollen tremendously, creating a puffy layer of insulation, and the soles of my feet were armored in callus. Things inside me were restructuring and streamlining as well. Even with that, I didn't have long, but the boat wasn't far and I could move very fast. I still wasn't breathing—or rather, I was breathing through my whole body. Absorbing. I felt tireless and light, as if the world was rolling beneath me and I was harnessed to a fixed point in the sky.

Bonfires were strewn all over the sea. Approaching the dome, I expected to find it burning, too, or flat as a jellyfish washed up on the beach, but it was still only half deflated, a lopsided soufflé. The lights were off and it appeared deserted. I had no impression of human life, inside or out. The Voice was silent. Other than myself, there was not even a Xombie to be seen, and I had an overwhelming desire to just lie down and join the scenery. I had already forgotten why I was here.

My feet frozen clubs, I slowed to a hobble, entering the towering breach made by the truck. The canopy was noisily tearing itself to shreds in the wind. It was dark inside, the grass crunchy. There were mutilated bodies everywhere, all stiff with cold as indeed I soon would be, waiting for spring. But something vast was stirring in the emptiness, causing the grassy tundra to heave like a waking leviathan. It was the submarine. The submarine was moving.

I could not see it in the near-total darkness, but I could find it easily enough by the escalating Biblical cacophany of ice splitting open and volcanic jets of air blasting from every fissure, as well as water boiling up, rising like the tide, to spread in glassy waves across the field. I could *feel* these things happen as if they were somehow an extension of myself.

With the water lapping over my feet, the Voice said, *Follow,* and I waded forward into the icy wash, struggling against atrophy. What did it want from me?

Then I paused, sensing something rushing up in the dark, bright as a torch in my consciousness, all teeth and fury. Not a Xombie. My fading reflexes were too slow to ward it off. A lithe, coarse-haired body slammed into mine, fangs sinking deep into my neck. I spun like a rag doll from the impact but kept my footing, grappling with the creature. Its strength was much greater than my own.

It was Don, the mandrill. And somewhere nearby I could hear a strained whisper urging him on: "Get 'em, Don old boy. Go get 'em. That's a good boy." Sandoval, lying half-dead. Don had been protecting him.

The ape was going to tear me apart. There was simply no way I could stop it. He would tear me to bits and I would never reach the sub. I tried to gamely push on in the hope that he would give up, but he ripped into me even more savagely, an engine of pure wrath. I had no feeling at all about him except an excruciating dreamlike sense of being held back; prevented from attaining my one vital goal.

Then suddenly there was a violent upheaval and I broke free. That Voice, achingly familiar, spoke to me again: *Go, Lulu. Hurry. While ya still can.*

It was him, Mr. Cowper, risen to do battle with Don.

He and the baboon were locked in brute combat, wreathed in briny spray that gathered on them like scales and tinklingly shattered with each blow. I hardly registered the fight—it was Mr. Cowper that had my attention, not as my father (I was immune to any such sentiment) but as a walking contradiction. He was neither a neutral presence like me, nor shiningly mortal like Sandoval . . . yet both coexisted within him, resonating something arresting and perverse: what Langhorne had called *Homo Perrenius*. Only now did I grasp the utter paradox of that. The fleeting aura of life—so delicate it could not be contained except in fragments of memory—clung to him along with his tattered robes, ennobling and elevating him to an exalted somethingness from which I was barred. Though dead, he had no reason to yearn for mankind. He was whole.

Hurry . . .

The baboon was gaining the upper hand—Cowper was nearly as frozen as I was, no match against that warm-blooded dervish. It broke his clutching fingers, ripped out his throat, all but tore his head off, but he maintained his grip, granting me time to escape. I moved away as quickly as I could, followed by the sounds of rending flesh and bone, sprinting across the water just as I used to do as a little girl, when rain made lawns into lakes and it was possible to walk on water if you just ran fast enough.

Then I did something very human . . . or perhaps it was Cowper's weird vestigial humanity that triggered it: I went back for him.

In a few long, loping strides I was upon them, seizing the animal's head under my arm and bending it backward; bending its shaggy neck double as Mr. Cowper and I pinned its body between us. At that moment, I felt vibrantly a part of the creature, warm and alive and full of feeling, squeezing it tighter and tighter in an ecstatic desire to merge. Leathery black paws flayed my face as the thrill reached a frenzied peak . . . then its neck snapped and the beast went limp. All those overwhelming feelings died with it, leaving a vast hollow gulf in the center of things, across which Mr. Cowper and I regarded one another.

In that look, he made clear to me the price of being real: mortal man's sorrows mercifully die with him, and a Xombie feels no sorrow. Cowper had no relief on either count. Happiness is a transient feature of youth and purpose—it is pain that accrues over time, tempered only by the ultimate refuge of death. What he had done to me in life was only one of countless sins that would follow him into eternity, forever replenished and compounded by the futility of his existence. Mr. Cowper was haunted; he could never escape himself. All he wanted was oblivion. I stepped forward and took his mangled head in my hands.

The boat was sinking, the flowerbed splitting open and dirt trickling down the fissures as gigantic blocks of ice upended, shedding their thin skin of turf. The broad sailplanes, now oriented vertically, slowly carved downward into the boiling swell until all that was left above was the bridge; the very top of the sail, where I had spent so much quiet time. Plumes of air shot upward like the spout of a sounding whale as the free-flooding compartments topped off. Almost gone now.

I ripped Mr. Cowper's head off.

Tucking it under my arm like a football, I scrambled up and down bucking slabs to the far end of the last iceberg . . . just as the highest point of the submarine vanished in swirling eddies. Mummy's dead voice spoke in my ear, *Come on in, sillybean, the water's fine.* The ice was closing again with a tumultuous racket, and any second it would swallow me up or grind me to paste between porcelain walls. Far away in the dark I could hear Sandoval screaming as Cowper's body found him. Untroubled, I stood up straight and let myself fall forward into the menacing surf.

Gone. The boat was gone. My body slipped downward through roiling bubbles; down into that dark where something told me I belonged. Then my free hand chanced upon the rim of the bridge cockpit and grabbed on. The sub had stopped descending—it could go no deeper here without scraping bottom. Now the giant propeller, the screw, began to turn. Though hundreds of feet away, I could plainly hear its *swish-swish* as it started to push the enormous bulk in my hand. The submarine began to move forward, pulling me along with it.

Feeling the current like a breeze, I slipped my stiff legs into the cockpit, then braced myself in that little space—a rajah in his elephant howdah—with Mr. Cowper's head between my knees. I could very nearly reach up and caress the slowly-passing ceiling of ice, while beneath me I straddled a vast tube of warm air and light and unsuspecting humanity. The crew within were more real than I was; they created reality, and their realness brushed off on me, even if this was the closest I would ever get to them. I did not believe enough in my own existence to feel shortchanged. I was a ghost. But I dreamed I could see myself down there among them, the living me, innocent of time, just celebrating our escape. In that way I was content to fade . . .

Lulu.

That Voice again. It was not Mr. Cowper this time—or at least not him alone. Now, as I leaned over the edge of the bridge, I fully understood the Voice and the collective will it represented.

There in the ocean gloom at the base of the sail I saw them: so many of the guys I had known in life, minus just a few, and many more I didn't know. All of them were wrapped around the sail by the cord that had been threaded through their bones, like early seafarers lashed down before a gale. Even Julian was there, clinging tight as a starfish. All my Xombie boys.

I remembered Utik telling me of ancient Netsilik shamans who fearlessly dove to the bottom of the sea to force favors from the goddess Nuliajuk, mistress of sea and land. Only I didn't think this goddess would cooperate, and the scouring sea would pluck us off, one by one, until we were reduced to our hardy elements: individual Maenad microbes, dispersed by the currents. That was the closest we could come to death. Yes, for all practical purposes this was death. The fellows had chosen wisely.

I closed my hardening eyelids and bid it come.

epilogue

DEAD? OBVIOUSLY NOT, or I couldn't be writing this. In limbo was more like it. Limbo—I always thought that was a corny word. What about purgatory? Too religioso. And terms like "netherworld" and "stasis" smack of cheap science fiction.

No, I was under a spell—I like that. That's what it felt like: an enchanted sleep. My body was a beautifully preserved relic, completely inanimate, yet I hovered around it like a half-awake roving eye, blearily taking stock of the surroundings. I missed a lot; there were big gaps in my awareness, and I wasn't absolutely certain any part of it was real.

For instance, how did I get into the submarine? It took me a while to realize that's where I was, and then I couldn't make sense of it. I was in the wardroom, laid out inside the long glass case that usually held an inscribed silver platter with the boat's King Neptune–themed crest. They had dressed me in a modest nightgown and put a satin pillow under my blue head. A tube from my neck carried blood the color of Concord grape juice to a spigot outside the case, where Dr. Langhorne appeared regularly to collect a bag, while the stern portrait of Admiral Rickover seemed to stare down disapprovingly from above.

At times I was alone. Other times a procession of men and boys, everyone I knew and some I didn't, filed by the case as if in mourning. I couldn't hear their murmured words, but it was fascinating nonetheless to witness my own funeral. So many sad faces—Coombs, Robles, Monte, Noteiro, Albemarle, Julian, Jake, Lemuel, Cole—some more surprising than others in that they were Xombies. Even Mr. Cowper was there, I felt him, somewhere unseen. The dead mingling with the living in perfect civility, if a little aloof; a little more alone in their blue skins.

How could this be? How was it that I too felt nearly at ease among all these mortals? How was it I didn't burst from the case and begin strangling, willy-nilly? No, I had changed; I knew something I hadn't before; knew it in every cell of my being: You can't take it with you. Dr. Langhorne had done it; she had inoculated me, and now the Xombie compulsion to salvage some rudimentary taste of life was debunked, futile, leaving me to rattle around eternity all by myself. The Xombie walks alone. That was the thought that filled my amorphous consciousness and defined my existence. That was my boogeyman, always there, always peeking at me through the cracks. Eternity. Empty eternity. No hope of salvation. That was the difference: I knew this was all there was, or would ever be.

The other Xombies also felt this hopelessness, I knew, and I sensed that they blamed me for it, that I was the source from which their existential fear flowed. Yet at the same time they loved me. They came forward with this strange mixture of resentment and reverence, each kneeling before Langhorne twice a day to receive a shot of human anguish, deep in the lungs.

Finally, witnessing this communion day after day, I began to realize I was the mother of all these Xombies; that is, I was being milked to provide them with the means of civility. That without my blood they would revert overnight to their guiltless, marauding state. They would lose themselves but gain oblivion . . . and peace. This was the conflict, the eternal war that raged inside of us: Was it worth it? And how long could our fragile undead souls weather such a storm?

Dr. Langhorne had completed what she and Sandoval had started out on the grass. It was far from the miracle they had peddled to the Moguls; it was closer to an addiction, with me the heroin. It might be driving us mad. At best it was a poor stopgap until we could get back to New England and hunt down Uri Miska.

For that was Langhorne's plan. Everything had been her plan, right from the start; and now at her bidding they sought the true cure, the one with the potential to restore humankind. The enzyme circulating in me was only a preliminary phase of treatment—a short-term means of suppressing symptoms. It was imperfect, but Miska knew more. Miska would know everything.

Come on, sourpuss! It's an adventure!

From time to time I would forget it was Dr. Langhorne talking to me (or talking to herself, as is more likely) and fall under the strange, vivid delusion that it was my mother by my side. For a brief instant the rift between present and past, living and dead, would be healed.

"You ever hear that joke, 'What's long and hard and full of seamen—A submarine?' It's no coincidence this thing is a giant phallus, Lulu. It's all about who's got the biggest dick. It's true. Hoo-boy, men, I swear to God. But you know what's funny? You know what I noticed? Look at this submarine straight on and its outline is an inverted Venus symbol. That means it's our job to shake things up; turn this can upside down. What do you think?"

She wasn't expecting an answer, and I wasn't expecting

to give one, but I felt my lips forming the words *Penis Patrol*.

"That's okay, kiddo. No need to talk. You rest. You just rest." In her voice I heard the same lonely mantle of déjà vu, of communication with spirits. It was all that held back the green vastness of the sea.

Then the moment would pass, and I would grasp after it, clutching at a wisp too fleeting to catch. I would feel the cold.

Here's a fairy tale:

Once upon a time I was alive. The end.